ELGIN

TWO THE SHUTDOWN
AND THEN WHAT!

ELGIN

TWO THE SHUTDOWN
AND THEN WHAT!

JOYCE ELGIN

ELGIN TWO THE SHUTDOWN AND THEN WHAT!

iUniverse books may be ordered through booksellers or by contacting:

iUniverse
1663 Liberty Drive
Bloomington, IN 47403
www.iuniverse.com
844-349-9409

ISBN: 978-1-6632-1693-9 (sc)
ISBN: 978-1-6632-1692-2 (e)

Print information available on the last page.

iUniverse rev. date: 01/21/2021

CONTENTS

Dear Readers,

You know Calvin from the last book, "The Elgin's Family and Friends Believe it or Not!" Calvin is the son of Kevin, the lawyer in the story with Jimmy Elgin, as the boss and possible alien with skills. Tim was the tall tale story teller but did he tell the whole story?

Remember the videos in the room full of tapes that the guys were working on for Jimmy, their boss? When Jimmy found his true love Sylvia, did the work stop on the tapes or did the guys continue for the fun of it? What happened after Jimmy got his true love? Where are they?

We all know Calvin had a plan to go slow with his true love Jay and all appeared to be as normal as it could be. What could go wrong? What could possibly go so wrong in our world that would have the world shutdown and people staying in their homes in the year twenty-twenty? Life doesn't go as planned even for someone as smart as Calvin. One can plan and work with all the facts they have but something no one could have guessed happens, then what?

Read about what Calvin did and learn about things in his life. Calvin still prays a lot and reads the Bible even more than before but now he has more interest in it. How to explain Calvin's need for the Bible? Calvin is very unsure of himself and the world around him. He knows one thing for sure. God is here. God is love. God is hope. Most of all, God cares for us all the time.

Calvin looks for answers only to find something that Jimmy's true love Sylvia once said, "The answers will not be found from overly smart people but from common sense everyday people as yourselves. You will have the answers, keep thinking and sharing the truth. That is the way God works. God does big things in small ways. God works with the nobodies and not the somebodies for answers to do his work on Earth."

Then Calvin noticed all those nobodies that are the heroes today. God bless you all. Remember you heroes that God is with you always. Thank you for doing God's work.

With God's love always,
Betsy Johnson, the cook.

MAIN CHARACTERS

Barbie Edson is Eddie's wife, Jimmy's old friend from his secret spy days.

Betsy Johnson is Kevin's married daughter who is a great cook with Jay.

Bonnie Carson is Kevin's new wife and Eddie and Barbie's only daughter.

Calvin Carlson is Kevin's son and the one Jimmy is training.

Cindy Peterson is Jimmy's silver daughter and the leader of their people.

C-Jay Peterson is Cindy's husband and they have kids: Aim, Kim. and Jim.

Eddie Edson is Jimmy's old friend from his secret spy days.

Edward Edson is Eddie's favorite grandson and Bonnie's only son.

Gail Anderson is Kenny's wife, Jimmy old friend Gerald's daughter.

Gary Anderson is Kenny's only son, Kelly's dad with Tammy.

James Edson is Eddie's grandson, falls in love with Sarah, kids: Rob, Ron, Roy.

Jimmy Elgin is the leader and maybe an alien who was a secret spy.

Kelly Anderson is Kenny's spoiled granddaughter with Calvin kids, Ken & Kell.

Kenny Anderson is Jimmy's old friend from his younger days as a secret spy.

Kevin Carlson is a lawyer and guards Jimmy, has son, Ricky.

Leo Edson is Eddie's oldest grandson who has a little son named Ed.

Lisa Edson is Virgil's wife and has daughter, Violet.

Marie Elgin is Michael's wife and Junior Tim Micky Kevin Elgin's mother.

Michael Elgin is Jimmy's only living son and a doctor.

Mickey Johnson is Betsy's husband and had a kid, Mitch.

Micky Johnson is one of the guys the computer genius and wife is Virginia.

Salina Edson is Victor's wife and a chiropractor, their kids, Christy and Mary

Sam Elgin is one of the guys, head of security and his wife is Vicki.

Samantha Edson is Leo's wife and a dentist.

Sarah Peterson is Jimmy's spoiled daughter who falls in love with James.

Suzanne Edson is Edward's wife, a mental health doctor their child, Ellie.

Sylvia Elgin is Jimmy's true love.

T-Jay Peterson is white suit guy and does import export, wife was Sally.

Victor Edson is Eddie's grandson and twin of Virgil. Good friends with Mickey.

Virgil Edson is Eddie's grandson and twin of Victor. Good friends with C-Jay.

CHAPTER ONE

NOTHING IS SIMPLE

Calvin was pleased with his life and he had a plan to take it slow with his true love, Jay. But as with all good plans, they don't always go as they should and changes need to be made. Calvin loved Jay and she loved Calvin but then there is life. Jay had ideas on what she wanted in life and that was to do something on her own. Calvin loved his work and did work a lot. But then can true love take a lot of anything? Calvin worked, Jay did her thing with her college and career.

Cindy started to take over her father's company which wasn't as easy as it sounds. Maybe working for a living is not that easy. Then being married has its ups and downs. C-Jay loved Cindy and she love him. Cindy worked a lot at the company that her father left her. C-Jay still worked on the farm with his grandparents.

Betsy and Mickey worked for Cindy which was good but Betsy loved to cook. Mickey loved to eat so that was going okay. Betsy wanted a baby. Why did she want a baby? Mickey wasn't sure, so we all know who he went to ask for help on a sunny day in August of twenty-nineteen.

Mickey said to Calvin, "You got a minute?"

Calvin knew right away he didn't want to talk to his brother-in-law about anything.

Calvin replied, "No."

Mickey said, "Calvin, don't worry so, Jay will find a job she likes and continue college with you working all the time, this can work for you two. Give it time. Love finds a way."

Calvin replied, "What do you want?"

Mickey got right to the point and said, "Your sister wants a baby, why? We are happy now. Why do we need a crying baby?"

All Calvin could think of was that he didn't ask me how to make the baby. What to say. Calvin wanted to say I have enough problems of my own with Jay. I don't like her new friends and I think her mother is back on liquor or drugs. I work all the time and I will never get married.

Calvin did reply, "I don't know. She is your wife. Try talking to her about it. If you are not ready for children, tell her that. You do have time. Did you ever talk about having children?"

Mickey answer, "Yes, but we never talked about when. As for talking to her, your sister does all the talking. I always agree with her. That has worked for me. A wise priest once told me in a marriage a husband should keep his mouth shut as much as possible."

Calvin said, "What do you want me to do for you?"

Mickey replied, "Talk to her. You are her brother. She can't leave you."

Calvin walked away and thought maybe Jay was right they needed new friends. This family was getting to be too much.

Calvin went back to work wondering, did his dad want grandchildren? Calvin worried about his dad because Jay's mom was a mess. What did his dad, Kevin, ever see in that woman? Calvin was not sure. Calvin thought about Sylvia, Jimmy's true love. She was very nice but sick all the time. All Jimmy wanted to do was be with Sylvia. They took naps twice a day and she had trouble eating with her stomach problems, breathing with her lung problems, heart issues, seizures, headaches. In other words, what did work on her besides, well it must have been very good sex for Jimmy. He was crazy about his Sylvia and Calvin worried what would happen if she died. Michael had a full-time job trying to keep that woman alive and walking even. But Sylvia did look good. At least Calvin's job was not as bad as Michael's, the doctor who had to care for Sylvia and all the other doctors she had. No bodies' love life was working out the way they had planned it, that was life. It could always be worse and it did get worse in our world.

Calvin decided to ask his dad Kevin if he wanted grandchildren from Betsy and Mickey now. So, he asked his dad as Kevin sat there quietly.

Calvin said, "Dad, Mickey told me Betsy wants a baby but he is not so sure they are ready. What do you think? Want to be a grandfather?"

Kevin looked up at Calvin and replied, "No. Please no. Not now. Tell them to wait a year. Boss thinks something bad is coming but he doesn't know what it is. Maybe we are over thinking things. But tell them to wait until they have been married for a few years. That would be better for the marriage. Thanks for asking me."

Kevin got up and walked out to Jimmy. Jimmy and Kevin were talking about something very low but Calvin couldn't hear it. Calvin worked that day and then went to find Mickey with his sister, Betsy.

Calvin said, "Dad and I were talking. They think something not good is happening but they don't know what. If you are thinking of having children, maybe you should wait a few years."

Betsy said, "I think Cindy and C-Jay want to get started with having those seven grandchildren that Jimmy wants from them soon."

Calvin replied, "Cindy, you should talk to Jimmy about it first. I don't know much more. I am not sure what is going on with Jay and me."

Betsy replied, "Jay wants to be a cook like me and work a little. She likes college but doesn't want to go from her mother's home to your house and be married without some life of her own. Can you understand that?"

Calvin agreed but he really didn't understand why Jay had to work. He made enough money for them to live on and she could go to school. What was the big deal? Nothing was simple in love, and women had a whole other mind wave that Calvin couldn't understand. Even with the love he had for Jay, he didn't really understand but he wanted her and for the first time in life, he needed her. But why? Is this what Jimmy was experiencing? The need for someone else he couldn't live without. Then, if Sylvia would die, what would happen to Jimmy? Sylvia was Jimmy's life and that was something a person should never do, let someone else be your whole life. Calvin's thoughts stopped as he saw Cindy go into Jimmy's office. Calvin knew he shouldn't but he had to listen.

Cindy said, "Dad, I think we should start on those seven grandchildren you want from us very soon. What do you think? Calvin said I should talk to you first. He said Kevin told him that Betsy and Mickey should wait a few years for the good of the marriage before having children."

Jimmy looked up sadly and replied, "I am glad you asked me. This is a two-person job and I mean you with your husband. But I agree with Kevin, a marriage needs time for a couple to be alone together at first before children. You have time. Take a few years. Wait, not now. Something is going on in our world and it is not good. It is not in my area and I can't help in any way. I am good at building weapons, helping people; saving lives is not my ability. You will prepare

3

the people, our people, on our place, and to stop coming here now. Understand me, start now, waste no time in doing it. Top of the list. Take Calvin to help you."

Jimmy started to write orders on how to do this and what to do in detail. Cindy left the room and went right to work, stopping all trips between the two places. At that home the people had to be kept safe. But from who or what, Calvin wondered? Did Jimmy even know?

As the work continued Calvin asked, "What is going on? What is the problem? Can we fix it?"

Cindy answered, "I don't think so. Our people have skills but because they have these skills, we are weaker in other areas of our body. My dad knows best."

Calvin went to Jimmy and he was with Kevin talking low again. Calvin asked, "What is wrong? Can we fix the problem?"

Jimmy replied, "No, we can't. If we get too close to it, we will get sick. I am not sure of much but I know something very bad is coming. I am trying to read minds on it but you guys shouldn't. Stay away and keep the people safe. We need to get ready for something so bad."

Jimmy had said a lot but who was our people? All Calvin noticed was the people at that place which no one could find without Jimmy and Cindy's help. They had skills like reading people's minds and disappearing then reappearing in a different place but that could have been learned. The supplies were different because these people never ate meat or any meat products. Calvin thought, was this because they had no animals there but the winged horses and they loved animals? The people were learning to grow food crops. Their soil was not good and they worked hard in big greenhouses. Building the greenhouses took time and then the canned food was all they would buy from stores, with flour to make bread. The children did love candy and sugar but that was not high on the list of things to get. Jimmy put a lot of his money into it and Kevin helped. Calvin was still not sure of it but he did as Jimmy asked him to. All the guys worked day and night on this, then Halloween came with candy for all. Jimmy and Sylvia were in church praying most of that time. Cindy bought so much candy that these children could never eat all of it, so she put most of the candy in big freezers for them later.

Then Thanksgiving came and all was good. Betsy and Jay were cooking up a good meal and church was wonderful. Nothing was different. The work was almost done. Jimmy was a shopping fool. He and Sylvia were buying all the Christmas gifts sooner and then they wanted to pray.

Calvin was busy working with the needed new greenhouses, and the canned food with flour, then all the freezers being put in place. The people were learning how to care for themselves with washing things. They were doing a lot of cleaning which didn't appear to be needed. Just trying to run this place was hard enough without the extra Jimmy wanted them to do but Cindy never questioned her father. She did as he said.

The other parts of the business were being left to other workers and it was as if Jimmy didn't care. Cindy started to sell some of the other parts of the business but it was doing great so why sell? Nothing Jimmy did was simple. Calvin continued to ask questions but most of the time Cindy didn't even know why she was doing what she was doing. Cindy did what Jimmy told her to do. Jimmy was even harder to understand then he had been before, and he was troubled about something bad. Was Jimmy too worried about Sylvia's health to be thinking straight? Was he so afraid she would die from some illness that he was over doing it? Who was to watch this? Kevin, was to watch Jimmy.

Calvin knew his dad had his hands full with Jay's mom. Teresa Mary was drinking again and possibly using drugs. She was hiding it from Kevin but he knew and was afraid to tell Jimmy. Teresa Mary was also bad to Sylvia, which made Jimmy mad and Kevin was in the middle of it all. Jay loved her mother but didn't know what to do with Sylvia so they stayed a distance from each other. Sylvia didn't want to fight with Teresa Mary or come between Jay and her mother, so things were not good for anyone, personally. Jay moved out to live with some friends. Betsy and Cindy were waiting to have babies because both of their dads' advice was for them to wait to be married a few years, so they did. Calvin was sure intelligent people planned their children and he know these women were intelligent.

Christmas came and all was good but Jay had an issue at her work place with licensing for cooking at a hotel. Calvin still didn't understand why she had to work. Calvin loved her so he stood by her decision with emotional support. Calvin wondered what he should do, ask Jay to marry him or wait? So, Calvin went to Jimmy and his dad, Kevin, for advice. Calvin knocked on Jimmy's office door as he heard them talking.

Jimmy said, "Come in, Calvin. We need to talk to you anyway. But you go first. What is on your mind?"

Calvin asked, "I want to marry Jay but I am not sure if she is ready. Should I ask her this Christmas or wait? What do you guys think?"

Kevin looked at Jimmy as if they were talking through their minds then Jimmy answered, "We are glad you asked us. We think you should wait until she is twenty-one years old then ask her. Our friend Tim once said if love is real and true then it will wait until it is right for both of you. We don't think she is ready. Jay needs to see life away from her mother. She needs to find herself as a person."

This Calvin understood and agreed with. If you love someone then let them go, if they come back, then their love is real and will stay with you always. Calvin wanted an always love and one woman in his life. Did Jay love him that way? If Jay didn't love him that way, Calvin was sure he could love another who did. Calvin believed in true love but it had to be both ways or it would never work at all. Jay had to love him as he did her. Calvin now understood Sylvia, that she loved Jimmy so much but because of her health she didn't want to take up all of his time and that is why she left him. Jimmy loved her and was not thinking straight when it came to his Sylvia. Was it Sylvia's beauty or the sex with her that Jimmy couldn't let go?

Kevin said, "Calvin, did you hear us? There is something going on in the world but we don't know what it is and we should know. Just because we are smart doesn't mean we know."

Jimmy talked now, "Calvin, it is very bad and I can do nothing to stop it. I am so sorry. I would tell someone but what would I say? I think something bad is happening but I have no facts. Where in the world should I start looking? I think it will hurt the people who are already sick, like my Sylvia and I could make her sicker if I got it. She could die. I can't do that. Please understand. I can't prove it. I can read minds and that is how I know something is wrong. They would cut my head open if they find out that I can read minds; but not just me, all our people."

Calvin could see Jimmy and his dad were very upset over this but there was nothing they could do at this time and they were out of time. Then what if they were wrong and Jimmy was overreacting? He worried about his Sylvia too much. Calvin left the meeting thinking he had no idea what was wrong so he checked with Betsy and Cindy to see if they knew anything. No one else felt anything or read any minds on anything bad happening. Not even Kevin read any minds on it so maybe Jimmy was overreacting.

Cindy and Calvin did do as Jimmy asked with the guys doing the work. They had a very nice New Year's Eve party and a New Year day. But work went on as always. Cindy, Calvin, and Betsy still had a rough time with running the companies without Jimmy. Kevin tried to help but he too was having a hard time without Jimmy. Jimmy and Sylvia were in prayer all the time. Betsy and Mickey had their first anniversary. Betsy was counting down the time to have a baby. In a few years, her dad and Jimmy had said. Well, to Betsy and Cindy, a baby did take nine months so when to make the baby was within months. Valentine's Day was great and Jay with Calvin had the best night. It all appeared to be going good for the first time in a long while. Ash Wednesday was a big church day and the last one they would see for some time. Teresa Mary was screaming at Sylvia and she turned away from her. Then the unthinkable happened.

A virus shut down the world. This didn't happen all at once but the word was out and Jimmy took action to close up the people under his care. Teresa Mary went home with little Ricky for the schools were all closing. Jimmy sent Cindy, C-Jay, Betsy, and Mickey to that place where they could go but not find without Jimmy or Cindy. They were to stay there, and not come back. C-Jay didn't want to leave his grandparents but he would never say no to Jimmy. T-Jay would take care of their needs and no one else. Sarah was to help T-Jay. Michael and Marie were to care for Sylvia. She couldn't stay at that place they now called Marci's because of her health or Calvin was sure Jimmy and his dad would have gone there too to live. The guys stayed because T-Jay was staying with the grandparents and Jimmy. Sam wouldn't leave Jimmy and Sam's wife didn't like it that the place was called Marci anyway. Sam's son and daughter did go there with their families to live. Micky and his wife stayed with Jimmy because her brother and sister's families were not able to go to the place called Marci that they couldn't find without Jimmy.

They had to move fast. All was ready to go but what the hell was going on and could they stop it? Jimmy, Kevin, and Calvin did go to Washington DC to talk with the president but there was nothing they could do to help this situation. This president was very nice to them about it, saying, if they came up with any ideas, to let him know.

Well, they lived in Seattle, Washington, a city hit first and hard. The guys didn't stay in Seattle; they left fast. And things got worse. T-Jay with Sarah went to the county to the grandparent to care for them. Sam and his wife to her parents to care of them. Micky and his wife to her brother and sister's families to be together. Jimmy took Sylvia to her home and he got a place close by with Michael and Marie. Kevin and Calvin stayed with Jimmy but it was at the old company where they could do work. They worked on what they could but this was a health issue. Sylvia may need them and for Jimmy, Sylvia came first. Things got worse as more people got sick and died. They were not in a good place as far as health because of their skills which made them physically weaker to the virus. If they got the virus they would die. Michael worked on the test and it was not good for anyone who could read minds or disappear then reappear. They had to sit this one out and wait with the world. What to do with all that time, Calvin thought.

Jimmy and Sylvia were in danger and he too could die if he got the virus. Then what about his dad, Kevin? What about his sister or Cindy or even himself? Calvin was young and a healthy guy but he had skills. Did that make him weaker with this virus? Everyone should be careful and that meant Calvin too. Who would be able to get their food? Well, they did have a good supply of everything. Michael wasn't going out to do anything for he didn't have these skills but he could give the virus to Jimmy or any of the others without even knowing it. Michael and Marie stayed home being very careful. Calvin knew he couldn't go see Jay, and what about his dad going to see little Ricky or his mom? Calvin was glued to the computer to learn all he could about this virus.

Calvin could e-mail, make phone calls, text Jay and other things. He couldn't go to see Jay, and he couldn't tell her why. Should he tell her the truth about his skills and this new danger for him? What to do? Would she believe him and should he show her his proof or would it be too much for her? Calvin went to talk to his dad and Jimmy about it to see what they thought he should do. Calvin knocked on Jimmy's office door and then went in.

Calvin said, "Boss and dad got a minute? I need a little advice about Jay. I can't go see her right now with this virus issue. Should I go anyway? Should I tell her about my skills?"

Jimmy looked at Kevin and this time Kevin answered, "Son, I am sorry but you shouldn't go see Jay because one of her friends may have the virus and not know it. They may not be sick and may never get sick but you would die from it if you get it. I love Jay too, but son, it is too much of a risk. Never tell Jay about your skills. I never told your mother. Thank God I never did. Jimmy's first wife Margo knew, then told a court Judge in the trial for Cindy and thank God that Judge didn't believe a word of it or what could have happened to Jimmy or us? Son, it is not just about you but all of us. Your sister and any of us, kept our skills a secret."

Calvin walked out with what his dad had said, wondering did Sylvia know about Jimmy? But Calvin wouldn't ask. Calvin wasn't even sure if Mickey or C-Jay really knew about all the skills and if they were real or a project Jimmy made for them. No one ever asked Jimmy. Were they aliens from another world and was this place they went to on another planet? How would Calvin be sure? Who could Calvin ask that question and find the answer? Well, Jimmy but we all know that was something Calvin would never ask Jimmy or Sylvia or even Cindy.

No one was happy with the stay at home situation but they all listened to it and did obey it. If you are not one of the people that could die, it is easy to say that it is overreacting but if you are the one who could die, it is a different story. Calvin thought there was one thing worse than death from this virus which was very bad, but that was giving it to someone else and having them die from it. Michael was there with vitamin C for everyone and they all took it, for Michael was a good doctor. Jimmy didn't give money to the cause because their people needed so many things and that cost him lots of money.

As the weeks passed, they got into a schedule which Michael had them all do. Do something like church and prayer in the morning then a project of some kind for work. Calvin kept up the company work as best he could, with what they could still do. Then a break for calling friends and keeping in touch with family. Calvin talked to Jay first thing in the morning and at night before bed. Calvin talked with Cindy and Betsy each day about work, sometimes with Mickey or C-Jay for some guy talk. Then they had to go for a walk which Calvin did with Jimmy and Kevin, his dad. They had their meals but not together, then a movie in the afternoon or night was good. Jimmy was with Sylvia a lot and she didn't go out much so he didn't either. She was worried too about getting him sick so they both were very careful. They had each other and that was good.

Calvin was alone a lot and he did talk with his dad, Kevin, more about his life and Jimmy's. Calvin read books. But Calvin was bored. Jimmy came to Calvin one day and took him into a room which had been locked. There was also a bookshelf over a door so no one would even know there was a door there. Jimmy removed the bookshelf and unlocked that door with Kevin coming over to help him. Calvin wondered what this room was about. In the room were video tapes, wall to wall tapes of something, but what and why was Jimmy showing it?

Jimmy said, "I know you need a project to do and I would like someone I can trust to review more of these tapes. Fix them up and if you need help, go to the guys or your dad. See my past and tell us something about the future. Sometimes the past helps us with the future and we have time to do this study."

Calvin replied, "Yes, I would love to do it. Thanks."

Calvin went right to work and he had a reason to wake up each morning to get these tapes usable. Calvin wanted to know the past. Calvin was surprised about a lot of things. The first thing he noticed was Marie, Michael's wife, was having a baby in this unbelievable time. Was this a good idea? Michael and Marie were so happy about it. Jimmy and Sylvia appeared to share their happiness. Calvin asked his dad about it. Kevin told him all about how Marie was a child found in Mexico living on the streets, homeless, hungry. Because Margo thought Marie had not enough food in her younger day, she might never be able to have children and didn't want her to marry Michael. But Michael didn't care about having children. Jimmy didn't care if he had grandchildren from Michael and Marie but Marie always wanted children. Now Calvin understood why this was a wonderful thing in the event of the world's pain from this virus. Michael had Marie take it easy, resting a lot. Michael took all his time caring for them.

There were the seven of them living together, Michael the doctor, Marie his wife, the nurse and the baby to be born soon. Jimmy the boss and his true love Sylvia were two people in love. Two teens as they once were, hand in hand, walking through life as the world was shut down. Sylvia was not the sick one anymore and Jimmy was not the genius being her caretaker. They were taking care of each other and were so in love, now Sylvia felt Jimmy needed her for more than sex. Which Calvin believed Jimmy always did.

Kevin was Jimmy's guard and would be at his side forever, never letting any harm come to him. That was Calvin's dad, Kevin's true life's work or mission in life and Teresa Mary did come second. He loved her but she, as everything else, came second in his dad's life. Calvin was sure he, his sister and little Ricky didn't come second in their dad's life. They were more!

Calvin started his work on the tapes in the video room. What did Calvin want to know about Jimmy's past? Well, maybe how Jimmy met Sylvia, his true love. Could she help him with Jay, Calvin's true love? Calvin knew they met in church, that they prayed a lot together which was something he and Jay didn't do. Was that their problem? Did they need God in their lives? Jay didn't pray much because her mother didn't pray. Was the child to do what the parent does? Calvin went to his dad and asked questions about his family, his dad's parents, his mom's parents. Were they alive? Where were they? Kevin looked at Jimmy then set a date to answer Calvin's questions and left the room. The day came for Kevin to answer Calvin's questions and he sat alone in a room waiting for Calvin. Jimmy was nowhere in sight. Calvin had talked to Jay and he did tell her about the videos with his new project. Jay was very interested in it and they were really talking again, not just saying nice things to each other. Calvin even told Jay about his talk with his father, Kevin about his grandparents, but Jay said nothing of what her mother had said to her grandmother, Sylvia. Did she not know about it?

Calvin walked into the room and sat down across from his dad, then spoke, "Are your parents still alive today? Do you have any brothers or sisters? Do I have cousins?"

Kevin replied, "Yes, my parents are both alive but my father is very sick with this virus. He is not going to live and I can't help him. Jimmy and I have sent help but he will die, then the body will be burned in a funeral cremation. My mother should be okay. They still live in their home with my sister. She got divorced years ago when I graduated from law school and I worked her divorce. Her husband left her for another woman and they had a couple of kids. Your cousins grew up and one killed himself, the other has a drug addiction problem. I don't know or care where he is. My sister is not doing good but I send them money each month to pay for things. My father had skills but not my mother or sister, just my dad and I. I am not sure why. Did my dad work for Jimmy's mom or what? That is why you need to review the videos. Jimmy doesn't really know everything. I never asked are we aliens or not?"

Calvin said, "Dad, I know my mother died when I was very little. Tell me about it and her family."

Kevin started slowly, "I met your mother at college in law school. We were both going to be divorce lawyers. The money with Jimmy was so good, your mother didn't have to work for any reason and she liked that. I married her because Jimmy wanted married guys to work for him around his pretty wife, Margo, at that time. Margo was fifteen years younger than Jimmy but they were married with three children when I started working for them. When I say for them, I mean Jimmy, Margo, and Tim. Tim was the guy that trained me at the company."

Calvin said, "Wait a minute, Dad, that is not the whole story. Tell me about where my sister Betsy came in. And did my mother have brothers and sisters? Are her parents alive now? I haven't seen my mother's parents for a long time. What is up with that? Why did my mother divorce you, dad?"

Kevin replied as he looked Calvin in the face, "You may have heard Jimmy and me talk of our best friend, Tim, who died from drinking. I did go out drinking at the bar a lot with Tim so your mother said if I went out drinking one more time with Tim then I was out of the house and her life. Well, I did and I saw my clothes were burning on the front yard as the cab driver took me home, so I went to the office to sleep. But Jimmy needed help and we flew out of there. My plane was shot down. As my plane went down, this pretty strawberry blond lady saved me and that is how Betsy came to be. Your mother was not over with me and was pleased I was not killed so we got back together. Then you were born but Betsy's mom had Betsy on the same day and she died after child birth. I told your mother she had twins. It was Tim's idea and I liked it but Jimmy told me not to do that. Jimmy told me to tell your mother the truth but, Calvin, the truth would have never worked on your mother so I lied. You guys had skills and I hired a woman with skills to care for you because your mother hated me. I am not sure if you were born with the skills or if Jimmy gave you skills to keep you alive because he was the doctor in with Tim who delivered the babies. I was in the delivery room but I fainted. Your mother caught me in bed with the lady I hired to watch you kids and divorced me. That judge gave your mother everything she wanted which was everything I had and was ever going to have but she died before our divorce was final. You were to live with your mother then I could visit you but when she died, we were still married so I got you and everything else. I sold our home and gave that money to her parents. Your mother was an only child. You visited your mother's parents but they were turning you against me and were not nice to Betsy. Then they wanted more money from me each month. They had a gambling problem and were killed in a car accident in Las Vegas after a night of drinking. I didn't have you kids come to the funeral and buried them by your mother. That is why I stopped taking you kids out to your mother's grave. We stopped seeing my parents because I was sure they would tell you all about it. My parents thought I killed them or that Jimmy or one of the guys did. Now, Jimmy was a secret agent for the British Government and he did work for the USA. Jimmy was like a James Bond 007. He had friends, Eddie and Kenny, but I don't know their last names. That is where to start with the videos."

Calvin knew that was hard for him but now Calvin understood more about himself. Calvin called Jay right away and he went over the facts with her. Jay asked one question that got Calvin to think after they were off the phone. Was

Jimmy a hit man for the government? Calvin rechecked and the woman who cared for them was taking his dad to court but before the court trial she was killed in a plane accident. His mother died by falling down stairs at the company, hitting her head. Who found his mom, Tim or Jimmy? His mother's parents were killed in a car accident and were taking money from his dad. Why would Jimmy or anyone do that for his dad?

Calvin talked to the guys and they always called his dad, Kevin, the boss' pet, but why? They had all been with Jimmy longer so why was his dad the one with Jimmy all the time, because he was a lawyer or was it something else? Jimmy was always so nice, could he have killed anyone? Then an answer came from Micky, Mickey's dad, his brother-in-law told Calvin that it was his dad, Kevin who first told Jimmy that his Sylvia was alive so many years ago. It was Kevin who helped Jimmy find his true love, Sylvia, and got her to be with him. Jimmy never forgot who helped him. But would Jimmy kill for someone? Could Jimmy kill?

Calvin went to all the kids and guys for any answers they may know. Calvin got information and wrote it all down. There were answers, but what was the question Calvin wanted to ask? It was like a big puzzle and Calvin had nothing better to do with his time but solve it. Who was Eddie and Kenny? What did they do with Jimmy? Why did Tim not ever tell them about Eddie and Kenny in his tall tales? Were they aliens from another world or people with skills?

Calvin's mind worked overtime and he wondered if this virus was worse for Jimmy and people with skills. Could it be that the virus had killed off more of the people with skills than without? So, maybe people born with skills died before the ones without skills did. As many of them didn't reproduce so most people who don't have these skills were the ones who populated the world. Could it be that simple?

Cindy called, crying. She had talked with Marie and was happy they were having a baby. Cindy had learned that Jimmy's mother, his biological mother, had seven children; where were they? Had they died? The children that had skills died one in four before they were born. Jimmy and this Marci had been looking into it before she was killed. Marci was who they named that place after.

Calvin and Cindy started to look into this to see what Jimmy was working on back then by the papers he left up at that place where Cindy and Betsy now lived with their husbands. Jimmy and Marci had those people have children because there were no children being born. They tested the women and only three hundred could have children and only one hundred men.

What was going on back then? Jimmy had the women each have a child with a guy but each guy had to get three women with child each year. Tim had a note saying that must have been the best speech ever, even better then President Kennedy's "Ask not what your country can do for you but what you can do for your country." And Jimmy's great speech was that we should, "Have sex for your people and reproduce for skills." Tim noted that he thought Jimmy's speech was better. Why was the birth rate so low and then why did one in four not live long enough to be born? Jimmy did question about why these babies with skills tried to disappear then reappear out of their mother before they were able to live outside of their mothers and die. Jimmy had three hundred children born this way a year and Jimmy didn't need to do this anymore. The population grew. But now, could this virus kill off people with skills again or was it something else that caused the lack of children being born with skills?

Cindy's concern was, would her babies die? Jimmy had two sons who died before they were born and in each of these cases, Jimmy had found the babies appeared to be trying to disappear and then reappear someplace else. Jimmy was looking for why his baby sons died and that was one possible answer. Other answers could have been the health of the mothers. Venus was Jimmy's first son's mother and he died before he was born. Jimmy thought there was something in the tea Venus drank which caused the baby to be born too soon. The unborn baby tried to disappear and reappear out of the mother, but why? Jimmy first questioned whether the baby boy was trying to get away from the tea that was killing him inside her. The second dead son's mother was the married woman who Calvin believed was Sylvia. She was too weak to carry the baby and the baby was trying to disappear then reappear out of the mother to save his mother's life. Which did work but the baby died. Sylvia almost died too but the doctors saved her and she was taken to another hospital. Calvin wrote this to Cindy and not to worry, she had Michael as her doctor. Calvin, as always, wouldn't ask Jimmy about his two dead sons and Tammy, Jimmy's daughter, who was killed. Calvin knew that Margo's boyfriend hit Tammy. One hit to a small child can kill them, which is what happened to Tammy.

Calvin told Cindy and Betsy about the video room and his work, and that maybe there were answers there. The work began with the tapes in the video room, looking for answers, if there were any. Cindy and Betsy, Calvin's co-workers on this from that other place, called Marci. Jay was Calvin's love and support on this project. Little Ricky, C-Jay and Mickey were his male friends.

The world was still shut down and all was not well. But there was a light at the end of it all and things were going better with this virus. Could the world reopen again? What would that mean for Calvin and people with skills? Could they pick up as before this virus happened? Nothing is simple.

CHAPTER TWO

THE BOYS ARE BACK!

Calvin walked into the room with the wall to wall video tapes. There must be thousands of them but who and why would anyone want to do this? That wasn't the question Calvin needed answered. The question Calvin needed answered was could or would Jimmy kill for something or someone? Were they aliens or was it a skill Jimmy gave them to help them to live? Something caught Calvin's eye that was on a shelf marker that read:

Calvin said it out loud, "The boys are back!"

Calvin looked through those video tapes and worked to clean them up. He called Sam, T-Jay and Micky and asked about them. But all Micky knew was of Jimmy, Eddy, and Kenny who a man named Mr. King called "the boys." Calvin knew these were the two guys who were secret agents with Jimmy long ago, which was what his dad had said. Calvin worked for days cleaning up the tapes to watch with his dad, Kevin. They started the first tape with three boys in a basement playing guitars and singing songs. But a song was going around in Calvin's head, not on the tape. "The boys are back in town," but where did Calvin hear that song?

Eddy said, "Jimmy, Barbie told me that you came on to her last night after the dance at school. She is my girlfriend. Did you?"

Kenny reported, "Come on guys, it is just a girl. Jimmy, you can have any girl you want, this is Eddie's girl. Let us not let a girl come between friends."

Jimmy replied, "I didn't come on to Barbie. You can have her, Eddie. I don't even like her."

Mrs. King came down the stairs to the basement and said, "Is anyone hungry? We have food for you boys upstairs whenever you are ready. The boys are back."

Mr. King waved the boys upstairs to eat and they follow him. Mrs. King is Larry's mother and Calvin knew this from pictures of her. Mr. King was Larry's step-father and Larry was Tim's boss. Tim was Jimmy and Kevin's best friend who drank himself to death. So, now Calvin knows who the boys are; it is Jimmy, Eddie, and Kenny. Larry is videoing all this but still, Calvin doesn't know why. Is it a hobby or because they are in his mother's home? Kevin shows Calvin the proof that Larry had someone named Karen kill Mr. King's first wife so Larry's mother could marry Mr. King and then Larry got Mr. King's money.

They were at the end of that videotape and Calvin wanted his dad to tell him more, so Kevin got the legal stuff out and showed Calvin everything. Larry and his mother came from London, England with Charles and his mother. They also had a friend who had a son that was Larry's lawyer and was killed along with Larry named Bob. This was after World War Two and in the fifties, then sixties. They had very little money, so Larry needed his mother to marry Mr. King who had a lot of money and she knew him from the war. Larry's mom was a British agent and her husband was killed in the war but she had four sons, one being Larry. The documents showed that Eddie's dad was named Lee and was Larry's mom's oldest son but Lee's wife died in child birth. Eddie's grandmother raised him. Her second son's name was Lawrence and he left to live in Italy. Larry was her third son who stayed with his mother. Larry's younger brother was Lonny and no one knew where he ended up.

Kevin said, "We should ask Jimmy about all this, then watch another video."

They went to Jimmy's office and knocked on the door. Kevin asked, "Who is Eddie and Kenny?"

Jimmy smiled and said, "It has been so long and yes they are my friends. We were called the boys by Mr. King and his wife, Larry's mom. Larry's mom was an agent of the British who got us into the spy business. I was a secret agent for about fifteen years of my life."

Calvin looked at Kevin then he had to asked, "Did you have to kill people?"

Jimmy smiled again and answered, "Yes, many people, but mostly bad men. Tim once told people I was a hit man but that wasn't true. We only killed if we needed to and we did need to a lot. Eddie was the company man, Kenny was the talker, and I was to be the smart guy. Kenny loved the excitement and I wanted to die because I couldn't find my Sylvia. This was right after that car accident."

Calvin asked, "Who was Charles' mother and Charles?"

Kevin looked down then up at the ceiling and said, "Wrong question."

Jimmy replied, "She was my lover after I couldn't find Sylvia. She was about thirty years older than me and a very pretty blond lady. It was my first summer home from spy college. Her son found us in bed together and that didn't go well. Charles was her son and later he became my partner in a university college teaching."

Jimmy got up and left the room. Kevin went after Jimmy but it was no big deal. Jimmy didn't have a boring life. Jimmy was trained to kill and could do it without being found out. Kevin and Calvin watched another video. This one started with Jimmy coming home to Tim's house when he was about thirty something. Not a boy anymore. Tim was waiting for him.

Jimmy said, "I said I would be here but Kenny and Eddie are coming later. Eddie was surprised you invited him and his family. Kenny is pleased you thought of him."

Tim replied, "It was Merit's idea. He thought you would come home for the wedding if the boys were there too. And I guess it worked. The problem you must deal with is, our sweet little Margo won't wear that bride's maid's dress for the wedding and we can't get a new one in time. Talk to her. Margo will listen to you. I have tried everything. She hates the dress."

Jimmy looked at the time and answered, "I will talk to her in the morning, it is late. Do you have enough money to pay for this wedding? How are you paying for it all? Do I need to buy them a wedding gift? What did you and Sue get them for their wedding gift?"

Tim stopped as Merit came in the room. Jimmy waved at Merit as he went into his room then called Margo, saying, "Margo, Jimmy is home and he noticed I am alive."

Margo replied, "I am on my way to your place."

She hung up the phone as Jimmy waited for Tim's answer, then Jimmy said, "You charged it all?"

Tim replied, "Larry's business isn't doing well; can you help us again? There isn't any money for me to take from Larry's bank accounts."

Jimmy looked at Tim and took a deep breath, saying, "But you put the money back that you took before and you stopped sleeping with his wife, Linda, right?"

Tim looked around then said, "Well no, I didn't put any money back as of now nor have I stopped sleeping with his wife. But I am going to work each day. Whereas before, I would pay myself and not even go to work. I now go to work most days."

Jimmy would have said something to Tim but Margo came through the door and threw her arms around Jimmy with a big kiss for him. Then a kiss for Tim on the cheek. Jimmy was still so surprised by the kiss he got. Merit came out but no one was talking and Margo was all over Jimmy. Jimmy appeared to be enjoying it. Merit's work was done for the night and he went to his bedroom.

Sue, Margo's mother, was at the door and said, "Margo, what are you doing here at this hour?"

Jimmy replied, "I guess I need to see this bride's maid's dress that Margo doesn't want to wear this weekend to her brother's wedding. I don't know if it can wait for morning. Margo, I got you this pearl necklace to go with your dress and these silk nylon stockings to wear for the wedding. I understand the dress is not long. Please try on the dress for me, so I can see it."

Margo went to put on the dress while Jimmy and Tim sat there. Sue was on the phone, calling home to let them know where she was. Margo came out in the dress and it fit her just right. Jimmy's eyes opened up wide and he sat up to see the dress on Margo. The sleeves were off the shoulders and the back was cut low to the butt. Tim sat up too.

Sue called out to them, "Make sure Margo wears that dress this weekend."

Tim replied, "Have you seen the dress?"

Sue answered, getting off the phone, "Yes in the box, why?"

Jimmy said, "Margo, I can truthfully say, I really like that dress on you. It takes my breath away. Please turn around in the dress. I want to see the back of the dress on you again."

Tim got up and asked, "Jimmy do you need ice water or just ice to cool you down? I know it has been sometime. Margo, my wife Betty will be here in the morning to buy you girls some jackets for those dresses. Jackets that tie and can't be taken off. Right, Sue?"

Sue was sitting down with her mouth open, then said, "That sounds good, Tim. Margo, let us go home now. Thank you for your help Jimmy, with the dress."

Sue took Margo out the door smiling and Jimmy called out, "No problem, any time at all. I am here for you."

They were gone before Kenny and Eddie came but it was quiet so Kenny asked, "Who died?"

Eddie said, "Thanks for inviting us to this wedding but we really don't remember Jr. Joey or his wife to be. Who are they? Can we take a shower and sleep here tonight? It is very late."

Tim smiled at Jimmy, saying, "I am sure there will be enough hot water tonight for showers for you two guys. Jimmy is planning a cold shower tonight, right?"

Then Tim went to bed. Eddie looked at Kenny who looked at Jimmy who was still a little too happy. No more was said and Jimmy found them both rooms to sleep and a shower. Jimmy only need a cold shower that night but he was good with it. In the morning, Tim was gone getting his wife from the airport to buy those jackets for the bride's maid's dresses. Merit stayed to watch the boys to see if they needed anything. Eddie was going to get his wife from the airport but he was sure Tim was upset about something; but what was it?

Kenny did ask Jimmy, "What happened last night?"

Jimmy replied, "I called Margo sweetheart; she didn't like the bride's maid's dress she is to wear this weekend and I had to see her in the dress. I really liked her in that dress. But Tim thinks the bride's maid's dresses need a jacket to cover them up because the sleeves are off the shoulders and the back is very low to the butt. I do really like her in that dress."

Kenny thought for a minute then asked, "Is that little girl I danced with at your engagement party with Venus, the woman richer than God, who lost your baby and dumped you, that you never married, is she a bride's maid at this wedding? What is her name?"

Jimmy called out, "Merit, do you know the answer to Kenny's question?"

Merit came out and said, "Yes, Gerald's daughters are both in the wedding as bride's maids. And the older one asked about you, Kenny. That is why I had dad invite you and Eddie, telling him that Jimmy would come for sure. I think she has the hots for you. I forgot her name."

Kenny asked, "Does she have a boyfriend and how old is she?"

Merit answered, "No boyfriend but Gerald is very protective of his daughters and Jimmy helps Gerald with everything. They are good friends. So, don't try anything with his daughters. I think the older one is twenty-two years old. That is the one who wants you, Kenny."

Eddie said, "I got to go get my wife, but isn't Jr. Joey the one who peed on my shoe at my wedding to Barbie? That must have been fifteen years ago. I need to do a pay back. Okay, I can't get away with peeing on his shoe at his wedding but I have a small son who could."

Eddie was out the door on a mission to get even with Jr. Joey. Teaching his small son to pee on someone's shoe wasn't the best fatherhood thing to do but then maybe his wife Barbie would put a stop to that before it started. Barbie would be a responsible parent, right? Kenny looked at Jimmy who smiled. Then they went to get something to eat and they took Merit with them. A gift for the wedding couple, which only Merit seemed to know, but as for most weddings, they were registered at a store for gifts. Jimmy picked out a butter dish because he was in fact paying for the whole wedding. The gift Kenny got was a candle set for candlelight dinners. They went shopping for clothes for themselves to look good at the wedding. Merit tagged along to keep them out of trouble. Eddie found them at supper time and they ate together because Eddie's wife with his three kids were visiting her family. Eddie's wife had gotten their wedding gift for this unknown bride and groom.

Eddie said to the boys, "Jimmy and Kenny, we decided that if anything happened to us that we were leaving our three children to you boys, okay. I have it in our Wills."

Jimmy looked at Kenny and said, "No, I think you should have a woman in that mix. Not two guys to care for your children if you and your wife die. Eddie, you should rethink this issue."

Kenny replied, "I am okay with it. What are the chances Eddie and Barbie would both die at the same time? Jimmy, we got this for Eddie. I like his children. They pull my finger and I fart."

No more was said. Then Eddie left to be with his wife, Barbie. Jimmy and Kenny went to Tim's place but Marci was there. Kenny wanted in the worst way to see Marci's whip that night. Marci talked most of the night but she did show Kenny something with her whip but with no sex. Merit watched it all and was disappointed too. They went to sleep after Marci left, and at about two am, Kenny and Jimmy heard a noise. There were two guys outside with guns. The boys had a rule of shoot first, ask questions later. So, they shot the two guys but didn't kill them. Merit was up and calling his dad, Tim. Tim had a room at the place where the wedding was to be.

Merit ran out to see who was shot and it was Joey, Tim's brother, the father of the groom shot in a place we won't say at this time. Larry, Tim's boss was shot in the ass. The boys had great aim and could hit a fly off the wall at many feet away. Their training as a secret agent was money well spent by the government. Larry was crying, Joey was bleeding, the boys looked on.

Kenny said, "Who are they? Why do they have guns at Tim's home? It is not hunting season and never in the city."

Jimmy replied, "Go back to sleep. It is not one of Tim's neighbors or anyone who lives in his home. It is just his brother and boss. Tim and I have an agreement that I can't shoot any of his neighbors or someone living here, but it said nothing about shooting his boss or brother."

Merit was trying to help Joey and stopped the bleeding with a clothes pin from a neighbor's clothes line. Then the neighbor's dog took the shot off part of Joey and was going to eat it. But a cat got it away from the dog. A bird got it from the cat and the bird dropped it for the rat which Merit stepped on with his foot. The ambulance came to take Joey and Larry to the hospital. Gerald, the company doctor was called. Tim was on his way to his home and mad.

Merit cried out, "Help me."

Kenny looked out the door and asked, "What should I do, Jimmy?"

Jimmy replied, "Take a plastic bag for Merit's shoe as we can sew Joey's you know what, back."

Kenny got a big plastic bag from the kitchen and took it to Merit for his shoe to put in. Tim and Gerald were there then. They had gotten the report from the police and the neighbors. The police agreed with Gerald and so did the neighbors. The boys did what anyone would have done if someone comes to your home with a gun at early morning hours. Tim wasn't pleased with the boys and took Merit's plastic bag to the hospital. Larry would be fine and Tim removed the bullet. Larry would be sitting differently but that was all. Joey, on the other hand, as Gerald stated would be a one baller. Gerald didn't like Joey and he blamed Joey for having an affair with his wife, Shella. Tim gave Joey medication and went home with Gerald to talk to the boys. It was about seven am in the morning. Merit got up and saw someone coming. He got one of the guns and it went off by mistake and shot a hole in the ceiling of the living room. Eddie had just gotten there and took the gun from Merit as Tim came in with Gerald right behind him.

Tim cried, "Eddie, you too and my ceiling. Who shot my brother? Who shot my boss?"

Eddie replied, "I hate to be left out."

Eddie winked at Merit. Eddie was not going to tell on Merit, for what could Tim do to Eddie? He was a secret agent and had a license for a gun but Merit had no license to shoot a gun.

Kenny replied, "I shot the guy's one ball off but just the right one."

Jimmy got up and said, "I shot Larry in the ass because he is an ass hole."

Gerald looked at Kenny and replied, "Thank you, my new best friend."

Kenny was please because this was the girl's father who Merit told him had the hots for him. And this girl was very close to her father which was what Jimmy had told Kenny that day. Linda, Larry's wife came to thank Jimmy for shooting her husband in the ass and all was good, but now they had to reattach Joey's unmentionable. They couldn't have Gerald, the doctor, help because, well he hated Joey so Tim would have to. But Tim delivered babies and this wasn't something he knew how to do. Tim knew push and breathe, then the baby comes out. Jimmy had been to medical school and was what kind of doctor?

Jimmy replied, "I am not doing that for Joey but Merit is studying to be a surgeon and I can talk him through it with Tim's help in the operating room. It will be good practice for Merit. And Merit is the only one who likes Joey to try to do a good job."

No one disagreed with Jimmy and they went right to work, for the wedding was that afternoon. The wedding had to go on as planned with no one knowing this issue for Joey. To the hospital they went, but Kenny took Gerald out for a drink of twelve-year-old scotch with Eddie. Gerald needed to be away from that hospital for the best interest of Joey's health. Sue wasn't pleased with this at all, but Jimmy, Tim, and Merit were working on it at the hospital for Joey. Eddie paid for Tim's ceiling to be fixed which Jimmy had Marci's people do it in an afternoon and a very good job they did. The surgery went alright for Joey and all was okay.

The tape ended there. Now Calvin knew all he was looking for - it was that Jimmy had a license to kill and did shoot people. Jimmy could shoot very good at any point from almost anywhere. Jimmy had a medical degree and was a doctor. Kevin told Calvin he never heard of anyone named Kenny, or even Eddie, but spies. He got documents on everyone but not these two secret agents. The song, "Secret Agent Man," was now in Calvin's head. Do they really take away your name and give you a number? Were Kenny and Eddie killed in the line of work? If you kill people then people may try to kill you, right? Not that great of a job.

Calvin checked again with the guys, T-Jay, Sam, and Micky. They knew no more about anyone named Kenny or Eddie in Jimmy's past. They did know that Jr. Joey got married to Jenny and had a lot of children but they were both killed in a car accident before Jimmy and Margo got married. The kids went to live with

Jenny's cousin, the one from their wedding who wore a hot pink bride's maid's dress with black hair. Micky found Calvin old wedding pictures. There were no pictures of Jimmy or Kenny, or Eddie at that wedding. Merit, Mark, Margo, and Gerald's two daughters were with Jenny's three family members, with Jr. Joey and his new wife Jenny in that picture. Margo had a pink dress on, one of Gerald's daughter had a peach dress and the other daughter had a crème dress on. That meant nothing to Calvin so he went back to the video room.

The video of the wedding was of the church; Jimmy and Kenny walked into that church and sat up in the singing area above the people. Tim was all upset and went to talk with Jimmy. Kenny wore a blue suit with a pale blue shirt and dark blue scarf and no tie. Jimmy wore a black suit with a black shirt and a white scarf with no tie. Tim was wearing the traditional wedding suits guys wore with the white shirts and tie.

Tim said, "What are you two doing sitting up here? Come down and join the family."

Jimmy replied, "No, I don't think we are in good with Joey and maybe the family. I think we will watch from here. It is safer for us. Maybe some anger issues."

Tim answered, "You better stay for all of this wedding or Sue will be upset. Just do it for Sue, Jimmy, and that means the church, meal, with the dance after. Got it?"

Jimmy nodded and Kenny asked, "What about me? Want me to stay too, right?"

Tim walked away without answering Kenny and went back to sit in the front row of the church next to his wife, Betty and his brother Joey, who looked a little sick. Then the wedding started and the bride's maids walked in. Jimmy and Kenny were looking at the girls but Tim's wife did have jackets on them to cover what needed to be covered. The girls did look great anyway and that kind of beauty is there for the boys to enjoy. The wedding was long and boring but the boys had eyes only for those two bride's maids. Kenny and Jimmy would have sat there all day if they could have looking at those bride maids. But all good things have to come to an end; out of the church they all went with Kenny and Jimmy there to assist the girls.

Gerald noticed Kenny and was okay with him around his daughters, which now Kenny called Peaches and Crème was the younger sister to him. Jimmy called Margo, sweetheart in her pink dress that Jimmy loved. Tim looked mad again. Was it because they did stay or was it because they were too helpful with the bride's maids? Jenny's cousin in her hot pink dress could have fallen off the world and they wouldn't have noticed. Jimmy and Kenny's helpfulness was limited which made Eddie laugh. Barbie was enjoying watching the boys doing what they do best, making a situation out of nothing at all.

At the meal, Kenny was sure to help Peaches and Crème to their chairs to eat, letting the two guys with them know that he was watching every move they made. Gerald's work was done and his daughters were safe for the night with Kenny around to protect them. Jimmy was sweetheart's protector always and no one touched Margo, not even her boyfriend, Steve. Steve did what Jimmy told him to, always and no more. Joey was sure his daughter Margo was safe from any guy but was she safe from Jimmy? Margo was almost twenty-one years old.

The boys ate together and appeared to be good. Then as Jr. Joey and his wife Jenny cut their wedding cake, Eddie's small son went up and peed on Jr. Joey's shoe. Everyone was laughing but he was a little boy so no one said anything about it. Eddie was pleased with himself.

The dance started and the wedding party started to dance. Tim gave Jimmy a look like "be good." Tim wasn't wasting his looks on Kenny, and Eddie had his wife to keep him in line. Eddie got the boys a drink from the bar, O'Doul's, non-alcoholic beer. The boys never drank liquor, not your James Bond type of shaken and not stirred. Why they never drank or very little was because they needed to be at their best at all times. A sip or two but never more than that.

Peaches came up to Kenny and asked, "Would you like to dance with me? My dad really likes you now. I really like you. Do you remember when you danced with me at Jimmy's engagement party and I was about thirteen? I am not a child anymore."

Kenny, the guy with always an answer, had a hard time with one and said, "Yes, oh yes."

To the dance floor they went and Sweetheart came for Jimmy and he took her into his arms and on to the dance floor they went. Eddie left to find his wife and the night was on. Tim stayed at the bar drinking way too much but then everyone was buying him a drink and what could he say, so he drank. Steve came to Tim at about midnight looking for Margo. Where was Margo? Tim looked for Merit standing outside and looked in the parking lot. Kenny was still dancing with Gerald's daughter who he called Peaches. Mark was dancing with Gerald's other daughter who Kenny called Crème and Eddie was dancing with his wife, Barbie. Where was Jimmy? Tim wasn't thinking good but he went to Merit.

Merit called out, "Tim is coming."

Tim asked. "Who the hell are you talking to?"

As Jimmy got out of Margo's car to talk with Tim, Tim had seen Margo sneak into the dance from her car. What was going on, Tim was thinking very slowly. Merit went into the dance too. Jimmy gave Tim some coffee which Tim drank but continued to question Jimmy about was he in Margo's car alone with her and what were they doing until he fell asleep? Jimmy had Kenny and Eddie help him get Tim home to bed. Merit made sure Margo got home okay and Mark made sure Gerald's daughters were safe at home because Gerald was drunk too.

The next day, the boys had to leave on a mission and Kenny with Jimmy weren't happy about it but Eddie was okay with it. His wife would come later with the children but they had to leave to be in London Monday morning. Jimmy left Tim a note on the table reading that he had to go to work and that Tim had drunk too which wasn't good for anyone. Jimmy and Kenny got roses for the girls. Jimmy got two dozen pink roses for Sweetheart or Margo. Kenny got two dozen peach colored roses for his Peaches and a dozen crème roses for her sister, which Kenny wrote "to my friend to take care of your sister, I will be back." They had to go to work and that was that. Eddie got the boys on the plane and to London they went. That was the end of that video.

Calvin would check if Gerald's daughters were married and to who. Did Kenny ever come back? What did Jimmy and Margo do in her car that night? Why did Merit cover it up and warn them?

Calvin knew Jimmy always had a few top people around him like now he had, T-Jay, Sam, Micky, his dad, Kevin, him, but Jimmy liked the number seven. Who were the other two? What about in those days, who was it? It looked like, Kenny, Eddie, Tim, Gerald, Jim, Charles, and Marci. Jimmy had a style he used and he was a doctor but he helped Tim deliver babies so Calvin looked at files and saw Jimmy was the baby's doctor. Could their skills be added at birth? Jimmy loved children and wanted to help with saving lives. Calvin had to know more about Jimmy's past and the boys. He checked files and dates but this was all before he was born. Kevin, his dad, knew very little about Jimmy's life before he married Margo. Calvin looked through more video tapes to find the one where it left off or at least when Jimmy came back from the mission. It had to be in nineteen eighty-four or five and then he found it. This video tape started with Merit going to Mrs. King to find the boys. Mrs. King makes some calls.

She turned to Merit and asked, "What should I tell the boys that is so important?"

Merit replied, "Tell Jimmy, Margo is late."

Jimmy, Kenny, and Eddie arrived at Mrs. King's door. The boys walked in and it appeared they didn't know what was going on and Mrs. King wasn't telling them on the phone. She got them something to eat and waited for them to pray then eat the food.

Kenny asked, "Are you in danger? Is Mr. King okay? What can we do for you?"

Eddie said, "Grandma, you got us worried. We came as soon as we could like you requested."

Jimmy looked down. Did he know or was Jimmy reading minds again? Jimmy's face got red and Mrs. King looked for Merit to come. Merit walked in and whispered something in Jimmy's ear. Kenny and Eddie were trying not to laugh but they couldn't help themselves. Did they overhear what Merit whispered to Jimmy? Mrs. King left the room. Merit sat down.

Eddie spoke first, "Jimmy, we know you love children and want to be a father. I know how much you love Sweetheart. Just get married. End of story. But she is not good for you."

Kenny said, "I could marry Peaches and we could have a double wedding. I love Peaches."

Jimmy looked at Merit and said, "Your dad will kill me. We didn't, but she did take off and things got out of hand. We went too far. I didn't enter."

Kenny was laughing and said, "Oh hell, Jimmy, I believe you. A virgin birth. You do pray a lot."

Eddie said, "What to do now? We are here for you, Jimmy."

Merit replied, "Maybe she is upset and wants attention."

After Merit left, Kenny said, "We can put Tim in his place because he has a wife and is sleeping with his boss's wife, we can prove it. I got pictures of Tim and Linda, Larry's wife."

Eddie said, "We could kill Tim. Is he not sick? An accident, he could bleed to death."

Jimmy said, "I will wait for Margo to talk to me. Merit is right. It may be she needs attention from me and that is all there is to it. I love her but I am not sure what kind of love it is - a friendship, a caretaker, or romantic love. I am so afraid she will die in childbirth like the last woman I loved. I just couldn't take it."

Kenny and Eddie looked sad and walked over to Jimmy sitting down with him not saying a word. Mrs. King came in to take them to their rooms to sleep for the night. The boys were back in town. In the morning Tim came to see why Jimmy hadn't come home to sleep at his house.

Kenny said, "Well, Tim, the last time we stayed with you, things didn't go so good, remember. I shot your brother and you were not nice to me about it."

Eddie replied, "I didn't want a repeat of a hole in your ceiling again. I think you were upset about it. You gave me a look that wasn't nice."

Tim said, "Kenny, you and Eddie are never welcome in my house again. But Jimmy, that is your home. You should come home to sleep without those two."

They left the room as Kenny replied, "Tim, that is cold, that hurt. We do have feelings."

Jimmy said, "Tim, I work with those guys, they are my friends. We had an agreement. I don't shoot your neighbors or anyone who lives in your home. I did pay for all of your nephew's wedding, even the gifts you charged. You can put up with Kenny and Eddie a little better than that. They do have feelings. We are working on a project to help get a contract for Larry's company, what more do you want from me?"

Tim answered, "I want you home at my house, safe. This secret agent stuff is going to get you killed. That means more to me than any project or contract for the business. I care about you. I worry about you when you are gone. You don't call and Margo cries all the time. You need to talk with her. You spoiled her so much not even Steve can handle her and he is her boyfriend. Jimmy, can't you find someone nice and get married, have a family? I know you love children. Quit that job. Eddie and Kenny should quit too. It just is not safe. Work with me. I will even work with Eddie and Kenny if you stay home. Please stay home, we'll find something you like."

Jimmy answered, "I will when this project is done. I am working in Russia. Big changes will happen for the good of all people, then I will retire. Boys, what do you think of Tim's ideas?"

Merit came in and said," Dad, it was me that shot the hole in the ceiling, not the boys. The gun went off. I am sorry. I should have told you before."

Kenny and Eddie stepped up to Merit and Eddie said, "It is okay kids, we got this."

Tim looked at Jimmy who nodded yes then Tim said, "You guys covered for my son. Why?"

Kenny replied, "He is a good guy. Why not. He did a lot for us."

Merit said, "Dad, I want to be like Jimmy, Kenny, and Eddie, a secret agent man. Will you guys help me?"

The boys looked at one another and then shook their heads no with Jimmy saying, "After this mission I am stopping this time, for myself."

Kenny questioned, "Do you mean it, Tim? You would help find work for me if I stopped being an agent? I want to stay here and marry Peaches."

Eddie said, "Kenny, are you sick? You, marry? Has hell frozen over? I better call the Priest and see. I am going to work in an office at MI-5 in Britain as soon as I can with Barbie. Get out of field work. We are getting too old for this stuff anyway, boys."

Jimmy said, "Kenny, call Peaches for a date. Where would you like to take her on your first date? I am sure Gerald likes you."

Kenny answered, "I want her to go to church. I want a lifetime with her or nothing at all."

Merit asked, "Why did you become secret agents in the first place? Tell me if it is so bad."

Kenny answered first, "I was born a mistake to my parents too late in their lives. I was just in the way and I felt no one love or cared. I was having fun. But I love someone and want to live."

Eddie answered, "My family has secret agents in them like my grandparents. My dad killed someone and was in jail. I wanted to marry Barbie but how do I get her family to like me? Being a secret agent was cool to them and I got to marry the love of my life. But I want to be home more with my family and see my kids grow up."

Jimmy answered last, "I did it to learn how to find people. It was after the accident with Sylvia and I didn't believe she was dead. I have tried to quit many times but the money is very good."

Kenny called Peaches and took her to church. Eddie visited his grandmother and looked at old picture of when she was a secret agent. Jimmy went with Tim and Merit to find Margo. The tape then moves to a Halloween dance at Steve's parents' home. Kenny is there with Peaches, Jimmy is trying to talk with Margo alone, and Eddie is running into the party looking for them.

Eddie asked," Where is Jimmy? I think someone is trying to kill my grandmother."

Kenny went to talk with Peaches and Jimmy said something to Tim then they left. Margo starts to cry and Peaches, with her sister, go to Margo then they go home. Steve stands there like what the hell is going on? Merit said something to him but Calvin couldn't hear it on the video, it was too low. The next thing on the video is Jimmy coming home and Margo waiting for him.

Margo said to Jimmy, "I am not, I was just late, I have it now. So, you don't have to worry anymore. Sorry, I know you don't have time for me. I asked you to make out with me and you never say no to me on anything. Then I took it too far, do you hate me now?"

Jimmy sat down by Margo and said, "No, I love you and I always will but I am afraid you would die as all the other women I have loved did. I have never been more afraid of anything in my life. I want to be a father again but I don't want you to die. I still have a broken heart. Please understand I need more time. It wasn't a mistake and yes, we went too far but not all the way. I did it because I wanted to. You will be twenty-one at your next birthday."

Kenny was with Gerald at a café and asked him, "Can I ask your daughter to marry me? The older one, Peaches."

Gerald replied, "I think you should learn her name. What do you think, Kenny? But yes, I am okay with your asking my daughter to marry you. Jimmy told me you will be teaching at the university he and Charles have, as an instructor for agents, students who want to be secret agents next school year."

Kenny replied, "Yes. I will start next September but until then I have to complete my work load. I will learn your daughter's name when the Priest said her name to me in Holy Marriage."

Then Kenny left to be with the boys. Kenny, Jimmy, and Eddie went through many things at Mrs. King's house. They found a bottle of wine with drugs in it to kill someone. It was in the wine that Mr. and Mrs. King drank before bed. Who would want them dead and why?

Kenny said, "I need a diamond ring for Peaches. I want to ask her to marry me at the Holidays. I already asked her dad and he is okay with it."

Eddie got down on his knees saying, "Praise the Lord, Kenny is getting married. I never dreamed it. Jimmy, do you need to marry?"

Jimmy replied, "No, no big deal."

But from the look on Jimmy's face anyone could see he was disappointed.

Next, they see Tim running to Jimmy telling him Charles' mother was shot in Paris, France and he is to go there right away. Jimmy doesn't want to but Charles is crying and Jim is there so the boys talk Jimmy into going. Kenny and Eddie go with, thinking this may have something to do with someone trying to kill Mr. and Mrs. King. Was Charles' mother an agent too in World War Two? Charles didn't know anything. Charles was a baby then. Jimmy went to Mrs. King before they left and yes, Charles' mom was Mrs. King's secretary at the secret agency. She was so young then. Jimmy, Kenny, Eddie, Jim with Charles left for Paris but when they got there, Charles ran to his mother in her hospital bed. Charles' mother looked at Jimmy standing in the doorway and she closed her eyes to die. Eddie looked at Kenny and they knew she just had to see her lover, Jimmy, one more time before she died. Jim was helping his friend Charles.

They went back but before the funeral Jimmy was sitting there with Eddie and Kenny, watching a guy drinking a bottle of wine. But was it the wine bottle with the drugs in it and who was the guy drinking it? Where are they? It looked like the one in Mr. and Mrs. King's home and then the guy left, but who was he?

The funeral of Charles' mom was where they were in the next video. Margo hadn't known about Jimmy and his older woman, lover. Was Jimmy going to tell her? No one said a word. The funeral was full of old friends from the spy agency and Charles' step brothers and sisters. Charles' dad was married before and his first wife died, then he married Charles' mother. They had Charles but his dad was killed before Charles was born in World War Two. Charles had always cared for his mother.

The funeral had whispers about Jimmy and Charles' mother's love affair. Kenny and Eddie with Tim stayed close to Jimmy. Merit was to be with Margo and Peaches with her sister that Kenny called Creme. Was Jimmy ever going to tell Margo? Well it looked like Jimmy wasn't going if he didn't have to. The tape ended and Calvin learned Jimmy didn't always tell people things he should have but if he didn't want to for no reason at all, he didn't do it. Like Jimmy should have told Teresa Mary she was his daughter. Or even tell Kevin but he didn't. What else was Jimmy not telling them that he should have. That the boys are back?

CHAPTER THREE

THE REST OF THE STORY!

Calvin had learned a lot about his boss, Jimmy, but nothing that made him a killer. Yes, Jimmy had an interesting life and his work as a secret agent did involve killing. Jimmy didn't kill people for no reason. If the boys did shoot, they would hurt them but it didn't appear they killed just to be killing. They took their work very seriously and didn't use it for personal gain or Calvin was sure they would have killed Tim for Jimmy to clear the way for him with Margo.

Kevin asked, "Do you think we should watch more. Are we getting any closer to what you want to find out? Or is it becoming entertainment?"

Calvin replied, "I think I am learning something about what I want to know. I need the rest of the story. But yes, it is entertaining. Jimmy was never boring."

They started the next video. It was Christmas and the boys were in church. Kenny held Peaches' hand. Eddie was with his wife and kids. Jimmy sat with Tim and Margo. After church, Jimmy and Margo walked away from the group. Kenny was on one knee, asking Peaches to marry him in front of Gerald and her sister. Eddie and Barbie were trying to get their children into the car. Tim was standing there with Merit, going nowhere, waiting for something.

Jimmy said, "Margo, we have to talk."

Sue asked, "What is going on?"

Tim replied, "Margo will start screaming in a few minutes and we need to help Jimmy."

Now Kevin and Calvin were thinking Jimmy was asking Margo to marry him. Is Tim okay with it? That wasn't the story they heard through the years. I am sure Margo thought the same thing.

Jimmy said, "Gerald's daughters, Merit, and Mark with you, have to go away to college after Christmas. It is not safe here for you anymore. Mrs. King has told us some things. My new project will cause some big problems for us. Please understand it is not forever. I love you."

Margo replied, "Not this shit again. You are sending me away. Hell no. I wouldn't go."

Tim heard Margo screaming at Jimmy as Eddie drove away. Kenny got his yes from Peaches.

Gerald walked over to Kenny and said, "I got this, Kenny, and I will be paying for the wedding."

Kenny smiled, letting Gerald handle it from there. Kenny had got his yes from Peaches to marry him. The girls were mad but Gerald's daughters did as their father asked. Merit and Mark did as they were told but Margo was the problem. Steve went to talk with the boys. But they did explain the situation and it was the only thing to do. Steve couldn't see Margo every day and maybe that was good. Margo was mad. Jimmy and his damn project. But that project brought in money for Tim at Larry's company and work. What was Jimmy's project? They went to Jimmy's office and knocked on the door. Jimmy waved them in.

Calvin said, "What was your project back then?"

Kevin could see Jimmy didn't want to answer but he replied, "Watch the videos and then we can talk about it. There is too much to say."

What did that mean? Calvin and Kevin did what Jimmy told them to as they always did. Back to the videos. This time the boys were with Tim in Mrs. King's home waiting for her.

Mrs. King walked in with papers and files, then she said, "I am very sick and the doctors can't do much more for me. But you are my boys and you need to continue. This is what I need you guys to do. Tim, Larry is videoing everything so you find these videos and hide them for later viewing. Kenny will have to be killed or make it look like you were killed and you can only tell Peaches but not her father or sister can know. You can't work here but we can get you a job training secret agents or spies someplace unknown. You can come for Peaches later. Eddie, I can get you and Barbie deep in British intelligence. I still have some pull in the agency."

Mrs. King then turned to Jimmy, saying, "You can't leave or die because of your people. What you need to do is be here with Tim. Complete the project and stay alive."

Jimmy asked, "How long do you have, Mrs. King? Does Mr. King know?"

As Mrs. King left the room she said, "He knows nothing about my health issues or my work. That keeps him safe. Larry knows nothing about this ether and I want to keep it that way."

Kenny replied, "We always have known that Larry knows nothing at all."

Jimmy said, "Tim, I need Kenny and Eddie on the Majestic Twelve with me okay? The group is where we will always stay in connection forever."

They all agreed and left the house to rest at Tim's home. The video tape ends there. What happened to Eddie and Kenny? They had to watch more. Tim knew and they were best friends! Calvin looks and finds another tape; is this right after or a later date? The video starts with Jimmy waking up and Kenny sleeping on a chair, Eddie comes up from downstairs.

Eddie called out, "Tim, food. Where is there any food?"

Jimmy replied, "Tim doesn't do food. I will make us biscuits and gravy or butter."

Kenny awakened with, "Food, did I hear food? I want biscuits. How is your tooth, Jimmy?"

Jimmy answered, "That dentist gave me something for pain. I think to shut me up. He did nothing for my tooth."

Eddie replied, "So none of us can eat because your mouth hurts? I am hungry. Tim, where is your wife? I want food."

Jimmy said, "Tim's wife doesn't cook and she lives in Paris, France. That is how Tim's marriage works. He believes in phone sex. Don't ask."

Kenny replied, "Please Jimmy, don't tell us more. But maybe you could marry a woman that cooks. Can Sweetheart cook?"

Eddie asked, "Kenny, can Peaches cook? Or is that something you haven't checked out? Checking everything but her cooking?"

Kenny laughed. Jimmy was smiling. Eddie continued, "Barbie can cook but Jimmy hates my wife, wonder why?"

Jimmy said, "Kenny, I need you to become a Majestic Twelve member this week so that is why I called you guys here. Eddie, go see your grandmother and she will give her membership to that group. She can do that. Mrs. King is the leader at this time of Majestic Twelve but unfortunately when she dies, I want that job, understand."

Eddie and Kenny agreed. Tim stood there saying nothing, the look on his face told a story of the fact that he had no idea what this Majestic Twelve group did or why Mrs. King was the leader but he asked no questions. They ate biscuits with butter and hot cocoa, then the boys left Tim. Eddie went to his grandmother's home and Jimmy with Kenny drove to the side of the hill where Jimmy stopped the car.

Jimmy said, "Kenny, I need to tell you something first. I need you to never tell Tim or anyone else. I will tell only Marci."

Kenny replied, "What, you got a child somewhere no one knows about? You and an unmarried woman have a kid? Okay, I am sorry. What is it really, my lips are closed."

Jimmy replied, "I have a daughter with that married woman who died having my son. My daughter is about seven years old. I need you and Marci to care for her if anything happens to me. She was married to this man so the child is with him. I did do the tests, the child is mine."

Kenny didn't know what to say to that, so he agreed to do it. Then they went somewhere in a building that wasn't on the video. Time passed and Eddie was at Tim's place as they returned.

Eddie asked, "How was it?"

Kenny replied, "Scary. Those people mean business. But it is at a different place each time. Very secure and secret. You find out the new place from time to time. But you meet so many times a year unless there is an issue and don't ask what is an issue. Trust me you don't want to know. What happened to the guy I replaced?"

Jimmy answered, "He died by drinking wine. We helped him to drink this wine that killed him. He was the one that shot Charles' mother. Yes, my old lover from my past. No questions."

Tim smiled as Kenny and Eddie looked at each other. Marci had come through the door. She looked around then stopped. What had happened? What had she missed?

Kenny said, "Tim, you have got to learn to lock that door of yours."

Jimmy replied, "With Marci it would do you no good. She comes on her broom and flies in like all witches."

Marci answered, "I love you too, Jimmy. Where in the hell have you been? You don't call me. Did you get anyone pregnant? Are you even trying? Get off your lazy ass and just do it."

Eddie spoke up, "Now, that is a conversation I never dreamed I would hear. Jimmy, what is wrong with you? Just do it. Do we care who it is, Marci?"

Marci answered, "At this point, no. You are not getting any younger, Jimmy. I have a list of women for you to try."

Kenny said, "If I wasn't engaged, Jimmy, I would help you out on this project for Marci."

Eddie replied, "Jimmy, I am so sorry, I am married but I wish I could help you too. Let me see that list. Maybe Tim could help. I know Tim has a wife in Paris, France and his boss' wife as a lover, but maybe he could help a little?"

Jimmy answered as he tore up Marci's list, "Very funny boys. Marci I will take care of it. I love children and I want some, just give me time. No to your list. No thank you."

Kenny asked, "Marci, maybe you could do it yourself with Jimmy?"

Tim was laughing and said, "They fight a lot, he gives her money, they raise children together, but they don't have sex anymore, so I think they are like married people. Marci has a husband, who is a good friend to Jimmy."

Eddie remarked, "That does sound like Jimmy's love life. Let me see, there was Sylvia, Charles' mother, Marci, Venus, and the married woman. Am I leaving anyone out?"

Jimmy replied, "I am sitting right here as you talk about me. I need to talk to Marci alone."

Marci was all smiles now as she and Jimmy walked out the door. The video didn't show where they went or what they said but it was at Tim's home where all the guys do is sleep until Jimmy comes back. Eddie and Tim look at Jimmy but Kenny knows what Jimmy told Marci about his kid. Maybe she would stop telling him to have a child now but why was that so important to her?

The next video was of Mrs. King dying with Larry crying at her bedside and Mr. King in shock. Tim had called the boys back. Eddie came in to be with his grandmother, the only mother he had ever known. Jimmy and Kenny stood by the door. It was happening now. Tim called Merit to bring back the girls for the funeral. Then Tim called all of Larry's brothers to come back. Eddie's dad, Lee, was let out of jail for the funeral with guards. Lawrence came from Italy. Larry's younger brother, Lonnie, didn't come home. Mr. King's daughter, from his first wife, named Joanie came, but not his son named Jonnie. They waited but Jimmy was sure that Jonnie, who had been Larry's partner in the business, was killed and at the bottom of the river by Mr. King's home. Jimmy also thought Lonnie and Jonnie were the same person. Jimmy laid out his theory for Kenny and Eddie with files, papers, and then his input. His idea was that Mrs. King, as they knew was a British agent in World War Two, and in those days, women agents did things like sleep with the enemy to get information. Eddie was shocked by this, but not his grandma. Jimmy showed that she married Eddie's grandpa who was a British pilot in the air force and they had Lee, Eddie's dad. But he was killed in the battle over London. She had baby name Lawrence who Jimmy believed was with an Italian father as the British tried to get the Italy government not to join Germany or at least find out what was going on. Then she had an affair with a German relative of who? Someone Jimmy believed was Larry's father. The British wanted the USA's help in the war, so agents went to America and that's when she met Mr. King. He was a military guy high up in the government. She got pregnant with Larry's younger brother but what could she do? It was known that her husband was dead. Mrs. King could pass off the three first children as her husband's but not the last one. Larry had to go live with his father for about three years as she had the baby, then the father who was Mr. King took his son to his first wife to adopt.

Eddie said, "Jimmy, I bet you believe in that paperwork somewhere that Larry killed President Kennedy and his brother Bobby. My uncle is not evil. I know you hate him but come on."

Jimmy replied, "Yes, I do believe Larry killed President Kennedy and Bobby because Larry needed the war in Vietnam for his business, making weapons with Jonnie. Larry found out this was his brother Lonnie so he killed him. The Kennedys were going to tell the world about aliens or UFOs and stop all action in Vietnam. Kennedy was looking into the Majestic Twelve."

Eddie shook his head in disbelief. Kenny didn't say a word but Jimmy was right about one thing and that was that the Majestic Twelve group work was something to do with aliens or UFOs. Kenny was the newest member and still in shock over that first meeting. He couldn't tell Eddie. Eddie would learn now that his grandmother died with him in her place at Majestic Twelve as its newest member.

They continued to review that paperwork of Mrs. King's sons and it showed only three sons but she gave birth to four sons. Where was the last boy, she named Lonnie? Larry lived with his mother after he started school and was good friends with Charles whose mother worked for Mrs. King. Charles' mother worked for her before and after her husband died. Charles' dad was a sailor and he was on the ocean looking for this German battleship called the Bismarck. There wasn't any information as to whether that was how he was killed in the war or not but he could have been killed on a ship by a battleship called the Bismarck or he was on the ship that sunk the Bismarck. It was hard to know at this point. The video tape ended there. All Calvin could think of was that song, about how they had sunk the Bismarck, from World War Two. The past was starting to come alive for Calvin because he was starting to know these people, who they were and how they lived. And that they knew Jimmy. Did he have any family in World War Two or even One? What about Vietnam or the other wars? What about 9/11? What did he really know, if anything, he was a baby? Could that be on a video if Larry already died? But who killed Larry? No one ever knew or did Jimmy find out and told no one? This wasn't like Jimmy to let something like that go without an answer but Jimmy was shot sometime after that. With more questions, to the video tape room they went. Tim was told by Mrs. King before she died to be in charge of the video tapes. Did Tim take them over and continue after Larry died, for what reason? Why do the videoing in the first place? Calvin recalled that Micky told him once about the video tapes. Jimmy and Tim wanted to know about the guys they worked with before. Did they mean Eddie and Kenny or who?

Kevin said, "We had a lot of people die in car accidents. The wine thing has me thinking that Tim died from wine. Whenever Margo needed Jimmy back, he came back to her when someone died. Like her twin brother Mark or her mother, Sue. Could Margo have been a killer? I feel something bad about her. She wanted Jimmy too much and would do anything to keep him. But your mother and her parents weren't close at all. No connection to Jimmy. That was Aaron's ex-wife April who married Jimmy. Taking Jimmy away from Margo."

Calvin thought for a minute and then asked, "Aaron is Margo's husband now. How do you know him? Because he married Jimmy's ex-wife?"

Kevin replied, "No, we were best friends in college and through law school. Aaron had a brother who was killed around the time Marci was killed by this Billy Joe. The same guy that took Margo for money, one billion dollars he wanted from Jimmy."

Jimmy looked in and asked, "How is it going? Getting boring? Find your answers?"

Calvin replied, "The videos are interesting. Did Tim continued taping after Larry died?"

Jimmy replied, "Not at first, I don't believe he did. But after I was shot, he did to find out things. Tim was never sure why I was shot by Larry's kids. If there was video, Tim felt he would have had proof for the police but there was nothing. That was good because Steve shot us."

Calvin asked, "Do you know who killed Larry and Bob at the meeting with Tim that day?"

Jimmy smiled and walked out of the room, handing Calvin three tapes. Jimmy must have thought this was too easy to figure out. Do you know the answer readers? Calvin started the next video at the funeral of Mrs. King and Larry is crying with Mr. King. Everyone is there but her son Lonnie and Mr. King's son Jonnie. Jimmy and Margo have a few moments but not much on the video, then Kenny talks to Peaches.

Kenny said, "My love, I got to go away now but I will come back for you. If you tell anyone their life will be in danger. Please don't tell your father. I am afraid for him. Wait for me then we will have to go away for some time. You can see your family but secretly. Please understand, I am so sorry. Do you still love and want to marry me?"

Peaches took her ring off, giving it back to Kenny and walked away. Kenny cried, Eddie and Jimmy came to his side. They took him away. Kenny left town with Eddie, and Jimmy went for a lot of long walks. Tim was so busy with Larry and Mr. King, no time to even think of anything else. Gerald had his hands full with Peaches crying and now wants Kenny back, but no one can find any of the boys. Merit was standing there with Mark doing the best he could with Peaches' sister, but then things got worse as they always do. News came that Kenny was killed in the line of duty. No one knew anything, just a letter to his parents and Jimmy sent Gerald a note. But the note was strange, it read something about, that Kenny was gone and he loves Peaches so much. He is very sorry if he hurt her. Talk to you soon, was all Jimmy wrote, with a bottle of twelve-year-old scotch which wasn't something Jimmy would ever send anyone. The note was even typed. Gerald wasn't believing Kenny was dead. Something was up and he was questioning his daughter. She did tell her father what Kenny had said to her before he left and she gave him back his ring. Peaches was a mess, crying all the time and her sister tried to help her but then the unthinkable happen again, Mr. King died. Gerald had to try to help Mr. King but the grief was too much for him over the death of his wife. Larry was an unbelievable mess. Tim had the kids come home hoping Jimmy would show up. Where the hell was Jimmy? The video ended.

Calvin looked at the next video of Mr. King's funeral. But all Calvin could think of was songs of guys dying after he gets a Dear John letter from the woman who was to have loved him. Could things like that happen to Calvin? Kenny could take down any guy, but the woman he loved could kill him with just a look.

Kevin said, "Son, I am sure Kenny is alive. They are trained spies and good at their jobs."

They went for the second video tape Jimmy gave them, of Mr. King's funeral. The weather had been warm but it got cold as the funeral continued. Mr. King's daughter was there but no son. Tim ran up to Jimmy as he walked in without any of the boys. Not even Eddie was there and Kenny was dead as far as they all knew.

Tim said, "Where the hell have you been? I have had my hands full with Larry. Gerald could have used your help too with his daughter."

Jimmy replied, "I had to get Eddie to take over with Majestic Twelve and his new situation with MI 6 or 5, or whatever, then his family. I just hate that wife of his, Barbie."

Tim asked, "Is everything done? Are they good?"

Jimmy replied, "Yes, and I will try to talk with Peaches. I have no idea what I will say to her. Who is all here for Mr. King's funeral? Everyone who wants money?"

Tim looked around and answered, "Mr. King did have a lot of money but I think it all goes to Larry and his kids."

Jimmy looked for Jonnie and then saw Mr. King's daughter crying but Jimmy wanted to hide from her as she walked up to him. Tim was all smiles now. Jimmy gave Tim a look like, stop it.

Joanie said, "Jimmy, I heard you were an agent and could you find my brother, Jonnie? I don't know where to start and I know he would be here for our dad's funeral so something is wrong."

Jimmy replied, "I would start by checking the river behind the house. I am sorry for your loss."

Tim said, "Jimmy and Eddie haven't been the same since this happened to Kenny. Sorry, give them time. Eddie can't come today."

She smiled like she understood and walked away. The funeral was a church thing then out at the burial ground. Margo came up to Jimmy and she was cold so Jimmy gave her his coat. Margo got as close to Jimmy as possible. Tim and Gerald were too busy with Larry to notice. But Merit and Mark were watching, taking his mom with his dad somewhere so they couldn't see what Margo was up to. Steve, Margo's boyfriend, had to work at his dad's company for something went very wrong that day. Peaches and her sister were talking to someone in the shadows. The video was cut there and stopped. Kevin looked at Calvin; could it have been Kenny, was he alive? This was too short of a video, even Margo's birthday party was cut off or just gone. Kevin was sure this was when Jimmy and Margo had their first night together, that is what Merit told Kevin. The night of Margo's twenty-first birthday. Then all hell broke out when Mr. King's Will was read and his son, Jonnie, was found at the bottom of the river by Mr. King's home. What to do but watch the last video Jimmy handed them.

It started with Jimmy and Tim talking to Margo and Steve about meeting Larry with Bob at this out of the way place. Jimmy didn't like the idea but Tim wanted to try and work something out with Larry over this company issue. Tim had won the votes for he now controlled the shares in the company with Margo's boyfriend, Steve's share he bought from Mr. King's daughter, Joanie. Margo left with him, to see Steve's parents. Tim went to see Merit and they talked but Jimmy went to see a guy in the shadows. And there was another guy with him. The boys are back is the rest of the story, now they can see it was Jimmy, Eddie, and Kenny. Kenny is not dead.

Jimmy said, "Kenny, you have got to stop doing this. She either goes with you or you stop coming here to see her. Eddie talk to him. He is not thinking straight."

Eddie replied, "Oh yes, Jimmy, you got this all under control. What the hell are you doing? Sleeping with who, Sweetheart? Is she marrying Steve or what? What head are you thinking with? I am the only one who has it under control but this Majestic Twelve thing has spooked me. I don't sleep well at night. I am not afraid of the enemy but I am afraid of aliens now."

Kenny input, "Well boys, we are fine secret spies so what do we do now? I think Eddie should take sleeping pills, Jimmy should kill Steve, and I will talk to Peaches tonight, okay."

They all agreed and leave, then Kenny is seen meeting Peaches, kissing her he said, "Peaches, my love, we have got to stop doing this. I will get found out. Please come with me tonight. You can come home and see your sister anytime you want to. I promise and she can come see us but it has to be without anyone knowing. I want us to marry soon. I want a family with you. I do work as a trainer for spies in the agency at an unknown place."

Peaches answered, "If you were here, my dad Gerald wouldn't have died. I know Larry killed him. Can you find out if he did? Jimmy isn't sure. Dad did drink and drive drunk. If you find that out then I will leave and marry you."

Kenny promised Peaches he will and if Larry did have anything to do with her father Gerald's death, he will kill him along with anyone else who helped him. But tell no one not even Jimmy. Kenny is sure Eddie will help him. Then they make out and they leave their different ways. The words were hard to hear because Kenny was talking very low but they were sure that was what was being said between the kisses.

The day of the meeting was happening and Jimmy was with Tim, as Margo with Steve waited for Larry to come with Bob. There were three guys in the car. Margo asked Steve to get her something from their car they left down the road and he went to do that. As if Margo knew Larry was coming by a signal of yes, they could see it now. Peaches and her sister signaled Margo with a mirror that Larry was on his way. Kenny and Eddie stopped the car before it got to Margo. Kenny took his gun out and shot. Eddie shot at the video camera so they couldn't see what happened. They can only hear the video sound after that.

Kenny said, "This is for Gerald from Peaches, die."

It sounded like the other guy was taken in a car with Eddie and Kenny, then they were gone. Jimmy was down there in minutes but they were gone with Larry and Bob dead. Margo was crying uncontrollable. Steve took her home. Tim found a phone to call the police. Were Kenny and Eddie trying to get information from this guy that was with Larry on how Larry could have killed Gerald? Margo knew all of this, but didn't tell Jimmy. Jimmy must have found out about it, but when? Where is Kenny now? Did Peaches marry him?

All Kevin knew was she married a nice guy, but who? Not much was ever said about it. And her sister did marry later but Kevin never knew more about it, they were Margo's friends. But Gerald's daughters were Jimmy's friends too or Kenny because Jimmy did go to his Majestic Twelve meetings several times a year and had for years. Kevin remembered Jimmy always went to his meeting there. Jimmy never missed a meeting ever, that Kevin could remember. But when Tim and Merit died, Jimmy went to more meetings at Majestic Twelve. Now Kevin understood why this helped Jimmy, going to those meetings, were Eddie and Kenny there?

Kevin was now questioning, did Margo kill her Uncle Tim with wine? Would she kill Merit? They did have a lot of car accidents. But driving is not really safe is it? Jimmy wanted them to see these video, was he unsure of how Tim died?

Did he question it? Was he having Calvin and Kevin look into it now? They did have the time. This virus had everyone at home and they were no heroes now. Just like everyone else, staying home and being safe. Life had been busy and life does go on but something like this virus stopped the world in its tracks. Good does come out of things and God is everywhere even in the worst of times. How we use those times is what God gives us and Jimmy was using it to relook at things. Jimmy was having Kevin and Calvin take a second look because maybe he felt too close to the situation. Sometimes emotion can cause us not to see things as clearly as we need to, so we go to a good trusted friend for help. But this too will end and you will wonder what did I do with my time? Well, Kevin and Calvin were continuing with watching videos. They wanted to know the rest of the story.

The video did have some breaks in it like someone didn't know what they were doing and started it up again in the middle of things. Like Tim trying to video Jimmy, and he was sick in bed. He was shot with Marci and her husband caring for him. Kenny and Eddie were there too. Well, that does explain why Jimmy was in good care at this hard time in his life when he almost died. The boys were there for him, not just Tim and Margo with Merit. It showed Jimmy waking up with Kenny and Eddie talking with him, but they stayed out of sight from Merit and the others. Then the video showed Jimmy and Margo's wedding. Not much of the wedding, a little with Kenny and Eddie in the shadows. The end of the video showed a small wedding with Kenny and Peaches marrying as Jimmy gave the bride Peaches away to marry Kenny with Eddie as best man. Tim was videoing. A very low-key wedding. Peaches' real name was Gail and she was wearing her grandmother's old wedding dress. There was a picture of her grandmother in that dress at her wedding and a picture of Gerald, her father, on a table as you walked into the wedding. Calvin sat back, pleased that Kenny got his girl. Kevin wondered how he missed all this, then why Tim never told him about Kenny and Eddie? Kevin was sure Tim told him everything. But then Tim was like Jimmy; some things they should have told about but they didn't. Things like, am I an alien from another planet or did you make up this tall tale like you love to tell people, Tim? Oh, how Kevin wished Tim was alive. So, they went to find Jimmy. He was praying in their church at the house they lived in. They waited as Jimmy came out.

Jimmy said, "I thought I should start with you two meeting them first and see how that goes. You can't go into the meetings with us but sometimes Kenny or Eddie bring one of their kids or grandchildren with them. They wait in the café until we are done but it is long. What do you think? Do you want to meet Kenny and Eddie? Kenny has a son and a granddaughter. Eddie has three kids and five grandsons."

Calvin said, "Oh, hell yes. When can I meet them? What great friends you have."

Kevin asked, "Boss, do your children know Kenny and Eddie? Were they at Tim's funeral?"

Jimmy said, "No, I want my children to meet Kenny and Eddie with their families and you guys. Margo and Gail had a fight right after Tammy was hit. They never talked again. Gail didn't trust Margo after that. Kenny made sure Margo couldn't find them. That is why Kenny or Eddie didn't come to Tim and Merit's funeral. Margo doesn't know how I keep in touch with Kenny or Eddie. So, this is between us and Sylvia knows."

Kevin asked, "Were they at your children's weddings?"

Jimmy replied, "I went to all of their children's weddings and they came to all my children's weddings."

Kevin said, "How could we not have noticed?"

Calvin replied, "There were so many people at all the weddings and there were Jimmy's people so maybe that is how. Counted as Jimmy's people. Do your children know them, Jimmy?"

Jimmy answered, "No, I have never told my children but now I have to tell Cindy. We each chose one child to know about us, in case they ever need help from the other two. Kenny has his son, Gary, because his son has some health issues. Eddie has his daughter, Bonnie, because her husband was killed in the line of duty as a spy. I am picking Cindy because of the work with our people at the place that we now call Marci's. We are to pick one grandchild too."

Calvin asked, "So you work with Kenny and Eddie at Majestic Twelve only and no more secret agent spy stuff? I still have questions and why did you let us watch the video now? Where have Kenny and Eddie been all this time?"

Jimmy answered, "I have seven trusted people I use to help me. Now I have T-Jay, Sam, and Micky. Then Kevin and you, Calvin, but I like the number seven so Kenny with Eddie are my co-workers. If I need anything or if they do, we help each other for life. We look out for each other's families. You watched in the video, them at my side when I was shot and how they helped me when I almost died. That is what we do. But it is time for you and your dad to join us.

They have been in what we call the shadows. I need Cindy to have seven people to help."

Kevin asked, "Why did Tim or you never tell me about them?"

Jimmy replied, "A need to know thing, it is secret agent stuff and nothing to do with you. They like you and are glad you are here for me. They are very pleased with you, Kevin, for helping me find Sylvia, something they couldn't do and they did try. They admire you, Kevin."

Calvin asked, "What do we do now?"

Jimmy replied, "Because I have questions about Tim's death and so do the boys. We aren't sure if Margo is a killer. But there is more to see about your mom. Kevin, I never wanted to hurt you. Kevin, you know Tim cared so much for you and Micky. This will hurt, but Calvin is old enough to know. So, watch more videos. Tim is not the best video person but he did try."

Kevin was speechless and we all know Kevin is never without words. Jimmy left the church with Calvin looking at his dad, wondering what is it? Did Margo kill his mom and why? Do women kill? That's not good. What is the rest of the story here about, Tim's death or others who have died? Or could the rest of the story be about the boys, Kenny, Eddie, and Jimmy?

CHAPTER FOUR

WHAT DOES IT MEAN?

Calvin was wondering what did it all mean? Did Jimmy want to know if Margo killed Tim with a bottle of wine after he got out of rehab for drinking? Why couldn't Jimmy say that, if he wanted to know. Jimmy had issue still with Margo for some reason, he didn't see her as this evil person. But then his dad didn't see Teresa Mary as a drunk with drug issues. Did Calvin have the same problem with his Jay? Is love really blind? Kenny got his true love, Peaches, and Jimmy got his Sylvia. Calvin wanted to know more about Kenny and Gail who he called Peaches. Then what about Eddie with Barbie and their three children? If Calvin asked Jimmy, would he tell him? Did Sylvia know Kenny and Eddie? She must have from before.

Kevin said, "Where do you want to start, son? Should we look to see about Eddie and Kenny's lives or try to find out if someone killed your mother first?"

Calvin asked, "Dad, what did it all mean?"

Kevin replied, "It means that there is crap we need to find out. We need to know if your mother was killed and if so, by who? Then we need to know about Kenny and Eddie. They are a big part of Jimmy's life and he is a big part of our lives. I am staying with Jimmy, are you?"

Calvin answered, "I am staying with Jimmy and I want to know all of it."

Calvin looked through the video tapes. What was he looking for? Then he saw the dates. What was the date his mom died? Calvin found the file in Michael's office of his mother with a picture of her, like the picture his dad gave him as a child. Betsy and he had different mothers, that his dad told them as small children. Betsy had a picture of her mother but the only mother they remembered was Linda. Kevin came in and they watched the video together.

It started with Kevin crying, holding Betsy and Calvin in his arms. They are about six months old. Betsy is playing with something on Kevin's desk but Calvin is half asleep. Alice, Calvin's mother walks in with very high heel shoes on, screaming at Kevin. It is hard to hear it all but she takes Calvin from Kevin. She then throws papers at Kevin and he sits there in shock. She walks out the door and sees Margo on the stairs. Margo gives her a push and she falls backwards hitting her head on the stairs. Tim sees it but Margo leaves and Alice is dead. Kevin comes out of his office and is thanking God on his knees for Alice being dead. Jimmy gets there and calls for help. Then Sam, Micky, and T-Jay come running.

Kevin asked, "If any of you guys killed my soon to be ex-wife, I won't be mad just tell me."

On the video, the guys all say no. Jimmy tells Kevin to bring Calvin and Betsy to his place to live. Kevin is a little uneasy with this now as Calvin is watching it. What to say to your son when he sees how happy you were when his mother is dead? Kevin even thanks God and prays, how do you explain that to your son watching it all? Kevin is not having a good day. A few days pass before Calvin talks to Kevin but he is not mad, merely shocked. Kevin doesn't give any reason why, just that he didn't want to lose his son, Calvin. They need to tell Jimmy, but why didn't Tim tell Jimmy? Kevin was Jimmy's lawyer, and cost her so much? They went to Jimmy and told him.

Jimmy said, "Maybe that is why Tim started drinking so much more after that. He didn't know what to do. I had my hands full with Sylvia leaving again and Sally's cancer. What a bad time. Margo was mad at Alice for not telling her about April and me. April had told Alice all about us. I had the affair to get Margo to divorce me. A guy can't walk away from a woman, she has to leave him or he will never get free from her. So, Margo killed your mother, I am so sorry. I can't say I liked your mother but I never thought of that."

Calvin wanted to know more about his mother. Why did people not like her? Calvin called everyone but no one appeared to like his mom. The wives of the guys were nice but said she was April's friend. So, where was April, this was Jimmy's second wife.

Calvin went to his Dad and asked, "Dad, where is April now that she and Jimmy got divorced?"

Kevin looked uncomfortable and said, "April killed herself before the divorce was over. She wanted a lot of money from Jimmy and he would only give her so much, not a penny more."

Calvin said, "Don't tell me she drank wine? Maybe Margo killed her too, for Jimmy."

Kevin said looking sad, "Maybe because Tim and Merit were the doctors then."

They both went for Michael's files and as they looked, Michael walked in and got the old boxes out for them. Tim had it that April killed herself by pills in her glass of you know it, wine. Margo could have put the pills in April's wine but then they had no proof. Margo was a crazy woman and had tried to kill Jimmy many times. Kevin and Calvin went to find Jimmy to talk.

As he knocked on the door, Kevin said, "Boss, we have found out Margo killed April by putting pills in her wine. We can't prove it but we can prove Margo bought April the bottle of wine as a gift. There was a card from Margo to April in that box which read to the ex-wives of Jimmy Elgin, drink on me, Margo. The bottle of wine is gone. Tim and Merit were the doctors then."

Jimmy looked up and answered, "Maybe she killed April. I never saw it, even after I was sure it was Margo that helped Kenny and Eddie kill Larry with Bob that day at our meeting with Tim."

Calvin asked, "Did Kenny or Eddie ever tell you they killed Larry with Bob?"

Jimmy replied, "No, but then Kenny had a rule: never admit to doing anything he could get in trouble for someday. I could see it in Kenny's face and Eddie wouldn't even look at me."

They left Jimmy's office but a few days later, Jimmy told them that the Majestic Twelve meeting was the next day. Kevin and Calvin agreed to go. The only one who knew was Sylvia. The night before Calvin didn't sleep at all. He was thinking of Eddie and Kenny with Jimmy, what great friends. Some good friend was better than money in the bank or even gold anywhere. In the morning, Kevin looked like he hadn't slept at all, either. Jimmy, Sylvia, Kevin, and Calvin got into the car to go, without Michael or Marie asking any questions. Kevin and Calvin slept all the way there. When they woke up, they weren't sure where they were. In the next car were two nicely dressed guys with the prettiest younger woman Calvin had ever seen. Her long brown hair glowed in the sunlight with her big blue eyes. Calvin couldn't breathe.

Jimmy made the introductions and the pretty young woman was Kenny's granddaughter, Kelly. There was some small talk and a few jokes from the boys.

They were very nice to Sylvia without looking at her much at all. They ordered food and ate, asking Kevin a lot of questions about things in the past with Tim. Then, Jimmy, Kenny, and Eddie left for their meeting up some stairs.

Jimmy said as they left, "Take care of my Sylvia, now you know why I brought you two along."

Eddie said, "Jimmy never lets us watch his Sylvia. He must really trust you two. But we know how jealous Jimmy is of his Sylvia. Don't even look at her."

Kenny replied, "I am trusting you two with my granddaughter. Kevin is in charge. Calvin, I know that look. I have had my breath taken away by a young woman too. I'll be back."

Kelly replied, "Grandpa, stop it. He is that way with everyone around me if they are guys. He scares the hell out of them. Then Eddie and Jimmy come over and help him."

Sylvia said, "I need to go to the bathroom, Kelly would you come with me, okay, Kevin?"

Kevin agreed as they walked to the ladies' room and Calvin had to go into the bathroom to check it first then the two women could go in. Kevin and Calvin waited by the door of the ladies' room. Calvin was sure his dad would say something like, son go home and make up your mind as in that old song where a guy is dating a girl and then gets distracted by her older sister. The father takes the guy aside and tells him to go home and make up his mind. Sylvia and Kelly were back before Kevin said anything at all to Calvin.

They went to the table then Kevin whispered, "Son, you got time. There are many pretty women in this world. Check them out before you settle down with one for life. I like Jay but if she is anything like her mother and not like her grandmother, well, maybe keep looking."

For Calvin, the time just flew by. Kelly and Calvin talked about everything. As they came back it was a quick good bye but Kelly kissed Calvin on the lips good bye. They were all laughing.

Kenny turned to Calvin and said, "I'll be watching you, Calvin, around my granddaughter."

Kenny was laughing too as he helped his granddaughter into the car to go. Where was social distancing there? But Calvin liked it. Kevin pushed Calvin into the car. In seconds they were gone and Jimmy was driving them home. No one talked all the way home. Calvin wasn't the kind of guy that if you aren't with the one you love, then love the one you are with.

Jimmy called Kevin and Calvin into his office. "I need to tell Cindy about Eddie and Kenny."

Calvin asked, "Jimmy, when do we tell the others about Kenny and Eddie?"

Jimmy replied, "I'm not telling anyone but Cindy, maybe C-Jay with you two. Kenny and Eddie don't want to come out of the shadows ever."

Kevin said, "Calvin, ask Jimmy. I can see what you want. I know you, my son."

Calvin said, "Jimmy, I guess you want Cindy to take your place in Majestic Twelve. Kenny would want his son or Kelly and Eddie, one of his family, to take his place so there is no room for me."

Jimmy smiled and replied, "Yes, we do want that but there is always someone else who dies that doesn't have anyone to replace them on Majestic Twelve. I am the leader and we have a guy who is very sick with no one he wants to give his seat to. I can talk to him about you for the job. But if it doesn't work out, you could give your seat to Kevin, your father."

Calvin agreed that was what he wanted. Jimmy nodded and they stopped talking about it as Michael came into the room. Michael looked at them but continued on what he was doing. Calvin continued to look through the video tapes and the night Tim died was on video. Tim was trying to video that night as Jimmy, Tim, and Kevin had come home to Jimmy's house.

Jimmy said, "We are so glad you are home. Kevin, let Tim be alone with his wife tonight, okay."

Kevin replied, "I understand but, in the morning, we are going to eat everything on that table."

Linda goes in as Tim calls out, "Kevin, this woman wants me. Help, Jimmy, I am not into this."

Jimmy knocks on the door and asked, "Is it okay if Tim comes out and plays before bed?"

Linda replied, "Yes, I am sure Tim has missed you guys more than me. But not too late, okay."

Tim came out happy. Jimmy, Kevin and Micky are there having the best time with takeout food. The video was long and there's a lot of laughing so they couldn't hear any words that were said. Then in the morning about five am, Micky goes home. They go to their bedrooms as Kevin hugs Tim before he goes to his room. It is very quiet on the tape but they let it run. Kevin and Jimmy sat there for hours watching this nothing but the room getting dawn. Then, Linda comes out of Tim's bedroom and gets the kids' breakfast. The kids eat and go back to their bedrooms to play.

Linda calls out, "Jimmy, Kevin I fed the kids breakfast and they are playing in their rooms nicely. I am going to help Margo cook this morning for Thanksgiving meal. Tim, I love you. You guys were up all night, sleep for now. I will see you guys later to eat."

Tim calls out, "I love you too, Linda, sleep guys."

Jimmy said, "Go to sleep."

Kevin replied, "I am asleep."

It is very quiet and then the back door opens with a key and Margo walks in very slowly into Tim's bedroom with a half- bottle of wine.

Tim whispers, "I can't have that, I promised Jimmy."

Margo answered, "Just a little wine and not a whole bottle, then never again." Margo said in a low voice at Jimmy's bedroom door but close to the video so they hear it, "You think that billion dollars of yours got Tim safe, think again. I win."

Margo leaves the house without anyone knowing she was there. The video runs longer but it ends with Merit and Margo after Jimmy brought Tim back from trying to recover him. Kevin is getting help. Micky, Sam, and T-Jay come running to take Tim to the hospital.

Merit picks up the bottle of wine and said, "I know what you did to my dad and I am telling Jimmy. No more Margo and you killed Mark. I know it but I don't know how you did it."

Margo replied, "Merit, I am so sorry. We can have this bottle of wine checked for anything. You are upset. Here I will get you a glass of water."

Margo puts pills in the glass of water then gives it to Merit to drink. He drinks it and leaves.

Margo runs to the neighbors, crying, "Help me, Merit said he is going to kill himself. Call the police. I am going after Merit. Call Jimmy or the guys."

The video ends there. Jimmy got up and went to Sylvia. Kevin called Micky and told him to come to see them as soon as possible then went to his bedroom. What would Calvin do? What would you do? Calvin decided to make copies of this video. He didn't want anything to happen to this information. The next day, Jimmy called Kevin and Calvin into his office with Sylvia there. Okay we all knew Jimmy would tell his Sylvia everything. She sat quietly by him.

Jimmy asked, "What should we do with this information?"

Kevin replied, "I called Micky last night and told him to come here to talk but I didn't tell him about what. He will be here today. I had to let him know. Micky and Tim were so close."

Calvin said, "I made copies of that video for us to keep safe with that information."

Jimmy answered, "But what do we do now? Margo is still Michael and Sarah's mother."

Sylvia spoke, "I think Calvin should take it from here. Jimmy is too close to the situation. Kevin, you are the lawyer, so find what is the legal thing to do with what facts we have. We need another lawyer for Cindy. Cindy is now the boss of the company and she needs her lawyer. I think it should be Kelly Anderson, Kenny's granddaughter is almost through with law school."

Calvin asked, "What about when Micky comes today? What do we tell him?"

Jimmy replied, "We show him the video and if we can, watch it again with him. Micky will need his support group, T-Jay and Sam. I don't want Michael or Sarah to know, maybe Cindy."

Calvin said, "Micky looking at that video with us is okay, but T-Jay and Sam would have to agree not to ever tell anyone else. Then Cindy, Betsy and their husbands, if they can keep their mouths shut. Just in case Margo finds out we are on to her."

Jimmy smiled in agreement with Kevin. Margo killed Tim because she was mad at Jimmy. Margo was crazy and dangerous. She needed to go to prison or a mental hospital.

Calvin said, "I think we should take a copy of the video for Kenny and Eddie to review."

Jimmy agreed. Calvin wasn't sure what they were going to do about Margo. Micky had come and they watched the video. Micky was upset and wanted to kill Margo.

Jimmy said, "We will have Calvin in charge of this with Margo because he isn't so close to the situation. I will have Calvin bring T-Jay and Sam here tonight to review this video. Want to see it again? I understand if you want to go home. But killing Margo now, we aren't doing that."

Micky replied, "I want to stay and see it again with T-Jay and Sam. See what they think of it all. Just you three know for now and me? Thanks, Kevin, for calling me right away."

Kevin answered, "I thought you had the right to know as soon as possible.

We just found out. Jimmy, doesn't want Michael and Sarah to know or anyone, really."

Calvin said, "We get the facts first. We will get that Margo and good, but we will do it smart."

They all agreed and Calvin got T-Jay and Sam to come in that night. They all watched the video again. Kevin had them sign an agreement that they couldn't tell anyone what was on that video tape but Kevin didn't have Micky, Jimmy, Calvin and Sylvia ever sign any agreement.

After the video, Sam looked at T-Jay and said, "Thank God you don't see that mother-in-law of yours anymore. I knew she was crazy but I never dreamed she was this crazy."

Michael was very busy with Marie and Sylvia was always sick. Then Jimmy asked Michael to do some research on the virus to help the cause. Just computer stuff but they had to try to be more helpful. Michael agreed with Marie helping him and Sylvia keeping an eye on Michael.

Jimmy had Sarah do some research on the ocean. There were animals on the beach of one of the states Jimmy said these animals were dying in large numbers. People had to help the animals back into the ocean to save them. Jimmy loved animals of all kinds, and this was very important to him. Sarah worked on the computer research with all kinds of groups. She was very busy with this work and Jimmy did call Sarah on updates. T-Jay kept a close eye on his wife, Sarah, for Jimmy so she wouldn't find out anything about Margo. Then before the Majestic Twelve meeting, Jimmy had Cindy, Betsy and their husbands watch the video.

Jimmy told Cindy his plan for the two new people but he didn't call them employees, he called them co-workers. In the morning, Sarah came and Michael met her, they talked about how important their work was to Jimmy. They told Cindy to keep up with the day to day stuff. Calvin was a little worried but they appeared to know nothing at all, but were there to show Cindy how important they were to Jimmy. The business Cindy did could run itself.

Sarah said, "Dad, it was not large amounts of animals but large animals on that beach."

Michael added, "Sarah, dad is old and he gets things mixed up. A man his age. And you know old people. I got this. Cindy, now keep doing the day to day things for the business. I am sure that company can almost run itself. Not so hard and if you need help, call Sarah or me."

Cindy wanted to hit her older brother and sister but Calvin winked at her with a smile. It was Cindy that Jimmy called to watch the video. It would be only Cindy that Jimmy would tell about Kenny and Eddie, so who did Jimmy trust the most? Then what about Teresa Mary and her children? Well, it would be Cindy that would have the grandchildren for Jimmy and Sylvia. And Cindy wasn't going to upset Sylvia. Cindy and Sylvia were best friends which pleased Jimmy very much. Cindy was the smart one and she would always be in Jimmy's favor as Kevin had been for finding Jimmy's true love Sylvia for him. Then they left again for Majestic Twelve but this time, only Calvin and Kevin went with. Kenny was there with Kelly and Eddie had a grandson named Edward there too. Edward was older than Calvin or Kelly but very quiet. They talked about Margo and had all seen the video.

Jimmy said, "It is time to go to the meeting. Calvin will come with us for an introduction. He will be our new member."

Kenny smiled and Eddie waved his hand, like let's go. Calvin followed them around a long hall to a big room with eight other people coming in and sitting down. Jimmy called the meeting to order and Calvin's membership was the first thing on the agenda. Kenny made the motion to have Calvin Carlson as the new member. Eddie seconded that motion and they all opened a folder then voted yes. The rest of the meeting was hard for Calvin to understand with files and numbers, then more voting. After hours it was over and they talked for some time. The tables were cleared. Jimmy locked things up in a briefcase.

Kenny said, "You did good, Calvin. You should have seen me at my first meeting. I was scared."

Eddie laughed, saying, "I was scared as hell but Jimmy and Kenny were there so I was okay. We are glad you are with us so now we have one third of the vote and not just one fourth."

Kenny and Eddie agreed as they left to find Kevin talking with Kelly about the legal stuff at the business with Edward listening, not saying a word. Kelly smiled at Calvin then waved goodbye as they left to go with the guys laughing. Even Kenny was laughing.

Jimmy said, "Calvin, you can show Edward and Kelly around Cindy's business when they come?"

Calvin replied, "I would love to."

Everyone was laughing and Edward said his first words, "I have that effect on people."

Jimmy couldn't look at Calvin without laughing.

When they got home Kevin asked, "Calvin, are you okay?"

Calvin replied, "I don't understand Majestic Twelve. I vote as Jimmy, Kenny, and Eddie do."

Kevin said, "They watch for UFO's. But I mean with Kelly, Kenny's granddaughter?"

Calvin was going to answer but Jimmy came in. It was time to go because Kelly and Edward were there. To Cindy's business they went and with Kelly sitting by Calvin, there was no social distancing there. Edward was laughing already. Kevin shook his head as Jimmy drove. Cindy and Betsy were there to greet them. Jimmy made the introductions and they were shown the business layout. C-Jay and Mickey took a look in at the pretty Kelly with Edward. Who were these special co-workers Jimmy had for Cindy? They knew Kelly was a lawyer but what was Edward's job? After they were all done showing them the company, they talked.

Calvin asked, "Do you want to do a walk around the business? I would love to show you."

Kelly smiled, saying, "Yes, I would just love that."

Kelly took Calvin's arm and Edward looked at everyone saying, "You know they want me to come with, right?"

Then he followed behind them. Jimmy was laughing so hard and even Kevin couldn't stop laughing. The others just stood there with their mouths open wide saying nothing. You know Betsy was on the phone to Jay the minute she could talk again. Jay was still into herself but Betsy got to the point with shut the hell up and listen to me now.

Betsy said, "Cindy got a new lawyer named Kelly and she is pretty. My brother Calvin is noticing her and she is after him. Got it, Jay? Get off your pity potty and make up your mind. Your mommy or your guy?"

Calvin was with Kelly and Edward after that most of the time. It was work, right? What were they going to do about Margo? She couldn't get away with this. That was what all the late-night working was about, right? With Calvin and Kelly, oh yes, Edward too.

Edward came over to Calvin and asked, "Women problems? Can I help? Look at it this way, guys like us in the world have to work overtime and not settle down so fast. With this virus we may need to repopulate the planet. Save your energy, the human race may need you."

Calvin looked at Edward, saying, "Are you full of something? It is better when you don't talk."

But for the first time, Calvin had a friend and he liked Edward. Calvin went to meet Edward's family, all of them, secret agents, spies, like their great, grandparents and parents were. What about Kelly? The Eds, as Calvin called them, guys all warned Calvin, hands off of Kelly, Kenny trains spies. Kelly was pretty but worth dying for?

Calvin went to Jimmy's office, knocked and asked, "When are you telling Cindy about Kenny and Eddie?"

Jimmy replied, "June twenty-first. I want you to take Kelly to the video room with Edward. Show Kelly and Edward about their families. Then we need to decide on Margo, what to do."

Calvin asked, "Who is we? Who is deciding on Margo? Not just you?"

Jimmy answered, "I have the final say."

Calvin left to meet with Edward and Kelly. Edward said, "Let's look for Kelly's dad's stuff first."

Calvin asked, "Kelly, give me an idea what period in time are we looking for?"

Edward was laughing as Kelly replied, "I was born before my parents got married. My mother is older than my dad and she was training to be a secret agent with my grandfather Kenny. My grandparents weren't married either before my dad was born. My question is why? No one will tell me why my grandpa Kenny was thirty-six and my grandma Gail was twenty-three?"

Calvin found the video of Kenny talking with Peaches, he was telling her how much he loved her but he had to leave because of an issue and he had to die in the eyes of the world. Peaches didn't want to leave her dad, Gerald. Later it showed on that video, Margo come to Peaches.

Peaches said, "I heard Jimmy was shot, what happened? I have to talk with Jimmy. He has got to find Kenny. I am pregnant with Kenny's child. I will marry Kenny. I don't want my dad to know. It was my fault before I knew Kenny had to go, we did. I told Kenny I wouldn't go with him because I didn't want to leave my dad alone. Please find Kenny and see if he wants me."

Margo replied, "I shot Jimmy and we had sex the night of my twenty-first-birthday. I thought it was someone else. I will tell Jimmy about you and the baby. He will find Kenny for you."

Jimmy and Tim had gotten out of the hospital with Merit to bring them home. Margo and Merit were planning to take Tim to another hospital for treatment. Margo was alone with Jimmy.

Margo said, "I should have told you sooner but things got in the way, like paying for Uncle Tim's medical bills, that damn school dance and Kenny's Peaches is pregnant with Kenny's baby."

Jimmy asked, "Tell no one, I can find him. I thought she told him to go away. Is the baby his?"

Margo replied, "Yes, she has been with no one else. It was before he left, find Kenny."

Jimmy answered with a smile, "I will let him know."

Then Jimmy left for a while that wasn't on the video. There was nothing until he came back and shook his head okay. That video ended but Edward handed Calvin another short video. This one started with Eddie and Kenny coming into town the back way not to be seen. Kenny goes straight to Gerald's home and crawls into Peaches' bedroom laying down beside her. She turns over and almost screams. Kenny puts his hand over her mouth. He whispers something to her. She hits him in the face and then kisses Kenny. Eddie crawls up to look in.

Eddie asked, "Do I have to sleep in the car or what, make out on your own time."

Peaches and Creme, as Kenny calls them, find a room for Eddie to sleep the night as the video doesn't show more than Eddie sleeping. But in the morning, no one notices they are there. Eddie gets up and puts something in the coffee so when Shelia and Gerald have their morning coffee they go back to sleep in their chairs. Eddie with the sister, Crème, help put them back to bed and Eddie goes back to sleep. The sister watches TV. Time goes by until Kenny and Peaches come out of her bedroom, kissing. Kenny lays out a plan as Eddie wakes up. Kenny's plan is for Peaches and her sister to come live with him. Telling their dad, Gerald, that they are continuing their education in London, England to be doctors. Kenny even has the paperwork for the University but it isn't the scholarship like it reads, for Kenny is paying for it all. The plan is set, then Eddie and Kenny leave but it appears a few weeks later Kenny comes for the two girls, Peaches and her sister. They all leave for Kenny's home. The video stops there.

Kelly asked, "Why didn't they get marry right away? Grandpa Kenny loved grandma Gail so why did they wait? Can we find more on it?"

Calvin and Edward looked but there was nothing on Kenny's home on the video or in London. On the next video, Jimmy and Eddie are meeting Kenny at a café.

Jimmy said, "Kenny, are you sure you guys want to wait until the baby is born to marry?"

Kenny said, "Peaches wants to wear her grandmother's wedding dress and she can't do it pregnant. I don't want to upset her because she was so sick at the start of being pregnant so we didn't marry. We will tell her father on Christmas and then marry after the baby is born."

Eddie said, "I think that will be a wonderful Christmas gift for Gerald to have a grandchild. I am sure he will forgive you and then his daughter marrying you in his mother's wedding dress. How nice and meaningful."

They all left. It restarted as Kenny and Peaches hold a baby, standing at Gerald's front door.

Kenny said, "Gerald, I love your daughter and we have a son. She was in school and lived at my place in London. Her sister stayed with us too and went to school but we asked her to get Shelia out of the house tonight so we could talk to you alone. Please give us your blessing to marry and forgive me."

Gerald replied, "Come inside, it is cold out there and let me see that grandchild of mine. It is a boy? I am so glad you aren't dead, Kenny. Jimmy was acting strange about it. Yes, oh yes, you can marry and I forgive you, Kenny, always."

It looked like all was good and Gerald was great with them getting married. Shelia and the sister come home but they couldn't hear everything, it was a good time. The next day, Peaches and her sister find the grandmother's wedding dress. They plan a small private wedding at the house. The baby is Baptized and named Gary Gerald Anderson, which is Kenny's last name, for they will marry in two weeks. Eddie and Barbie are the Baptism sponsors because Jimmy can't be there with Margo due to the issues with Larry's company. Jimmy will be there for the wedding as Kenny's best man at Gerald's house. Gerald is so happy but Shelia meets with Larry and tells him all about it. Larry and Bob talk too low to hear. They are planning something. Kenny, Eddie, and Barbie have to leave for a mission to complete one more thing because Jimmy is busy helping Tim with the company problems, the vote for control is that New Year's Eve. After they leave, Gerald goes to vote at the company. Gail stays home with the baby.

Sheila said, "I'll meet you there, Gerald, I am dressing too slow tonight."

Gerald leaves but on his way, Larry stops Gerald with his limousine. Larry calls out, "I hear from Shelia you are grandparents. Can I buy you a drink? A grandson. How nice for you."

Gerald replied, "I am very pleased but let's not say more. I promised Jimmy I would stop drinking and now I have the best reason in the world to stop, my grandson. So, thanks, but no."

Larry said, "Okay how about a coffee? I wouldn't tell anyone, Eddie is my nephew, you know."

They meet for coffee and all looks good until they see Bob talking to a guy, then they see the guy put water on the bridge that Gerald will drive over to the meeting to vote that night in a few minutes right out of that cafe. Gerald goes to the bathroom and Larry puts something in his coffee. When Gerald comes back, Larry has them drink up their coffees so they can go.

Larry said, "Don't waste any of this special coffee I brought you for your grandson's birth. I may lose my ownership of business and be poor."

Gerald drinks the coffee laughing and then leaves. The car is driving fine but Gerald looks like he is sleeping. The car hits the ice on the bridge then hits the side of the road. Gerald's head hits the inside of the car. Someone checks and they drive away, but who is it? Calvin calls his dad in but Kevin goes to get Jimmy.

Jimmy said, "That is Lawrence, Larry's son. He was in jail for the death of Merit's wife."

Kelly asked, "What do you mean was in jail? Did he get out? Did he serve his time?"

Jimmy answered, "No, he killed himself. Or did someone with secret abilities kill him in jail?"

Jimmy and Kevin reviewed the video again as Calvin with Edward took Kelly home. This was the first time Calvin met Kelly's parents, Gary and Selene. Gary was very nice, Selene was tall with dark hair and eyes, looking like she could handle anyone as a lean mean fighting machine. Edward got Calvin out of there as soon as he could and home safe. The next few days, all Kelly wanted to do is see why her grandparents didn't marry then. Everyone was surprised as Kenny, Eddie, and Jimmy walked in to sit down to talk with the kids that day.

Eddie said, "Your grandmother told Kenny to hit the road. If he would have been there, her dad would have never been killed. So, we took care of Gary until your grandparents worked it out."

Jimmy talked next. "When your great-grandfather, Gerald, was killed I told his daughters I would pay for his funeral. Eddie, Kenny and your dad as a baby, came to the funeral. Kenny wouldn't let me pay for Gerald's funeral, he did. Your grandparents worked it out for love."

Kenny didn't talk and they left the room. Jimmy and Eddie stayed close to Kenny as if this was hard for him to have Kelly know about his past. The work started again on what they could do to Margo for what she had done. Edward would have to wait to see about his family history but Kelly had gotten her answer. They closed the video room and reviewed Margo's case facts. But Calvin heard the boys. Mrs. King called Jimmy, Eddie and Kenny were talking so they went to listen to them first. Jimmy, Kenny, Eddie, and Kevin sat in the garden in the sun drinking hot cocoa. They never drank liquor or even coffee. Why, Calvin wondered but then there was no drug use either or smoking of any kind. Their work was too important and they needed to be sharp at all times. They did love non-alcohol beer; they just sipped it for appearances.

Eddie said, "I told you guys all these years ago to date a woman with no sex then marry her, have the sex, wait a year or so then have children, that really works. That is what I did. Barbie and I have been happy most of our years together. I love it."

Jimmy replied, "That is the advice we have given to our children. Right, Kevin?"

Kenny asked, "But did you give Calvin that advice or just your married daughters? I like Calvin but I see the way he looks at my granddaughter. I know that look of love sickness."

Jimmy said, "Okay, I married Margo, heaven help me. But she is the mother of my three kids."

Eddie replied, "Edward, Kelly, and Calvin will come up with something for Margo that is justice. I mean thou shall not kill is in the Ten Commandments."

Kevin said, "There are Ten Commandments? I thought there were just five?"

Kenny answered, "I like this guy, Kevin. But he has to keep Calvin in line around my Kelly."

Eddie said, "Maybe, you should talk to your granddaughter and not let her do as she pleases."

Kenny replied, "No, I have spoiled her rotten and I will continue to do that."

Jimmy said, "Remember my don't kill list and Calvin is on that list of don't kill, understand?"

Kevin said, "There's a list?"

Eddie replied, "Yes, we have agreement lists and understanding in writing. Here is your copy."

Kenny said, "If someone was trying to hurt a child you would stop them even if you had to kill them, the commandment we shall not kill is misunderstood. We must kill in war, right?"

Eddie replied, "Kenny you are going to a hot place when you die."

Jimmy answered, "Why don't we talk about the Ten Commandments another time. But for now, remember the list, no killing, Calvin. We want him on Majestic Twelve and if it is too much for him, Calvin can hand it off to his dad, Kevin. I need Calvin as my go between, Cindy working the business for me and my life away from it. I don't want Margo killed, because she is the mother of three of my children. What to do? I trust Calvin, Kelly, and Edward to come up with something everyone can go along with, even Micky. He can't know about you guys for now."

They walked away to talk about this, Kelly, Calvin, and Edward. They shouldn't have listened.

Kelly said, "Life in jail or locked up in a mental hospital. Jimmy doesn't want her killed but Grandpa Kenny will vote to have her killed. Eddie wouldn't vote to have her killed so that is it. They vote on everything as equals so that is the vote."

Edward said, "I don't think Jimmy wants Sarah or Michael to know, that is what a trial would tell them, so it is the mental hospital. We need her to put herself in the mental hospital, but how?"

Calvin said, "It would be best if Margo signed herself in and then signed Michael as her doctor."

Both Kelly and Edward agreed as they got the facts together for Jimmy to review with Kevin. Jimmy did just what Calvin, Kelly, and Edward believed he would, he had Eddie with Kenny's input. Kenny wanted to kill Margo. Eddie liked the mental hospital idea. Micky wanted Margo killed but Kevin went with the hospital because that is what he thought Tim would have wanted him to do so that was it.

Jimmy called Kelly, Edward, and Calvin into his office, saying, "Set it up at the mental hospital for life. But if Margo ever gets out, they will kill her and I agreed to that."

They went to work on it. Within a week, Margo was in a mental hospital for life. Michael was the doctor and Sarah was in shock but in full agreement with Michael. Margo had tried to kill herself. She said she had seen Tim coming back from the dead and Merit was with him. Margo tried to jump out of a window at her home and then she tried to kill herself by pills in her wine. Eddie's grandsons smiled and all was done. Now Calvin had Eddie's grandsons help and they enjoyed every minute of scaring the hell out of Margo. Margo was in the mental hospital under Michael's care for life. Margo was sure Tim and Merit had come back from the dead.

Micky was noticeably mad at Kevin because he didn't know about Kenny and Eddie but did know Kevin gave input on what to do with Margo. T-Jay and Sam were on Micky's side that Margo should have been killed for what she did, but they did all understand why Jimmy couldn't vote to have her killed. Kevin was in the dog house so to speak and only Cindy besides them knew why, but Kevin took it. T-Jay, Sam, and Micky still called Kevin, Jimmy's pet, but now they knew why because he was the one who told Jimmy that his Sylvia was alive. Kelly and Edward stood by Calvin as they continued their work for another day. They smiled, it was up to Calvin on the work they did for Cindy and Jimmy.

CHAPTER FIVE

THINGS ARE DIFFERENT, OKAY?

Edward said, "I think it is time to look into my great-great-grandmother Mrs. King. Are we done with Kelly's question? We took care of Margo. We got her so upset by seeing the ghosts of Tim and Merit, I thought she was going to kill herself."

Calvin replied, "Thank your cousins for all their help. They are good secret agents. But the drugs and liquor Margo had taking herself almost had her over the edge anyway. Just a push."

Kelly said, "I know, Edward, it is your turn but I would like to see that house my grandmother grew up in someday. Is it far from here? Do you know where it is, Calvin?"

Calvin went to look at old papers. One thing he did know it was in the same town as where Tim lived. This old home that Jimmy, Micky, and his dad restored with the help of Kelly's dad, Gary. Calvin looked up Gerald's named and found the house. Calvin knocked on Jimmy's office door.

Calvin asked, "Jimmy, do you have a minute? I need to know if it is okay for us to drive out and see this place of Gerald Dogenmeier's home which is now owned by JG Dogenmeier?"

Jimmy replied, "Thanks for asking. I need to talk with Kenny about it. I will get back to you."

Calvin, Kelly, and Edward were working on Edward's question about his family's past. The papers on Mrs. King showed she was a spy for the British government in World War Two and her father was in World War One, also an agent in the British government. Mrs. King's first name was Victoria and she married a fighter pilot. Her last name before she married was Winton and was after Churchill. When Victoria came to the USA her last name was Ewing. Eddie changed his last name to Edson but friends called them the Eds because all of the grandsons were secret agents. Edward's oldest cousin was Leo with his brother James, then the twins Virgil and Victor. All were between the ages of twenty-two and thirty. Calvin wondered if it was inherited the fact that every one of Eddie's kids were spies. If kids understood their family, they might know themselves better. Calvin told Kelly and Edward about the videos he and his dad Kevin watched on this and learned about their grandpas. They watched those videos. Kelly loved seeing her grandparents meet and fall in love. Edward enjoyed seeing Mrs. King being the leader of Majestic Twelve. What was the question Edward wanted to know?

Kelly said, "I think, Edward, we should look in detail about your great-great-grandpa."

Edward replied, "I think you are right. I am not sure where to start or what I am really asking."

Calvin replied, "That happens to all of us when we are too close to the situation. We will check into Eddie's dad, Lee's father, the pilot. When was he killed, we should find information on when they were married and go from there."

Family history did matter if you wanted to know health things or why you were the way you are. Why did I like to be a secret agent in Edward's case? Calvin learned that secret agents aren't hit people and don't kill people unless they may have to kill only to protect someone. But Majestic Twelve was to meet and Jimmy with Calvin only left for a new location. This time they talked on the way there about the files. Jimmy explained it was about UFOs.

Calvin asked, "Can we go to JG Dogenmeier's home?"

Jimmy replied, "You have to asked Kenny that question."

They were at the café eating, waiting to go to the meeting as Kenny said, "Calvin, ask it. Yes, you can take Kelly and Edward to JG Dogenmeier's home. It is my wife's sister's son's home now. She did marry but her husband cheated on her so I took care of it. She changed her name back to her maiden name and had her baby. It was a son that she named Jr. Gerald and they lived in that house all this time. Kelly's father redid that house for them."

It was time for the meeting and they went into it. After the meeting, they talked a little about nothing much and went home. Calvin was still mixed up about the meeting. He did understand what they did there. They checked on

UFOs to see if there was something someone should look into or not on each situation. The files had the facts on each issue. Calvin and Jimmy did talk on the way home about the different things they voted on with Jimmy explaining a lot of it. Calvin was glad that someone was doing it and he was pleased it was Jimmy as the leader. Kelly wanted to go out to the Dogenmeier place so Edward and Calvin drove out with her. They were greeted at the door by an older woman who said she was Kelly's grandma's sister. She showed them the house and it was a very nice, older large home. Her son Jr. Gerald owned the home now with his wife, Judy, and their son, Gerald the Third. Judy had her sister with her three daughters over at the house that day and one of them caught Edward's attention. Calvin noticed but they were looking at many pictures of Gerald Dogenmeier. They were all doctors. Then before they left, Crème as she called herself, showed Kelly her great-great grandma's wedding dress that her grandmother wore when she married Kenny. The older woman told Kelly that the dress was hers for her wedding. Crème, the older woman, had a grandson only. Kelly laughed but Calvin could see she wanted that dress and would be back for it when she married. Kelly even tried the wedding dress on and Calvin had never seen anyone look so beautiful in a dress. Kelly closed her eyes in dreamland as they drove home. Edward was still looking back at the girl from that place who Calvin wondered who she was and did Edward know her? The girl stood waving good-bye to Edward as Calvin drove with Kelly in the front seat and Edward in the back seat waving back at her.

Kevin was waiting for Calvin and asked, "Want to talk?"

Calvin replied, "I am a little mixed up about women. Did you love my mother when you married her? Why did you marry and have me?"

Kevin answered, "I think all men are mixed up about women and no two women are the same."

Calvin smiled and thanked his dad. Calvin was glad he had his dad and Jimmy. Calvin did feel unsure of himself and went to pray to his best friend God, then Calvin heard voices. Calvin listened and Kevin wanted Michael with Marie to name their baby Tim because Michael's last name was Elgin. Jimmy or Kevin couldn't bring themselves to ask Michael or Marie to do that. Calvin decided to write a note to Michael about what he heard. The next day Michael and Marie told Jimmy and the family that they wanted to name their baby, Tim Micky Kevin Elgin. Could Micky and his wife, Virginia, be the baptism godparents and Kevin be the confirmation sponsor? They all said yes and were overjoyed. Calvin had only seen Jimmy this happy with Sylvia and when each of his children got married. Michael winked at Calvin and Marie gave Calvin a big smile. Calvin thought he did something right and it felt good. He didn't have to save the world, just help make it a better place for someone else, anyone else with God's help.

Work continue on Victoria King and her first husband and on their son, Lee. What was Mrs. King's first husband's first name? Calvin, Kelly, and Edward found it with old papers in that old house Larry once had which was almost falling down. It looked like someone had lived there after Larry died. It was his daughter, Loretta, and her husband, Jr. Charles. They left there when her brother, Lawrence, was killed in jail by a secret agent person in question. Calvin and Edward guessed could it have been Kenny that killed this Lawrence but not the uncle? They said nothing.

Edward said, "I don't care about Lonnie, Larry, or Lawrence. I care about my family great grandpa Lee and great-great-grandpa Edward Churchill. I think I was named after him."

Calvin looked at Kelly and they knew it was time to ask Eddie. Edward had to do that for himself. Edward was afraid but then he also had to admit he wanted to stop being a spy or secret agent and become a priest. The only time Edward was happy was in church but then what about that girl Calvin saw Edward waving at? Calvin wasn't sure he could tell Eddie this or even Jimmy or Kenny. Edward had to do. Somethings a guy has to do for himself and that is all there is to it. Kelly and Calvin would be there for Edward always as his friends or forever co-workers. But who was that girl and did Edward know her? Was she there to meet Edward? Should Calvin ask Edward? Maybe Edward was praying to be with this girl. Calvin had never seen Edward look at anyone like he did this girl. Calvin made a list that Victoria King's married to Ewing, Larry's father. Who was Lonnie's father? Lawrence was born out of marriage and Lee was Edward's son, the fighter pilot who could have been related to Prime Minister Churchill.

Calvin knocked on Jimmy's office door and Jimmy said, "Come in, we should wait for Eddie."

Kevin, Kenny with Eddie came in, saying, "I guess I am up for the questions. Go for it, Edward."

Edward asked, "Was my great-great-grandpa Edward who I was named after related to the Prime Minister Churchill in WWII? I know he was a fighter pilot killed in the war. Do you know how many times his wife remarried?"

Eddie answered, "Yes, but not that close, related. He was killed in the battle for Britain. They won that battle and he died a hero. Victoria married three times and had two sons out of marriage. Lawrence with the Italian guy and Lonnie, which Jimmy thinks was Mr. King's son who he and his first wife adopted. Jimmy believes Lonnie and Jonnie were the same person but when we found Mr. King's son's body, it was too bad with those day's technology to know."

Edward answered, "Thank you, Grandpa. I want to become a priest in our church."

Kenny said, "Eddie, remember we are secret agents, not hit men. We don't kill."

Jimmy replied, "Calvin, take Edward and Kelly home now. Eddie needs to calm down. Kevin, help Calvin now out the door fast!"

They were out of Jimmy's office and out of the house within minutes to go home.

Kenny said, "Why don't you want Edward to be a priest? You have other grandsons to give you great-grandchildren."

Jimmy replied, "Just give Eddie some time. He is in shock. This grandson Eddie raised as his own child after Bonnie's husband was killed. Edward's father was killed even before Edward was born. Do you think that is why Edward doesn't want to be an agent because that is how his father was killed? We have always told Edward his dad was in heaven with God."

Eddie replied, "How would you feel, Jimmy, if your son wanted to be a priest? Your only living son, Michael. I know that isn't nice to say because you have two dead sons and a daughter that was killed. Kenny, what if your only grandchild wanted to be a Nun or sister in the church?"

Kenny answered right away, "I would be happy and I would drive her to that church right away. It would be a happy day for me. No more worry about guys like Calvin. I would thank God."

Jimmy was laughing with Eddie now and Kenny was thinking with prayer, could this be the answer to his problems with his pretty spoiled granddaughter, Kelly? What was one guy's nightmare could be another guy's dream come true with Jimmy thinking, oh my God! They met later and Edward was still worried about Eddie. Kelly was thinking Edward had a right to be a priest if that was what he felt was his calling. Calvin would need to talk with Edward.

Calvin said, "Edward, it is none of my business but that girl at Crème's home. You appeared to like her a lot. Is this priest the kind you want to be, that marry? She appeared to like you a lot."

Edward replied, "I told her we would be there so we could meet. You were so busy with Kelly that I could get away to be with her alone. They always told me my dad was in heaven."

Calvin said, "You want to be a British priest that marries or a priest in your grandfather's church that doesn't? Edward think about this. I think you are in love with the girl. What is her name?"

Edward answered, "Suzanne is her name and we met in college. She is learning to be a mental health doctor. Her family is out of money and she wouldn't take money from me for her schooling. I don't think she loves me."

Calvin replied, "You don't think she loves you because she wouldn't take money from you for her school? So, you want to become a priest. Have I got that right?"

Edward answered, "Yes, and God is the only one I can talk to. You don't understand. You are so good looking you can have any girl you want. Suzanne is the only girl I will ever love."

Calvin said, "Why didn't you ever tell me about her? I understand love. But are you sure she doesn't love you? She came out to see you at that home."

Edward replied, "Suzanne is a very nice person and feels sorry for me, that is all. We are friends. We do things together alone. We wanted to see each other. Please tell no one."

Calvin agreed, then went to knock on Jimmy's door with Eddie, Kenny and Kevin said, "Come in, son. It is plain to me that Eddie is not for his grandson being a priest. As I understand it, you three vote on everything so vote on if Edward should look into this as a career. Jimmy had more than one career and so did Kenny. Okay, Eddie, you and I didn't but most people do."

Kenny said, "I think that is a good way to go. Let Edward keep working to being a spy and a priest, why not? But Jimmy, it is time to tell Cindy about us."

Jimmy answered, "I don't think being a spy and priest go together. Calvin, come in here and join us. You tell Cindy what you know about Eddie and Kenny so I can fill her in. Got it?"

Calvin said, "I will talk to Cindy but there is a girl in Edward's life I am not to tell you about but I have to. Her name is Suzanne and I know they see each other alone a lot. She came out to the place at Gerald's home and Edward is in love with her. I think she loves him too. Edward doesn't think she loves him because Suzanne wouldn't take any money from him that she needs to go to school to be a mental health doctor. So that is why he really wants to be a priest and be with his dad who is in heaven with God. I shouldn't have told you. I am a bad friend."

A big smile came to Eddie's face and he replied, "Thank you, God. A girl that wouldn't take money from my grandson for her college. Now that is a lady. Calvin, you are a good friend to Edward and we aren't letting him throw away love. Time to vote on this."

Jimmy replied, "I vote Edward takes classes to be a deacon in our church and mental health doctor so he can be with this Suzanne more. Edward can still work for Cindy."

Kenny answered, "I vote to agree with Jimmy on all of it. We can get a scholarship for this Suzanne for school to be a doctor. We need a mental health doctor in the family. I know how to do it. I did that for Peaches and her sister, Crème, years ago. I got this."

Eddie said, "I agree, thanks, Calvin, for telling us. We will never tell Edward you told us. So, we all vote for Edward and love, thanks again all of you."

Calvin was pleased he told them to help Edward. Edward wasn't thinking straight. Then Calvin went to find Cindy. How would Calvin tell Cindy about all this with Eddie and Kenny? They were great guys and cared about their families like Jimmy with his dad, Kevin. Should Calvin tell Cindy about Edward and Suzanne? What would he say? Then what about Kelly and that wedding dress from her great grandmother that she looked so beautiful in? Why couldn't Calvin get her in that dress off of his mind?

Calvin said, "Cindy, we need to talk, alone. You can never tell anyone, not even your husband or my sister what we are going to talk about. Promise me for your dad, Jimmy. I am the go between your father and you. This is what he wants?"

Cindy say, "It is about Kelly and Edward with who they really are, right?"

Calvin replied, "That is a good place to start, thanks. Kelly is the granddaughter for your dad's old friend named Kenny and Edward is the grandson of your dad's old friend named Eddie. Kenny and Eddie are on Majestic Twelve with your dad as the leader of the group. I am the newest member. It is a group that watches for UFOs to see what could be real or not. They vote on what needs to be checked out but I don't know who checks it out. Kenny and Eddie are part of a close group your dad has which is seven people. He has the guys with my dad and I."

Cindy asked, "Why am I finding out this now? You said Kenny and Eddie are Jimmy's old friends. Why did my own dad never tell me about his close friends or see them? Were they at my wedding? I don't remember anyone different but there were so many people."

Calvin thought then answered, "Now that I have seen them, yes, they were at your wedding. Both even danced with you. But like you said, there were so many people."

After their talk Cindy had their Mother's Day lunch with Jimmy and he said, "I know Calvin told you about my oldest friends. So, ask your questions."

Cindy asked, "Why tell me now? Why didn't I know them before? I do remember dancing with them at my wedding. Kenny is funny and Eddie is very much a gentleman. Like an English gentleman but Kenny was so funny and I remember charming."

Jimmy replied, "Yes they are both that. We were secret agents together or spies. We had to go away out of sight. Being a secret agent is not at all like on TV or the movies. It is very different. It is a need to know thing for your safety and theirs with their families."

Cindy asked again, "Why tell me now?"

Jimmy answered, "The business and you need seven people you can trust around you. To call on for help. Edward needs your help and understanding. He wants to be a deacon in our church and a mental health doctor. There is a girl named Suzanne which Edward is interested in and my old friend Eddie wants his grandson to marry this girl. Kenny will help with a scholarship to medical school for Edward's girlfriend, Suzanne. Keep Edward and Kelly, I trust them."

Cindy asked, "So, who should be my seven trusted people?"

Jimmy answered right away, "Sarah and Michael but they aren't going to be your paid employees but co-workers like Kenny and Eddie have been for me all these years. Calvin, Betsy, Kelly, and Edward. For now, I am the seventh one. I want to be close to you and involved with the business making decisions."

Cindy was pleased with that and they had a wonderful day as they always did but Jimmy didn't stay long. He was home to his Sylvia, Cindy had given her beautiful flowers for Mother's Day. Cindy's plan was to always be nice to Sylvia then she was sure Jimmy would be there for her. There were things Calvin couldn't tell Kelly with Edward and they knew it.

Kelly said, "Kenny, Eddie, and Jimmy were very secretive. Don't ask too many questions."

Edward replied, "Old guys are like that, still living in the spy world, trusting no one. In their day, things were different but now I think it is safer. Oh yes, we are shutdown in a world with a stay home virus. Maybe the old guys are right?"

Calvin answered as they all went home their own way, "I think we should listen more to older people. They may understand more than we think about our world. They may know more."

Edward was seeing his Suzanne again and from what Calvin could make out, she got a scholarship for mental health college. Now that money wasn't an issue for her and Edward, they we seeing each other all the time. Now, readers, we all know who knew what when.

Kelly asked one day as they were working, "Is Suzanne your girlfriend, Edward? I like Suzanne."

Kevin walked and said, "I think we should meet this Suzanne, see if she is crazy. Sorry Kelly."

Kelly was laughing and said, "I am not worried, Grandpa, Kenny would take care of any guy who wasn't perfect. He always said the Bible is misunderstood. Eddie tells him he is going to a hot place. But you know my grandpa tells Eddie it is a sin to judge because that is God's job. It has been fun growing up listening to them, then Jimmy come in it gets good."

Calvin wished he had heard them. But would Edward ever bring Suzanne around to anyone to meet?

Betsy knocked on Jimmy's office door and the door was open as he looked up at her. Betsy did go to Jimmy and ask, "I think Mickey and I should start now to have a baby. No more waiting, we have been married awhile. What do you think? Not your area of thinking?"

Jimmy replied, "I think if you asked me then I would answer you and give you my advice which is to wait. You have only been married a short time. What is the hurry? It was hard enough on your father, Kevin, when you got married and now you want to make him a grandpa. Let's wait a little longer on that. That is what I think. Thanks for asking me."

Betsy didn't know what to say so she asked, "What about Cindy and C-Jay with the seven grandchildren you want from them? How much longer are we to wait?"

Jimmy replied, "Michael and Marie are giving me a grandson for now, that is enough. Cindy should wait too. We have time to enjoy this but not all at one time, please."

Betsy agreed but then with Jimmy she never got the last word in and he always had her speechless with thinking it over. She went to tell Cindy about her father, Jimmy's wishes.

Calvin was listening and he was sure there was more to it but he wasn't asking anymore questions.

Edward was sitting in church praying as Calvin came in to pray. Calvin needed to talk to his best friend, God. As Calvin was done praying to God, Edward can over to him.

Edward said. "I am not sure about me being a deacon. I am not good. What do you think?"

Calvin replied, "I think we should meet Suzanne's parents. You are the best person I know."

Edward asked, "No, I don't think they will like me because of my work as a secret agent or spy. But maybe because I now work for Cindy it could be different. Would you and Kelly come with me to meet them? Suzanne would like you two to come because she is afraid too."

Calvin and Kelly agreed to meet Suzanne's family but first they went to Edward's family. Edward was an only child of Eddie's only daughter. Edward was Eddie's favorite grandson with no question. Eddie was nice to Calvin. Calvin whispered to Eddie about meeting Suzanne's family with Edward and Kelly. Eddie was pleased. When they left, Calvin knocked on Jimmy's door.

Calvin asked, "Jimmy, got a minute to talk?"

Jimmy replied, "First, what about? I don't want to talk about when you should or shouldn't have kids, okay like your sister did. Or about my daughter Cindy's sex life, no we can't talk."

Kevin came in and asked, "Son, did you get a girl in trouble? Which one, Kelly or Jay or was it someone else? Oh my God. What are we to do now? Kenny will kill you. And Jay's mom is crazy. Jimmy do something."

Calvin said, "No, dad, I didn't. I just want to talk about Edward meeting Suzanne's family. Kelly and I are going with him. What should we do?"

Kevin was on his knees thanking God. Promising God anything and to be very good from then on. Jimmy looked like he wanted to say, get the hell out of my office crazy people, but he took a deep breath. Calvin did see Sylvia smile at Jimmy when he was breathing and looking at her.

Jimmy said, "Calvin, we have got to find more work for you. Edward will have to work this out himself, just go with him and be nice. You are a good friend but that is it. Pray for him."

A few days passed and Calvin was waiting for the night to go and meet Suzanne's family. He continued his work with the people at Marci's. Cindy came in and walked over to Calvin, pointing at her dad's office. They went to listen as Jimmy and Sylvia were going into the office talking.

Jimmy said, "I want to talk with you alone. I think I should move my office out of the house that we are living in. It worked great when the kids were growing up but now that they are all married, it is becoming an issue for me."

Sylvia replied, "No, I don't think so. These people need you. Calvin needs more work to do. He is a young man with girls on his mind. I think we should have a party with Kenny and Eddie for Cindy to meet them. Just Calvin, Kevin, and Cindy with her husband, C-Jay. Then Kenny and Eddie with their families. Eddie's daughter's husband was killed, right Jimmy?"

Jimmy answered, "Sylvia, what are you up to? Yes, Bonnie doesn't have a husband now and has not been with anyone for years. That is why Eddie is so close to Edward. He almost raised that grandson himself. I don't think Bonnie knows about Edward's girlfriend."

Sylvia said, "I don't think my daughter is ever going to be anything good for Kevin. He needs a good woman. Eddie's daughter is a good woman. Maybe Edward would bring his girlfriend around if his mother wasn't so involved with his life. Kenny should train Calvin as a spy."

Jimmy looked at Sylvia, smiling, he said, "Woman, you got this all figured out. I love you and you are right. Let's do it. What about more to do for Calvin? He is too smart and needs more."

Sylvia replied, "Kenny can train Calvin to be a secret agent, his work on Majestic Twelve and with Cindy. Have Calvin, Kelly, with Edward plan a party for Cindy to meet Eddie and Kenny."

Jimmy answered, "Sylvia, you must be there with me. Okay, I will talk to Calvin. I wouldn't move my office out of our home for now. I love you."

Sylvia smiled and kissed Jimmy. Calvin looked at Cindy and they didn't say a word but went their separate ways. Cindy looked back at Calvin with a wink of the eye. Calvin smiled and nodded.

Jimmy called Calvin into his office and said, "Calvin, I would like you to be trained as a secret agent or spy but Kenny will have to do the training. Kelly and Edward are there a lot."

Calvin replied, "Yes. Oh yes, I want to do that. Sign me up now."

Jimmy continue, "I want you, Kelly, and Edward to plan a party for Cindy to meet Eddie and Kenny's families. Could you do that and when?"

Calvin replied, "Yes, oh yes, I can do that too. How about Memorial weekend. No one is still going anywhere. Where would you want it?"

Jimmy answered, "I am not sure. You talk to Kelly and Edward, come up with ideas. I will tell Kenny that you are ready to start training."

Calvin agreed and left fast to find Kelly and Edward then said, "We have this party to plan."

Kelly said, "Cindy will be hosting this party so where will we have it? The guest list is here. So, we can't have it here because not everyone is coming. Food, who will make the food?"

Edward said, "We need a secret place that we have never used before. Like you do with Majestic Twelve. A different place each time and no one knows where it will be with security."

Edward was a good secret agent and he did know his stuff. Edward was to find the place with the security. Kelly invited the people without knowing where it would be like a puzzle or game. Calvin was to do the food for he did know two good cooks, Betsy and Jay.

Edward had great locations which he would have Jimmy, Eddie, and Kenny choose at the last minute from what had been used in the past with Majestic Twelve's meetings and there was always a café to use. But it wouldn't be open Memorial-weekend. Calvin could check to see if they could rent those cafes that weekend for a large fee. Kelly had made up complex maps and games for the families to find the location of the party as a party game. What fun it was, no two maps were to be the same but all ended up at the same place. Who were they meeting and why? What a guessing game with clues to solve. What to wear was on the invitations, anything goes, but be respectful. What did that mean? More clues to solve. Sunday was the day it started with church, then meet and greet, the meal with your hostess. The fresh vegetable would come from C-Jay's grandparents' farm in their greenhouse. Jimmy, Kenny, and Eddie requested fish for the meal with vegetable and dark chocolate cake to eat. The girls would get the fish from Sarah. Sarah was pleased she didn't have to go and asked no questions. Michael didn't want to go because Marie was so big with the baby. Sam, Micky, and T-Jay were assigned by Jimmy to take over the business so he could take this time off. Everything was going as planned and Calvin liked it when a plan came together. It was Jimmy meeting some old friends with Cindy. No big deal. Everyone was sure they would be at the graves looking at dead people Jimmy had known like Marci. Calvin had the girls go out on Saturday and made arrangements for them to stay the night to be able to cook the food for them. Sarah's work with the oceans got them the best sea food. Edward gave the location and Kelly gave the invitations out. Cindy did the drinks which was flavored water, strawberry, lemon, and peach.

The day came and the girls did the cooking, all was going well. Edward was there with Suzanne but everyone was so busy, no one noticed but Eddie and all of Edward's cousins. Kenny loved the peach water. Eddie was sure the lemon water was for him and Jimmy had to have the strawberry water because Sylvia had strawberry blond hair in her younger days. Sylvia even remarked that was before her hair started to go white as Jimmy told her that was just more blond. There was laugher and joke telling with fun for all. Jimmy had Sylvia and Kevin at his side most of the time. Calvin stayed close to Cindy with C-Jay but they danced, singing songs of golden oldies. Jimmy, Kenny, and Eddie sang so good together. Calvin did dance with Kelly but so did all of Eddie's grandsons. Edward only danced with Suzanne. Kevin danced only with Eddie's widowed daughter, Bonnie. Where was the social distancing?

Calvin made sure everyone got home safe and with their new map it was another game to find their ways home. Calvin loved that about Kelly but then he took another bite of the dark chocolate cake to die for he loved, that Jay had made, which was so good. Memorial Day Monday they were cleaning up and that too was fun. Eds all volunteered to help.

Edward said, "You know why the Eds volunteered to help? It is so they can be here with Kelly. I would watch her. They also want to know who was the angel who did the cooking besides your married sister, Betsy. I have to go but remember we meet Suzanne's family soon."

Calvin replied, "I am here for you. What about all these volunteers? That's not good for me."

Edward said, "You think that's bad for you. Remember you start your training to be a secret agent with Kenny this week. I'll be with you, don't worry too much. I will pray for you."

Calvin smiled but thought why should I be worried. Should I be worried? How bad could it be? Edward said he would pray for him. That didn't make Calvin feel better.

Kelly said, "My grandpa is very nice and helpful. You'll see. He is very good at what he does."

Calvin wasn't feeling it. Where was his dad, Kevin? Calvin thanked Kelly and Edward. He left to find Kevin and saw his father was with this Bonnie, Eddie's daughter. Was this to happen out of the controlled area? What were they doing? Did Jimmy know this? It was only Tuesday and Calvin's having a bad week. The weekend party couldn't have been better but now what was this? To make Calvin's day worse, Jimmy wanted to see him right away in his office.

Jimmy said, "Calvin, come in and sit down. The party was great. I think we should have more. What do you think? Was it a lot of work? You look upset? Something wrong?"

Calvin looked at Jimmy for a minute then said, "My training starts with Kenny this week. Is that hard or bad for me? Why is my dad with that Bonnie? Is that okay? I liked the party too and no it wasn't that much work. We enjoyed doing it. Edward's gone to be with Suzanne. I don't know when we meet her family."

Jimmy answered, "I didn't know your father was with Bonnie today. I will look into it. Kenny is very good at his job and you will be fine. Edward and Kelly will be there with you. Don't worry. I am glad the party was fun for you guys to plan and do. Jay and Betsy are very good cooks. Kenny and Eddie loved the food. Thanks for having them do the cooking."

Calvin agreed and left to go to sleep. When Calvin awaken, he heard voices so he went to check it out. Cindy was there pointing. Jimmy, Eddie, and Kenny were talking in Jimmy's office. Calvin wasn't sure why, what had happened? They looked upset or at least serious. Cindy was listening so Calvin listened with her where no one could see them.

Jimmy said, "I called you here for something I think is maybe a big deal."

Eddie said, "Jimmy it better be, the risk is high."

Kenny asked, "What is it? Who died?"

Jimmy answered, "Calvin told me that he has seen his dad, Kevin, with Bonnie, your daughter, Eddie, here at my home. He didn't say what they were doing but my guess is they weren't cleaning my house."

Kenny was laughing now and said, "I see the big problem. We needed to come right away. Things could happen!"

Eddie answered, "We all choose a child to know where the other one lives. I chose Bonnie because her husband died when they were married and before

76

Edward was born. I am sorry she came to your home, Jimmy, but not to see you for help or anything. Do you think Kevin went to get her then came here?"

Jimmy replied, "No, because Calvin told me and he is the only one who Edward may have shown where he lives. Kevin doesn't know where she lives unless Bonnie told him. Which isn't to happen, they all know that."

Kenny said, "I picked Gary and he has no reason to see Kevin. Jimmy you picked Cindy. Now we are on grandchildren, I picked, Kelly. Eddie picked Edward. Who do you pick Jimmy?"

Eddie said, "Slow down, we are back to Bonnie. What to do about this?"

Kenny said, "Well, we know Bonnie, she takes what she wants and I don't think she came here to play cards with Kevin. Kevin is a great guy, so how do we do this with him?"

Jimmy replied, "Well, Bonnie did come here. Kevin didn't walk away. Bonnie is very pretty. Kevin is a normal guy. What to do?"

Kenny answered, "Kevin is on Jimmy's don't kill list. So, we be adults about it. I like Kevin."

Eddie replied, "Kenny, when it is your granddaughter, Kelly, I will tell you how much I like Calvin, okay, but for now what should we do?"

Jimmy said, "We can't ask them not to see each other, they are adults but they must do it safely. They must be very careful."

Kenny said, "Yes, I have always been one for safe sex."

Eddie replied, "Kenny, I am going to hurt you if you don't see this as an issue and stop laughing."

Jimmy answered, "Kenny shut up, I mean seeing each other in a safe place and time. Secret is the issue and not sex, I think. I will talk to Kevin. Eddie you talk with Bonnie about it. They can see each other if that is what is going on but in a very secure way for the safety of the group."

Eddie said, "Thanks Jimmy, for telling Kenny to shut the hell up. Yes, I will talk with Bonnie and I don't want to hurt her feelings on this. If she likes Kevin then that is okay with me."

Kenny replied, "Those last few words were so hard for you to say, Eddie."

Jimmy answered, "Then we agree how to continue with this issue."

Eddie and Kenny agreed then they left. Kenny was laughing and Eddie gave him a look like "stop it that is my daughter." Jimmy went to find Kevin.

Calvin said, "Cindy, I would love to hear what Jimmy said to my dad but I think we should have your husband with us on this listening stuff. I don't want him to get the wrong idea about us."

Cindy answered, "Okay Calvin, I will go and get him, you find your dad. Let me know by telling through our minds where he is and we will come to you. Remember, we can talk through our minds to each together, got it. We don't share that with our new friends."

C-Jay came back with Cindy but he said, "Calvin, I trust you with my wife. I don't want any part of this listening in on Jimmy. I am in question of that Edward. I am leaving you two now and going to help my grandparents with the animals. I like animals and not so much people."

Cindy said, "Meeting Kenny and Eddie's families was a shock to C-Jay. He doesn't do will with new people. Just give him time."

Calvin replied, "I can see that. C-Jay should get to know Edward. He will like him. But there is dad and Jimmy is coming to talk to him."

Cindy and Calvin hid out of sight to listen.

Jimmy said, "Kevin, got a minute to talk about something personal?"

Kevin replied, "Oh, you know. Does Eddie or Kenny know?"

Jimmy answered, "Yes, Bonnie is coming here to see you. Are we talking about the same thing?"

Kevin replied, "Yes, she is a wonderful person and it was all my fault. I will tell Eddie and Kenny if that need be."

Jimmy said, "I am not going to ask why she was here or what you two did, that is none of my business. I am going to say that it has to be very secret and secure, you're seeing each other. The issue here is security. But Bonnie goes after what she wants and always gets it, which I think she wants you. What do you want Kevin? Or am I misunderstanding this situation?"

Kevin looked down but answered, "No boss, you are not misunderstanding this situation. Bonnie is so wonderful and somethings are worth dying for. Maybe I could handle it with your help. What does Eddie and Kenny think? What about Teresa Mary, your daughter and I?"

Jimmy replied, "I think her drugs and drinking is too much for you. I understand you can't put up with it. So, Eddie is talking with Bonnie but he will do what she wants. She needs to do it safely. Kenny really likes you and he is okay with it but I see a few issues to think about. Like if you want something more like marriage, what about little Ricky and his mother. Then Betsy with her husband, what do we tell them? Just something to think about. None of us know where this is going and take your time to find out. Bonnie is a great person and so are you."

Kevin smiled and they worked on something else. Cindy and Calvin went their own ways but Calvin wondered what would happened if Bonnie was his step-mother and Edward his step-brother? What a mess? Life was messy. People got themselves in all kinds of situations without even trying. Calvin went to his best friend, God, to pray.

CHAPTER SIX

THEY GOT MARRIED!

When Edward came into the church, Calvin said, "Edward are you sure about Suzanne?"

Edward replied, "Yes, I am in love with her and I want to marry her. Mental health is a big problem in our world and if treated, maybe people can be helped."

Calvin thought that Edward did have the right idea and he was a good guy. Calvin's training started with Kenny and that was different then he had thought. Kenny was training mostly about prevention and detection before any violent action could happen. There wasn't killing but instead to prevent killing and to help people. It wasn't like on TV or in the movies, shoot them up or kill whoever. They did detective work. They got the facts and then they took action fast. They learned to move quickly and make fast decisions with close detail awareness. But what Calvin loved most about this training was there was always prayer involved as they learned.

Calvin noticed his dad Kevin was alone together with Bonnie at Jimmy's home on evenings. She would come there to meet him and they would go for walks in the garden when Jimmy made sure no one else was in the area. They did dance together in Jimmy's big house with music and they watched movies. But then Kevin came to Cindy and Calvin to talk. Calvin and Cindy were working in a part of Jimmy's home that Cindy was using as an office.

Kevin said, "I know you two know I am seeing Bonnie and she is Eddie's widowed daughter. We both have a lot in common. She raised her son Edward with the help of her dad, Eddie, as I raised you and your sister with Jimmy's help. We like each other a lot."

Cindy asked, "Do you want to talk with Calvin alone? I can leave, no problem."

Calvin said, "Dad, this is up to you and maybe Jimmy, Eddie or even Kenny, but not me."

Kevin continued, "No, I need you two to talk to the girls about cooking a nice meal for us from time to time. We can't go out to eat. So, it is easy to tell the girls because of the stay home order. Can you two make that happen for me? Tell the truth, Bonnie and I are dating."

Calvin said, "Yes, I can do that but you should tell Jimmy and then when do you want the meal?"

Kevin said, "Thanks, I will talk it over with Jimmy and we can get back to you." Kevin left the room and Cindy went to talk to Betsy. Calvin sat there praying, oh my God.

Betsy came through the door and said, "Dad's got a girlfriend other than little Ricky's mom? When did this happen? How long did you know this, Calvin? Does she have children?"

All Calvin could think of was please shut us up at home or let us go free, no more steps in reopening or I will have to need mental health care myself. How he now wished Kenny's training was more of killing someone, anyone, but mostly the one who came up with these steps on reopening the world. Edward walked in to see Betsy standing over Calvin.

Edward said, "Calvin, breathe, she is your sister and you love her. Hi, I will be going now. I am in the other room if you need to talk later, Calvin, Betsy or anyone."

Calvin said, "Dad met Bonnie at that meeting you and Jay cooked for with Jimmy's friends. They can't go out to eat because of the shutdown order so dad wants you or Jay to cook a nice meal for their date. Dad, I think is lonely and needs a woman's attention for a man of his age. Jay's mom drinks and uses drugs again which dad can't put up with. I don't know a lot more."

Betsy asked, "What does she look like? Do you know her? Are they having sex?"

No way thinking of your parents having sex, but Calvin answered, "Bonnie is very pretty and she is Edward's mother. I am not sure if Edward knows so after we talk, I am going to talk with Edward. Dad and I don't talk about his sex life or mine, but a man his age, I guess, maybe. If you cook, I will taste the food first so don't put anything not nice in it to make me sick."

Betsy agreed. But Calvin could see she was on her way to find their father, Kevin. Calvin said a fast prayer for him. Then Calvin went to talk with Edward.

Edward smiled and said, "I know about your dad and my mother. She told me. I don't know what to say. Old people, what can we do with them? If Jimmy, Eddie, and Kenny are okay with it then I am good with it too. Would it be so bad to have me as a step-brother? I do really like your dad, Kevin. My mom is nice but she is a secret agent and a spy like all the Edson or Eds."

Betsy had found Kevin and he wasn't having a good day with question after question about his personal sex life. Kevin looked around for help and just then Jimmy came rushing in. Marie was having her baby. Kevin got on his knees again to thank God for the timing of that little baby Tim being born. They all hurried to the room where Michael was delivering his son. It was the best day of all for little baby Tim Micky Kevin Elgin to be born to Michael and Marie. Jimmy came out holding his grandson. Sylvia was all smiles. A grandchild for them to spoil. Calvin thought how fast the day went from the worst in no time at all to becoming the best. Calvin knew his first job would be to make a big party for the baby's baptism at their home church. Kelly, Edward, and him were on it. Calvin knocked on Jimmy's door and went in.

Calvin said, "Need a big party for the baby Jr. Tim Micky Kevin Elgin's baptism? When do they want it? We can do that for them. The girls can cook."

Jimmy smiled and said, "That would be great, have the girls cook together again at my home this time. The guests will not be Eddie or Kenny's families, just them. Maybe Bonnie and Gary with Edward, Suzanne, Kelly. They will be helping you, right?"

Calvin answered, "Yes, but why Bonnie and Gary? Michael, Marie, and Sarah with the guys will be there, right?"

Jimmy answered, "Yes, but I need to blend them in. Your dad is still dating Bonnie, and Gary does work on homes."

Michael and Marie wanted Mexican food because Marie was from Mexico. Jimmy requested Mexican food with beef hot dogs and chocolate chip cookies for the meal. Jimmy wanted the beef from C-Jay's farm and all the fresh vegetables. Betsy was eyeing who Edward was with. The day of the baptism came and they stayed their six feet apart and had their face masked on. All safety rules were followed closely for good health with this virus in the world. Jay and Betsy did get a good look at Bonnie with Kevin and she was pretty. They even sat together. Calvin, Kelly, Edward and Suzanne were busy being sure everything went as planned.

Jay asked, "Betsy, I see who Bonnie is. She has blond hair with blue eyes and is dressed very nice. She must be rich. But where is Kelly? Is she still after your brother and what about him?"

Betsy looked around but Bonnie was there in front of the girls and said, "Hi, Betsy, I am Bonnie. I am dating your father. I am glad to meet you. I am Edward's mom. I love your cooking. I don't cook at all. How do you feel about me dating your father? I know about Jay's mom and little Ricky, Kevin's other son. I know Calvin a little. Hi, Jay, nice to meet you."

Betsy stood there with her mouth open but nothing came out. Bonnie smiled, nodded, then Kevin came and they went to sit down to eat again. Kevin smiled at Betsy and Jay. Betsy still couldn't talk. Jay was still looking for Kelly but she never saw her. They were so busy. Calvin got Kelly's plate for her. How considerate of Calvin, right? Kevin gave Calvin a big smile but the day was great and all went well. Maybe all the praying Calvin did helped or was it the training he was getting from Kenny on how to react fast without anyone getting hurt in anyway.

Edward came to Calvin and said, "Kelly had me check Jay out before that first dinner with Kenny and my grandpa Eddie. Jay does date other guys. Do you think Suzanne is ashamed of me?"

Calvin said, "No, Suzanne loves you. I can see it in her eyes. Are you checking out Jay? We never talked about dating other people, if we should or not. I guess it is her right to."

Edward said, "Now you know why Kelly isn't asking questions about Jay. She already knows. Kelly is like all the women in Eddie and Kenny's families, they take what they want."

Calvin was thinking was he jealous of who Jay was dating? Did this mean he could or should date Kelly? What could they do during this shutdown time? Then to Betsy, Calvin went for help.

Betsy said, "Women problem, my brother. Dad told me to listen to you. He also told me that Teresa Mary has been cheating on him for some time as she does with every man she has been with before him. I felt so sorry for Dad but he was okay with it. I think Dad is way over Teresa Mary and for the first time in Dad's life, he is in love. We may have to like Bonnie for him."

Calvin replied, "Bonnie is nice to Dad. They do enjoy being together alone a lot. He is happy."

Betsy replied, "Okay, back to your problem. I have been reading Bonnie's mind and she does love our dad. I read Kelly's mind and she is in love with you, Calvin. They want men like the boys, Jimmy, Kenny, and Eddie. Now who wouldn't? But I am pleased with my Mickey just the way he is anyway. Is Edward dating Suzanne?"

Calvin said, "Yes, Edward has been for some time. If Jimmy finds out, he will be mad at you. What about Cindy? Does she know you read the minds of Bonnie or Kelly? Any more?"

Betsy replied, "No, Calvin, I didn't read Jay's mind or anyone else's. Yes, Cindy knows. I asked her first before I did it. But if Jimmy finds out, I am afraid. So, don't tell him. Is Edward in love?"

Calvin said "Edward is very much in love with Suzanne but we haven't met her family. Do the women in Eddy and Kenny's family take what they want? Edward said they do."

Betsy answered, "What I read is yes. The women in those families are in charge. Eddie is so much in love with his wife Barbie and spoils his daughter Bonnie. Kenny is no different with his wife Gail or with spoiling Kelly, his granddaughter. But Jimmy loves his Sylvia and spoils her too."

Calvin walked away but what would he do if Jimmy asked him? Calvin would tell Jimmy the truth but if Jimmy didn't ask him, why bring it up? Betsy was his only sister and he cared for her. Calvin wasn't that lucky and Edward was looking for Calvin because Jimmy wanted to see him.

Jimmy said, "Calvin, come in and don't worry. I know what Betsy and Cindy did. I don't agree and they should never do it again but I am not mad about it. They were trying to help you."

Kevin was with Jimmy and said, "Son, you have time with women and they change their minds so wait to see what women will do. I know Bonnie thinks I am like Jimmy, Kenny or Eddie but I am me and in time I will see if just me is what she really wants or not."

They talked about women and then went their separate ways. Calvin was glad he had these guys to talk to and wondered if he could ever talk to Eddie or Kenny this way but he knew one thing, that he could always talk to God. The next day was Father's Day and Kevin came in to wake Jimmy up at seven am.

Jimmy said, "Why, Kevin? I want to sleep with my Sylvia. Go away. What could you need at this hour?"

Kevin said, "I need to asked you something. I want to ask Bonnie to marry me. She wants to come here tonight to sleep with me because she is going to work all day today after breakfast with Eddie. We can't see each other before midnight."

Sylvia whispered to Jimmy, "Be nice or I won't be nice to you, if you know what I mean."

Jimmy got up to talk to Kevin and was very nice as he looked at his Sylvia. She had never said that before to him and he was sure she meant it.

Jimmy said, "Let us go into the other room and talk so Sylvia can sleep. You two can't go a day without seeing each other?"

Kevin got all red in his face and replied, "No, I don't want to. She is working all day, so guys can have Father's Day off. Bonnie will have breakfast with Eddie and her brothers this morning. It is what they do every year. She and Edward sometimes have a lunch at her work but today I am having lunch with Edward and Calvin, then dinner with Betsy and her husband. I am having breakfast with little Ricky before his mother wakes up in our secret place. I will take food with me that Betsy made for us. That is why I needed to talk with you now. Calvin is going to be with you when I am gone with little Ricky. Calvin has your day laid out for you. I am training Calvin, Kelly, and Edward to help me with watching out for you."

Jimmy was still trying to wake up and said, "I can take care of myself and Sylvia. What is my day today?"

Kevin replied, "Calvin will be here in a few minutes to tell you. He didn't want to wake you. But what do you think about me asking Bonnie to marry me? And can you help me find a ring to give her?"

Jimmy answered, "I think I would like Calvin helping me if he lets me sleep as long as I want. What happened to taking it slow and seeing where this goes with Bonnie and you? Taking your time on this?"

Kevin looked down then answered, "Sleeping together is the issue and I don't think Eddie will like it if we aren't married. So, if she has a ring from me then we can rest together and not do anything. What do you think of that idea? Can you come with me today after dinner to get her a nice ring?"

Jimmy replied, "Oh, hell yes, that will work. Rest together at night in the same bed with the woman you can't resist, good idea. I think you should ask Edward about marrying his mother first before asking Bonnie and he may know what kind of ring she would like. I got a great idea; let us take Edward, Calvin, and maybe if we can get little Rick away from that mother of his, with us to get that ring for Bonnie."

Kevin agreed as Calvin walked in and Jimmy said, "I am going back to bed with my Sylvia and I don't need any help, understand Calvin?"

Calvin looked at Kevin who winked at him and nodded yes. Then Jimmy left them, closing the door to his bedroom.

Kevin left to be with little Ricky with food from Betsy. Betsy was going to ask questions but they had to be with Cindy and her husband somewhere. Micky walked in the door to sit by Calvin.

Micky said, "I think I will help you this morning until your dad gets back because you are learning. Jimmy is very important to us. He can be hard to understand and gets not nice if we get too close when he is with Sylvia. Understand me, Calvin?"

Calvin asked, "Don't you have to be somewhere for Father's Day this morning?"

Micky replied, "I hate Father's Day. My wife's brother and sister with their families are at my home. I will be with Mickey and Betsy for lunch, oh my God. At least your sister is a very good cook."

Calvin understood this. His sister Betsy was a handful but then she did cook good. Micky did love his wife and did as all the guys did, what their wives wanted, to a point, so he was here to help with Jimmy if he needed to or not! Kelly was with her parents on Father's Day, then with her grandpa Kenny for the rest of the day. Edward was with Eddie for breakfast then would be with Kevin and Calvin for lunch. An easy day, nothing much happened, Calvin thought just another Father Day's lunch with his dad as always but now with Edward. Micky and Calvin sat there by Jimmy's bedroom door with the TV on very loud and no one was really watching it but Micky wanted the TV on loud. Micky was different they all said and now Calvin saw it. Sam and T-Jay both called Micky to see how it was going. He talked long with them but let that TV go on so loud. Calvin tried to turn down the TV but Micky took the remote away from him to turn it up even louder. Then Mickey talked more on the phone. Calvin walked around to check the windows and doors. All was safe and secure. After a few hours, Micky was off the phone and Jimmy came out of his bedroom and turned the TV down. He must have taken the remote away from Micky but he said nothing about it and got something to eat for him and Sylvia. Sylvia was up, in a black bathrobe, and they sat down to eat at the table outside in the garden for their breakfast.

Kevin came back and Micky left without saying a word. Jimmy and Sylvia went for a walk then Edward came in the door. He looked at Kevin for a long time and then smiled. What was up with that, Calvin thought and did he really want to know? Jimmy and Sylvia came back from their walk and Jimmy said something to Kevin very low. Jimmy and Sylvia left again for a drive with Jimmy's people.

Kevin said, "Edward, can I talk with you and Calvin?"

Edward looked confused but said, "Yes?"

Kevin said, looking a little nervous, "I want to ask your mother to marry me tonight; what do you think?"

Edward replied, "I think that is up to my mother. But as for me, I am very good with you marrying my mother. What do you think, Calvin?"

Now all eyes were on Calvin and he wanted to hide but he answered, "I am okay with it too."

Kevin looked a little less uneasy and said, "Bonnie is coming here tonight but we are just sleeping, nothing more, understand boys? Edward, do you know what engagement ring, your mother would like?"

Edward replied, "Yes, I do. I will know the right ring when I see it. Take us with you to pick the ring out."

Calvin gave Edward a look like what the hell are you doing? Then Calvin thought maybe Edward's mother had told him she wanted to marry his dad and that was what his sleeping here tonight was all about, getting Kevin to ask Bonnie to marry. Women can be tricky in that way. They get a guy to do something and make him think it is his idea when all along it is what the woman wants. Calvin's dad had his hands full with Edward's mother and she was clearly in control. Calvin couldn't even help his dad, just stand by watching him go down in love and marriage. Bonnie was an Eds' woman and they got what they wanted which was in this case, Bonnie wanted Kevin with no waiting. They had lunch with small talk about where they could live as a family. Kevin talked about Jimmy, Kenny, and Eddie together in one place. Eddie was British, Kenny's wife may want to be closer to her sister and Jimmy could never leave Sylvia who would never leave her grandchildren Jay or little Rick.

Edward spoke, "My mother thinks you are one of them too. This grandpa Eddie will do and it is close to Kelly's grandma Gail's sister's home and not too far for Sylvia from her grandchildren Jay or little Ricky for you, Kevin. We could call it a vacation home then a retirement place for them to live safely."

Calvin was sure this wasn't Edward's idea but Bonnie's and she had it all figured out. But Bonnie was right Eddie, Kenny, and Jimmy were getting older with Kevin, his dad, trying to watch over all of them at once. How could Kevin do that even with their help? Yes, they did have time but they did need a plan.

Was this Jimmy's plan too, for he did want Gary included with them? Gary built homes, could it work?

When they were done eating, Calvin said, "Let us look into it all. I mean Edward, Kelly, and me on the homes."

Jimmy and Sylvia came back with Jimmy going to eat with Cindy, C-Jay, Michael, Marie, Sarah, T-Jay. Sylvia went to sleep with little Tim, the baby. Kevin went to eat again with Betsy and Mickey. I guess for fathers everywhere, it could be an eating day. Calvin and Edward looked over plans to start the new project. There wasn't a lot of locations that fit the need, just a few so they would look at paying large amounts of money for those areas. Then Calvin and Edward heard Betsy screaming. Kevin must have told her too about asking Bonnie to marry him.

Edward said. "What should we do first? Run to help your dad or pray to God?"

Calvin replied, "Pray to God first then go. I am not sure what kind of scream that is, joy or mad?"

Calvin and Edward went to pray to God, then they went to help Kevin with Betsy. It appeared to be screams of joy! How was a guy to know this? Calvin looked at Edward who looked back at Calvin like, it is your sister, don't you know her?

Kevin said, "If Bonnie said yes to my marriage proposal then I will ask her if you can make the wedding cake and dinner, okay, maybe with Jay. If that is what you want. The boys are helping me pick out the engagement ring tonight as you are busy. It is Cindy and C-Jay's first wedding anniversary."

Jimmy came in and asked, "Kevin, are you ready to go get that ring for Bonnie? Want to lay down a few minutes first? We have time."

Kevin replied, "Yes, please, I think I ate too much today."

Calvin and Edward were sure that wasn't what was wrong with Kevin. They were sure it was a little stress in this situation with everyone. Then Calvin was sure Jimmy was having a meeting with guess who? Kelly had come in, so it was Edward, and Kelly with Calvin who listened to Jimmy, Kenny, and Eddie talking. Readers, I am sure you know what they were talking about at this special meeting, Kevin and Bonnie getting married? How to start this meeting was Jimmy's problem, what to say?

Jimmy said, "Thanks for coming on this Father's Day. It is also Cindy and C-Jay's first wedding anniversary."

Kenny replied, "Peaches got them a nice card; here it is but why are we here? Something happening that can't wait again?"

Eddie answered, "Here is my card with Barbie but what are Kevin and Bonnie up to? Bonnie and Barbie have been talking about something very secretively. What are my women up to? Is Kevin involved?"

Jimmy replied, "This is what I know. Kevin asked me about him asking Bonnie to marry him. Eddie do you need to get some air or can I continue?"

Eddie replied, "There is more? No, please, continue with what you know, Jimmy."

Kenny said, "Yes, Jimmy, we are all ears. How interesting."

Jimmy said, "Bonnie is coming over to my house tonight at midnight to sleep here with Kevin. She had to work all day today for all the guys who are fathers. Eddie, do you want a drink of water?"

Kenny replied, "Jimmy, I think Eddie could use a drink a little stronger than water. Eddie, are you okay?"

Eddie said, "Water, I need water now!"

Calvin, Edward and Kelly ran in with glasses of water for Eddie. Eddie drank all three glasses of water.

Kenny said, "Thank God we have three helpers with water in Eddie's time of need. Praise the Lord."

Jimmy replied, "Thank you, Calvin, Kelly and Edward for the water. I am not going to ask any of you how you knew Eddie needed water. But sit down as we talk about this situation of Kevin with Bonnie."

Kevin walked in with Gary, Kelly's dad, and they sat down too. Calvin was so glad to see his dad but maybe Kevin should run for it because Eddie didn't look happy.

Kenny asked, "Gary, my son, why are you here? What is it that we don't know? Maybe I need water."

Gary said, "Dad, we were thinking that you guys need homes closer together as vacation houses I could build for each of you. Homes for Jimmy with Sylvia, Eddie with Barbie, Kenny with Peaches or mom, and Kevin with Bonnie. I know Bonnie wants Kevin to ask her to marry him."

Kevin replied, "Bonnie may say no to my marriage proposal. Eddie, I guess I should ask you first. I did ask Edward and my kids. What do you think, should I ask Bonnie to marry me? She is coming tonight and we will sleep beside each other but I promise I will do nothing more than sleep beside her."

No one said a word, they all looked at Eddie, then he said, "There is nothing to vote on, this is up to Bonnie. Kevin get your ring and ask her. I have no idea what kind of ring Bonnie would like."

Kevin replied, "Thank you, Eddie, for not disagreeing with me about asking Bonnie to marry me. But I am taking Jimmy, Calvin, little Ricky, and Edward with me. Edward thinks he may know what kind of engagement ring his mother would like."

Jimmy and Kenny could hardly stop laughing. Eddie was laughing now too. Kevin looked around wondering what were they all laughing about. From very serious to now laughing and Kevin was sure they were laughing at him.

Edward replied, "Don't worry, Kevin, I am sure we will find the right ring for my mother. I even have a few pictures from a book on engagement rings."

Calvin looked at Kelly and she smiled. Jimmy couldn't stop laughing and Kenny was making signs of someone being reeled in as a fish being caught. Eddie shook his head in disbelieve.

Eddie handed Kevin the water and said, "Son, you need this more than me. Good luck."

Kenny replied, "Eddie, we all know Bonnie leaves nothing to chance. Bonnie always gets what she wants."

Jimmy, Kevin, Calvin, Edward and Kelly went to find the ring because little Ricky couldn't get away from his mother that night. Or had Jay told her mother all about it? They went to that diamond place of Jimmy's which he had ownership shares in. If you buy a lot of diamonds, just buy shares in that business, it is cheaper. Kevin thought he had enough money with him but it wasn't enough for this ring. Jimmy gave him more and said he would be taking the money out of his salary for life. Edward found the perfect ring but the cost, well, let us never tell anyone that. Calvin was thinking getting married was costly, or at least the ring was. Kelly was looking at all the diamonds for herself. Kevin was happy that he had the perfect ring for his Bonnie. And why shouldn't it be? Come on readers, we all know Bonnie picked it out herself and gave pictures to Edward. Jimmy continued to laugh all the way home. Eddie and Kenny were waiting there at Jimmy's home. Was it to see the ring Kevin got or to know how much that damn ring cost? Kevin was happy. Edward was very pleased with himself. Kelly was in dreamland for someday her engagement ring. Eddie and Kenny joined them at Jimmy place. Eddie took one look at the ring and shook his head.

Kenny said, "Only Kevin could love Bonnie that much. Bonnie couldn't have picked anyone better."

Eddie answered. "That is my Bonnie. She has always known what she wants and gets it."

The kids were outside in the garden making things look nice for Kevin to ask Bonnie to marry him that night at midnight and little Ricky was there helping too. Bonnie came in at midnight in a black negligee and Kevin took Bonnie out to the garden, got down on one knee asking her to marry him. She said yes. Now, you would think there was a night of great sex but no, Bonnie was on the phone all night with her mother and the other ladies in Eds' family. Kevin crawled up beside Bonnie and went to sleep. Nothing more happened but little Ricky got lost or was hiding in Jimmy's house and Calvin with Edward couldn't find him until seven in the morning. They got little Ricky home just in time before his mother looked to find little Ricky in his bed at her home sleeping.

The wedding plans were on and it was going to be a big wedding. Eddie agreed he would be paying for this wedding. Kevin agreed with anything Bonnie wanted. Kenny and Jimmy couldn't look at Kevin or Eddie without laughing. But when would the wedding be? Betsy was baking the wedding cake with her and Jay doing the cooking for the meal. A wedding this size would take time to plan and Calvin was glad of that. There were many questions to answer like where will they live? Then where will they have this big costly wedding? Who would be in this wedding? Did Calvin like or even know his new step-mother?

Calvin said to Kevin, "Got a minute to talk about this wedding for you and Bonnie?"

Kevin said, "Yes, son. You can be my best man if you want to be. Calvin, are you okay?"

Calvin replied, "Dad, are you sure you want to get married again? Maybe you should wait a year."

Kevin answered, "I told Bonnie to have the wedding of her dreams so whenever she wants, I will do. She should tell me when then where she wants the wedding and I will be there."

Edward came in and said, "I was hoping you would wait until I was a deacon or I could marry Suzanne. It would mean so much to me. I want to ask Suzanne to marry me now that my mother is with you."

Kevin replied, "Yes, I understand that, Edward. I will talk to your mother about it. Great idea and big weddings do take time. I want Bonnie to have the wedding of her dreams."

Calvin said, "That is what we all want – a wonderful wedding for you, Dad and Edward's mother, Bonnie. Edward needs to ask Suzanne first and maybe marry first. You can wait, Dad."

Calvin was going with his dad, Kevin, to meet the Eds and this was fun but Edward needed to tell Bonnie about Suzanne. Everyone in the Eds already noticed Suzanne with Edward but not Bonnie. The next day the old priest died in his sleep and Jimmy was all upset. How could this priest die at the age of ninety-eight? He had a few good years left, right? Everyone was so upset, but they all knew this man served God for so long and good. Edward was ready to become the deacon and could do the wedding. After the funeral for their priest they were all sad. Edward did try to help everyone with the grief of the loss of their spiritual leader. Who would they tell their sins to? Then as always, things got worse. Jimmy got off the phone and called Kevin into his office. Calvin, Edward and Kelly listened.

Jimmy said, "Sit down, Kevin."

Kevin replied, "Is it bad? Do I need to sit down?"

Jimmy answered, "Kenny and Eddie are on their way. Three Majestic Twelve members were killed this week. I am concerned someone is after us. I need to replace them fast with you, Bonnie, and Gary."

Kevin said, "Why Bonnie? Are you sure they were killed? Has this ever happened before?"

Jimmy replied, "No, not ever have three members died in the same week. I need at least one woman and Bonnie is the only one I can think of for the job. Sorry Kevin."

Kenny and Eddie come in and Kenny said, "We got to stop meeting like this or people will talk."

Eddie replied, "Edward, Calvin and Kelly come in and sit down with us. No more listening."

Edward, Calvin and Kelly walked in to sit down. Jimmy explained the issue of the three people killed from Majestic Twelve. They talked about it then voted and all agreed on having Kevin, Gary with Bonnie, to replace the dead people on Majestic Twelve. If someone was killing people on Majestic Twelve then they needed their people to help them. Gary always protected his father, Kenny, as Bonnie always protected her father, Eddie, and we all know Kevin was there for Jimmy. Calvin is Kevin's son and the newest member. They voted on Gary building the new homes for all of them in a circle with the back of the house closed but not the fronts. The home wouldn't be square but a triangle. Gary would start right away. The wedding would have to wait until it was safe. But Edward wanted to marry Suzanne. They needed to know who killed these people and why. Could Jimmy have killed these people for not voting his way? No, not Jimmy, Calvin thought. Kenny or Eddie maybe? No, Eddie didn't kill unless it was needed to save a life. Kenny trained to not kill people in his work of training spies. Gary worked on the houses for them and Kevin with Bonnie helped him. The fourth of July was coming and Calvin wondered should they have a party? Edward was busy with Suzanne trying to meet her family and she was afraid he wouldn't love her because her family was very poor. Edward didn't care about money. He loved her.

Edward went to Calvin and said, "I want to meet Suzanne's family this Fourth of July, help me set it up."

Calvin replied, "I can ask Jimmy if he wants a party and we can invite them."

Kelly said, "No, they wouldn't want a party because of these Majestic Twelve deaths. But this issue of not meeting Suzanne's family is because they are very poor and she is afraid Edward wouldn't love her when he sees how poor they really are. They have a Fourth of July block party each year for their street and this year they have very little food. What about all those hot dogs left, we never used from Jr. Tim's baptism? We never even cooked them. So many hot dogs are in those big freezers. Could we give them to her family to eat for the Fourth of July street party with their neighbors?"

Edward replied, "I don't care about money. I love Suzanne and I need her. Calvin, I can pay for the food for them from Jimmy. I will go and ask him. We are not so perfect. My dad wasn't this young secret agent as you may think. My dad was an older guy who was killed because he had many enemies. My mother, Bonnie, moved up in the British agency because she was his wife. Kelly, tell Calvin the truth about you."

Suzanne walked in the room and sat down. The Eds had brought her for Edward. The four Eds' cousins stood there with Suzanne and her two sisters, listening to all of this talk. Did they hear what Edward had said? From the look on Suzanne's face, the answer was yes.

Kelly answered, "Suzanne, we are people with difference problems in our families too. You heard what Edward is not proud of with his mom and dad.

Now this is me. My mother had me when my dad was very young and she gave me up for adoption. My grandpa Kenny and grandma Gail adopted me so I am their child. My dad and mom ran away to get married but they didn't want me. My grandparents did and then after some time, my parents came back or did Eddie and Jimmy bring them back?"

Edward went over to Suzanne and kissed her. Calvin fell to the floor. Kelly ran over to Calvin. What is wrong with Calvin? Suzanne helped Calvin and he was okay but feeling weak. What was it? Could it be if Calvin wanted to marry Kelly, he would need to ask Kenny, not nice Gary, for her hand in marriage? Oh, what would Calvin do? Well, readers, you know what Calvin did as he got up and went to pray to his best friend, God. Then Calvin saw the three wise men, as Calvin called them, which was a joke. Sam, T-Jay, and Micky came over to Calvin with Edward. Edward looked at them, thinking who are they, the guys? Suzanne ran over to Edward with her sister and the spy guys, the Eds.

Sam said, "Calvin, what is wrong? More women problems? Is Edward marrying this Suzanne? Suzanne did you know Michael, Jimmy's only living son's wife, Marie, was a homeless child in Mexico at first?"

T-Jay replied, "My first wife, Sally, was a farmer's daughter and very poor but I loved her so. She died of cancer. But who is Edward and Suzanne? Calvin are you okay?"

Micky answered, "That is Bonnie's son, the woman Kevin is to marry this time. Let us see if that really happens. My beloved wife, Virginia, with her brother and sister were homeless when I met them. She felt she was not good enough for me and I almost died before she married me. Let's don't do that again to anyone, okay, Suzanne? We need a mental health doctor and deacon."

Edward said, "They got an older priest who is only ninety years old. I am the deacon studying with Suzanne to be a mental health doctor. I want her to be my wife."

T-Jay called out, "Kevin, this time not too long in confession at one time. Only an hour a day. Sinless. As the deacon, Edward, make sure Kevin doesn't wear out this priest and we need a mental health doctor, welcome to the group with your wife to be."

Sam answered, "Kevin, I know you are Jimmy's pet but we need a priest and not just for you. Try to be good this time. Don't wear out the poor guy with all your problems. We could use mental health help."

Micky replied, "Guys, leave Kevin alone. He is getting married. Kevin is

Edward's new step-father. I know we want to keep Edward and Suzanne, so that is it. I think this Bonnie doesn't stink, or drink, or use drugs, so maybe this time it will work for Kevin."

Jimmy came out and said, "Guys, stop talking about Kevin and go back to work. What, Calvin?"

Calvin said, "Do you want a Fourth of July party? We can do that for you."

Edward said, "We can have one at Suzanne's family if that is okay with you. I can buy all those hot dogs we didn't use for the baptism of Jr. Tim."

Jimmy replied, "No Fourth of July party, thanks but no thanks. I don't think we want fireworks or big firer sounds or lights in our ears this year. We are a little too jumpy on the deaths of three Majestic Twelve people. Help Suzanne's family have their party. You can have the food and all of it or it will get old. My Sylvia eats one hot dog a month and we have hundreds of hot dogs. Take all that food out of my freezers. Do it for the Fourth of July but can we stop by, Sylvia and I for one hot dog?"

Edward looked at Suzanne and said, "Yes, please come, do you think Kenny or even grandpa Eddie would come?"

Jimmy replied, "Yes, but come see me after you guys get the food to Suzanne's parents."

Edward, Suzanne, and the others went out to her family. Everyone liked Edward and he loved her family. Calvin was not sure where to sit, everything was very clean, not new. Kelly and the Eds were right at home. Edward came to Jimmy and they went out to get Suzanne an engagement ring but this time with Eddie, Kenny, Calvin and Kelly. It was a very nice, big ring which cost too much but then Edward would be paying for it forever, working it off with the boys, Jimmy, Eddie and Kenny, just the way they wanted it. The Fourth of July came and the party was for the neighborhood which Betsy cooked up a mess of food for. The Eds did the security. Edward was with Suzanne's parents, asking them if he could marry their daughter, and they agreed. Edward got Suzanne alone to get down on one knee to ask her to marry him. Suzanne said yes. It was midnight at the church at Suzanne's hometown with the boys, Jimmy, Kenny, and grandpa Eddie, as all were there with Suzanne in her mother's old wedding dress marrying Edward. Bonnie and Kevin came in time to see it all. Well, this wasn't what Calvin could have even guessed would happened.

Calvin whispered to Edward, "What are you doing? We should talk about this first."

Edward replied, "I am getting married now. The priest told you to get me the ring from the little boy holding the pillow with the rings on it. Do it now, Calvin."

Calvin did what Edward told him to, as everyone was looking at Calvin. Kelly was holding flowers. The Eds were ready to help Edward and his new wife out of there so the priest married them.

Calvin came back from taking Edward to an airplane and he flew away with his new wife, Suzanne, but where? Kelly and the Eds waved good bye to them. Calvin didn't even know Edward could fly a plane. Now who were these Eds anyway? The only person as upset with this as Calvin was Bonnie, his mother. Jimmy came in to check on Calvin. Then he went to his Sylvia. I guess this night, Jimmy watched over Calvin for a change because Kevin had his hands full with Bonnie crying her eyes out for her only son marrying without even telling her first. I don't believe, reader, those were tears of joy.

Bonnie asked, "Kevin, did you know about Edward marrying this girl?"

Kevin replied, "I knew about the engagement ring but I never dreamed it would happen tonight. I was so sure Edward would tell you himself. He never said anything about marrying tonight. I am so sorry."

In the morning, Kevin did talk to the Eds and I guess they all knew Edward's plan. Marry fast and get out of there before his mother had time to make a problem. Edward was in love and that all there was to it. Kevin went to check with Jimmy, Kenny and Eddie to see what they were up to. They were as surprised as anyone and Eddie was pleased. But he didn't see this coming either. Was it the wedding he wanted for his favorite grandson? Well, a wedding is a wedding to Eddie and it was a church wedding in Eddie's faith which was all he cared about. Barbie, Eddie's wife, was with Bonnie, her daughter, and weren't so pleased but it was done and that was it. Now, to meet the family of the woman who took their Edward. Kevin went back to Bonnie and told her that Jimmy, Kenny and Eddie knew nothing about it, being as surprised as she was but they were okay with it.

Bonnie asked, "Then where did the dresses come from for the girls to wear as brides' maids? Calvin and the Eds had nice suit coats on with Edward. She had a wedding dress and a boy with the satin pillow."

Kevin wanted to say no flower girls, you notice, but he knew better. Then Kevin did notice a wedding cake by Betsy. So, what was up with that? That couldn't have been done at the last minute. The Eds.

Kevin said, "I need to talk to Betsy about that wedding cake they almost cut and ate as they ran out of the church to the car. I was sure one of the Eds cut that cake and Kelly gave two pieces to Edward as he took his bride to the car. Or did Kelly carry the pieces of cake? I know Calvin ran after them and went with as he helped Kelly into the car then drove away with the Eds."

Bonnie asked, "What the hell are you talking about with this cake thing?"

Kevin replied, "I like cake. It was a very good cake. Betsy made the cake so she knows something."

Bonnie answered, "Good plan, Kevin. Get to bottom of this."

Eddie came over and asked, "How is it going for Bonnie? Barbie is disappointed to say the least."

Kevin replied, "I am to get to the bottom of this, so I am on my way to see the cake maker."

Kenny said, "That was great cake. I liked it. Is there any left?"

Jimmy replied, "I liked that wedding, food first, rest, church wedding, then cake. They were off."

Kevin left to find Betsy and she asked, "Need anything, Dad? More cake?"

Kevin replied, "Yes, Kenny wants more cake, any left? How did you know to make a wedding cake?"

Betsy replied, "Kelly told me. But it was a secret so I wasn't to tell anyone but Cindy. A girl thing."

Kenny replied, "Kevin, I got this, thanks for all the cake. Bonnie, it was a big secret and we think some girls were in on it but we aren't sure who all knew what when. But we are on it, right, Jimmy?"

Jimmy answered, "Yes, I will question the cake maker personally with Eddie and Kenny."

Bonnie looked at Eddie and Kenny eating the cake with Jimmy and said, "Bull shit, you just want more cake. I see right through you three. None of you see this as a big deal, you have your cake."

Kevin replied, "I can go with them and help find this all out for you, my love."

I think, readers, Kevin would have done better if he wasn't shoving cake in his mouth as he promised Bonnie. She had her hands on her hips. They left to get answers or more cake. Calvin came in as Jimmy handed him a fork to eat cake then the cake was gone, but the new family didn't share their cake.

Calvin asked, "Kelly, do know anything about the cake and the wedding for Edward?"

Kelly was all smiles, answering, "Wasn't that romantic? What kind of cake would you like for your wedding, Calvin? I want a chocolate cake with white icing for my wedding. That cake was so good."

Okay readers, Calvin needs to get the hell out of there. Weddings bring out something in single women and you don't want to be the one they are looking at if you are not ready. Calvin was not ready.

Kevin said, "Let it go, son. Edward is a few years older than you are and that does make a big difference. He was ready to marry and he loves Suzanne. Now, how to make her family feel welcome?"

Calvin replied, "If you go to their home, sit on the white chair, the other chairs are old but the chairs are very clean. Kelly and the Eds sit on any chairs with Edward at Suzanne's parents' home."

Kevin said, "Good to know, son. I will sit on the white chair only. Jimmy wants Suzanne's dad, John, to help with some building with Kelly's dad, Gary. Bonnie and I are to be there too but I am a little worried about Bonnie with Edward's new in-laws. I guess John is out of a job. We don't want to be too pushy."

CHAPTER SEVEN

NEW FAMILY AND HOMES

After the first few nights, Calvin was thinking he sure should have gone with them. Edward took Suzanne into his arms and carried her over the threshold, as they say, onto that airplane, then flew away. Edward could fly a plane himself. What other things didn't Calvin know about Edward, his best friend? Kelly with Calvin were now to take care of Jimmy. This new family, who were they? There was a father and a mother with two other daughters. Suzanne, Edward's wife, her sisters were Samantha and Salina. Kenny had given each girl a scholarship to a university to be some kind of doctor. Suzanne was mental health, Samantha a dentist and Salina a chiropractor. The father was to work with Gary, Kelly's dad, on the new homes.

Calvin went to Cindy and asked, "How long are Edward and Suzanne going to be on their honeymoon? How many days did you give Edward off of work? We need him, Jimmy has a tooth problem again. I think maybe he ate too much wedding cake."

Cindy replied, "Edward is a co-worker and he will come back when he wants to. I guess whenever. Calvin, Edward doesn't need your help on this one, he knows what to do with his wife, Suzanne, on his honeymoon. Edward is an Eds and these guys aren't shy about some things."

Calvin and Kelly went to get Jimmy some stuff for his tooth until he could see the dentist. At the store on their way out, six guys tried to take Kelly into their car. Calvin told Cindy by his mind reading to call the Eds to help him then he went into action. Calvin was all over those six guys before they knew what hit them. Calvin could disappear and reappear behind them and he did, as Kelly was fighting them off of her. All six guys were down in minutes as the other four Eds came to help. The police came too. Leo Edson showed his agent's license and badge. The six were taken to the hospital and then jail. James Edson had called Kenny Anderson and his grandpa Eddie Edson to come with Jimmy Elgin. Kelly wasn't hurt at all, not even a hair on her head was out of place. Calvin was like a mad man in action and the Eds said nothing but they knew Calvin cared more for Kelly then he was letting on. No one was ever going to hurt Kelly with Calvin around, not ever. Kelly maybe could have taken those street guys down herself but then it is always nicer to have a knight in shining armor to come to your aid. Kelly was so impressed with Calvin. All Calvin was concerned about was Kelly. He called Gail, her grandmother, right away to come. Kenny was all smiles. Jimmy had his tooth medication and Eddie with the other Eds were watching it all as Kevin and Bonnie had gotten to do some legal stuff with the police.

Jimmy went to the dentist but Michael had the sister, Samantha, learning to be a dentist go with. Samantha told them she didn't know much but they told her it was what she did know about being a dentist they needed. They would cancel their next Majestic Twelve meeting and they had done that before so it wasn't a big deal with everyone understanding why. Jimmy's mouth may have been more of the problem than the deaths of three people but then who knows for sure? Jimmy was down with his tooth problem but now Samantha, learning to be a dentist, had a big crush on Jimmy. Jimmy never saw that coming, she was his dentist and no more. Calvin noticed it first, then Sylvia. But when they told Jimmy, he said it was a dentist caring for a sick person and he was old enough to be her grandfather. Leo was all jealous. How to get Jimmy to take this serious before something got out of hand? Calvin called Kenny and Eddie to meet. Kevin was there too in Jimmy's home.

Jimmy said, "Why are we meeting? My teeth are still healing."

Kenny replied, "Calvin, what is it? Is Kelly okay? Thanks for being there for her."

Eddie said, "My grandsons say that is some advanced training you got there, Calvin."

Kenny answered, "I didn't train Calvin with all that. He must have gotten that from Jimmy."

Calvin said, "I guess I don't have a right to call you here but I see a big problem which Jimmy isn't taking serious. His dentist girl, Samantha has a crush on Jimmy and Leo is all jealous."

Kenny replied, "Jimmy is very cute, what is up with Leo?"

Eddie added input, "Jimmy has always had a way with women of all ages. Leo is my grandson."

Jimmy replied, "I am her first patient. She feels sorry for me. I see the way Leo looks at her."

Kevin asked, "Calvin, are you sure she feels this way? Leo is Eddie's oldest grandson?"

Jimmy replied, "I am not giving up my dentist. She should marry Leo. He cares for her."

Eddie said, "My back hurts. I am not having a guy touch me. I need a chiropractor. I like that chiropractor girl as a doctor. Calvin, which of my grandsons wants her?"

Kenny answered, "I think that is Victor who likes the chiropractor. I did notice that at Edward and Suzanne's wedding. Okay, we keep the two girls and Calvin gets them husbands. Good plan and we all vote yes to that. I need some work on my neck from that chiropractor one."

Calvin cried, "Okay, I will get them together but I need Edward's help."

Kevin said, "I'll have the Eds tell Edward we need him back as soon as possible."

Jimmy was sick with his teeth and Eddie and Kenny with their pain. Edward and Suzanne came back. Kelly, Calvin, with Edward started the project to marry off two of the Eds, Leo and Victor.

Edward said, "The Eds say there is a problem with the two sisters and I think they are jealous."

Calvin replied, "Yes, they think we should get the two sisters' husbands now. Jimmy wants his dentist but only as a dentist. Eddie and Kenny need the other one for their back and neck."

Kelly said, "Did you hear how Calvin saved me from six street guys trying to hurt me?"

Edward asked, "Are you okay now, Kelly?"

Kelly replied, "Yes, I am shaken but not stirred. I'll be fine with Calvin close to me always."

Calvin asked, "What are we going to do? Eds for husbands but they aren't the marrying kind."

Edward said, "I have only been gone a week. I guess a lot happens in week."

Kelly asked, "Doesn't one of the Eds have a little son somewhere? He may need a wife. Maybe it is time to tell Eddie about his great grandson named after him, Ed."

Calvin said, "One of the Eds has a son? Oh my God. Which one and where is its mother?"

Edward answered, "Calvin, you are a bit of a tattle tale and your dad, Kevin, is the pet. When you know something, Calvin, it is the same as Jimmy, Kenny and Eddie knowing it or maybe even Kevin. We Eds don't do that."

Kelly replied, "Oh Edward, that isn't Calvin's fault. It is his job that he is always doing."

Suzanne knocked on the door and Edward let her in but they had to kiss first as Suzanne said, "We have a problem with my sisters, they have a big crush on them."

Calvin said, "We'll get them husbands."

Kelly replied, "The Eds are cute."

Suzanne answered, "I don't think the Eds are interested in my sisters. They aren't the marrying type or not with my sisters. Not their type."

Edward replied, "They are the marrying type and these two girls are their type but that isn't the issue. My oldest cousin, Leo's son's mother, died so he has a broken heart. Victor likes the younger sister but is too shy to talk with her."

Kelly winked at Suzanne and said, "I think we can help Victor but Leo, that is up to the dentist girl. Does she like children?"

Suzanne said, "Yes, but we aren't anyone special. I don't even know what Edward sees in me."

Edward walked over to Suzanne and kissed her, saying, "Love, that is all we need, love. Leo needs love to heal his broken heart and Victor needs love to help him not be so shy."

Kelly's mind was working on how to get everyone together but we all know where Calvin was going to go when no one was looking, into Jimmy's office and Eddie with Kenny were still there. Calvin knocked on the door and Jimmy waved him to come in.

Calvin said, "Am I a tattle tale?"

Kevin came in and answered, "No, son, now tell us all about it."

Calvin said, "Your grandson Leo has a small boy, I don't know where he is but his mother is dead. Leo has a broken heart. We think he loves the dentist. Victor likes the other sister but is too shy to talk with her so we think we can help there too. Two husbands for two sisters. I am not a tattle tale, am I? If I know something, I don't tell you everything, do I?"

Eddy spoke, "No Calvin that means you are a valued person. I have a great grandson?"

Kenny spoke next, "That makes you our ears to the world. We need to know this."

Jimmy wasn't talking but was that because his tooth still hurt or his mouth and Kevin was all smiles. Okay, readers, we know Calvin is the tattle tale and Kevin is the pet, so what, who cares?

As Calvin left Jimmy's office, Edward came up to him and said, "That is okay. Calvin, I understand. Jimmy, Kenny, and my grandpa Eddie are your whole life and your dad's. But Leo isn't the only one with a broken heart. You have a broken heart too from Jay when she dated other guys, this hurt you very much. It will take time to heal."

Kelly came in and they went to work on who could have killed those three Majestic Twelve people. Bonnie wasn't going to work out for Majestic Twelve and Kevin was putting a stop to having her on that group so it would be Edward, Kelly, and Kevin. Gary, Kelly's dad, wasn't really that mentally stable and he couldn't handle it with UFOs. Kelly could be the woman on the team. Cindy wanted to be but Jimmy said no. Leo was to bring his five-year-old son to meet Eddie the great grandfather and Eddie was so thrilled about having a great grandson. Why didn't Leo ever tell Eddie or his parents about his son? Edward took Suzanne, Calvin, and Kelly to the convent where Leo's little son lived with the nuns. Ed was the boy's name and he was so happy to see Edward. The boy looked so much like all the Eds and he was a nice kid. Edward talked to the nun first and gave her more money, then he went to Ed.

Suzanne whispered to Kelly, "I saw that boy at our wedding, Edward's and mine. He had our rings on a satin pillow which Calvin took off and gave to Edward when the priest told him to do it. Edward had told me who the boy was. That it was Leo, his cousin's son."

Calvin replied, "Why didn't I ask about the kid?"

Kelly answered, "Because it all happened so fast. I knew about Ed, Leo's son. His mother was an agent. After she was killed, Leo took the baby to the convent of the Sisters of Holy Mother."

Calvin asked, "Are there any other secrets I should know about with the Eds?"

Kelly replied, "Yes, I am sure there are many but the Eds love their secrets."

Ed asked, "Who is the woman that is to marry my daddy? Is she pretty like my mother was? Is she nice? Does she like kids? I know she is a dentist so I will brush my teeth before I meet her."

Leo came in the door and Ed ran to his dad with a big hug for him. Leo held his son for a long time. Calvin had never seen this side of Leo. He was so nice like a parent. The Leo Calvin knew was a party guy and always on the go. But this Leo was there for his son, Ed. Leo walked with Ed to his bedroom and got his things to go to see Eddie with the family. Leo was talking to his son about things like what he had for supper and what he wanted to take with him to see his great grandpa Eddie. Leo was a dad with a son and he was helping his son with his coat on to go. Who would have ever guessed he had a son to care for and the nuns knew Leo very well? Ed waved good bye to the nuns.

Ed looked up and asked, "Where is the woman to marry my daddy? I do need a mommy. I brushed my teeth. Do you think she will like daddy and me?"

Eddie replied, "She would be crazy not to. I am your great grandpa, Eddie."

Ed said, "My daddy is very handsome. All women love him. But me, I am not sure about."

Jimmy spoke now, "Ed, you are so handsome like your daddy and all women will love you too."

Kenny replied, "I want a great grandson like Ed too. He is perfect."

Calvin and Edward came in with Samantha and she smiled at Ed with his dad, Leo. It was a good start. Ed liked Samantha right away and she took to the boy as if she had known him all her life. Now would Samantha like Leo? Jimmy and Kenny talked to Eddie to let Leo and Ed stay at Jimmy's home for the night. Samantha was happy and was trying to help care for Ed already which the little boy did like. Ed was missing a mother and Leo had seen that right away. Samantha was the motherly type. Leo was impressed. Jimmy smiled; his work was done. Eddie appeared to be pleased and Kenny was looking at Calvin differently. Should Calvin be worried? Victor had started dating Salina which appeared to be going good after that night and Jimmy, Kenny and Eddie would get to keep their chiropractor. But what other kind of doctor did they need? Eddie had two more unmarried grandsons and the boys weren't getting any younger. Eddie's grandsons were good looking young guys and why waste them? They needed more doctors in the new family, so marry more. The four of them met to talk about it.

Kevin stood by the door, saying, "What other kind of doctors do you think we need?"

Kenny replied, "Let me see, where are my glasses? I know, an eye doctor."

Eddie asked, "Why is it always my grandsons who have to marry a doctor?"

Jimmy replied, "Because my only son is our doctor and his son is too little."

Kevin said. "Maybe another doctor to help Michael out. We are a handful."

Kenny asked, "What do you mean, Kevin, that we are falling apart from old age?"

Jimmy answered, "Maybe someone who can help us eat better, healthier. So we can live longer. But I do like the naps with Sylvia each day."

Eddie replied, "Jimmy's naps means sleeping and not just sex all the time."

Jimmy answered, "Shut up, Eddie. Naps are what I say they are."

Kenny replied, "Thanks, for once telling Eddie to shut up for a change and not me all the time. Sex is good for you. Maybe not eating so much wedding cake next time would help us."

Eddie answered, "So, that is why you two have a need for more doctors. Limit your activity. I only have two more grandsons to give. Try to rest at nap time and eat less cake."

Kevin said, "But what fun would that be. Oh shit, I should keep my mouth shut. We aren't married now and my daughter is the cake maker, the cook."

Jimmy called Calvin, Edward and Kelly into his office and said, "We need a party for our new family. I would like to invite more of Crème's relatives like those who have granddaughters becoming some kind of doctors. Let us have a party to get to know them and the new family. August fifteen is a holy day week-end, have it then with a meal after church."

The meal was to be lobsters, shrimp, green salads, hot baked bread, butter, fruits, and no cake. They would also have non-alcohol beer to drink with caffein free ice tea. Sunday, it started with church, then meet and greet, the meal and dancing. Jay came with a boyfriend named Al and Ricky. The Eds were all very nice to Al and Ricky. Little Ed loved following Ricky around everywhere and Leo was pleased his son had a friend. Kevin was please Jay brought Ricky there. Calvin tried hard to make Al feel welcome but then the Eds were too funny to be believed. The Eds told Al all about how they were being sold off to doctors to be married by their grandpa Eddie and his old friends, Jimmy and Kenny. Al couldn't stop laughing, it wasn't how pretty the girl was, but how much education she had and what kind of doctor she was going to be that they were being sold for. It did appear to be hopeless for them.

As Virgil said, "There will be no more fast cars and women. No more sex and love in every city. Just a wife and crying babies for us. Our young lives are over. Grandpa Eddie has spoken."

James replied, "No more shaken and not stirred. No more James Bond 007 life. My life is over. Time to come home to hell. Grandpa Eddie has laid down the law. No more fun."

Leo answered, "I do need a mother for little Ed. I could use a wife now. She is very nice. Okay, she is a dentist which is what they want. So why not, I do really love her."

Victor said, "I like her. I want her. I'll keep her. She is a chiropractor, they need that."

Edward spoke now, "See why I told no one until I married first? Family is pushy. But I got a mental health doctor and boys, we do need that in our family."

Calvin looked at Al and said, "We are lucky we aren't in the Eds' family."

They sang oldies but goodies and Jimmy, Kenny, and Eddie with Kevin sang so nicely while Virgil and James found themselves a wife that had a doctor's degree of some kind to date. Calvin danced with Kelly and Jay. Kelly danced with all the Eds and even Al. They all had a good time but Edward only danced with Suzanne. After the party, they all helped clean up.

Crème did have a lot of female family members studying to be doctors, which ones would they choice? Ricky had a great time and wanted to see Ed more and the two boys were friends now. Ed followed Ricky all over. He was about five years younger but still a boy to play with. Ricky was nice to Ed like a big brother as Calvin had been to him. Ricky could tell his mom he had a new friend named Ed and his dad named Leo who was dating Samantha, a dentist. Teresa Mary was good with them, taking Ricky with because Leo told her the truth that he knew Kevin but not well and the boys were friends.

Jimmy called Calvin, Edward and Kelly into his office and said, "The schools may not be opening so have Ricky go to a private school here at the house with Ed. Samantha can get the boys together each day. Kevin, you talk to Teresa Mary about it. I think she will go for it. Jay needs to continue her education. I don't care in what. Make it happen."

They all agreed but Edward said, as they left Jimmy's office, "I will talk to Leo about Ed and Ricky. Kelly and Calvin, you two talk to Jay about her education. Anything, but continue it."

Calvin and Kelly went to Betsy then Calvin said, "Betsy, Jimmy wants Jay in college and for more than a cook. I know she loves art so maybe some art classes too with anything else she wants."

Kelly asked, "But how to pay for it? I am sure Jay wouldn't take money from Calvin or Jimmy. How about my grandpa and his scholarship to any university? Grandpa Kenny knows how to write them out that makes the paper work look so real."

Betsy replied, "Kelly, you would do that for Jay? Ask your grandpa Kenny to pay for her schooling? You have got to be a saint."

Kelly answered, "No, you know the old saying, keep your friends close and not friends closer."

Calvin went to see Jimmy as he motioned Calvin in and said, "What is Jay to learn for?"

Eddie answered, "Well, maybe Jay can learn to be an eye doctor. Okay, Kenny and Jimmy?"

They all agreed but then Kevin spoke, "Bonnie wants our wedding in the fall, in September. Is that okay with you guys?"

No one was talking now so Edward spoke, "Sound like a good time. We can help with the wedding. The girls can cook again. Any issues?"

No one said a word so the wedding was on and Calvin, Edward and Kelly started to plan this big party at a new church. With social distancing and wearing masked, everyone could come without everyone knowing who was all there. The church was very big and nice with a stain glass window of the Holy family. Jay called Calvin this time and was so pleased with her scholarship to college and the classes to be an eye doctor. Okay readers, we all know that Kenny was paying for it all but then they did need an eye doctor, they were getting older. Jay would also be cooking with Betsy but Betsy promised to never tell Jay about the scholarship for Calvin. The wedding was on a beautiful September day, when Kevin Carlson married Bonnie Edson. Eddie walked his daughter down the aisle of that new church to Kevin, waiting at the altar. Calvin, Ricky and Edward stood as best men, the brides' maids were Betsy, Jay and Suzanne. Little Ed was the ring carrier and he was so proud of his job. There were no flower girls but there were flowers everywhere. It was so nice in that new church they used for the first time. Kelly sang the wedding song as they walked into the church. Teresa Mary wasn't there and I am sure that Bonnie didn't invite her. The food was great with almost anything you could think of: fish, steak, lobsters, ham, and chicken to eat. The wedding cake was lemon and it was seventeen layers tall with a water fountain in it. The old priest did a wonderful wedding service with a full mass, and a lot of dancing. Jimmy, Kenny, and Eddie did a lot of singing of oldies music. Bonnie's wedding dress was very nice and long with a long train which would have put any royal wedding to the test, who had the nicest wedding dress. Costly, oh yes. New, oh yes. Brides maids in fall colors of the way the trees change in the fall from summer to winter. The most beautiful fall colors of nature. The guys were in black suits with fall color shirts. It was perfect.

Kevin and Bonnie were off on their honeymoon. Calvin did know how to find his dad if needed. But did more happen behind the scenes that we will find out later, readers? As for the new homes, Jimmy wanted an old fashion style home, Eddie's home was very modern, and Kenny's place was like a castle. Suzanne didn't get a home, she got a new house to make anyway she wanted and now she knew Edward wasn't a poor man. Suzanne went to the church to thank God for her wonderful new husband. Edward was the man she loved and he was rich. Samantha was now dating Leo and he was very nice but secretive.

Calvin said to Samantha in church, "True love will heal Leo's broken heart. Just give him time."

Salina was happy with Victor. She even liked his twin brother who had a different girl all the time. James took too many chances even more since Kevin's wedding. Kelly stayed close to Calvin. Edward was sure Calvin and Kelly were in love. Jay had missed out on something great with Calvin because of her mother's craziness.

Sam, Micky and T-Jay were pleased to have new homes and it was so close to Jimmy with Cindy, so to keep them safe would be easier. They could stay out of sight by most people and if you didn't know they were there, you could miss them altogether. Sometimes it is better to be prepared then to complain about what has happened to you. The guys were taking no chances and they were more ready for anything this time, even a virus. Leo looked at Samantha who was playing with Ed. He was all happy because he had a mommy now. What should Leo do? He still had a broken heart. Eddie wanted Ed to come live with him and not go back to the nuns at the convent of the Sister of the Holy Mother. Leo knew he would have to leave and go to work again soon, so what to do?

Victor came in and said, "Leo, let us have a double wedding with the two

ELGIN TWO THE SHUTDOWN AND THEN WHAT!

sisters this October. I do love Salina. We should get married at their family church like Edward and Suzanne did. No big deal, do it. What do you think?"

Leo walked to the window and replied, "Yes, that sounds good but I want to talk with Edward, James and Virgil first about it, okay?"

Victor replied, "Don't tell Calvin. We all know the first thing Calvin will do is tell Jimmy, Kenny, Grandpa Eddie and Kevin. If Kelly knows she may tell Calvin and we are back to them knowing. If Grandpa Eddie gets little Ed then you may never get him back. But you have to go to work soon so what to do with your son, and that is leave Ed with a new wife, Samantha."

Leo answered, "I know Ed loves Samantha as his mommy. The question is does she love me?"

Victor explained, "You will treat Samantha right. You will be good to her and give her anything she wants. Spoil her rotten. Samantha couldn't do better than you, Leo. You will give her a nice home. All Samantha has to do is love your son and you, which I believe she does."

Leo said, "Samantha went from loving Jimmy to loving my son with me, I am not so sure."

Victor answered, "It sounds like you care a lot about Samantha and her feelings. Isn't that some kind of love? You have had sex with many women since Carol, so what is the big deal?"

Leo walked into the church with Calvin there and Edward whispered to Leo, "Want to talk?"

Leo nodded yes. Calvin kept praying and explaining to God why he just had to read Leo's mind. After they left the church, we all know where Calvin went as Leo and Edward went to talk. Okay, Calvin was a snitch, and he ran to Jimmy's office which was Jimmy's new office with Eddie, Kenny and Kevin in it. Calvin knocked on the door.

Jimmy replied, "Calvin, come in. You are out of breath. You ran from where?"

Kenny asked, "Is Kelly okay? What happened?"

Eddie answered, "My grandsons again? Do I have any more great-grandchildren?"

Kevin said, "Son, just breathe and then answer us. Take your time. Thanks for coming."

Calvin rested a minute then said, "Victor wants to marry Salina this October with Leo and Samantha. But Leo thinks Samantha is not in love with him. Leo still has a broken heart. Samantha is now in love with Leo and his son Ed, not you anymore, Jimmy."

Jimmy replied, "Well, boys we are on the right track. Leo is very handsome and charming. A guy with a broken heart always gets the woman. Then Leo has the cute little boy, Ed, who needs a mommy. What is there not to love for a woman."

Kenny said, "So what is the problem? They all get married. We have a dentist and a chiropractor. I see no problem here. How is your tooth, Jimmy? My neck feels better. Your back is better, right Eddie?"

Calvin cried, "What about love? Jimmy, stop thinking about your mouth. Kenny, your neck is fine and Eddie, your back will be okay, this is your grandson's life."

Kevin asked, "Son, what do you want us to do for Leo? We all like Leo and Samantha."

Jimmy said, "I am not losing my dentist. Then chiropractors are also hard to find that are any good. We are getting older. We need these ladies. Eddie, you can give up two grandsons."

Eddie answered, "Yes, I can. No problem. They should get married. End of problem. Love will come later or we could kill that grandson of mine."

Kenny spoke up now. "No, we can't. I think Jimmy should talk to Leo about love."

Jimmy replied, "Why me? I know nothing about love. I have my Sylvia for love."

Eddie said, "I never dreamed I would say these words but Kenny is right. Jimmy talk to Leo."

Kenny input now, "Jimmy do you want to keep your dentist or not? What is it with that mouth of yours anyway? Which of your teeth have you not had problems with?"

Jimmy replied, "At least I have my teeth."

Kenny answered, "Now that was just mean and low down not nice."

Eddie said, "So it is, Jimmy will talk to Leo about love and he will marry the dentist woman."

Calvin left Jimmy's new office thinking he shouldn't have even told them. Maybe Edward was doing better with Leo. Calvin went to find Edward who sat there with Leo not talking. Leo looked at Calvin like what the hell did you do to me? I am afraid of Jimmy. He is too moody. Now, I got all that with just a look but I am not sure what you got from this, readers?

Calvin asked, "How is it going?"

Edward answered, "We are not talking and I am not sure where to start this conversation."

Calvin said, "Jimmy wants to talk to you, Leo, in his new office now."

Edward, Victor, Virgil and James went with Leo into Jimmy's office. Calvin looked around and saw Kelly walking with the Eds. So, Calvin walked with the Eds and Kelly into Jimmy's office.

Jimmy looked up and said, "Oh great. Let us all talk. I think I am going to move again."

Leo said, "It is about me. Victor thinks we should get married to the sisters, Samantha and Salina. You may know them better as the dentist and chiropractor. I do love Samantha."

Jimmy asked, "Then what is the problem?"

Leo replied, "I think Samantha should be with a man she loves and not me, I not good enough."

Jimmy asked, "Should we look for the best man for her? Maybe God would work?"

Leo answered, "No God wouldn't work. He is in heaven; she needs someone here to love her."

Jimmy replied, "Boy, we got problems. Maybe you should do it until we find the perfect guy."

All the Eds were now smiling with Calvin and Kelly. Calvin thought so this is why they had Jimmy talk with Leo. It wasn't rocket science or genius work but work for the heart. Samantha did love Leo and he did care so much about her so maybe Jimmy wasn't so interested in his dentist but in Leo's happiness with his little son, Ed. Leo smiled and thanked Jimmy for he loved Samantha and she cared for him with his son, Ed.

Kenny asked, "Are we getting the rings?"

Edward replied, "Yes, they are going out to ask John today."

Eddie asked, "Who is John?"

Edward answered, "My father-in-law, Suzanne, Samantha, and Salina's father."

Calvin said, "Edward's wife's dad, the dentist and the chiropractor's dad. Same guy."

Victor came running up to Edward very happy and said, "John told us both yes to marrying his daughters. But now we need nice engagement rings. I don't have money but Leo does."

Kelly replied, "Don't worry, I know four men who will be happy to help you out with that problem if you have the wedding where they want it."

Leo walked over and said, "Calvin did you tell on us again?"

Edward answered, "They knew. They will help with the rings but they want a big double wedding at the new church so grandpa Eddie can find wives for James and Virgil. Talk again?"

Leo replied, "No way. Let us do it their way."

Victor asked, "What do we need to do?"

Calvin said, "Come with us and get the engagement rings. Which will cost too much money but you will pay them back for the rest of your lives. We will plan the wedding."

Kelly said, "In other words, just ask the girls to marry you, if they say yes then shut up, be at the church when we tell you to and do what we tell you to. Get it?"

Edward replied, "I know, guys, it sounds bad but the honeymoon is all worth it. And then afterwards it is just one honeymoon night after another. That is so good."

Victor asked, "Do we have to tell our parents?"

Calvin replied, "No, I think we take care of all of that. Get the rings and ask them to marry you."

Leo asked, "Do you think either of these women can cook?"

Kelly replied, "Too late now to find out. Betsy does the cooking here anyway."

Victor said, "That works for me. I love Salina. Leo got cold feet? Get some warm socks."

Leo shook his head no and walked away. He knew it was all over for him and he did love Samantha. Maybe it wasn't love but it was very close to love that he was feeling for her. All the Eds went with to get those engagement rings and each time those rings' cost were going up as Calvin saw it. Jimmy's investment was really paying off in this diamond place. Leo took Samantha out to eat at a nice place with his son and asked her to marry him which she cried but said yes. Victor took Salina into the noon light for a walk to asked her to marry him and she said yes. So, the wedding was on and the girls agreed to whatever Jimmy, Kenny, Kevin and Eddie wanted for they were paying for it all, with their father John being pleased.

Leo said, "Let John and Mary pick out the home they want but not far from their daughters."

John was sure he couldn't pay for one of those homes but then Edward let him know he wouldn't be. His new sons-in-laws had this covered. John continued to work with Gary.

Calvin answered, "I have found several doctors who are unmarried females but Edward said they will never do because they are money grabbing, lying, cheating, not nice women. Kelly said they aren't nice looking, ether. No more mother Teresa women left in the world."

Jimmy called, "Kevin get in here. Find ladies that can be seen without a bag over their heads."

The next day was the Majestic Twelve meeting and Edward Edson was to be the newest member. Edward needed a majority of the votes to win.

Calvin asked Edward, "Do you want this job?"

Edward replied, "I don't want my mother to have to do it. So yes, I will do it if they vote me in. If not, I am okay with that too. Really Leo would be better for the job then me."

Eddie said, "Edward, you are the best for this job. I trust you the most of all your cousins."

Kenny said, "We are here for you. Calvin is here and you guys are best friends."

Jimmy spoke last, "I think we got the vote. Not all the vote but I got two out of the five."

They walked in together. The other five sat down looking afraid. As if someone was out to get them but who, they didn't know. Jimmy called the meeting to order. First on the agenda was the new membership of Edward Edson. Jimmy told the group this was unusual to have two members of a family in Majestic Twelve as members but then these are unusual times, and Edward Edson has training as a special secret spy agent to help them feel safe if possible. Calvin nominate Edward Edson and Kenny second it. They all opened their files and to everyone's surprise all voted yes for Edward to be the next member of Majestic Twelve. Then the other voting continued. Edward was confused but he did what Calvin did as Calvin followed Jimmy, Kenny and Eddie. It was a proud day for Eddie to have Edward with him in Majestic Twelve as his grandmother Mrs. King was once. They talked a little then left but the other members appeared to be pleased to have a trained active agent on the membership with them. Somehow it put everyone at ease. When they got home, Edward and Calvin went right to sleep. In the morning Kelly went to see Calvin and Edward.

Kelly asked, "How was it, Edward, the Majestic Twelve?"

Edward replied, "Confusing and scary. But I can do this with their help. We need you, Kelly, as the woman for the group. But why can't we leave Virgil and James alone? They are happy not being married. Just give them time and they will find someone their selves."

Calvin had found two women who did go to Eddie's church and were good girls so he worked them into the wedding as brides' maids to walk with Virgil and James. The surprise two ladies from the university where Suzanne and Edward met. Friends, how romantic. Edward was sure Calvin was full of shit but he went along with it and Suzanne and Kelly didn't believe either.

The meal was to be chicken and fish with two wedding cakes; one was an angel food cake with the other a chocolate food cake. White and black were the colors. All the brides' maids wore black. The guys were in black suites with white shirts. The brides in white and grooms in black. It was pretty. A black and white wedding with red roses everywhere. An October double wedding. Samantha wore Barbie's wedding dress which was really Mrs. King's wedding dress from her first husband Edward, the pilot killed in WWII. Salina wore Mrs. King's wedding dress that she wore marrying Mr. King. Edward got to help with the wedding for the old priest had a cold and couldn't talk. Edward got to say the marriage questions to his cousins. Suzanne sang the wedding song. Betsy and Jay did the cooking.

But Virgil and James appeared to be so busy with singing, not their beautiful dates as bride's maids. Then James was outside for air a lot. Virgil and James did most of the singing with Ricky helping on the drums. They left for their honeymoon but no one said where they were going. Leo and Samantha took little Ed with them and his friend Ricky. Victor and Salina took no one with them. Edward and Suzanne drove them to the airport to their planes.

Then everyone went home to their new homes. The home would be all done by Halloween and they were all busy moving in. But Sarah said she had to work and hadn't moved into her and T-Jay's new home. Sarah was working hard at her office and I guess that was important clean water. Sarah hadn't been home to sleep with her husband T-Jay since Kevin and Bonnie's wedding. What was going on there? Work or maybe the good-looking handsome James Edson who Sarah danced with at Kevin and Bonnie's wedding?

CHAPTER EIGHT

WHERE FROM HERE, NOW?

Calvin's first question was where do we go from here? Three of the Eds were married and there were two more to go but that would take time. Virgil was dating lots of girls but what was James doing? Love can't be hurried, can it? Virgil still ran after every woman he saw but not the women in their new home's area. Out of sight, so I guess it was out of mind.

James said to Virgil, "Stay away from Kelly and Jay, then Calvin won't tell them."

Virgil replied, "We will be good guys at our new homes but raise hell as always everywhere else. James what is happening with you? Settling down with one woman, or shouldn't I ask."

Victor answered, "I love it. This married life is so good. I have no idea if she can cook or even knows where the kitchen is or what to do in that room. We got the bedroom going great."

Edward asked, "Where is Leo? Does anyone know how he and Samantha are doing with little Ed? I know they came back and he left for work but that is all."

Kelly came in and said, "Maybe we should ask Jimmy, she is his dentist. You know how important his teeth are to Jimmy."

Calvin was right behind Kelly and asked, "What are we talking about?"

James replied, "We are talking about you, Calvin, as always. When you aren't in the room, we talk about you. What a big tattle tale you are to them."

Edward said, "Stop it or Calvin will kick the shit out of you and you know he can do it."

Virgil replied, "What are you saying, that Calvin isn't a snitch?"

Kelly answered, "We didn't say that. But Calvin is a very cute snitch."

Victor said, "Now I am getting sick. Let us find out where Leo is okay, no more talk."

Kelly took Calvin's hand and with the Eds followed into Jimmy's office. He looked up and said, "What now, I could be sitting here in my underwear. What happened to knock first then enter?"

Victor replied, "We have seen guys in underwear before, Jimmy."

Jimmy answered, "But you have a lady with you. Calvin what is this?"

Calvin replied, "The Eds called me a snitch again. I was going to knock but they entered. Kelly, are you okay? Jimmy isn't in his underwear. Jimmy sleeps in sweat pants."

Jimmy called out, "Kevin, where the hell are you?"

Kevin replied, "Still in bed with my new wife, why are you up at this hour in the morning?"

Calvin said, "Dad, it is noon, twelve noon. Time to get out of bed. Why are you still in bed?"

Kelly said, "Eds, one of you guys have to have a long talk with Calvin very soon, okay?"

James replied, "Kelly, that is Edward's job. Calvin is his best friend."

Jimmy remarked, "Why am I even here? Oh yes, this is my office, so why are you all here?"

Kevin came into Jimmy's office as Edward said, "We don't know where Leo is. He came back from his honeymoon then left for work. He is not back and he should be. Where is Leo?"

Jimmy answered, "Why the hell would I know where Leo is? He doesn't check in with me."

James replied, "Because his wife is your dentist."

That made no sense to Jimmy as he looked at Kevin who just shrugged. Kevin called Eddie and Kenny to come over, that Leo was missing. Jimmy called his dentist not for his teeth but to see if she heard from Leo. But she hadn't heard anything from Leo nor had his son, Ed. Eddie and Kenny got there with Kevin, meeting them at the door, telling them all that was going on. Jimmy wasn't happy. Eddie and Kenny came in with Kevin to sit down.

Jimmy remarked, "I got to get a bigger office. Have you lost a grandson, Eddie, before like this?"

Eddie replied, "No, never. James where is your brother?"

James answered, "I don't know, that is why we are here. His dentist is my brother's new wife."

Virgil said, "I think Leo ran away from home. He didn't want to get married and you made him."

Calvin said, "They called me a snitch again, a tattle tale. They didn't even knock on Jimmy's office door before they entered with Kelly, a lady. Jimmy could have been in his underwear."

Edward said, "He was working on who killed those three Majestic Twelve people with a lead."

Eddie said, "Leo was following it alone. What did I teach you guys? Never go anywhere alone."

Jimmy got up, walked around and said, "Do you know, Edward, where he was going start there?"

Out of Jimmy's office they all went to find Leo. Jimmy called Sam, T-Jay, and Micky into his office and told them to help the Eds with Calvin. Kelly was to stay at Jimmy's office. She wasn't happy but she did it. Kevin was to take Sam, T-Jay, and Micky to the place Leo was last.

Kelly went to see Samantha and did a girl's thing then right back to the boys, Jimmy, Kenny, and Eddie. Leo was gone only a few hours. He left in the morning and they went looking for him about noon that day. The Eds and Calvin found Leo tied up in an old warehouse. Leo was black and blue in the face but not dead, just hurt. As was their style, they kicked the shit out of the guys in that place, asking no questions. Calvin became a mad man again and the Eds were with him all the way. Within minutes it was all over and Leo was going home. They took the twelve guys who had Leo with them and that wasn't pretty but then it looked like Leo had put up a fight before he went down with a gunshot to his left leg. What happened to the twelve guys? The Eds took them somewhere but my guess is it wasn't to the police. Edward and Calvin took Leo home as Kevin, Sam, T-Jay, with Micky cleaned up the warehouse of anything. Michael was waiting for Leo and he was cleaned up before seeing Samantha with his son, Ed. Leo kept telling Samantha how sorry he was but all she did was kiss him and Ed was there to hug his dad. Leo would be fine, just a few bad bruises. After Leo was asleep, Samantha went you know where, readers, to Jimmy's office. Jimmy wasn't having a good day.

Samantha did knock first and Jimmy replied, "Who is it? What do you want?"

Samantha said, "It is me, your dentist. I want Leo at home and not getting hurt anymore. Can't he do an office job? Isn't his grandfather Eddie the head of this secret agent stuff?"

Samantha was crying as Jimmy opened the door with Eddie and Kenny there. Eddie was crying too but what could they do? This was the job. Jimmy, Eddie and Kenny walked Samantha back to Leo and put her in bed beside him. As he was sleeping, Leo's arm went around Samantha. I think the boys were all crying now. Readers, I am sure it was crying and not raining indoors. Gary continued the work on the new homes as John helped him with Mary, his wife, worried about their new son-in-law, Leo. Leo was to stay down for some time but that wasn't Leo. Calvin was in, helping Leo who said he was fine but Calvin would help anyway. As Calvin helped Leo, they talked about women and love. That long talk that someone needed to have with Calvin. He knew the basics but the details he wasn't thinking, so Leo gave him that information as a big brother.

Calvin asked, "I know you have been with many women but is it all the same and can you be in love with two women at the same time?"

Leo answered, "I think you can love and truly love two women at the same time. But no two women are the same. Carol was my partner and the mother of my son. But Samantha is Ed's mommy and the woman I am in love with."

Calvin replied, "So, I love Kelly and Jay but which one am I in love with?"

Leo smiled and said, "I am not sure, that is what you have to find out. But I don't believe this Venus had anything to do with me being taken but killed the three Majestic Twelve people. She thought the woman was Jimmy's true love and the two guys were Kenny and Grandpa Eddie."

Calvin left Leo and went to Edward and said, "Do you think Carol could be still alive? It looks to me like a woman who is mad at you to hit a guy in the face only, then they shot him in the leg but clearly didn't want to kill Leo. Just wanted him to have pain. This is what women who are jealous do. They don't want the guy but they don't want him with anyone else."

Edward said, "Two different situations, Leo being taken and Majestic Twelve people killed."

Calvin went on his way to knock on Jimmy's door, Jimmy said, "Come in, Calvin. What is it?"

Eddie said, "I guess teaching my grandsons how to knock on a door wouldn't kill me."

Kenny replied, "I am not sure if that is possible. I know your grandsons."

Kevin said, "Calvin, what is it? What did they do now? Sorry, Eddie. But who did what to who?"

Calvin answered, "I think Leo could teach them to knock first. He is kind of the leader of the Eds. But I was talking with Leo and I think because they hit him in the face, shot him, but didn't kill him, so it was to hurt him only. A jealous woman? Secret agents do fake their deaths. Then with Venus, a different situation. She thought the woman in Majestic Twelve was Jimmy's lover and the two guys were Kenny and Eddie. So, she hired someone to kill them."

Eddie said, "I will check with the agency and see if that is possible."

Kenny asked, "Do you think Carol wants Leo and Ed back if she is alive?"

Jimmy answered, "No, Carol is one of those women and will never be any good for either."

Kevin asked, "What do we do? Find this Carol and put her away?"

Calvin said, "I think that is best for all. But we also need to find Venus and take care of her."

Kenny asked, "Jimmy, what is it with you and crazy women?"

Eddie answered, "Oh, Jimmy has the touch like Leo. They draw crazy women to them like magnets."

Jimmy spoke now, "Guys, I am sitting right here. Don't talk about me until you leave my office at least. Try to talk behind my back."

Kenny asked, "Now what fun would that be, Jimmy?"

Eddie explained, "We need you in on the conversation as we talk about you."

Calvin left and knocked on Edward's door saying, "Edward, we have work to do."

Edward called out to Calvin, "Come back in a few hours. It can wait. Or is someone dead? If not come back in two hours for me."

Calvin went to find Kelly and she was reading so he laid his head on her lap then went to sleep. Edward came and was checking doors as Kelly noticed someone small sneaking into Leo's home so Kelly pointed to Calvin and they went to check it out. A dark-haired woman had a gun and was going to shoot the little boy. But why? Kelly shot her gun several times as the woman fell to the floor. Calvin ran to Kelly to help her. Little Ed didn't even notice it because Kelly had put on the silencer for her gun before shooting the woman. Leo had Samantha take Ed in another room and went over to Kelly with Calvin. By that time, Edward was there too and had called Michael, the doctor. The woman was shot dead and she was this Carol, the child's mother. Calvin was all worried about Kelly and we all know it was the only right thing to do. It was to save a child's live. This time, Edward called Jimmy, Kenny and Eddie to tell them all about it. Leo never even looked at Carol but did thank Kelly for saving his son's life. Then he went to Samantha and Ed. I guess, readers, you don't have to be the child's mother to be the child's mommy. Leo held his family close which was little Ed and Samantha. By now everyone knew that Carol had set this all up so she could find out where they lived and kill her son with his new mommy. The Eds were on it but it appeared Carol hired the guys herself to take Leo then came to kill them alone. It must have been Leo's marriage to Samantha that set her off. Kenny was very proud of Kelly and Calvin was worried this upset Kelly too much but the Eds were sure Kelly could handle it with no problems, she was trained to protect. Kevin went to pray to God.

Edward was in the church praying and turned to Kevin, saying, "I know what you are thinking, that my mother taught the girls how to kill but think again. Who were they after, these women? Jimmy's dentist's husband and Jimmy. So maybe sweet Sylvia is their leader, not my mom."

Kevin prayed harder to God, what the hell was going on with the women? Or in other words, don't mess with their men. No, Sylvia was too sweet and Teresa Mary was totally wrong about her mother, right? Sylvia was like an angel. She was a good girl who went to church all the time. She had a lot of health issues. Was Sylvia born that way or was she a secret agent with Jimmy too in his past? Why was it so hard to find Sylvia for them if she was just a nobody? Kenny and Eddie were very good at their jobs and so was Jimmy, then why couldn't they find Sylvia? In the morning, Kevin walked into Jimmy's office as Kenny and Eddie came in.

Jimmy said, "We are here to talk about Thanksgiving Day. I want the girls to cook a nice meal so Sylvia and I can sleep in late again. Would you guys all like to eat together this year? We can't do much for Halloween but church again. Cindy will do candy for all our kids with Betsy."

Kevin asked, "What about T-Jay, Sam, and Micky meeting Eddie with Kenny at Thanksgiving?"

Jimmy answered, "I will have them do the security to be sure and then have a supper meal with them only. Want to eat two big meal on Thanksgiving, Kevin?"

Kevin replied, "I could do that. Yes, that would work."

Jimmy called out, "Calvin, Kelly, Edward, we need you. Please do Thanksgiving with two meals."

Calvin looked at Kelly who looked at Edward and they agreed it would work. Cindy was still trying to get all the candy to the children from Halloween which they didn't trick or treat but had a big haunted house which Ricky and little Ed got to go to with Kevin to give Leo and Samantha some alone time. Calvin would also be helping Cindy get all those pumpkins for Halloween and then to cook for Thanksgiving because they didn't eat meat at the place called Marci. Things weren't back to normal but for them it was still very good.

The Majestic Twelve next meeting went well and everyone appeared to be calmer with secret agents around that were two younger men. Edward didn't understand any of it but Calvin was starting to know what was really going on now. Jimmy had half of the members and it was never hard to get one of the other five to vote Jimmy's way so having only ten members on Majestic Twelve had given Jimmy almost complete power and he liked it that way. Jay came to help Betsy with all the cooking but Betsy whispered to Jay, we need to talk.

When no one was around Betsy took Jay for a walk and said, "Kelly killed someone named Carol and I know she did it to show us she will kill for her man, which I think is my brother, Calvin. Jay, I don't trust Kelly. She is acting too sweet around you. Watch yourself."

Calvin looked in on the girls and said, "Jimmy wants us to eat in this big church place because he wants our homes more secret. How are you girls doing? Jay, do you want to bring a date?"

Jay replied, "I guess my mother is out of the question. What about Ricky?"

Calvin said, "I will ask Jimmy."

Calvin left for Jimmy's office, knocked on the door and Jimmy said, "Come in, Calvin. Is the meal going okay? Do the girls have everything they need?"

Calvin replied, "Yes, but Jay asked about Ricky coming and then her mother?"

Jimmy answered, "Yes, Ricky will be coming with Leo and his family for Ed to play with but no on Teresa Mary. Bonnie wouldn't like that and Sylvia is still upset over how Teresa Mary treated her last February. Does Teresa Mary need a place to go or food or anything?"

Kevin said, "I will check with Ricky and see what his mother needs for food, no drugs or liquor."

Jimmy looked at Kevin and said, "You should talk with Bonnie on how to handle Teresa Mary and Ricky with money. I don't want Teresa Mary at our Thanksgiving meal at all. Am I clear?"

Then Calvin left to talk to Kelly about it. Calvin wrote Jay a note, if your mother needs anything let us know but not liquor or drugs so that means no cash. Jimmy doesn't want your mother here because of the way she treated Sylvia last February, if you didn't know. You and Ricky are always welcome. Calvin signed it and so did Kelly. They gave the note to Betsy for Jay. Betsy showed the note to Cindy then gave it to Jay.

Thanksgiving started with church then the meal was so good with turkey and all the food that goes with it. The supper was as good, more turkeys and all the food that goes with it. Sarah was going outside a lot at supper for air but it was cold out there. Sam, T-Jay, and Micky did the security at lunch and the Eds did the security for the supper. Then it was the Eds outside doing the security as Sarah was always out there getting air that cold November Thanksgiving. What is going on with Sarah? Jimmy's people did the cleanup both times so no one was talking. Jay didn't bring a date this time but there was so much food she could take whatever she wanted home to her mother to eat. Did Kevin give Teresa Mary anything for Thanksgiving? Hell no, over Bonnie's dead body. Ricky got whatever he wanted but nothing for that mother of his. Bonnie didn't care if Teresa Mary rotted in hell or drank herself to death but I think, readers, Bonnie had wished she would. But Bonnie was so nice to Sylvia. Well we all know whose side Bonnie is on with that issue, the side that she gets to keep Kevin. Bonnie went home to her new beautiful home with Kevin. Kevin was now one of the boys, with Jimmy, Eddie and Kenny. Just the way Bonnie wanted it at the top always. The guys liked Bonnie and she was so nice to everyone, even their wives liked Bonnie, Kevin's new wife. Betsy did have to say that she too liked Bonnie, her new step-mother. Bonnie was so nice and understanding about Betsy wanting a baby so Bonnie talked to Kevin about it. Leo with Samantha and his son, Ed, would be taking Ricky home. Bonnie liked that and Kevin liked the idea that Ricky could come.

Someone knocked on Jimmy's office door and Jimmy called out, "What now?"

Calvin replied, "Christmas and New Year's, what do you want us to do, another party?"

Jimmy answered, "Come."

Calvin asked, "Parties, do we need two of them or more? Do you want the girls to cook? I have to get something for Kelly's birthday in two days, help me. Where is my dad?"

Jimmy replied, "Sleeping. Your dad is sleeping. I can do this myself. I have all of you here to protect me now. Yes, four parties, one for Christmas Eve after

Church, Christmas day, New Year's Eve at midnight and New Year's Day after church. A gift for Kelly. I can ask Kenny but I think she wants pearls, real pearls, eighteen inches long. White pearls. We can fly out to get them."

Calvin said, "My dad sleeps as much as Edward does now that he is married. Always in bed."

Jimmy replied, "Calvin, you need to talk again with Leo about all that sleeping, got it?"

Calvin agreed and went away to plan four big holiday parties. It was fun having Jimmy's old friends around with their families. Calvin saw Leo in the yard and walked over to him.

Leo said, "What now, Calvin?"

Calvin asked, "Jimmy told me to ask you about my dad and Edward always sleeping now that they are married. I noticed you sleep a lot too but then you got hurt."

Leo answered, "Calvin, they aren't sleeping, just having a lot of sex with their new wives. Jimmy, Kenny, and grandpa Eddie call it napping. Anything else?"

Calvin was all ashamed now, he should have known as he went to find Edward and said, "Can you come with me to get Kelly a necklace of pearls, eighteen inches long, which I know will cost me way too much money for her birthday. Jimmy wants four parties for the holidays."

Edward replied, "I know the necklace to get Kelly for her birthday. I will know it when I see it. We can do the four parties for the holidays if we start now."

Jimmy came to get Calvin and Edward, then they left. Jimmy said, "No picture for Calvin to see on the necklace, Edward?"

Edward laughed and to that place they went by airplane. They got a beautiful snow-white pearl necklace which was eighteen inches long for Kelly's birthday from Calvin which cost Calvin way too much money but he paid for it without Jimmy or Edward's help. Home they went. Then Calvin called Jay to meet her at Betsy's home. Jay agreed to meet the next day. Betsy and her husband worried if Kelly found out, would she kill Jay? Jay came there with Ricky.

Calvin said, "I think you have to work something out with Sylvia for Jimmy. I am not sure what but an understanding that you don't tell your mom. We aren't asking you be a liar but don't tell her about it. That could work. You and Sylvia have a friendship."

Jay answered, "I don't know, I will think about it. Is that what you want me to do?"

Before Calvin could answer, Kelly walked in and she did look mad. She looked at Calvin and Jay. Betsy ran in with chocolate cake for Kelly's birthday. It had Happy Birthday Kelly on it and Betsy was acting all surprised to see Kelly there, as if her and Jay with Calvin worked on this cake for Kelly. Calvin was in shock but saved by his sister, Betsy. So, Calvin gave Kelly a small nicely wrapped gift. Kelly opened it and was so happy. She kissed Calvin and Jay left. Ricky was playing with Ed. So, who told Kelly that Calvin was talking to Jay? Maybe Leo did or was it Samantha or Edward? There was no more talk about Jay being there and Kelly had a very nice birthday at Kenny's home. They were all there, the Eds, Kelly's parents, Jimmy, Sylvia, Kevin, Bonnie and Calvin. Kelly got many nice gifts but the one from Calvin was the gift she loved.

Edward came up to Calvin and said, "My best friend, you are running out of time now with those two women. Choose one and let the other one go find someone else."

Calvin thought, whatever happened to "Calvin, you have time"? Be sure she isn't crazy before you choose. How did it go from you have time to you are out of time? Calvin went to pray to God.

Betsy came over to her brother and asked, "Women problems?"

Calvin replied, "I feel like I am being pushed and I am not ready. Sorry, but I need more time."

Betsy said, "Calvin, you are a smart guy. Stay with what you believe and let no one push you."

Calvin saw Edward going into Leo's home and thought, what now? Edward was in Leo's home with Victor, Virgil and James. Kelly came to Calvin and stood there watching them not talk.

Calvin said, "What is up with the Eds?"

Kelly replied, "Well it is the holiday session and they are on the not good list. How to tell Grandpa Eddie the latest issue with which woman? In other words, who did what to who? Is Victor or Leo cheating on their wives or is Virgil and James having problems with another girlfriend? It is always about women. What did they do that they shouldn't have?"

Calvin asked, "Should we go in to them?"

Kevin came and looked then looked again, and he asked, "What is going on?"

Calvin replied, "I think one of the Eds has a woman problem."

Kelly said, "I don't think they can solve the problem because one guy is one brain. Two guys together have three fourths of a brain. Three guys together have a half of a brain. Four guys together have a fourth of a brain but five guys, is no brain at all. Now Calvin wants to help, that would be six guys with no brains at all. What do you think, Kevin, should we go for seven guys or just one woman to solve this problem?"

Kevin asked, "What would you do, Kelly?"

Kelly replied, "What we will have to do in the long run. Get money to buy that woman off."

Calvin asked, "Has this happened before?"

Kelly laughed, "Oh yes. But how to get the money or tell Eddie is the biggest problem."

Kelly and Calvin looked at Kevin as Edward came out of the meeting with his cousins, the not good boys. Edward smiled at Kevin and he knew he would be the one to tell Eddie, oh God Merry Christmas. How bad could it be? What could they have possible done in this shutdown world? I mean social distancing, right? But then these Eds never founded any rules, ever.

Edward said, "Dad, can I now call you dad, Kevin? You and my mon are married."

Kelly was laughing as Calvin whispered to Kelly, "What is it?"

Kelly replied, "The Eds have decided to have your dad, Kevin, tell Eddie. So that is what Edward has been sent out here to do."

Calvin asked, "Will Eddie be mad? When this has happened before what did they do?"

Kelly replied, "Have your dad ask them."

Kevin must have been reading minds for he knew he was set up and he went with Edward to talk to the Eds. Calvin and Kelly stayed out as Cindy came to find them and listen.

Kevin walked in and asked, "I know this has happened before. I don't need to know who is having the problem with whom. How did you solve the problem before and how many times has this happened? It is not Edward's problem, is it?"

James spoke first, "No, but you are now Edward's step-dad, right? Edward is an Eds and we help each other all the time without telling on each other."

Kevin replied, "I am Edward's dad now, so how can I help the Eds?"

Leo spoke next to Kevin, "We need one million dollars to shut her up."

Kevin said, "Paying them off, has that worked before and is there a child involved?"

The Eds all got up and went to a corner of the room and talked very low to each other. Then they came back and sat down.

Virgil replied, "No, but she is married. And her husband doesn't know about the affair."

Kevin asked, "What is the problem then?"

Victor said, "He wants to break off the affair but she will tell her husband and grandpa Eddie."

Kevin said, "So you think a million dollars would heal her broken heart?"

Leo replied, "That is what she said will heal her broken heart and keep her mouth shut."

Kevin asked, "You said this has happened before so where did you get the money from, your grandpa Eddie?"

James replied, "Hell no, Grandpa Eddie would kill us first. We got the money once from my parents then Victor and Virgil's parents, Bonnie and Kenny, but that is only a one-time deal."

Kevin asked again, "How old are you guys?"

Victor said, "Just the past years or so for Virgil and I but James and Leo are good at this. They got their money from first, Kenny who we had to promise never to touch his granddaughter Kelly or he will tell. They got it from Bonnie but we can never take Edward with us on this."

Virgil said, "Then we went to our parents with a promise never to do it again or they would tell grandpa Eddie. We are afraid of Jimmy. We think he can kill with just a look. Not going to him. Can we have it? We promise never to do it again. We will be good from now on, trust us."

Kevin said, "I want to see all four of those other situations on paper. I don't need names just what happened and did the money work. But again, was Edward ever involved in any of it?"

The Eds all shook their head no. Not Edward on any of these kinds of problems. So, Kevin agreed to get them the money himself but he had to see the other cases first and they had to keep their hands off of Jay. Kevin wouldn't tell Eddie. Kevin didn't have to because he was sure Calvin would do that for him. Cindy and Kelly left and we all know where Calvin went as they all went their own way. Calvin headed straight to Jimmy's office. Calvin knocked on the door.

Jimmy said, "Come in, Calvin, and tell us all about it."

Kenny asked, "What are the Eds up to today, Calvin?"

Eddie just closed his eyes and said, "What now?"

Calvin told them the whole story and Eddie started to look sick. Kenny was thanking God he had a granddaughter not grandsons. Jimmy smiled that they were afraid to come to him for money. What would Kevin do with this wild group of guys? Well, at least Kevin was a very good lawyer. This was his area and I think, readers, that woman with the broken heart who needed a million dollars to heal her broken heart had met her match. Kevin had never lost a case and with Calvin's mom, she died so that was that. I guess they could kill this money grabbing woman but that wouldn't be their style or at least not Kevin. Kevin would take her to court if she didn't leave the Eds alone and as for telling Eddie, well, he knew from Calvin but Eddie would never tell his grandsons that he already knew. Kevin went to see this woman with her husband, then they had a not so nice talk but no money did they get. Kevin did put a million dollars in an account of the Eds to use if needed, but all the Eds had to sign that money out to use. Kevin trusted Edward and the Eds were pleased to keep their agreement. The bad Eds boys may have gotten black coal in their Christmas stocking but that was all. The Eds promised to never do that again. There were five Eds but Edward didn't ever do that, so one Eds hadn't kept his promise from before, could they do it now? Eddie did ask Calvin, Kelly and Edward to check to see if he had any more great-grandchildren running around that he didn't know about. If the Eds could get into problems in this shutdown world what could they have done before that virus? How hard could this be to check, all the women the Eds dated even once.

Edward replied, "How many years do we have to check all the women they dated?"

Eddie looked sick as Kenny said, "We need someone to watch the Eds for Eddie. We don't want to lose Eddie over his wild grandsons."

Jimmy called, "Kevin, please come into my office for a minute. We want to talk with you."

Eddie replied, "Kevin did a great job on that issue for my grandsons and they trust him now."

They all agreed and Eddie felt better as Kevin walked into the office but Kevin knew but he didn't mind at all. He was sure he could watch the wild Eds, for Kevin was a little like them himself in his younger days. Maybe next Christmas, the Eds would all be on the nice list for Santa but I wouldn't bet money on it, readers.

Barbie, Eddie's wife, the Eds' grandmother wanted to know how her grandsons were treating women. So, Barbie went to Kevin. Kevin was not having a good day again. Barbie is now Kevin's new mother-law, Bonnie's mother. Okay, we all knew the mother-in-law would come sooner or later in the picture. Kevin is a good lawyer and he sat there listening to Barbie. Calvin and Kelly wanted to help Kevin but Edward wouldn't let them go anywhere near. Edward knew his grandmother and if grandpa Eddie took orders from her, that was it.

They did listen and Kevin replied, "All the Eds appear to be respectful to women but they like women a little too much. The problem is the Eds like all women and can't find one to love. But I have high hopes for Edward, Leo, and Victor now that they are married. We will pray for James and Virgil to find nice women to marry."

Eddie came in the room and said, "Barbie, leave Kevin alone. He has a full-time job watching our grandsons. I trust Kevin with our only daughter and watching our grandsons."

As Eddie and Barbie left, she asked, "How will we know anything?"

Eddie replied, "Kevin's son, Calvin, tells us everything right away, great guy."

Calvin, Kelly and Edward started their work on checking to see if Eddie had any more great-grandchildren which wasn't as hard as Edward thought it would be. Micky helped them with the computer to check if anyone had a baby or abortion that the Eds were ever seeing, and it looked like no. The guys, Sam, T-Jay and Micky were a big help to Edward, Calvin and Kelly but they were more pleased when the Eds were gone on a mission. The guys didn't trust them around their wives. These Eds were too handsome with a James Bond 007 look.

The Majestic Twelve met again and Jimmy could tell that the other members wanted the two unused chairs filled. But Jimmy wanted to wait for Kelly to be older but could he make the group wait or lose out on filling the spots himself? Eddie told the group about the virus and were they sure it is over or what? A new person they didn't know much about, where they had been and they couldn't ask them by their rules. Kenny talked about the killing of these three members and were they completely done checking into it. No one went to jail for it. More time was needed there. The other members really trusted Calvin and Edward, two young men with security training. Jimmy had Kevin and Kelly drive with them and wait in the café. Kevin was reading minds and it was to introduce them to the other members without doing it by words. The other members would see Kevin and Kelly, then they would find out they were lawyers and this would be a good thing for Majestic Twelve. Not so many spies or science people. A mixed group of people in this age and time, a lawyer was always useful. The meeting went good and Jimmy was pleased but the other members did look at Kelly and Kevin.

Calvin had gotten both Jay and Kelly a Christmas gift.

He went to Leo for help and said, "You know that you should take the girls out to eat. Just a Christmas lunch to give them their gifts with no one knowing it."

Calvin asked, "Are you sure that is okay to do?"

Leo answered, "How will you truly know who you love? You aren't a liar or having sex with anyone, just eating. Nothing wrong with that. A guy has to eat and give them their gift."

Calvin did as Leo told him to and it worked out great. Both girls loved the dinner and gift. No one knew and Calvin's secret was safe with Leo. Now Calvin understood why the Eds were so close. No judging, for that was God's job, but tell God first? Then word came that one of the Eds got shot and they had to go get him, where was he? Calvin didn't understand what was going on. What was the big deal? Edward was packed and leaving. Suzanne came to Calvin crying.

Bonnie ran to Calvin and said, "Don't let Edward go on this one. Please, Calvin, talk to your dad."

Calvin knocked on Jimmy's office door and he said, "No, Calvin, this isn't for you. Go back to bed. No more talk, leave us now."

The way Jimmy talked was so much like he wasn't open for any conversation on this so Calvin went to find Cindy. But he couldn't find Cindy. C-Jay had no idea what was going on or where Cindy was. Calvin with C-Jay went to find Betsy. Mickey was awake looking at C-Jay and Calvin.

Betsy said, "Calvin, what the hell are you doing in my bedroom? I am in bed with my husband."

C-Jay replied, "We went to bed together but Cindy is gone."

Calvin said, "Something happened to one of the Eds and I think Cindy is helping Jimmy now. I think Cindy is okay but working. I want to help too but Jimmy told me to go back to bed."

Betsy said, "Okay guys, Calvin with me. C-Jay stay with Mickey."

Calvin asked, "What should we do?"

Betsy asked, "I will read Bonnie's mind and any of the other women to find out but you don't. Let us not make Jimmy mad at you. Go back to your bedroom and wait, please trust me."

Calvin went back to his bedroom but waiting was like hours for each minute.

Why was he waiting in his bedroom like a child? Calvin wanted to help the Eds. He could fight too.

Betsy came back with Cindy to Calvin's bedroom, and said, "One of the Edson guys are shot in a county which isn't good for us but what they are really after is to kill you, Calvin."

Cindy answered, "Jay and Kelly are in their bedrooms safe. They don't even know this is happening. We should have James Edson home by the end of the day. He was trying to find out who had a hit on Calvin Carlson. James is home now and Sarah came running from her office crying, but why? Michael is ready for the hurt people. I think there are more shot."

Calvin asked, "Is James hurt bad?"

Cindy replied, "There was a shootout. Not Eddie or Kenny but I think Leo and Edward got shot. Dad and Kevin did go in and disappeared out again to stop killing."

Betsy was crying as she asked, "Was anyone killed?"

Cindy looked tired and said, "I don't know, my dad stopped talking to me through our minds."

Cindy was crying too now. Sylvia came to the room and hugged Cindy, then went to Sarah. Michael was waiting for the hurt people. Jimmy and Kevin came back first and it looked like they both had been in a fight. Then Eddie and Kenny flew in with the other Edson guys. Edward with oxygen as he came out and Leo wasn't walking. Victor and Virgil were helping him. Then James came out of the plane and he was shot but walked to Michael for treatment. Sarah ran up to help James Edson. Michael went to work and Gail with Marie helped. It was a long night. Kevin went to check on Jay and Ricky. Jimmy helped Eddie. Sylvia stayed with Suzanne who now understood Edward was hurt very bad and could die. Calvin thought this spy work is no good, we have got to get those Eds another job. But then why would anyone want to kill him? Calvin was no one special, or was he? Jimmy walked over to Calvin and stood by him.

Calvin asked, "Why?"

Jimmy replied, "Money, power, and greed. Someone payed them to kill but who and why."

Calvin went to pray to God, his best friend, but this time Calvin prayed for Edward's life as Suzanne sat by Calvin crying.

She said, "Edward can't die, he is going to be a father."

Kelly came into the church and sat by Calvin, praying for Edward. God help him. All Calvin could think of was that this can't be happening. Edward can't die like his father did before he was born. Calvin took Suzanne's hand and they prayed together for Edward.

Michael came in and said, "There you are, Suzanne. Calvin and Kelly make sure Suzanne rests now, we don't want her to lose her baby. Edward is going to want that child of his."

Bonnie with Kevin had come into the church to pray too. Calvin and Kelly took Suzanne to lay down by Edward in his bed. The Eds all found places to lay down around Edward as Calvin sat by Edward's bed with Kelly. Bonnie was so afraid her son would die as his father did before he was born to never see his child. Days passed so slowly as they all cared for Edward. The other Eds were doing better but still moving very slowly. Eddie sat by his favorite grandson day and night praying. The Eds were all in church praying and promising God anything for Edward. I am sure each one of the Eds asked God to take them and let Edward live but I don't think it works that way. Then Edward woke up to see Calvin, Kelly and all the Eds sleeping in his bedroom with Suzanne by him. Michael and Marie came running over to Edward.

Edward said, "I know I got shot but I thought at least I would get a private room with my wife. How mad is grandpa Eddie at me? How many people am I sharing this room with?"

Jimmy replied, "Times are hard because of the shutdown with that virus, no one gets their own room now days. No, I am joking, they are all here for you. They wouldn't leave your side when you were so sick. But Suzanne has something wonderful to tell you."

Edward looked but Suzanne was still asleep, so was Kelly and the Eds, then Edward looked at Calvin who was in tears. Calvin couldn't stop himself from telling, you know the tattle tale.

Calvin said, "You are going to be a father. Suzanne is having your baby. How great."

Edward whispered to Calvin, "I know. Why do you think we got married so fast?"

Edward closed his eyes to sleep and held his Suzanne close to him as Michael rechecked everything. When the Eds woke up we all know who told them what. Okay, Calvin was a tattle tale but the Eds already knew. Eddie was overjoyed and they all could have used a little joy at that time. Christmas was very joyful and the parties were fun as always. All the Eds were home and Sarah helping care for

James Edson only. Did Michael need help? No one noticed this with Christmas Eve and day with the two big meals. Sarah stayed with Michael to help with the shot Eds. Calvin did notice Suzanne was big with the baby. Why had he not seen that before? When was this baby coming? No one said much about it because Edward was so sick and no one wanted to upset Suzanne. Everyone liked Edward. I guess all those prayers really did help because Edward was shot many times and it did look very bad for him but God must have saved the day or maybe a little credit goes to Michael, the doctor. Each morning all the Eds were in church praying thanks to the Lord our God. Maybe Eddie couldn't make his wild grandsons be good but Edward could with God's help. Calvin thought we should never wait for a loved one to almost die to pray like that to God. We should always be praying like that to God, thanking God for our loved ones, each, for they are a gift from God. God is there for us in the worst of times. Calvin felt not alone when Edward was so sick because his best friend God was there with Calvin holding his hand through it all. This old priest was so pleased, full of Eds' confession.

Eddie said, "Do you think we should get the old priest that hearing aid he needs?"

Kenny replied, "I think we should wait a little longer. Your grandsons are still going to confession each day. I don't want the old priest to fall over and die hearing their confession."

Jimmy answered, "I do agree, I mean that is why we always get a priest over ninety-years old, to make sure he will never really hear in full our confession. I don't feel good about telling things I have done that way and now to someone who could hear me."

Eddie, "I am not sure if we have the right idea here on this."

Jimmy said, "Maybe not, but God forgives."

Kenny replied, "I know, let's get the old priest a new car for all his hard work."

Kevin said, "Another new car for the priest? He is doing better than a lawyer with those sport cars you guys buy him and he loves them. But he doesn't need any fast, nice cars to pick up women. The old priest doesn't date, he is a priest and way too old to care about dating."

Kenny said, "Only you, Kevin, would think of something like that. He gets another new car."

New Year's came and all was good but Sarah came to help Michael with the gun shot Eds or should we say, Sarah came to help James Edson. Sarah went up to James Edson and they danced together very slowly. I guess, readers, it was the pain of that gunshot wound for James to dance slow and very close to Sarah.

Sarah asked, "James, do you have a date with some woman coming tonight?"

James replied with a smile, "I thought you were my date tonight."

Sarah kissed James on the lips as Michael saw this, he was all upset about social distancing and no kissing unless it was your wife. Michael put a stop to it just in time to get the Eds under control. James and Virgil Edson did leave right after that. The next day after church it was very quiet and Sarah told Jimmy she wasn't feeling good so she would stay at work. Jimmy sent Michael to check on her but Sylvia volunteered to go for Michael. He looked upset with Sarah.

Sylvia walked in to see Sarah and said, "I have seen James Edson and I am a believer. Now eat."

Sarah smiled at Sylvia and they ate together. Jimmy came later and ate with them too. They were checking on who had a hit contract on Calvin Carlson. Leo told them about the two dinners with the girls and maybe Jay or her mother had something to do with it. Kevin would check it out.

CHAPTER NINE

LOVE IS WHAT IT IS

Jimmy was to go and see the president of the United State of America. He was putting it off as he always did. But this time it was because of Calvin. Jimmy wanted to take Calvin with him again but was that safe for Calvin? Who or why did someone want to kill Calvin? Kevin hadn't said much after talking to the Eds. Kevin went to see Teresa Mary and all they did was fight about nothing at all. Teresa Mary was worse than ever. Kevin read her mind and she had nothing to do with Calvin being on a hit list. Teresa Mary was drunk and on drugs. Ricky was doing great with little Ed as a friend and Leo to watch him. Ricky loved to be with the big boys like Calvin and the Eds. Kevin wondered what did he ever see in this Teresa Mary? Kevin was having a lot of sex with different women so what attracted him to her? Then Kevin saw it as Teresa Mary turned to throw him out of her home, she had a little of Jimmy in her, a slight bit and that was what Kevin loved about Teresa Mary. She was as moody as all hell.

As Kevin was on his way home, Teresa Mary called the phone number Leo had left her for when Ricky was with him. Leo and little Ed had left to get Ricky as the phone rang and Samantha answered it. Teresa Mary wanted Kevin's home phone number so Samantha looked it up on Leo's desk and gave it to her but then she called Leo on his cell to tell him. Leo called the Eds and told them to tell Kevin to get the hell out of there because Bonnie was going to kill him. There would be no questions asked, just death for Kevin seeing his old girlfriend Teresa Mary. Teresa Mary had called, and Bonnie answered the phone. Teresa Mary went off on her over the phone; who knows what the hell to call it but screaming fits.

Bonnie listened carefully and then asked, "Did Kevin come to your home to see you?"

Teresa Mary, answered, "Yes, but I have no idea why. He should be killed for that."

Bonnie replied, "I couldn't agree more with you and he is my husband now, so that is my job to do. If Kevin ever comes near you again let me know. Men are pigs."

The women agreed that Kevin was a pig and should die but that was Bonnie's job to do. Then they hung up the phone as friends. Not good for Kevin. Readers, the last thing a man wants is his ex-girlfriend, who is the mother of his young son and his wife, now to be friends at all. By now Leo and Ricky had the news that Bonnie would kill Kevin for seeing Teresa Mary. The Eds ran into Jimmy's office as Jimmy looked up to see who was there, as there was no knocking on the door first.

James said, "Jimmy, you have to go to Washington DC to see the president as you always do. Take Kevin and Calvin with you, now. Please, we are concerned."

Virgil said, "We are concerned about the country. So, I will pack your things; go for a long time."

Victor said, "Enjoy the sites. I heard there is a lot to see in Washington DC."

Jimmy replied, "I thought you Eds were British?"

Leo answered, "Our hearts are in the United State of America."

Edward said, "Now on to the airplane, it is ready to go. Don't upset me, I am still very sick."

Jimmy, Kevin, and Calvin got themselves ready and got on that plane but what was going on? The plane took off as Bonnie came through the door for Kevin. Was Bonnie mad? Oh, hell yes. The Eds had gotten Kevin out of there just in time and Ricky's dad would live another day. What is love? Well, it can make you do silly and crazy things. Unbelievable warmth, concern, but don't forget anger and hate. Trust, kindness and the desire to kill someone? Very strong emotions come from this simple feeling of love. But then what can melt the heart fastest?

Bonnie asked, "Where is Kevin going?"

No one of the Eds answered but Ricky said, "Step mommy, can I talk with you about something? You are so pretty. My mommy screams and smells bad but you smell like an angel, so nice."

Bonnie replied, "Yes, Ricky what is it? You can tell me anything. I am your mother too."

Ricky said, "My mommy screamed at my daddy when he came to my home to talk about Calvin. Is Calvin okay? I am afraid for Calvin. Jay and Calvin aren't good together and dad is trying to help but I don't understand. Jay has other boyfriends as mommy had with daddy that I was never to tell anyone. But because you are my mommy too now that you married my daddy, I can tell you everything, right? You are like my guardian angel."

Bonnie's heart melted as Ricky sat on her lap talking, then he hugged her and went to play with little Ed. Eddie looked at Kenny who smiled. They both were thinking that has to be Jimmy's grandson, he is as charming as Jimmy can be with women.

Cindy came in and said, "My dad called, they are on their way to Washington DC."

Eddie said, "How convenient for Kevin. What a nice little son he has. Smart kid."

Kenny replied, "Kevin is the luckiest guy I have ever met. God must be on his side. Or maybe it was your grandsons, the Eds?"

Leo came to talk with Calvin and Edward after Jimmy, Kevin with Calvin got back. "I think we need a meal every month or so, the girls do cook great. A time to enjoy everyone."

Edward said, "Is that safe for everyone?"

Leo answered, "If we have it at our church and someone other than Calvin brings Jay there."

Calvin replied, "Not Virgil or James are getting Jay. Maybe Edward with his wife, Suzanne."

Virgil said, "We think it is Jimmy's old lovers that are trying to kill you, Calvin."

Calvin asked, "Why?"

James replied, "Why do people fall in love? Can someone stop and not fall in love. My guess is Jimmy must be a good lover. I think Venus and Margo got together. Venus has the money to hire hit men or women and Margo is the mastermind of this plan."

Virgil had to add his two cents, "Maybe we should try to watch and learn from Jimmy. I used to think Kenny was the greatest lover because he didn't marry until he was thirty-six then maybe grandpa Eddie was, because grandma Barbie loves him so much but it has got to be Jimmy."

Victor spoke now, "Only a woman would hire a hit person, a guy would try to do it himself. But this woman hired many hit people so who has so much money, unlimited amounts of gold?"

Leo said, "Only this Venus, so it has to be her but is Margo involved from the hospital? We will check if anyone sees Margo in that hospital."

Calvin answered, "Edward and I can do that with Michael. Michael is Margo's doctor."

Virgil asked, "What about watching Jimmy and his love making to learn?"

Calvin replied, "No, you are never doing that. That is sick. You need mental health help."

Virgil looked at the Eds and said, "You guys think so?"

Leo replied, "Yes, but then we all do, don't worry about it."

Calvin and Edward went to Michael and he looked, no one else ever tried to see Margo in the mental health hospital. Calvin went to tell on the Eds. The Eds were being bad or thinking it. Kelly was in with Jimmy, Eddie, and Kenny, helping them with some paper work. Calvin knocked on the door and Jimmy knew it had to be Calvin because the Eds never learned to knock first.

Jimmy said, "Come in, Calvin. Kelly is almost done helping us with this legal stuff."

Eddie said, "Calvin, is something wrong?"

Kenny replied, "Calvin, Kevin will be here in a few minutes. Kelly, go check on Edward, please."

Kelly answered, "Yes, grandpa Kenny. Is everything okay, Calvin? You look worried again."

Jimmy called out, "Kevin, get in here now."

Calvin said, "The Eds think Venus with all her money paid hit men to kill me, and Margo may have something to do with it but only Aaron with the twins have ever seen her in the hospital."

Jimmy replied, "That is very upsetting but why?"

Calvin answered, "This is the bad part. The Eds think Jimmy is too good of a lover for women and they would like to watch in order to learn."

Eddie replied, "I am going to kill those grandsons of mine, all but Edward."

Kenny was laughing so hard now and said, "I vote we all watch, okay Jimmy? Maybe a video."

Jimmy replied with a very red face, "Kevin, tell them no and this isn't to ever be talked about again or Eddie will kill them. Shut up, Kenny. Eddie, we will vote on it if this ever comes to light."

Calvin replied, "Before they thought of you, Jimmy, it was Kenny the great woman lover and then Eddie with Barbie loving him so much. Sorry to say this but it upset me."

Kevin said, "I will explain to the Eds why this kind of talk isn't okay. Thanks, Calvin."

Calvin answered, "They also think we should have an eating party for all of us to enjoy with the girls cooking but not me picking up Jay."

Jimmy said, "Okay, they are back to their stomach, that is good. We can have one at the church and the girls can cook. Have Betsy call Jay on her work schedule it is a job for her."

They all left Jimmy's office but what was Jimmy doing? Helping Calvin see Jay safely or just feeding the Eds? Kevin went to talk with the Eds. There was no information on what Kevin said to the Eds but Calvin wouldn't be told anything, for he was the ears of Jimmy, Kenny, and Eddie was the message Kevin delivered. What you say to Calvin, you say to them, to make a long story short. The Eds did take down all the hit people after Calvin but now they needed to kill Venus because she would never stop with her unlimited money and gold.

Calvin came to the Eds and said, "Cindy knows where Venus lives. Betsy and I can go with her. You guys watch Margo and her family. I think she is in on it. But why me, I don't know?"

James said, "Because it was you, Calvin, who found the proof that she killed Tim. Before that Jimmy didn't know. They would have never looked at that video, but you had the time and did."

Calvin left to pray to his best friend, for he knew Cindy would kill Venus, was this a sin? Maybe but if Cindy didn't, then Venus with all her money would kill him. Jimmy and Sylvia went to eat with Cindy only. Micky came to be with Calvin. Tech people are different, to say the least and Micky is way over the edge. Then T-Jay and Sam came in, just sat there looking at Calvin. So, Calvin got cards out to play and they played cards without betting money. Calvin was so pleased when Jimmy came out and the guys left at the end of the game. Not a word was said.

Jimmy said, "Cindy needs you, Calvin, and Betsy now. Help her go find Venus, take her out."

Jimmy and Sylvia went to pray, and they were crying about something. But Calvin had his orders and Betsy went with Cindy. They all left for Venus' place and it was filled with gold. Cindy said nothing to Venus when they got there. Cindy just looked at Venus hard and Betsy was on Cindy's left with Calvin on her right side, then they left again. What had happened? But later, the Eds told Kevin that Venus died on that day. Could Cindy kill with just a look? Betsy looked at Calvin, but he was sure they had done something that killed Venus that day. The Eds made sure Margo got the news of Venus's death, even the details of Calvin on Cindy's right and Betsy on her left. Jimmy and Kevin went to the funeral. Calvin was sure he could find that place if he had to for Jimmy. When they got back, Kevin didn't talk for a while. Jimmy went to Sylvia.

Calvin said, "How was the funeral? Is Jimmy getting any of that gold or is it a wrong question?"

Kevin replied, "Tim never told me this ether. The funeral was like no other I have ever seen. Yes, Cindy will have an invasion for the gold there. Let us never make Jimmy mad or Cindy."

Calvin went to Eddie with Kenny and asked, "What do we know about this Venus?"

Eddie said, "I don't know much, just that Jimmy said she wasn't bad to look at but when Venus opened her mouth, he couldn't stand her."

Kenny replied, "Jimmy was flirting with Venus to break up with this Marci who he was sleeping with and it worked. But how to get away from Venus was Jimmy's new problem back then."

Then with a bang, Edward and Suzanne's baby came. It was a girl, so Calvin and Kelly were the Baptism sponsors which they named Ellie Kelly Mary Edson. It was a good day and the girls cooked a great meal. No one was counting the months from the wedding to the birth of the baby for Edward and Suzanne. Michael did say the baby came early because Suzanne was so upset over Edward being shot and hurt so bad.

But what is love? Calvin saw it in his best friend's eyes how he held his baby daughter in his arms with his wife, Suzanne, at his side, now that was love. Calvin wanted that kind of love. Leo came over to Calvin with the other Eds, Victor, Virgil and James. They all wanted that too.

Leo said, "You'll find the right girl, Calvin, give it time. Edward always knew right away what he wanted and went for it. I guess you have to without a dad in your life."

James said, "I am never getting married. Love is a silly idea and no more than that."

Virgil replied, "I am waiting as long as Jimmy and Kenny did for someone and then I will marry."

Victor explained, "Being married is kind of fun. Love is being true to one person."

Calvin said, "My sister and Cindy are happy and married. It isn't who but I need time."

They looked around and saw Grandpa Eddie with their Grandma Barbie being so happy. Kenny and Gail were talking about something, that Kenny couldn't take his eyes off of Gail. Jimmy was with his Sylvia truly happy. Kevin was with Bonnie, holding hands. Sam and Vicki did appear to be happy, as different as they were. Virginia and Micky, as weird as he was, were happy. T-Jay, Mr. White suit guy and Sarah, were they happy after his first wife's death? This had James Edson all upset, seeing Sarah with her husband T-Jay talking and not touching at all.

Leo came over and said, "Not all marriage are happy ones, look at my parents or Victor and Virgil's parents, they aren't happy. Then see Kelly's dad, he isn't a happy man either. I don't think Bonnie even loved Edward's dad, she married him for his job. Then the nightmare I had with Carol, the mother of my son. Take your time. My grandpa Eddie was married fifteen years before Jimmy and Kenny got married, they were still best friends always. Take all the time you need, Calvin, for love is here to stay in our world even if it doesn't look like it most of the time. But there are many kinds of love too."

Calvin liked his talks with Leo. Calvin decided to ask other people how they knew they were in love with who they married. We know where Calvin went first, to Jimmy's office and knocked.

Jimmy replied, "I am moving this office out of here. What is it, Calvin?"

Calvin asked, "What is love? How did you know you loved Sylvia only?"

Jimmy replied, "I knew I shouldn't answer that door. Kevin get in here. Your son wants to know what is love and he is asking me of all people, not my area, go ask someone like Eddie."

Kevin said, "Son, Jimmy is feeling a little down about his past and all the problems with Venus."

Calvin replied, "But Jimmy is the smartest person I know and he loves his Sylvia so much."

Jimmy answered, "We are happy now but all that time without her. I don't understand love."

Kevin said, "You know, son, I have lost at love but I may have it right with Bonnie this time."

Eddie and Kenny walked in and Eddie asked, "What is it, Calvin? What did my grandsons do?"

Kenny said, "Calvin, you can tell us anything."

Calvin replied, "How did you know you loved your wife that you are married to and stay with?"

Kenny answered, "Gail picked me out to be her one and only love. It seemed like a really good idea to me. I loved her golden hair and diamond eyes of blue. That was all it took for me."

Eddie said, "I met Barbie in grade school and loved her always. We played together as best friends and then we became more. She was my only love and I never loved anyone else. And Barbie said she felt the same about me, best friends first then lovers for life with marriage."

Calvin went to Bonnie and his dad's new home to knock on the door. Bonnie came to the door. I don't think anyone ever knocks on the doors in the Eds' family. They walk in whatever.

Bonnie asked, "Calvin, is your dad okay? Is Edward alright? Come in, tell me all about it."

Calvin replied, "Bonnie, you are Edward's mother and my step-mother so Edward said we share parents so I have a question about real love. How did you know you loved my dad?"

Bonnie replied, "The minute I saw your dad, I fell in love with him. He was so handsome and standing by Jimmy, so guarding his boss. Then the way Kevin looked after my dad, Eddie and Kenny, I knew he was the only man for me forever. I had to let him know how I was feeling."

Calvin asked, "Was it at the party where you first danced with my dad?"

Bonnie replied, "Yes, it was, and I asked him to dance with me. Your dad said, yes why not and Jimmy laughed. Then we danced all night together. As he held me in his arms, I couldn't talk."

It was time to asked Edward how he knew Suzanne was for him. Calvin went to find Edward in the church praying. Calvin sat by Edward and prayed too. After praying Edward noticed Calvin.

Edward asked, "Want to talk or are you here to pray?"

Calvin replied, "Both, but now I need to ask you how you knew Suzanne was the woman for you to marry? I did ask your mother how she knew my dad was the man for her and I wouldn't ask that again, but it is very romantic. A woman thing, I think."

Edward answered, "Did you asked Jimmy, Kenny, my grandpa Eddie and your dad, Kevin?"

Calvin said, "Jimmy said love wasn't his area. Kenny with your grandpa Eddie were helpful."

Edward replied, "Before I met you, I talked with Jimmy about love and he said when he met Sylvia it was like life first started for him. She was so beautiful, and her big brown eyes were the light in his very soul. Jimmy told me he knew that he could never truly love anyone else like her. But I think Jimmy didn't say that to you because he thinks you are too young and that was his problem, too young to love that much. I talked with others too, like grandpa Eddie, Kenny, Leo, and my mother, Bonnie, at the end so I knew she loved your dad. But I never asked your dad, I was afraid to. But with Suzanne it was more like Jimmy had experience. My life opened up and I was a new person. When she smiled at me, I knew she was the only one for me forever. But would she want me because it has to work both ways and it did for us."

Calvin went to find his dad and asked, "Dad, how did you know you loved Bonnie?"

Kevin replied, "I was never truly in love before, just having fun with love, but Bonnie makes me understand myself. It is like I was lost but now I am found by her love. That makes no sense."

Calvin replied, "Love makes no sense but that does. I am happy for you, dad. I like Bonnie too."

Calvin knew one thing about love, that it was different for each couple and each person, but to make it work right, both had to really feel it to be true love. Calvin wanted true love. What is love? Calvin thinks love starts with knowing the love of God. Working on a relationship with God, friendship with God is the key to knowing real love.

The new year had started off good. Eddie and Kenny didn't come out of the shadows but Jimmy did go into the shadows with them. The group was coming together and it had its good points with not so good things. Calvin didn't want Edward to go out on any more missions with the Eds and he was going to talk to Jimmy about it with Suzanne's support. Calvin was sure Jimmy would agree. Calvin went to Jimmy's office and knocked on the door, but Calvin heard voices.

Jimmy said, "Calvin, please come in and tell me what you need, now."

Calvin said, "Is everything okay? The Eds again? What did they do this time?"

Jimmy replied, "They helped us move and they moved the video room which means they watched as many videos as they could until Sam found out. They didn't ask first. Sam, Micky, and mostly T-Jay don't like the Eds. They want them all gone on missions. What do you need?"

Calvin looked up and said a little prayer then replied, "I want you to have the Eds stay home all the time or at least Edward. I know Suzanne has asked that of you."

Jimmy answered, "Yes Suzanne has, and I see her point, but Edward will always go to help his cousins. Calvin, read minds and find out why the guys don't like the Eds and tell me but just me."

Calvin replied, "I am on it, sir. I wouldn't let you down but first, what kind of job do I do for you, anyway? I am not a tattle tale, or am I a go to guy, or the between guy?"

Jimmy replied, "You don't know. You are my replacement. I am training you to take my place but not with our people, that is for Cindy to do but in all other areas. On Majestic Twelve I want you, Calvin, to be the new leader after me. I want you to be the one who sees the president."

Calvin was so surprised he went to see Sam first and he was concerned the Eds would get information that Jimmy didn't want them to know, like the place called Marci. The idea of something in their heads like his wife had that could read minds was information Jimmy didn't want them to know. Calvin did have to agree with Sam, it was a security issue. Calvin went to Micky next to see why Micky didn't like the Eds. Micky was thinking more about the location and the building of the homes. Gary knew it all and that worried Micky. Gary was kind of a weak person, his wife, Micky didn't trust. Even Edward didn't trust Kelly's mom. Calvin went to T-Jay and he was very worried about his younger wife Sarah around those handsome Eds. Mostly James Edson. Sarah was many years younger than him and Margo, Sarah's mother, had cheated on Jimmy. Jimmy was fifteen years older than Margo so maybe like daughter like mother. Could that happen to him with Sarah? That was another good point. What to do but write it up in a report for Jimmy. Calvin couldn't tell Jimmy. Calvin would write it up and keep a copy.

Calvin took the report to Jimmy's office and knocked on the door, then said, "For your eyes only."

Calvin left Jimmy's office thinking what did I do? Jimmy will be mad at me. Then Jimmy talked to Calvin through his mind and told him it was right what he did, somethings have to be written down to be believed.

Edward came over to Calvin and said, "The Eds were bad again. They watched some video without asking as they helped with the moving. They said that Sam, the security guy, came in screaming. T-Jay the white suit guy was turning colors in his face, mad. Micky, the computer guy, took all the videos away, locked up the room as they left. Why don't they like my cousins?"

Then Calvin and Edward saw Kevin coming out of Jimmy's office going for the Eds. Calvin pointed to Edward for them to listen. Kelly came over to join them as they hid to hear.

Kevin said, "Why did you guys watch those old videos?"

Virgil replied, "We wanted to see Jimmy having sex with some woman so we could learn."

Kevin asked, "What did you learn?"

James replied, "Nothing good, some people at funerals. A man named Bob did the videoing for Larry. Who were they? Wasn't Mr. King my great-great-grandmother's husband?"

Kevin asked, "Did you see anything else?"

Victor answered now. "No, because Sam started screaming at us. Then the white suit guy turned colors in his face and the computer guy made us leave."

Leo asked, "What is wrong with watching old videos anyway? I liked seeing Jimmy so young."

Kevin replied, "You know how secretive they are, and this isn't okay to do ever. As for not liking you, well, they still don't like me either. But I don't care, maybe I don't like them."

James replied, "Yes, we don't like them either."

Kevin said, "So we stay away from them. We do our jobs. They are no fun."

Virgil replied, "Yes they are no fun at all. All that screaming."

Leo said, "We will go our way and they go theirs. Got it, guys. No problems."

Victor added his two cents and said, "We got this with you, Kevin."

Kevin said, "But the videos is Calvin's job so don't watch the videos without Calvin."

They all agree and then left. But now what to do about them being around so much? Kelly knew Calvin was the one Jimmy had shown them the video. Calvin worried, would Edward have to go with the others to work? Jimmy called Calvin into his office the next day.

Jimmy sat there with Kevin and said, "We can get Edward to stay but not the others. Edward was hurt very bad and can be Eddie's security. The others, that is how they make their money."

Calvin replied, "Thanks for telling me and for Edward."

Calvin saw his dad leave Jimmy's office and Sam, T-Jay, with Micky go in. Edward took the news well that he was to stay and be the security for Eddie but who was to do Kenny's security?

Kelly replied, "I can do the security for my grandpa."

Edward said, "Calvin and I will help you, with Kevin training us as always. Jimmy has those other three, Sam, T-Jay, and Micky. Cindy has Betsy, Mickey, and her husband C-Jay, right?"

Calvin never thought of it that way but he replied, "Yes."

Then Calvin noticed changes in the buildings that Sam, T-Jay, and Micky were doing by themselves with Jimmy's people. The changes were only in Jimmy and Kevin's part of the homes not Eddie or Kenny's areas. The Eds did all have to go back to work and it was all out of the area. T-Jay was very pleased to see them go, especially James Edson. Sam and Micky were on T-Jay's side to help get those Eds out of there. Jimmy and Kenny waved goodbye, but Eddie did cry a little to send his grandsons out on another dangerous mission. Eddie worried about them, but it was the job and he had done it too with their grandma. Were things worse in the world now than back then? Readers, your guess is as good as mine. Where were they going and what were they going to have to do? But one thing we know for sure, it was to keep our world safe for us. Thank God for them. Calvin and Edward went to the church to pray for his cousins. They could be back maybe for church on the first Thursday of next month. T-Jay had volunteered to be the security for the next church that first of the month. Edward missed his cousins even with his wife and daughter to care for. Calvin understood why Kelly had no interest in Victor or Virgil who were great guys, even James and Leo were very nice to her but it was their jobs. It was a hard life. Calvin had only seen the parents of Edward's cousins at the first meeting and two weddings. But then he didn't remember Kelly's mom there. He met her at her home with Kelly's dad, Gary, two times. She never came to anything at all, just Gary did alone. Calvin decided to asked Edward, so he went to find him in the church, praying as always.

Calvin said, "Edward, tell me why does Kelly's mom never come with you to anything?"

Edward replied, "You tell me why Jimmy is mad at my cousins and wants them gone."

Calvin replied, "Because T-Jay is worried about his wife, Sarah, with your cousin, James Edson."

Edward said, "It is just another jealous husband, they get that all the time. When Leo was only eighteen, Kelly's mom came on to him. Leo told her husband, Gary. Kelly heard Leo and told Kenny. Well, I guess all hell broke loose and Kenny told Grandpa Eddie. She can never come to anything my cousins will be at. I don't think any of the parents know, not my mom."

Calvin replied, "I understand, your cousins are good guys too."

Edward said, "They are my family. I was with them for all my birthdays, holidays, and everything at the boarding schools. At least we all went to the same boarding school. My mother and grandpa Eddie came to see us the most. I did go home more with them. My cousins never went with their parents ever until they went to Kenny's to study to be agents."

Calvin didn't know what to say. The Eds did have secrets, did Jimmy know this? Kelly did, she wasn't pleased with her mother but was good friends with Leo and all of the Eds. Calvin wanted to hug Edward but then these guys didn't do that at all. Just a hand on a shoulder or they sat by each other.

Betsy and Mickey had their second wedding anniversary and all Betsy and Cindy were talking about was babies. Mickey was still a little unsure of it, afraid of little Tim but C-Jay wanted to be a father in the worst way. He loved little Tim and would babysit the kid all by himself.

The first meal at church started. Calvin would watch James Edson and Sarah Peterson to see if there was anything going on. How many times could Sarah have seen James anyway? Another jealous husband, that was all it was.

But the minute the Eds walked in that church, Calvin noticed Sarah was all smiles and James Edson did turn to smile back at her. Oh shit, Calvin looked at Edward who was watching too. They weren't the only ones watching, Sam and Mickey were watching very closely too. Calvin prayed to God to let them at least get through church. After church Calvin and Edward moved fast to find James but it was too late, James was in a side room alone with Sarah. Edward was in the room with Sarah and James as Sam and Micky got there. When Calvin came in no one was talking. Leo, Victor, and Virgil came in, then Sarah left to go to eat as Jimmy came in. They all stood there and Sarah had a yellow rose in her hair which was now on the table. Other than the yellow rose in Sarah hair, she wore all white as T-Jay always wore his white suits.

James picked up the yellow rose from the table and said, "I have to go to work now. Can someone drive me to the airport?"

Jimmy asked, "Not going to eat first, James?"

James replied, "No. No thank you."

Leo left with James. Victor, Virgil, and Edward looked down. Calvin looked at Jimmy but he wasn't mad, just sad. Eddie and Kenny came in, Kenny appeared to understand but Eddie looked confused. The meal was very good but quiet. Now Jimmy knew why the Eds really wanted that meal for the get togethers. James and Leo were on an airplane to God only knows where.

James said, "Leo, you have a wife and son back there. I am fine. I have a job to do."

Leo answered, "My wife and son understand my job and my family which is you guys. Tell me about the yellow rose you took from that table."

James replied, "I don't want to talk about it. There is nothing to say anyway. Nothing happened. She just smiled at me so I smiled back, no law against that."

Leo said, "She is married, Jimmy's daughter and we don't mess with Jimmy at all, never."

James answered, "Understood, got it. The end. Go home. I am good."

Leo replied, "No, you aren't good. Damn, that is a beautiful woman. Oh shit. I am here for you."

James closed his eyes to sleep but a little tear came out without him knowing it for Leo to see. Cindy was talking to Calvin now back at the church and Calvin was telling her the truth but through their minds. Then Cindy went to kill her sister Sarah. Jimmy tried to stop her but he waited a minute to think should I stop her? What to do? What to do? Kids these days.

Michael asked, "Dad, what is going on? Cindy is mad at Sarah and it is going to be a fight."

Cindy said, "What the hell do you think you are doing flirting with James Edson? Your husband is my father-in-law. This would kill him."

Sarah sat down and replied, "I am totally wrong here. It is all my fault. James did nothing wrong. He was nice and a gentleman at all times. James is so handsome with those dark blue eyes, dark brown hair, and he is so tall. He has the cutest smile. I am so sorry."

Cindy turned to Jimmy and Michael then said, "Let us kill her. She is like Margo, cheating."

Jimmy said, "Sarah your husband is my best friend and he has been through so much with his first wife. You told me you loved him only, remember?"

T-Jay came to the door to see what was wrong. Jimmy sat down with Sarah. Michael stayed close to the door. Calvin talked to Jimmy through his mind about what do you need me to do? And Jimmy replied have your dad go see James Edson wherever he is as soon as he can get away without being noticed by anyone, even Bonnie. Calvin talked to Kevin by their minds.

Michael replied, "The sisters are fighting, you don't want to help. Trust me, stay out of this."

Jimmy turned and said, "Thanks T-Jay but no husbands or wives needed for this issue."

Sylvia looked at Marie and said, "Thank God that means we don't have to go in there either."

Jimmy said, "Cindy, you can't kill your sister. Sarah, you stay with your husband and I mean it."

Michael said, "I did treat James Edson with that gunshot wound he had, and he is a nice guy."

Jimmy replied, "Shut the hell up, Michael. When I want your input, I will ask for it."

Jimmy left the room and slammed the door closed. Cindy followed her father out with another slam of the door. Michael gave Sarah some tissue as she cried, and he sat down beside her. Calvin was reading the minds of Michael and Sarah. All Calvin thought about was that song, for it to be a shame to find the right one then being married already to someone else. Kevin had gotten away from everyone and Edward had told his step-dad where they were, Leo with James Edson. Edward and Calvin wanted to go with. They flew by plane to God only knows where again. Edward called Leo to tell him they were coming. Leo came to the door and they came in.

James said to Kevin, "I guess we should talk. Nothing happened between

Jimmy's daughter, Sarah and me. Her husband has nothing to be upset about, well, maybe a little."

Kevin asked, "How did you get to know Sarah in the first place?"

James replied, "We danced together at your wedding with Bonnie and went for a walk. We talked about having a baby."

Kevin asked, "Did you asked Sarah to dance with you or did she ask you to dance?"

James answered, "She asked me to dance then she wanted to get some air, so we went outside."

Kevin asked, "Did you know Sarah was married and Jimmy's daughter?"

James replied, "No, not at first. There were so many people and Bonnie does have a lot of friends. But then Sarah talked about an older husband and becoming a grandmother was a little too much for her. She was rethinking having children herself because her brother and his wife had a baby son. She is a very beautiful woman, we talked like we had known each other all our lives so I check into her life after that night and that is when I knew."

Kevin asked, "What is your plan on this?"

James answered, "To stay away from Sarah because she is married and Jimmy's daughter."

Kevin asked, "Is that why the Eds wanted the church meals?"

James replied, "Yes, I did that out of weakness for a beautiful woman."

Kevin asked one more question, "What about a yellow rose?"

James replied, "That is my favorite rose, one yellow rose, I don't know why or how Sarah would have known that, but it is like she knows my mind."

Kevin answered, "Thank you, let us stay in touch and you take care of yourself. Come home when Sarah isn't around. I can do that for you. No one needs to know. It is your home too."

James thanked Kevin and they left. On the way home Edward was sure to tell them that it wasn't James's fault, which Kevin and Calvin agreed. Now how to tell Jimmy the problem.

When they got back, Kevin went right to Jimmy's office. Edward went to his wife and kid but Calvin listened. Kevin did tell the truth, the whole truth and nothing but the truth. Calvin was proud of his dad. Jimmy looked shocked. Then Kevin called Michael in.

Michael asked, "Dad, are you alright?"

Jimmy replied, "Michael, I am sorry I got so upset with you, the problem is

I really like James Edson too. But T-Jay is my best friend. My spoiled daughter. What can I do?"

Michael said, "Dad, James' gunshot was to his chest and spies are always supposed to wear a bullet proof vest. James knows that. Why wasn't he wearing one the night of the shootout?"

Kevin replied, "Jimmy, I read James' mind and he is in love with Sarah. James wants to become a father but that was before he found out Sarah was your daughter. James thought she was one of Bonnie's friends at our wedding. James got an engagement ring for Sarah with diamonds from Mrs. King's old ring. Gary did a ring like this for a girl he loved named Tammy."

Jimmy asked, "Did Sarah asked James Edson to father a child with her?"

Kevin replied, "Yes, and Sarah disappears and reappears in James' bed a lot at night when he is asleep. James thinks he is dreaming about Sarah."

Michael asked, "Can't you stop her?"

Jimmy replied, "No, she may not even know she is doing it. Sarah may think she is just dreaming about James. Sarah has skills like me. That kind of deep love you can't fight."

Kevin asked, "Is Sarah like Margo, cheating on her husband?"

Jimmy answered, "No, Sarah is like me. In love and can't help it as I am with Sylvia."

Michael asked, "Can we help Sarah somehow, dad?"

Jimmy replied, "We have to, she is my daughter and I love her. I want Sarah to be happy and with the man she truly loves. But I don't want to hurt my friend T-Jay."

Kevin replied, "What can we do?"

Jimmy answered, "I have an idea. I think I know something about Gary's situation that will help us. I will talk to Sarah and we will help her. I need time to work this out. Michael, talk to Gary about his ring and this Tammy. Kevin, read Sarah's mind on her relationship with T-Jay and James Edson. Don't give me all the sexy details just the overall picture."

Jimmy went to find Sarah. Sarah was crying in the church and praying for James Edson. Jimmy sat down beside her and prayed for patience. Sarah looked at Jimmy then cried more.

Jimmy said, "I know how much you love James Edson. I am here for you. Just give me time."

Sarah replied, "You hate me? I don't know what to do, T-Jay is a good man but the passion I have for James and he has for me is uncontrollable. I am so in love with James, what can I do?"

Jimmy replied, "You know your work with water on the place Marci? I used it to help me with things. I couldn't save people I cared about at the time. But I think I could try again."

Michael walked in and sat down, saying, "Dad, is my twin sister Tammy still alive?"

Jimmy answered, "I think so. I put Tammy in water on that place Marci at a hospital. We buried an empty box. Tammy can disappear and reappear as you know and I think was doing that with Gary, Kenny's son, but why him?"

Michael answered, "We are very small, Gary played with us all the time and Tammy loved him. The ring and he talked about a girl who sounds like my twin sister Tammy."

Sarah said, "How does that help me with James Edson?"

Jimmy answered, "I have Sally, T-Jay's wife, there. I couldn't help her at that time but I can now."

Kevin stood by the door and asked, "Is Tim there too? Please say yes."

Jimmy turned to Kevin and answered, "Yes. We have a lot of work to do."

Eddie and Kenny walked over then Eddie asked, "What the hell is going on, Jimmy?"

Jimmy replied, "James, your grandson wasn't wearing his bullet proof vest when he was last shot and why? It is what they know as a secret agent to wear all the time on the job. I think he wanted to die. We have to stop him now. I think the other Eds know about it."

Eddie said, "Why, because of your daughter, Sarah? What are we doing to do?"

Jimmy replied, "I have a plan but first I need time and one of the Eds to always stay with James. Can you get James on less dangerous missions? I want the guy alive. Eddie, could you stand being an in-law with me?"

Eddie replied, "Yes, but Barbie maybe not. The Eds are already planning to be with James."

Jimmy turned to Kenny and said, "Stop laughing. I got some unbelievable things to tell you. But I have too much to do first. We are getting your son a new wife."

Michael walked in and smiled. He was thinking of his twin sister, Tammy. It was time to change people to stay with James Edson on his missions and Jimmy wanted Calvin with Kelly to go for some training as secret agents. Eddie was surprised but Kenny agreed they were ready and it was the next move. They got on a plane with Michael the doctor to recheck James Edson's gunshot wound. The Eds got to go with and Sarah with Calvin then Kelly to see Leo with James Edson. Virgil called Leo and told him Sarah was coming to see James with Michael her brother.

The plane landed and Sarah ran to James' arms and he ran to her. The other Eds got off the plane and looked at the sky. Kelly looked at the sky too. Michael worked with his medical stuff. Calvin looked around. Sarah and James were now kissing.

Calvin asked, "What are we doing?"

Kelly replied, "Acting like we aren't noticing them kissing, Sarah and James."

Calvin asked, "How long do we do this? It is getting very hot."

Now did Calvin mean the weather was hot or the situation was very hot? I am not sure but all the Eds, Kelly, Calvin and Michael went inside but not James and Sarah. They were still saying hi to each other. Very hot. Kevin mind read to Calvin and he replied that all he knew was never say anything not nice about Sarah or James Edson would hurt you very bad. He loved her and she loved him. Calvin also wouldn't be needing anymore long talks, he had learned. The others flew back home. Michael, Edward, Kelly and Calvin did stay with James and Sarah then they heard them talking between the kisses that night. They shouldn't have been listening but were.

Sarah said, "I want a baby from you. Do you still want to become a father? Could I be the mother of your child? I am in love with you, James."

James replied, "Yes I want you very much, but I don't want you to be pregnant with my child living in your husband's home with him. I can't live with that. I am so jealous of you with him. I can't think straight and it makes me not sleep at night thinking about it. You in bed with him. Him touching you. Sleeping with you each night."

Sarah answered, "James, what can I do? I promised my dad to give him time to work something out. Dad has T-Jay's first wife in a hospital like place and he is sure he can now get her back to health. We had an extra king size bed and I sleep on one end with him on the other. We never touch and just kiss in the air to each other. As for sex, we haven't had since I met you and he hasn't noticed, like his husbandly job. I got this gold star dust chain for you."

James replied, "I love this. I got you this ring to marry me, it is your birthstone, emerald. I guess asking a married woman to marry you is just wrong and then in bed, not the place."

Sarah answered, "Yes, James. I will always say yes to you and I will marry you as soon as I am free to do so. I am sleeping at my work place and not with him ever since I met you. I understand how you feel. We can make this work, I promise."

James said, "You are starting to sound like an Eds. We are always promising but keeping it?"

Sarah kissed James and said, "Well, that is what I want to be, is an Edson, your wife for life."

Michael came over, making them stop listening then had Kelly go to another room to sleep. Calvin and Edward stayed away from the room Sarah was in with James. Michael sat there all night.

In the morning Michael took Edward and Sarah home on the plane as Kelly with Calvin stayed to work with James Edson. It was one of the best weeks of Calvin and Kelly's lives, working with James as secret agents. Now Calvin understood why the Eds loved the job so much even with the risk. Back home T-Jay said nothing and was sure Sarah was working a lot with Michael and her dad, Jimmy. Jimmy did tell T-Jay all about their work but T-Jay didn't understand a word of it, he smiled in agreement to Jimmy. All appeared to be good with everyone. Working hard on what no one understood for Jimmy, but they all did what he asked them to. A lot of import and export of stuff for T-Jay, extra computer stuff for Micky, and more security for Sam to do. Edward was sent out to get Kelly, Calvin, and James Edson, but Jimmy wanted them to come home before the next mission. Edward got them home.

Kelly said, "James, if T-Jay's first wife is still alive then his marriage to Sarah wasn't legal."

James smiled at Kelly and said, "Thank you for telling me that. But I don't have the kind of money he has to give Sarah for a home and life."

Calvin replied, "Sarah makes her own money. T-Jay doesn't pay for Sarah's stuff. Sarah doesn't even need money from Jimmy, and I don't remember she ever did. Sarah works with the oceans and water. It is a big deal. She loves her work."

Edward said, "Sarah is the one that has been living at work because of the water situation for safety. Clean water is a big deal. Or doesn't she want to be with her husband? I saw that bed they had, extra king size, like they were sleeping in different countries. That big."

As they got home Kevin said, "No one knows you are here but us. Not even Sarah, so go home and rest. Calvin, how was the trip or mission? Kelly, are you good?"

Kelly answered first, "I loved working with Calvin and James. Thank you."

Calvin replied, "It was the best. Dad, I just can't wait to go again with Kelly and James, please."

James asked, "I have a home here? Or go to my brother Leo's place?"

Kevin replied, "You have your own home here. We built you a house. It is right next to Calvin's home which he hasn't seen either. Go and get some rest before you start the new mission."

James looked at Calvin and asked, "Where is it?"

Calvin said, "I'll take you there as we take Kelly home. It is by my house. I haven't seen it."

Calvin went to his new home and walked into an empty house. Calvin was going to need a bed to sleep in tonight. He turned to get a sleeping bag from Edward as James went into his house but James had a bed in his living room. Calvin stopped and looked. James walked in and looked, there was Sarah sleeping in the bed in his living room. Well readers, we all know what James did, bad, bad Eds. James crawled into bed with Sarah.

Edward asked, "Calvin, what is wrong?"

Calvin said, "I have no bed to sleep in. Got a sleeping bag for me tonight?"

Edward asked as he handed Calvin a sleeping bag, "Does James need one too?"

Calvin replied, "No James is good. He has a nice bed in his living room with Sarah in it."

In the morning Betsy asked as Virgil was getting all this food for himself, "Virgil, are you hungry?"

Virgil replied, "I am eating for three today."

Mickey said to his wife, "I think all those Eds are crazy. Which one is this one?"

Kevin asked, "Virgil, where are you going with all that food?"

Virgil replied, "I am hungry."

Jimmy looked with Kenny and Eddie then he said, "They are up to something again."

They followed Virgil to James' house. In the house, Virgil went with the food as Sarah woke up.

James said, "Virgil, how did you get in here? You can't come to bed with Sarah and me."

Virgil replied, "You weren't having sex, I checked, you were both sleeping. I got food. You have to feed women or they die. I like Sarah for you. You aren't so crabby when she is around."

Sarah said, "Thanks Virgil, that was very nice of you. James let it go. He means good."

James said, "Virgil, when we are done eating, you can go. I want to talk with Sarah alone. I have to heal from my wound first. Michael said I can't make love or I will open the stitches and I can't sleep by you again without wanting to make love to you, so February twenty seventh. It is a Saturday, marry me? I am not sure where we will live but I will find someplace good, I hope."

Sarah answered with a kiss, "Yes, I will marry you, live anywhere, and be very happy."

They started kissing as Virgil left and came up to Jimmy, Kenny, with Eddie then sat by them.

Jimmy said, "Virgil, what are you doing?"

Virgil replied, "We have a problem here. We don't want them to run away, do something."

Jimmy replied, "I can get T-Jay's wife back and him to see her on February twenty-seventh, then they run away to marry here. Okay, it isn't a great plan does anyone have a better plan?"

CHAPTER TEN

SARAH AND JAMES EDSON

Sarah and James have planned to run away and get married. Kelly said that Sally is asleep in a hospital. Jimmy's plan is to bring Sally back to T-Jay on the twenty-seventh of February while Sarah and James marry at home. Jimmy has the wedding dress James' great-great- grandmother Mrs. King wore for Sarah, which is what she wants. James is coming home one more time before they run away and marry to change agents. It is Victor to go with before they run away but Leo wants to be with his brother, James. Virgil and James come home late Friday night. Calvin and Kelly have gone to get them, as they land all the Eds are there to meet them.

Leo said, "Go home and get some rest, then we have to talk, James."

James replied, "You can't talk me out of it. I am running away with Sarah and getting married."

Virgil said, "Let us go home and sleep, then talk."

Calvin walked Kelly home and they kissed goodnight. James went to his home and Sarah was waiting.

James called to Virgil, "Go to your home tonight. Edward, give him a sleep bag if he doesn't have a bed in his home. I want to be alone with Sarah. I do mean alone with her only."

Virgil called back, "Remember James, no sex because of your stitches from that gunshot wound. It needs to heal or there will be no sex on your wedding night. You want to make your baby."

James replied, "Virgil, that is between Sarah and I, not you, okay?"

Virgil answered, "Just trying to help. You know how you are with Sarah. You don't think straight in bed with her."

Sarah replied, "I got this, Virgil, thanks. Good night."

Virgil answered again, "Good night, but how are we going to get that baby if we don't concentrate?"

Leo called out, "Virgil, leave James alone with Sarah. I have a son and this isn't thinking."

Edward called out, "I have a daughter and Leo is right, leave them alone, Virgil."

Victor called, "My wife is crabby again and I have been taking those pills Michael gave me, whenever she isn't nice and it isn't helping."

Calvin replied, "If, Michael, the doctor gave you those pills to take, they should work, take more."

Kelly called out, "Victor, you aren't to take the pills, your wife is to take the pills. What did Michael say about it?"

Victor replied, "I wasn't listening to Michael, but I read the bottle and it read take one pill with symptoms. Each time she was crabby I took a pill and I did feel calmer."

James called out, "Victor, take no more pills and talk to Michael in the morning. Please go to sleep everyone, now. I have to leave again soon and I want time with Sarah."

Virgil said, "I don't think you care about us anymore, James."

James replied, "One more word from any of you and I will hurt you. Get it. Goodnight."

It was very quiet until morning. They all went for breakfast as Betsy was cooking in the big room of the church. Victor went to see Michael and told him his problem taking the women's pills for female issues, as all the Eds stood there but James with Calvin and Kelly. Michael tried hard not to laugh.

Sarah asked, "Where is James? I thought he was with you guys helping Victor."

Victor asked, "Am I going to die or worse?"

Michael replied, "No, you will be fine, but I want you not to go on the next mission with James because I have never had a case like this before. You took the whole bottle over a month of time? I should check and keep an eye on you."

Leo said, "I will go with James this time."

Victor cried, "But it is my turn."

Edward said, "Victor can't go because you took a bottle of pills for women's issues. You stay here. Michael needs to watch you."

Eddie, Kenny, and Kevin came out to see what was going on and to get their food. Eddie looked at his grandsons standing there with Michael and he was afraid to ask.

Eddie said, "Do I really want to know what they did this time?"

Kenny replied, "I don't think we do. Michael is holding a bottle of empty female issue pills not looking at Kelly but Victor. I don't want to know more."

Kevin asked, "Where is James Edson? Who lost James?"

Virgil replied, "Sarah did. She misplaced James. Sarah just asked us if we have seen him."

Eddie said, "It is like talking to two-year-old, my grandsons."

Kenny said, "Come listen with me. I see James is talking to Jimmy. Very quiet."

They all tried to hide to hear. James had come into Jimmy's office but he didn't knock for the Eds had never learn to knock on a door before going into a room. Jimmy had got there and he walked in with the door still open as James looked in.

James asked, "Jimmy, can I talk with you this morning about Sarah?"

Jimmy was thinking, be nice, I want more grandchildren from this James Edson with my daughter Sarah as Jimmy turned to see James Edson standing there. Should James run?

Jimmy said, "Yes, James, please sit down, let us talk."

James asked, "I want to marry Sarah and could you agree to it?"

Jimmy replied, "Yes, but run away and marry here. I will have T-Jay with his first wife."

James was about to thank Jimmy as Virgil and Victor fell into Jimmy office from their hiding place with Edward falling after them. Calvin, Kelly, and Leo were trying to help the other three up with Kenny laughing so hard, then Eddie stood there as Sarah ran to James' arms.

James said, "Thank you, Jimmy. I am sorry about this."

Jimmy replied, "These seconds we had alone, James, were so memorable but now go with them. Please go out of my office and take my daughter Sarah with you."

Michael came in and said, "Dad, I had nothing to do with this. I was writing my report on Victor's issue with this medication. Never seen this before."

Eddie answered, "Yes. Those are my grandsons and they are each, one of a kind."

Kevin helped get everyone out of Jimmy's office and back to eating the food which was now lunch. Victor was still upset because he couldn't go with James this time, but Michael wanted to watch him for a few days. Victor hadn't taken too many of the pills for he did read the label, but these kinds of pills weren't for guys. Calvin, Kelly, and Edward were busy planning the secret wedding for Sarah and James Edson. All James told Leo was to be sure to get him to that church on time. It was Saturday February twenty-seven at seven pm at their new church with a meal and dancing. T-Jay, Sam, and Micky would be seeing Sally. Jimmy's plan was to tell C-Jay who was Cindy's husband and T-Jay with Sally's only child the truth on Friday night. James didn't want a Bachler party before his wedding, he wanted to learn how to change diapers and feed a baby. Eds were ready to learn. Virgil had gotten dolls to practice on. Michael came in to see Virgil crying in the worst way. He had dropped a doll and broke it.

Michael said, "Virgil, it is just a doll. We can get another doll for you to practice with."

Virgil said, "That not it. What if I hurt the baby? Sarah and James will be mad at me. Edward never let me touch his baby girl. Leo only let me touch little Ed after he was three years old."

Michael replied, "I am sure that isn't true. You just forgot."

Virgil answered, "No I didn't. Victor never got to touch little Ed either until he was three years old. Just Edward and James got to help. I know how to change a diaper. Edward let James and Leo hold little Ellie not me or Victor. I can clean up the stuff that comes out of babies."

Michael asked, "Did you want to hold my son little Tim?'

Virgil said, "I can't, little Tim isn't three-years-old."

Michael wanted to cry, he felt so sorry for Virgil who was now lost for all the Eds were married but him, with James marrying Sarah this weekend. Michael had to help Virgil somehow.

Michael said, "What did you do for the other bachelor parties?"

Virgil said, "For Leo's first one was learned how to change a diaper. For Edward's we learned how to be quiet around a baby sleeping. For the double wedding we learned how to not talk around wives. Calvin told us his brother-in-law said a husband should keep his mouth shut."

Michael went to see what the other Eds were doing for Virgil. James had kissed Sarah goodbye and he with Leo were going on a mission before he was to get married to Sarah that weekend. At home they were busy, the bride's maids were, Samantha, Cindy, Marie, Salina, Suzanne, Kelly, and Jay. The best men were Leo, Virgil, Michael, Victor, Edward, Calvin, and Gary. The two ring boys were little Ed and Ricky. No flower girls but yellow roses everywhere. The colors were blue and yellow. The cake was yellow with mint chocolate, sea food and non-alcoholic beer. Now this was to be a small wedding and they were running away to get married. The honeymoon was to be on a yacht that they, Jimmy, Kenny, Eddie, and Kevin got them for a wedding gift. Not the poor, I guess.

Then the day before the wedding James and Leo were trying to get home. All James was thinking about was get me to that church on time. But one thing after another went wrong and Leo continued to work through all the issues until they called Calvin to come to get them. Sarah was waiting with Jimmy, walking back and forth. Sarah didn't care about the wedding or the cake or the dresses, just James coming home safe. It was time for Jimmy to take T-Jay, Sam, and Micky to see Sally. T-Jay, Sam and Micky were all surprised as they got to the hospital. T-Jay ran to Sally and they were now talking.

Micky asked, "Is Tim here too at this hospital?"

Sam asked, "Is Tammy, the little girl I didn't keep safe that I failed in this hospital?"

Jimmy answered, "Yes, Tim and Tammy are here too. Sam, don't keep blaming yourself."

T-Jay came to hug Jimmy but he backed away and said, "No, I don't do the touching thing."

Jimmy left them, going to pray and then home to sleep with his Sylvia as James' plane landed with all being good. Sarah ran to James as they kissed. Sarah showed James all the wedding stuff and the church was so pretty. The ladies had a silly bridal shower with silly games and jokes but no liquor. The guys were serious, learning how to feed babies with a bottle if needed. Victor was the best at bottle feeding babies. C-Jay and Mickey came but now Mickey wasn't so afraid of babies and this was a different kind of bachelor party, one any woman would love. The Eds clearly had, as Kelly called it, baby fever. They wanted to become fathers but not Victor.

The next day was a busy day but James stayed in bed with Sarah most of the day. No one said anything about it but I guess they started the honeymoon first for this wedding. At seven pm Sarah was in her wedding dress for Jimmy to walk her down that church aisle. James was waiting at the church for his bride and that was all he wanted to do was stay at that church until he was married. James and all the Eds along with Calvin sat at that church praying as good boys. Michael showed up with all the other people. No small wedding. Sarah and James Edson were married with T-Jay as happy as he could be, holding his wife Sally in his arms once again. Jimmy sent word with one of his people to T-Jay that Sarah and James Edson were married today. T-Jay replied with Sally congratulations to you both. Sarah and James Edson left on the yacht for their honeymoon with Victor, Salina, and Virgil driving boats alongside to protect them from any problems.

Jimmy called out, "Leave them alone, I want grandchildren. I didn't do all this work for nothing."

Eddie replied, "Just give the guy time. He is an Eds, he will get the job done."

Kenny cried, "What the hell happened to romantic love? Come on guys, give them time."

Kevin said, "Michael can check Sarah when they come back, Jimmy wait."

Jimmy said, "Cindy, what are you doing just standing there, go make me grandchildren. C-Jay is more than ready. He wants to be a father. No more waiting."

Sylvia came to get Jimmy to bed.

Sarah and James were gone for three weeks on their honeymoon and during this time T-Jay, Sam, and Micky came home to get things ready for Sally. James was back to work and Sarah got sick a lot.

Jay had a surprise twenty-first birthday with chocolate cake. They ate and danced all night. Sarah was there but still did not feel the best. James was at work with Victor but he would start to train new students with Kenny as his job was to be home more. Calvin gave Jay a gift but they all listened in. Kelly wanted to know what Calvin was saying to Jay and what would she say to Calvin? And readers, we all know how the Eds love to listen with Edward showing them how to do it better.

Calvin said, "I got you this gift. It is from me only but in the future, I will ask Kelly to help me pick out gifts for you too. I want to see you happy."

Jay said, "Thank you, Calvin. Would you be upset if I asked you who is that guy with the Eds? I have never seen him before. He isn't tall and has blond hair. He is quiet and shy."

Calvin replied, "I don't know but I will find out and get back to you. He does appear to be nice. I did see him at the home where Kelly tried on this wedding dress of her great-grandmother's."

Jay asked, "Did Kelly look nice in that dress? You remembered it."

Calvin answered, "I have never seen anyone look more beautiful in a dress then Kelly did in that wedding dress she tried on that day. But that guy was there and that is where he lives."

Virgil fell again and made a big noise, so Jay and Calvin stopped talking to go back to the group. Now Kelly was sure to make that guy, Gerald the Third to dance with Jay all night. Jay and Ricky left for their mother's home with security to be home safety so Calvin took Gerald the Third to Jay's mother's home. Calvin waited in the car as he had Gerald the Third help carry in Jay's new birthday cake to her mother and to meet Teresa Mary which did go well. I mean, is he studying to be a doctor from a rich family? When they got back, Calvin knocked on the door.

Jimmy replied, "Come in Calvin, how did Jay's surprise birthday party go?"

Calvin replied, "Very nice but she met Gerald the Third. I think they like each together a lot."

Jimmy asked, "Is that a problem for you, Calvin?"

Calvin answered, "I am not sure. I like him and he is very nice."

Jimmy said, "Gerald the Second and Third will be coming a lot. They will be doing the work with us on Tammy. Could you be nice to him? Gerald the Third is alone a lot and studies hard."

Calvin replied, "Yes, I can be nice to him if he is nice to Jay always."

They agreed as Calvin left Jimmy's office. The work with Sally was done and she would be home for Easter. James came home all worried about Sarah but people were too happy, what was up? James was looking for Sarah as he went home to her as all the Eds met with Calvin and Kelly.

Virgil called, "Calvin, you tell him, you are the tattle tale."

Calvin replied, "This is something Sarah should tell her husband not me."

Virgil called back to Calvin, "When is Sarah going to tell James she is having his baby and it is more than one? I see three babies, and all are boys in that picture of Sarah's stomach. Good work James did but when is Sarah going to tell him? I can't wait."

James said, "Thanks Virgil. Where is my Sarah?"

Virgil answered, "Throwing up in the bathroom again."

Edward said, "Virgil, you shouldn't have said anything that is for Sarah to tell him, not us."

James replied, "I am standing here, that is okay, Virgil. I want to talk to Sarah alone, please."

162

Virgil said, "When the babies come, we can help. I can change diapers the best of any of you."

Victor said, "But I can feed babies the best of anyone. And there are three babies and she only got two of you know what, so one has to be bottle fed."

James said, "Go home now. No more talk about it and what Sarah has or doesn't have. She is my wife. No more thinking about it. Bad Eds."

Edward asked, "Is James mad at us?"

Leo replied, "No, he is overwhelmed with finding out about Sarah and three babies at once."

Calvin asked, "James, are you okay?"

Kelly said, "I think we should call Michael. James doesn't look so good."

James went into the bathroom and Sarah got up to see if James knew about the babies. James tried to get down to Sarah but he hit the floor. Sarah was by his side as they sat on the floor together.

Sarah said, "I didn't know how to tell you, we were having a baby and then more than one or even two but three baby boys. I didn't want to tell you on the phone so I knew you would be home for Easter. I guess someone told you."

James replied, "Yes, they did let the news slip out but they didn't mean to. I love you, Sarah."

Sarah replied, "I love you too, James. Are you okay?"

James was on the floor as Michael got there to help James to the bed and put Sarah with him. Michael checked James and Sarah out and then went out to talk with the group waiting.

Michael said, "That would have any guy pass out, having three babies is scary."

Virgil was there to help with anything for three babies and James with Sarah were happy to have him around. He helped with baby beds and baby proofing the home. But Virgil did have to go to work out of the area and he would call to see if James or Sarah with the unborn babies were okay. Virgil was buying baby clothes on his mission which did get him a lot of women. Readers, don't feel sorry for Virgil because my guess, he was getting a lot of sex with this issue. James was teaching now with Kenny at the spy school so he could be home with Sarah as she got big with the babies. Sarah was a happy woman and was never mad at James Edson for he was the one who made all her dreams come true. James prayed all the time, so worried that Sarah would die in childbirth. As Jimmy sat in his office, James walked in, he tried to knock but had no idea how.

James asked, "Is this a bad time?"

Jimmy said, "No, you can talk to me anytime."

James said, "I am worried about Sarah having three babies. I can't lose her, help me."

Jimmy replied, "I have been working on an idea. Tim is the best doctor to deliver babies I have ever seen. Now I am not saying Michael isn't good at delivering babies, but Tim has done more than one baby at a time, he is the master. We will have Michael, Gail, Tim, and I for delivering those babies for Sarah. Don't worry James, we got this."

James thanked Jimmy, leaving feeling better but Kevin heard this all which had Kevin so pleased. Tim was next on the list thanks to Sarah and James Edson with their three baby boys. As Calvin was there to help Sally move back home to T-Jay's house with C-Jay, her son. Now C-Jay was always closer to his mother than his dad T-Jay. So that is why he told his mother first.

C-Jay said, "Mom, Cindy and I are going to have a baby in December of this year. We did it. You are the first to know except for Michael her doctor. I am sure Michael has told Jimmy by now."

Calvin stood there and thought what about Betsy and Mickey; were they having a baby now too? How could Calvin ask them this, but then Kelly called Calvin all upset so he had to go.

Kelly was crying. Had someone hurt her? Calvin would kill them. But they were safe here.

Kelly said, "Calvin, something is wrong with me."

Calvin asked, "Have you been with a guy?"

Kelly replied, "No, my head. I have gold things coming out of my head, see."

Calvin looked and she was like them. Kelly was one of them, she had skills. What could Calvin say but take her to Jimmy to explain this.

Calvin said, "It is okay, I got this. I have them too."

Kelly was still crying and asked, "What the hell are they? Am I going crazy?"

Calvin said, "No, I love you so much. Please believe me, it is okay. We will go and talk with Jimmy. Have you ever seen them before?"

Kelly stopped crying and said, "In my dreams with a woman but she looked like my mother but was more of my mother, I am so confused."

Calvin held Kelly close and took her to Jimmy's office with a quick knock on the door and in they went. Jimmy looked up at them. Kelly's gold things were in her head now and she had stopped crying. Calvin told Jimmy through their minds what was going on. Jimmy smiled at Kelly.

Jimmy said, "Kelly, we have some unbelievable things to tell you and show you, but first Calvin show her yours. I have silver ones and so does Cindy. We are the leaders with silver ones."

Calvin showed Kelly his gold things from his head and Jimmy showed his silver. Kelly was looking and not talking for a long time. Then Kevin knocked on the door. Jimmy's mind told him to wait.

Kelly asked, "Does my grandpa know? What am I?"

Jimmy replied, "I don't think your grandpa Kenny knows but maybe your grandma Gail knows. You are my people, the woman who gave birth to you wasn't your biological mother. Tammy my daughter is your mother. Tammy was too sick to carry a baby so this woman, Selene did."

Kevin came in and Calvin took Kelly away to rest. Jimmy went to talk with Gail and Kevin was to keep Kenny and Eddie busy. Kevin went out but how was he going to do that until Sally came.

Sally said, "Kevin, could I meet Jimmy's old friend Kenny and Eddie now?"

Kevin replied, "I guess so. Come with me."

They went to Kenny's office this time and Eddie was there talking about keeping James home until those babies were born. Kevin walked in with Sally. They both stopped talking and looked up.

Kevin said, "I didn't knock because Eds don't do that. This is Sally, T-Jay's first wife who was sick and now is back. She wanted to meet Jimmy's old friends."

Kenny said, "You could have told us first before bringing a lady into my office. I have a mess here."

Eddie said, "I am Eddie Edson, James' grandfather. He is the one who married Sarah."

Sally smiled and said, "Yes, I know and be sure to thank him for that. I hear James Edson is very good looking and handsome like all the Eds are. Kenny, your office is a nice place to be, so warm and full of things about God, that surprised me with the work you do as a secret spy teacher."

Kevin said, "Now that we have all met, want to get something to eat? My daughter Betsy is cooking up a mess of all good things."

They went to eat. Sally was enjoying the charming Kenny and the gentleman that Eddie was as Kevin had kept his word to Jimmy that they would be kept busy. Jimmy talked to Gail then she helped them with Tammy as Gerald the

Second and Third did. After a long day of surgery, Tammy would be okay. Betsy told them she and Mickey were having a baby. Calvin and Kelly went to the others.

Virgil said, "Kelly, your mom was killed in the line of the job in Paris, France this morning. Very sorry. I will go get her today."

Victor said, "I will go with Virgil. She was doing a pick-up and it went bad. She was shot in the head many times. Killed right away. About three this morning."

Leo talked next, "I will go with them and help. We will get whoever did this."

Edward looked at Calvin and he was holding Kelly close. Michael checked but she was shot several times. Kevin checked but a letter came to the family from the agency on Selena Anderson's death.

Kelly went to pray at the church but wanted to be alone, so Calvin went to find Edward.

Edward said, "What is up with Kelly and you always being alone, in love?"

Calvin replied, "Yes, I am in love with Kelly and I want to ask her to marry me. I am thinking of a long engagement. Can you come with me to get the ring she wanted from that place of Jimmy's with the diamonds? I have saved the money."

Edward replied, "Yes, I can fly us there but maybe you should ask Jimmy first."

Calvin went to Jimmy's office and knocked on the door. Jimmy motioned him to come in, the door is open. Calvin walked in very slowly like he was afraid. Jimmy noticed something was up with Calvin.

Jimmy said, "Sit down, Calvin, and talk to me."

Calvin replied, "I don't want to talk to my dad, just you about this. I want to get the ring that Kelly wants from your diamond place for her. Can I?"

Jimmy answered, "I think that is an engagement ring and very costly."

Calvin replied, "I have saved the money up and Edward can fly me there. I want to marry Kelly."

Jimmy was thinking fast and said, "Yes, you can get the ring. I will even fly with you."

But Edward told Kelly's dad about the engagement ring Calvin got her and Gary told Gail. Gail went to tell Kenny and wanted him go to be nice to Calvin for she knew Calvin would talk to him first.

Gail said, "Shut up, Kenny. Calvin got Kelly an engagement ring today with

Jimmy and Edward. The one you and Kelly picked out. He is waiting to ask her to marry him on Kelly's birthday."

Kenny asked, "Would Jimmy give Calvin that kind of money? That ring we picked out is way too much money for anyone. Way over the top."

Gail replied, "Talk to Jimmy about it now. Go, Calvin is a nice guy and Kelly loves him very much. I want her to be happy and not end up like our son did."

Kenny said, "I will talk with Jimmy in the morning. He is in bed with Sylvia now, my love."

Gail replied, "Go now."

Kenny left the house to go to Jimmy's place alone. Kenny knocked on Jimmy's door and Kevin answered. Kevin was looking for Eddie. Why would Kenny come without Eddie?

Kenny said, "I am here alone to see Jimmy alone without you, okay, now."

Kevin went to see Jimmy and he was out of bed dressed as if he knew something was up. There was another knock on Jimmy's door and Kenny came to the door. It was Sally, T-Jay's wife.

Kenny said, "Come in. You are Sally, I remember you. Jimmy, you have a busy home."

Jimmy replied, "Sally, please come in, Sylvia is in the garden waiting for you. Kevin, go put a don't enter sign out by my house or don't pass or I will kill you. If anyone does, please kill them for me and I don't care who it is."

Kevin looked at Jimmy but did do as requested. He was making a sign and standing by the sign as Virgil walked by and looked, then looked again with a wave. I guess Kevin was now an Eds, crazy like they all are.

Kenny said, "I am here to ask you about what you and Calvin with Edward did today."

Jimmy replied, "I can't tell you, it is a secret, but Calvin will be talking with you soon about it. Be nice. He loves Kelly very much and she loves Calvin. You could do worse for Kelly."

Kenny asked, "You gave Calvin that kind of money for that ring of all the silly things to do."

Jimmy answered, "No, Calvin saved all the money up himself for the engagement ring."

Kenny replied, "Kevin doesn't know?"

Jimmy answered, "No and we aren't telling him. Anyone who works that hard to save that kind of money for a woman should have the time to do this right without anyone telling him what to do. Be nice and go home."

Sally left too but the next day she was talking with the guys' wives about bringing the group together at the church for meals each first or third Thursday of the month.

Sally asked, "What do you know about the other people? I mean, we all like Kelly and Edward."

Vicki said, "It is the Eds they don't like. The handsome Eds like Virgil who still aren't married and as cute as can be but my son's age. Then James with Sarah."

Virginia replied, "They are the secret agent spy guys and they are hot. Virgil is the wildest and funny, but he is my son's age too. I know your son C-Jay and Virgil are friends. They are talking together all the time. Mickey, my son, likes his twin brother Victor and they do things together."

Sally asked, "Is it because of Sarah and James Edson? Is T-Jay upset about it?"

Virginia answered, "No, he is happy for them. I think if it wasn't for James and Sarah, Jimmy would have been too afraid to try with you for your health. Jimmy didn't know the legal stuff of it all and he never told Kevin about it at the hospital."

Vicki said, "James Edson is Sarah's type which is like her dad, Jimmy. Sarah loved T-Jay, but I don't think she was in love with him. When Sarah saw James, it was uncontrollable for her."

Sally replied, "What happened and when?"

Vicki answered, "It happened at Kevin and Bonnie's wedding. James Edson was singing songs."

Virginia said, "He is a very good singer and sexy. Then his grandmother, Barbie, told him to check if the meal was ready. James walked back past Sarah and Marie with baby Tim. James couldn't take his eyes off the baby and then Sarah."

Vicki said, "I saw them too. Sarah and James' eyes met. James smiles at Sarah that cute smile he has, and it is very hot just watching them. When he walked back, he winked at Sarah."

Virginia reported, "When the music started the guys said they would do security, so Sarah asked James to dance with her and he did. Sarah and James danced a few fast songs but then they played slow songs. Sarah put her body so close to James and he didn't pull away."

Sally asked, "You two never told my husband about this?"

Virginia answered, "She kissed James several times on the dance floor and he didn't try to stop her. Virgil got a white hanky from Kevin to give James to remove all the lipstick from his neck."

Vicki said, "Then they went outside for some air and talked. We listened. Sarah asked James to give her a baby. James said it would be his pleasure, to tell him when and where. He did say that he didn't think the dance floor would work but he could try if she wanted to."

Sally said, "I think you heard a lot. Why didn't you say anything to anyone?"

Virginia said, "We had to go and eat because the meal was ready. Our husbands were back with T-Jay so Sarah kissed James Edson then came back into the hall."

Vicki said, "The guys wanted to sit far away from the Eds. James Edson was sitting by his grandparents. Eddie was mad at James for all the lipstick on the collar of his shirt."

Virginia said, "We left after the meal. Mickey told me James Edson didn't dance, he went into a room playing cards with himself. He was looking out but never came out again."

Vicki said, "Sarah never said anything to us about it and we never asked her."

Virginia said, "James Edson did get shot around Christmas time in the chest because he wasn't wearing his bullet proof vest, they are supposed to wear all the time on the job as secret agent men."

Sally replied, "Well, is there anything else you can think of about this issue with Sarah that could help me get everyone together as friends?"

Vicki said, "At the double wedding of the Eds, Sarah was walking a lot around that area and James Edson looked so cute in his suit, he was one of the best men. James sang songs most of the night when he wasn't outside for air. Sarah and James were making out in the garden."

Vicki said, "At Thanksgiving Sarah was outside for air all the time as James with the other Eds did security out there."

Virginia said, "I saw Sarah grab James behind a tree to kiss him and he didn't stop her."

Vicki said, "Then James, Edward and Leo were shot at Christmas time. Sarah volunteered to help Michael. Sarah took care of James Edson. She gave him a bath; he has a nice chest."

Virginia said, "Sarah went to the New Year's Eve party for the Eds to help

Michael with the hurt Eds. She danced with James and asked him if he had a date that night. James said he thought Sarah was his date for the night with his cute smile. Michael got all upset over social distancing, then James and Virgil went home."

Sally asked, "Do you know anything else that could help me maybe?"

Vicki said, "James Edson did the first church and meal security with Sarah meeting him outside making out. I thought they were going just do it right there but they did stop before sex. I think it was that gunshot wound of James' not healed that made them stop. I was watching a little."

Virginia said, "The next time we had church and the meal, T-Jay did the security because Sarah asked him to for her dad, Jimmy. When James and the Eds walked in Sarah was all smiles. James turned and smiled back at Sarah with his cute smile. After church something happened."

Vicki said, "There was a yellow rose in Sarah's hair which is James Edson's favorite flower and she laid it on the table for him, then left the room. James took the flower and went back to work out of the area on a mission."

Virginia said, "Kevin was sent to talk with James and then Michael went to see James, but Sarah was with him. Sarah ran to James' arms and it was hot love. I heard Victor tell Mickey this."

Vicki said, "Sarah and James Edson were going to run away and marry because they found out you were alive, so T-Jay wasn't really married to Sarah. Jimmy didn't understand this legal part. He is a genius but doesn't know law. Kelly and Kevin the lawyers explained it to him."

Sally replied, "So I guess I have Sarah and James Edson to thank for my life back with their love for each other. T-Jay and I are very happy again together just like old times. You girls did good."

Sally went home and wrote a letter to Sarah and James Edson thanking them for their strong love for each other. She explained her reasons with how happy she and T-Jay were together again. Sally sent the note with her son C-Jay as Sarah opened the door, C-Jay was standing there with a dozen yellow roses and the note.

C-Jay said, "Thank you for being who you are, Sarah, and always helping me. I have my mother back because of you and James Edson. You are the best person I know."

Sarah was in tears as James came to the door and they read the note from Sally of thanks with all her love.

The guys, Sam, T-Jay, and Micky started going to the church with the meals. The Eds still stayed away from them at the church and meal, with Victor or Virgil doing the security. C-Jay or Mickey were always outside talking with Victor or Virgil and bringing them food.

Jimmy said, "I only hope it is as good for Tammy as it has been for Sally coming home."

Kevin replied, "Sally is a very wonderful person. She alone can bring this group together with love and understanding. Just think, it all started with Sarah and James Edson."

CHAPTER ELEVEN

TAMMY'S IN LOVE, TIM IS BACK!

The surgery went good for Tammy and she was awake asking questions to Michael. The fourth of July was coming up and Tammy would be coming home but how would this work? Calvin, Kelly, and Edward knocked on Jimmy's office door, for he was finally in his office.

Jimmy replied, "Come in."

Calvin asked, "What about the Fourth of July for a party? Edward's wife's family doesn't live in that neighborhood anymore so what do you want? A party for Tammy coming home?"

Jimmy replied, "No, Tammy doesn't want a party. She wants to go slow into meeting people. Everyone is new to her but Michael, Sarah, and me. Have Suzanne's family do the Fourth."

So, a nice party at the same place Edward got married. Jimmy with Sylvia, Eddie with Barbie, and Kenny with Gail came to the Fourth of July neighborhood party to eat hot dogs. Calvin waited and when Kenny was alone, he walked over to him and sat down beside him.

Calvin said, "Mr. Anderson, I would like to ask Kelly to marry me on her birthday. I got the engagement ring she and you wanted for her. What do you think, sir?"

Kenny replied, "I do like the ring, but this is a little too costly. What do you think?"

Calvin answered, "But we will be married forever like you and Gail. I can get Jimmy to have Gail's dad to be done next at that hospital after Tim, if you let me marry Kelly."

Kenny looked up and said, "Yes, that is it. You get Jimmy to do Gerald and you can marry Kelly."

Calvin answered, "I can do that. Thank you, sir."

Calvin left happy as Gail went over to Kenny and asked, "What did Calvin want with you?"

Kenny answered, "To ask Kelly to marry him and I said yes, if he gets Jimmy to do Gerald."

Gail said, "You sold our granddaughter for Jimmy to do this work for you?"

Kenny replied, "I didn't see it that way, honey. It was Calvin's idea. We can get your dad back."

Jimmy and Eddie walked over but Gail with Kenny weren't talking. Kevin whispered, "What is up?"

Jimmy answered, "I am not sure but Tammy is here with Gary? They are talking to Kelly."

Kevin asked, "What should we do?"

Jimmy replied, "I don't know about you but here comes Michael with Marie and the baby Tim. Oh good, Sarah with James Edson are going their way and it is time for my nap with Sylvia."

Sarah hugged her sister Tammy and introduced her to James who smiled his great smile. James, Gary, and Michael were talking as the women do. Tammy walked over to Kelly with Calvin.

Tammy asked, "Is this your boyfriend, Kelly? Your dad tells me he is Calvin Carlson."

Calvin replied, "Yes, ma'am."

James said, "Calvin, if Sarah and I can make it work, you with Kelly can too. Love is worth it."

Eddie was upset that the Eds weren't being good again. Kenny was seeing his son in a new way, happy and with Tammy. Why is Tammy with Gary today? Kevin was trying to keep the Eds under control but Virgil was now dancing on the tables. T-Jay, Sam, and Micky drove by, shaking their heads; what a mess, those Eds were out of control and wild boys. Sam was looking to see if Tammy was okay, he would protect her this time for sure. Edward and Suzanne got away from the group to pray in the church. The Fourth of July is fun in the USA. After the party, Jimmy went to see Michael.

Jimmy asked, "Michael, do you know what is happening with Tammy and Gary?"

Michael replied, "Yes, Tammy has been coming to see Gary, that is why he is so mixed up. They got married when she was fifteen years old and she got pregnant. Tammy couldn't carry the baby, Kelly, so she had this other woman do it as you did Margo with Cindy."

Jimmy got up, walked around and said, "If Tammy was only fifteen, then the marriage wasn't legal. I never signed anything for her to marry."

Michael answered, "Oh but you did, dad, grandma had you sign it with other stuff for Tammy."

Jimmy sat down to think this through before the next Majestic Twelve meeting. Kevin's name was on the agenda to be the newest member. Kevin was a good lawyer and a fun guy. Bonnie went with Kevin to meet with each member for a nice dinner which he paid for. Kevin wasn't a poor man. Back home before Tammy and Michael's birthday, Tammy went to Jimmy's office to talk with him. Tammy knocked on the door.

Jimmy said, "Come in, Eddie and Kenny are here."

Tammy walked into Jimmy's office and said, "Tammy's in love."

Eddie said, "We should go, Jimmy."

Tammy said, "No, I want Gary."

Kenny replied, "You can have my son, Gary, Tammy."

Jimmy said, "Wait, Kenny. Tammy, we should talk about this."

Kenny said, "Nothing to talk about. Take my son, move in with him. It is all good."

Tammy answered, "I want to remarry Gary on my birthday in the church."

Eddie said, "I like it. Great idea, let us just do it. I vote to let Tammy and Gary remarry."

Kenny replied, "I vote to have Gary and Tammy remarry on her birthday too. That's the vote."

Jimmy sat there and looked, then said, "Okay, if that is what you want, Tammy, you got it. Calvin, Kelly, and Edward we need a wedding for Tammy and Gary on Tammy's birthday, whatever she wants. I will pay for it, get the bills for me."

As they all left Jimmy's office, they saw Gary was waiting to see Jimmy. Jimmy looked like he was thinking, oh shit, this again.

Kenny said, "Be nice, this is my son."

Jimmy said, "Please come in."

Gary said, "Could I marry Tammy? I know you were tricked by her grandma the first time."

Jimmy replied, "Yes, I know you love my daughter Tammy very much and she loves you, yes."

The wedding for Tammy and Gary was family only, which was now a big family. Okay, in other words, a full church. The cake was dark mint chocolate with chocolate frosting and dark chocolate roses. Black roses everywhere. Everyone was to wear black but the bride and groom. Tammy wore Marko's wedding dress she wore to marry Jimmy the first time. Michael, the only best man, and Kelly was the only bride's maid. Little Tim was the ring boy. Jimmy walked his daughter Tammy to her husband Gary and the priest married them in their new church. The dance started with singing of the oldies but goodies. They didn't go on a honeymoon but home to Gary's place. Virgil enjoyed dancing with George and Marci's granddaughter. Jimmy did talk with George. He was pleased that Venus was dead. Jimmy had put off Majestic Twelve as long as he could but they had to meet and Kevin's membership was at the top of the agenda. Kevin got ready to go to Majestic Twelve and be voted on. He didn't sleep the night before. What would Kevin do if he lost the vote? Who could take his place for Jimmy? Kevin called Micky to tell him if he loses the vote Micky must step in for Jimmy. Micky agreed to do it. A computer guy would work. Micky went with and waited in the café. Sam and T-Jay came with Micky. Jimmy called the meeting to order and first on the agenda was voting on the membership of Kevin Carlson. Who Jimmy did point out was Calvin's dad. Calvin nominated his dad, Kevin Carlson. Edward seconded it. They all opened their folders and voted yes to Kevin Carlson being the newest member. Maybe telling the truth does help. Or was it all the time Kevin put into getting to know the other members?

Kenny said to Kevin, "It is okay, I was scared as all hell but Jimmy helped me. He will help you."

Eddie said, "I still have nightmares about aliens coming to kill us. I use sleeping pills from Gail."

Edward said, "It is okay, step-dad just vote as Calvin or they do. I don't understand much of it and I don't want to."

Calvin said, "Dad, we got this. Thanks for helping. We are all in this together. Jimmy got his vote now and we wait for my Kelly to be the woman of the group, got it."

As the meeting ended, all the members were nice to Kevin but he wasn't talking. Kevin was afraid now and thought aliens are out to kill him. Kevin nodded okay. Calvin let them know it is okay.

Micky said to the others, "Kevin's not talking? It must be bad. I am so glad they voted for Kevin."

T-Jay said, "I would never want to be in that group. If it shuts up Kevin, that is good."

Sam replied, "Let us get out of here and never come to these meetings ever again."

Back at home, Virgil was having a guest and Sarah said to James, "Virgil asked me to help him get furniture for his home. I think Virgil has a girlfriend. I saw him dancing with a blond."

James replied, "Is the girl over twenty-one years old?"

Sarah said, "I don't know. Virgil is very sensitive about it. He looked down when he asked me to help him with the furniture and I can do it over a phone."

James answered, "Okay, but only by phone. I guess that would be good for you to do this."

Then James went to Virgil and said, "Sarah can help you with furniture but only by phone."

Virgil replied, "Sarah is my friend. I can help with the babies. I have my shields on for baby boys to go all over. Remember when we change little Ed's diapers to keep our mouths closed."

James answered, "Yes, I remember, with three boys it will be an issue, so face shields needed."

Virgil replied, "Okay, but I am still not touching the babies, just diaper changing."

James said, "I am sure you wouldn't drop our babies. But do you have a new girlfriend coming here to see you? This is none of my business."

Virgil stood there all red in his face and said, "Yes, I do. Is that bad? We can't go out on dates, so I want her to come here to my home. Is that wrong?"

James asked, "Where did you meet her? How old is she? And no, it isn't bad or wrong."

Virgil replied, "I met her at Gary and Tammy's wedding. I don't know how old she is. I know I can't date anyone under twenty-one, agency rules. I would like to have a baby one day."

James didn't know what to say but, "I understand. Do you know her name or where she lives?"

Virgil answered, "Lisa is a very good kisser and hugs me. She lets me touch her anywhere. But tell no one because they will laugh at me. I am not unlovable, am I?"

James sat by Virgil and said, "Virgil, you are a very nice guy and lovable. We will help you."

Virgil smiled and said, "I don't want to date anyone else anymore, okay. I want her."

James replied, "This I understand, come with me and let us eat something."

Now James had to find out who this Lisa was and how old she was. Who will James ask? He went to Calvin, Kelly, and Edward for they planned the wedding. Sarah was helping Virgil with furniture for his home. Virgil wanted furniture a woman would like, nice things for his new girlfriend.

James asked, "Are you busy, Calvin and Kelly? I need to find a person for a friend. Her name is Lisa, how old is she? She was at the wedding of Gary and Tammy. She danced with Virgil."

Calvin said, "Okay, let me get the names of all the people there."

Calvin was really reading Virgil's mind to see who the girl was. Calvin replied, "I think it is Jimmy's old friend George's granddaughter. They have never been here before. I don't know her age."

James asked Sarah on their way home, "Do you think this girl is coming here to see Virgil?"

Sarah replied, "Yes, I do and I think they are sleeping together."

James asked, "How in hell is she doing that? Security is very close around here. Sam is tight."

Sarah replied, "I think she wants Virgil bad and he is a cutie."

In the morning James went to work but stopped by Virgil and he asked, "Up early this morning?"

Virgil was red in his face and answered, "Yes, I slept good last night."

James asked, "Are you hungry?"

Virgil replied, "Yes, very."

They went to get something to eat but they didn't talk much. Virgil was busy eating. James looked worried. That night all the Eds, Kelly with Calvin met at James and Sarah's place for supper. Virgil was with C-Jay doing guy stuff. Kevin was invited too but no one else.

Kelly asked, "What do we know about this girl Virgil is dating?"

Leo asked, "What girl? Virgil has so many."

Victor replied, "No, he has stopped that since Gary and Tammy's wedding; it is one girl now."

Edward added, "She is a little blond with big eyes. She was all over Virgil at that dance."

James replied, "What are we going to do? I think they are sleeping together at his place."

Sarah said, "We know Lisa is George's granddaughter. I have a call into him, but I don't know her age. She is sneaking out to be with Virgil. George doesn't know. Sam isn't getting alarms. We meet next Friday at church with George. Someone let Sam know, George is coming."

Halloween came and Victor with his wife helped with the candy for the children at the place called Marci. Micky and Betsy brought them to help Cindy. C-Jay called Cindy and asked if she could bring Virgil with Lisa to help. Cindy went to get those three. They all went home after having fun with the children.

Jimmy called Kevin at eight in the morning then Micky that he had Tim. Kevin and Micky rushed to the hospital. Tim was talking a mile a minute and so happy to be back.

Jimmy asked, "What the hell is going on now? Tell me? Why was George's granddaughter here last night with Virgil giving out candy to our children at our place called Marci?"

Kevin looked at Micky who looked at Tim who said, "I am waking up to action. What fun."

Jimmy said, "Just ask Calvin and Kelly what the hell is going on? I am going home to sleep."

Tim replied, "You got a lot to tell me, Micky and Kevin. Leave no sexy details out."

Sarah met with George on Friday and he said, "I didn't know Sarah was having a baby now?"

Sarah replied, "Yes, I have three baby boys in me and this is my husband James Edson."

George smiled and asked, "Where is Lisa, my granddaughter? Is she still with Jimmy, your dad?"

James asked, "How old is Lisa your granddaughter?"

George answered, "Twenty-one-years old last summer, why?"

James, with all the other Eds, were on their knees thanking God in that church. George looked confused as Jimmy walked in. George smiled but was still looking for his granddaughter, Lisa.

George asked, "Where is Lisa, Jimmy? I hope she hasn't been too much trouble."

Jimmy replied, "Lisa hasn't been staying with me. Sorry, I didn't know she was coming here."

Calvin said, "George, I think Lisa had another reason for coming here. Lisa forgot to see Jimmy."

George asked, "What the hell did he say? Jimmy what is it? Why did Sarah call me?"

Eddie and Kenny came in and Kenny said, "Jimmy, we have a problem with Majestic Twelve."

Eddie said, "What are we going to do? How could things be worse?"

Jimmy replied, "You would think nothing could get worse but guess again, Eddie. This is George and he is going to kill one of your grandsons today."

Kenny said, "I will tell Majestic Twelve we will have that meeting. Good luck, Eddie."

Eddie asked, "Which one of my grandsons are you planning to kill?"

George answered, "The one that has my granddaughter Lisa."

Eddie looked to see which one wasn't praying in that church and replied, "That would be Virgil."

Sarah replied, "Your granddaughter Lisa has been coming here to see Virgil. He is very cute."

George asked, "Where has Lisa been sleeping at night if not at Jimmy's home?"

Sarah called her husband James, "James, George has a question for you."

James came over and replied, "We aren't positive but that is why we called you. We think Lisa is sleeping at Virgil's home with him. We called you as soon as we found out about it."

Eddie said, "George, if you don't kill Virgil, I will. I should have done that a long time ago."

George replied, "No, I am her grandfather. I will kill Virgil for sleeping with Lisa not married."

Jimmy said, "James, is there anything you want to say for Virgil before they kill him?"

James replied, "Well, Virgil really wants to be a father. He wants to have a baby."

Eddie said, "Is Virgil crazy? He can't even take care of himself now, a baby and a wife?"

Sarah added, "Virgil had me get furniture for his home that a woman would like. I think your granddaughter comes there to sleep with Virgil at night. Virgil is very hungry in the morning."

Jimmy said, "Maybe, guys, we should wait a month or two before you kill Virgil."

George asked, "Jimmy, did my granddaughter Lisa ever talk with you or even see you here?"

Jimmy replied, "I saw her at Gary and Tammy's wedding, dancing with Virgil and doing candy."

George asked, "Can someone take me to see my granddaughter?"

Calvin said, "We will go get Lisa and Virgil for you now."

Eddie replied, "Calvin, you better bring them back. I am keeping Kelly with us until you do."

Calvin agreed and all the Eds went to get Lisa and Virgil as Kenny came back from talking with Majestic Twelve members on the meeting issue.

Kenny asked, "So what is happening now?"

Jimmy replied, "They are holding Kelly until Calvin and the Eds bring back Lisa with Virgil. Sarah went with but I think she is going to rest. I believe they are coming or making a run for it."

Kenny asked, "So they aren't killing Virgil?"

Jimmy replied, "They aren't sure if Lisa is pregnant or not. Virgil wants to be a father."

Kenny was laughing and said, "Oh hell, that will work. Eddie, things got worse."

George was looking sick and asked, "How bad is this guy?"

Eddie replied, "I have to tell you he isn't my best grandson. He does have a lot of energy."

George asked, "What does he do for a living? Does he have a job?"

Eddie replied, "Yes, he has a job as a secret agent or spy for the British. He makes okay money."

George sat down and said to himself, "At least he has a job and a home to live in."

Calvin walked in with Lisa and Virgil. Lisa looked at her grandfather and hid behind Virgil who said, "I guess you want to kill me. But I love Lisa and she loves me."

George said, "So I guess asking if you have been good isn't the question to ask?"

Virgil replied, "No, we haven't been good. We have been very bad. I am in church, I can't lie."

Victor came in and said, "Virgil and Lisa, I got the car out back, run. Leo is waiting at the airport."

Edward said, "Calvin are you ready to distract them?"

Calvin said, "Kelly bit Eddie in the hand and ran to the car."

Kenny said, "Kelly don't bite Eddie. George don't fight with those kids or they will run for it."

Virgil said, "Can we talk about this? We have been bad Eds. We promise never to do it again."

George said, "Well, if you promise never to do it again."

Jimmy said, "No one said anything. George, if you don't kill Virgil, I will work on Marci right after Gerald. I need Gerald to help Marci for he is the doctor I need."

George replied, "I will do that, but Virgil promises."

Jimmy answered, "I will put that in writing so there is no misunderstanding. No killing Virgil."

Well readers, George doesn't know about how good Virgil's promises are. George is staying there to be with Marci at that hospital. I think there will be black coal in one of those Eds' stockings this Christmas again but we all know Virgil promised to be good. But we heard that before so readers don't bet money on it. Majestic Twelve is meeting and Jimmy takes Tim.

Tim said, "I am Tim Elgin, a doctor, but I deliver babies and don't think any of you men are going to have a baby anytime soon. I have been in a coma but awake now. I am here to help if you want me. Your leader and I have the same last name, not related but know each other."

Kevin nominated Tim Elgin as the newest member, Edward seconded it. They all opened their folders and voted. Tim won all the votes. I guess his bull shit does still work. Kenny and Eddie were laughing but said nothing. Jimmy was very pleased he now had seven out of the twelve members. No one asked about a woman in the group. Maybe no one wanted the job.

Tim said, "Majestic Twelve is as scary as I thought it would be. I'll be back for Thanksgiving."

Kevin replied, "I have problems with Majestic Twelve too and I don't know if I can take it."

Micky answered, "I am not worried, Jimmy, Calvin and those guys are on it. I trust they are smart."

Kevin went to George as Micky stayed with Tim and said, "George, give Jimmy a little more time please. He is so tired. He needs Gerald the doctor to help him. Go home for now."

George replied, "Okay, but I am taking my granddaughter, Lisa, with me. I don't trust that Virgil."

Kevin replied, "Good, we have our hands full with Majestic Twelve it scares the hell out of me."

George answered, "If you understood all of it, then it would do more than scare the hell out of you, it would kill you. Stay close to Jimmy, always in Majestic Twelve."

Then George got ready to go and look for his granddaughter. That didn't make Kevin feel any better about Majestic Twelve. But that wasn't the worst of his problems. Kevin saw Gary and Tammy walking hand in hand, so in love. Calvin was in the church with Kelly praying on her birthday. Then they went into the garden as Calvin asked Kelly to marry him. Calvin was now down on one knee to Kelly. I think Kelly knew this was coming. Who told her, Kenny or the Eds?

Calvin asked, "Will you marry me, Kelly? I am so in love with you."

Kelly replied, "Yes, I am in love with you too, Calvin."

Calvin gave Kelly that very costly ring and they prayed together at the church. Calvin had the woman he loved to pray with. They went to Kenny's home for a birthday party for Kelly as she showed everyone her ring from Calvin. Kevin came to Kelly's birthday party for some cake. Kevin saw the ring and didn't want cake, now he was crying. George took his granddaughter home kicking and screaming all the way. Virgil tried to stop him but they pulled Virgil off of George. The Eds got there late and told Virgil they would get Lisa back for him somehow. They went to Sarah to find out where George lived but she wasn't feeling good at all so they were going to wait until Sarah was feeling better to find George and Lisa. Virgil was crying now for his Lisa. The Eds were all sad. But then Lisa showed up and Virgil was all happy again.

The next day Eddie came into Jimmy's office and asked, "Should we tell George we have his granddaughter, Lisa?"

Jimmy replied, "I know Eddie, that you are an Eds but please knock first then come in my office. I will talk with George about his granddaughter, Lisa, coming here to see Virgil."

Eddie said, "Jimmy, Virgil can't be a father. He is still a child himself and she is no different."

They all left and Jimmy left word for George to meet him at their church because he had found George's granddaughter Lisa again. George didn't need to guess where.

Jimmy said, "How is it going George?"

George replied, "Like hell. I need Marci, or to kill my granddaughter, Lisa. Can I kill Virgil?"

Jimmy answered, "No, Sarah's three baby boys are almost here and that would upset her. Tim is being a pain in ass. Then let us get Lisa on the pill. I can't stop them and Lisa has skills."

George replied, "You can't stop her at all? You have more power and are the leader."

Jimmy answered, "I can't do it. If I could, I would have stopped Sarah or Tammy."

George asked, "Lisa is coming to Virgil at night in his bed?"

Jimmy replied, "That would be my guess. Virgil wants Lisa so much he is not thinking straight."

George said, "Jimmy, you make the deal with Lisa."

Jimmy answered, "I will through our minds but I will have her see Michael, the doctor."

Jimmy did and Lisa agreed through their minds and told Virgil she was going to see Michael the doctor for a check-up. Virgil was all happy, hoping for a baby.

Sarah was crying "The babies are coming, the babies are coming, go get Michael and dad."

James Edson went into action with calling all the Eds. One went for Michael the other went for Jimmy and still one went for Gail. But they needed Tim too, so one went for Kevin. James got his wife Sarah to the car to go to Michael at their hospital. Tim, the master, was doing his job of delivering those three baby boys. James was in the delivery room but he faints before the first baby boy comes out. I guess these secret agent guys can do anything but see a baby come out. It was hours and James was very worried about Sarah and the babies.

Edward said, "Why don't they tell us something by now?"

Tammy and Gary had come and she said, "I think two boys are out and one is coming now. They are all good. Three baby boys are out now and Sarah is good."

Virgil asked, "How does Tammy know that?"

Lisa replied, "She is Michael's twin, you know, how you and Victor are."

Well, for some reason that made sense to Virgil and everyone else, not that Tammy could read minds. No one guessed that one. But now who was telling the father his sons had skills?'

Tim came out and said, "Three healthy baby boys and a healthy mother, Sarah. All Is good."

All the Eds were smiling but James wanted to see Sarah. Tim took James aside then winked at the others, like give us a minute alone, so they all went for something to eat.

Tim said, "Sit down, James. Give Michael and Jimmy some time to clean up your family. Sarah and babies are good. Sarah is Jimmy's daughter. Jimmy is different."

James looked at Tim and asked, "What are we talking about?"

Tim replied, "You are a smart guy and I think you know about the gold from Sarah."

James answered, "So Sarah likes to put gold in her hair when we make love, so what?"

Tim said, "If you don't want the babies, Jimmy will raise them, but tell no one for safety. You and I both know that the gold comes from her head. You must have seen it many times to make three baby boys with skills. Now, skills are the gold in their head that help them read minds or disappear to reappear someplace else. You need to know this because the babies could be a handful at first. We will teach them how to use their skills."

James looked up at God and replied without thinking, "I want my family. I want Sarah and the babies. I don't care."

Tim asked, "Are you ready to go in and see your wife and babies? You can't tell your cousins or even your brother or grandpa. I am not sure why, but Jimmy will decide what is best with this."

James smiled, agreed, then entered the room to see Sarah with the babies as she held one of the boys, Michael had the other, and Jimmy held the third one.

They all looked at James but he kissed Sarah and lay beside her on the bed. They let everyone come to see the babies.

Sarah said, "Each Eds with his wife can walk with a baby boy to the nursery and that is the baby they can be the baptism sponsor for if they want. Okay, James?"

James agreed and they all walked with the nurse to the baby nursery but Virgil crawled into bed with Sarah and James. He was going to be taking care of them for he was sure he would drop a baby. Calvin was sure they weren't ready for a baby but Kelly was all smiles at the babies. Mickey was afraid of the babies again. C-Jay was following the babies to the nurse's station, watching every move.

Michael said to Lisa, "Ready for that?"

Lisa replied, "Nope."

Michael said, "Want to go on the pill after I have Marie check you?"

Lisa answered, "I love Virgil but we aren't ready for a baby. Yes, I want go on the pill."

Lisa went to pray at the church with Kelly and Calvin, then Virgil came to pray too. Were they all praying for the same thing? My guess is not, readers, but that is okay. That is God's job. The next day was Thanksgiving. Jimmy was having food on the church tables after church from noon to six pm and anyone could come anytime. George was going to do security and Virgil wanted to help. Kevin had told him to try to be nice to Lisa's grandpa. Virgil was good at his job so that did go well. Tim stayed the whole day eating with everyone. It was Tim's day and he enjoyed it completely. Lisa and Virgil were dancing on the tables. The party had started and it was wild. Christmas was right around the corner and shopping was a big deal but then the Eds didn't buy Christmas gifts because they always got black coal in their stocking. James Edson told the group they had to learn how to buy Christmas gifts for his baby boys because Sarah was still very weak. All the Eds met at Sarah and James Edson's home. Tim knocked on the door.

James said, "Calvin, come in."

Tim replied, "It is me, Tim Elgin, the one that delivered your baby boys, Sarah's Godfather."

Sarah said, "Come in great uncle Tim. No one here knocks but Calvin, my dad or Mickael."

James said, "We need Christmas gifts for the baby boys."

Virgil replied, "I think a gun may be nice. I can teach them how to shoot it."

Victor said, "I think a set of knives would be better. I can teach them how to throw them."

Leo said, "No, guys, they are too little. They need stuffed toys or something to bite on."

Edward said, "My daughter is getting dolls for Christmas but she bites on everything and me."

Calvin looked at Kelly and she said, "Guys, baby toys that make noise."

Calvin said, "But the babies make their own noise when they cry."

Sarah was trying not to laugh as the Eds worked on this. Jimmy, Kenny, Eddie with Kevin came.

Jimmy asked, "When are you having the boys' baptism and what are their names?"

Eddie said, "You have to name your children, James."

Kenny added, "I do like the color thing. Yellow, green, and blue for the boys."

Jimmy, Eddie, and Kenny left. James was now walking around in a circle. Virgil was jumping up and down by the window. Leo had his hands on his head. Victor was looking at the ceiling. Edward closed his eyes. Calvin looked at Kelly and she was smiling. Kevin and Tim ordered food to eat.

Sarah asked, "James, do you have any ideas?"

James replied, "Okay, I have been thinking about it for names, Roy, Ron, and Rob?"

The food came and they all ate as Sarah said, "I love those names but who is who?"

James replied, "The first-born boy was in a yellow blanket, so start of the alphabet so it would be Rob. The second-born boy was in a green blanket, next in the alphabet so it would be Ron. The last-born boy was in the blue blanket, the end of the alphabet so it would be Roy."

They were eating as Sarah called Jimmy to tell him the names as she got off the phone looking sad. James asked, "Sarah, doesn't Jimmy like those names?"

Sarah replied, "Yes, he likes the names for the boys but asked what are their middle names?"

James said, "Sarah, could you please pick those?"

Sarah replied, "Yes, I have it. Rob Calvin Edson, Ron Gary Edison, and Roy Michael Edison."

Tim said, "I hate to be a kill joy but if you call Jimmy, he will ask what for confirmation names?"

Kevin said, "I got this one. We say it is Eddie, Jimmy, and Kenny in alphabet order for the boys."

James asked, "Christmas gifts, I go to the baby store and buy whatever I like for newborns."

They are started to go home as the first baby boy started to cry for milk. Then the second one and they woke up the third baby so they were all crying with a diaper change needed. Virgil went right to work for he was the best diaper changer and the fastest with his face shield. Victor was working on the bottles and he was ready with the milk at the right temperature. Calvin cleaned up the mess getting Sarah with James to bed for it had been a long day. Now readers, don't you wish your family was like this even if they weren't perfect, but they did try.

Sarah said to James, "You know we have to do the next feeding ourselves."

James replied, "Yes, but we can sleep for a few hours before they want to eat again."

Virgil came back to sleep on the couch. What if they didn't hear the babies cry? Christmas was coming and Victor was cutting down Christmas trees this year and sang a song while doing his work.

Calvin said, "Victor is enjoying cutting down those trees a little too much. He attacks them like they are people to kill. Then Victor cuts them up with so much energy like cutting off a head."

Mickey said, "I think it is the singing while Victor works that has Calvin a little upset."

C-Jay said, "Maybe if we could get Victor to sing a different song than I am going to kill you and cut you up for Christmas. I have never heard that song before."

Leo asked, "Who wants to help with buying the food for the cooks for Christmas?"

Calvin replied, "I want to go with Leo to get the food. I have money. Please take me with you."

Virgil was standing outside, listening to the women tell him where all the Christmas decorations on the homes should go. The women looked happy as they all went inside and Virgil had his paper of notes. Virgil studied his notes then walked over to the trash can to throw his notes away. Edward, Mickey, and C-Jay went over to Virgil to see what they were to do.

Virgil said, "You put this stuff on those homes. Got it."

The guys went right to work with lights and got stuff out. The women came out and cried it is so pretty. The guys stood out of their homes as Victor came with their nice cut Christmas trees.

Micky said, "Well, maybe the Eds aren't so bad. We didn't have to get any trees because Victor loves doing the Christmas trees and he even carries them into the homes for us."

T-Jay said, "Look how nice they decorated the homes the way the women wanted them to. I see Virgil taking notes and everything. What a nice job Virgil did."

Sam replied, "I've never seen Virgil do any outside decorations, just Edward, Mickey, and C-Jay. What is that song Victor is singing about Christmas and cutting?"

Kelly called out, "Guys, if you are done with your work, I need you to taste the cookies I made with the ladies. Does anyone have time to do this for me?"

All the guys came running to help eat the cookies. Some jobs need more men than others at Christmas time. Now readers, we know what the ladies were doing, baking lots of cookies. Tim was the first one to eat cookies and loved this new family, these guys were the greatest.

Things were going great until Cindy cried, "It hurts."

Virgil said, "You ate too many cookies. Cindy stop eating before your stomach hurts, no more."

Michael came over and said, "No, I think the baby is coming out."

C-Jay said, "Now? Is it Cindy's birthday today?"

Victor replied, "So we get cake too."

Tim said, "I think the baby wants to come out so to the hospital we go, okay C-Jay."

James called to C-Jay, "Don't go in there with them to that delivery room. Don't do it, man."

C-Jay did try but he hit the floor before anything happened as Cindy was screaming. Virgil snuck in and pulled C-Jay out. The group was okay waiting, they had cake to eat. They named the baby girl Aim Marie Sally Peterson. Betsy and Mickey were baptism sponsors. Then Christmas and the party started, it didn't end, going into Christmas day with Virgil and Lisa dancing on the tables. Jimmy went to sleep with Sylvia and Kevin was in charge but he liked to party too.

The week between Christmas and New Year was a sleeping week. They were all getting along but they still had cookies. The New Year's Eve came along with food and party dancing. They went home to shower and change clothes before church, then more food with dancing. Betsy was complaining about still being pregnant and questioned who was praying that this baby stays in her? They all looked at Mickey. Then everyone went back to work and it was Betsy and Mickey's wedding anniversary. They planned a nice night at home to eat a meal and watch a movie. The minute they sat down to a quiet romantic night, Betsy's stomach hurt and the baby came. Now we all know who Mickey should have called, the doctor, Tim. But he called Victor, who come right away with Virgil. Then the others came as they were standing there thinking. Kelly called doctors, Tim and Michael. But it was too late and the baby was coming out. Jimmy walked in to help as the baby came before Tim and Michael got there. All was good for mother and baby.

Kevin said, "Jimmy, put the baby back in Betsy. I am not ready to be a grandfather. Do it now."

Tim was laughing so hard as he said, "Michael, take Kevin home and give him a shot to calm him."

Jimmy had Gerald's surgery; it did go well with the help of Gerald the Second and Third. Jay had her twenty-second birthday with Gerald the Third asking her to marry him and she said yes.

Eddie came in and said, "Jimmy, I think we should kill Virgil or Victor or both. They aren't being good. They didn't take down the home's Christmas decorations and it is almost Easter."

Kevin said, "I am on it. We will have those Christmas decorations down by the end of the day."

To work they went and if they weren't good, no Easter bunny. Now who in the hell was the Easter bunny? The Eds knew very little about this. They knew the church stuff but not about a rabbit.

Virgil asked, "Do we get food? I liked Valentine's day with a lot of kissing, flowers and candy."

Kevin said, "You take everything down very nicely and the Easter bunny will bring you candy."

The Eds went right to work, then all the homes had their Christmas decorations down in boxes so nicely and put away for next year. They waited for the Easter bunny. No rabbit. They got their guns out to shoot that bad rabbit who forgot their Easter candy.

Calvin said, "Dad, I think you forgot to tell the Eds that it happens on Easter, not before."

Kevin went to talk with the Eds. Hadn't their parents ever done anything like this with them? But then what parents? They were at boarding schools all the time. Kevin explained the Easter bunny to them. The Eds put away their guns but if that rabbit didn't show up, he was toast.

Sarah took Kevin aside and said, "What are we going to do? They really don't know and will be embarrassed if they think it is a joke. I don't want James to feel bad or sad about it."

Kevin left for Jimmy's office but did knock on the door and Jimmy waved him in.

Kevin said, "Jimmy, we have a problem which some people may find funny but I don't. Our new friends have let their guard down and joined us with good will but they are different. Easter is only a church thing for them and I told them about the Easter bunny. They waited but didn't get Easter candy, so they got their guns out to shoot the damn rabbit that forgot them."

Jimmy replied, "Kenny and Eddie don't do those things. Tim is a Jew. They don't have Easter."

Kevin asked, "Can I do Easter baskets and an egg hunt with candy after church? Calvin can help me with Sarah. I will have a meeting at Sarah's place that James is going back out with his cousins and Edward will be teaching for Kenny. Sarah doesn't like the female students around her good-looking, handsome husband. Calvin will do the Easter bags."

Kenny came in after that asking, "What the hell is going on? Why is James leaving, he is good?"

Jimmy answered, "I will give it to you straight. Sarah has seen too many pretty women that James will have to train to be spies. James wants to be back out with his cousins. So, Sarah is being very understanding about James going back out there. Got it?"

Kenny asked, "Is anyone going to help me?"

Jimmy replied, "They have decided Edward will teach for you. Maybe you should stay there."

Easter come and Calvin put candy in bags inside their homes the night before as Kevin had the meeting about James going out with his cousins. When Virgil got home, he ate his candy.

At church on Easter, Kelly asked, "Who is this egg hunt for, the little kids or our big kids?"

Jimmy replied, "The big kids mostly. Tim, put down those candy eggs, you are a Jew."

Tim answered, "Just because I am a Jew doesn't mean I don't like candy."

Eddie asked, "Do we have enough candy?"

Kenny replied, "I hid a lot of candy but this is so silly to do. Tell me again why people do this?"

Jimmy answered, "Because it is fun."

Eddie asked, "Are we having fun now?"

Kenny said, "Well, it looks like they are having fun, our big and small kids."

James left with his cousins after Easter. Betsy and Mickey named their baby boy Mitch Mickey Micky Johnson with Cindy and C-Jay baptism sponsors.

CHAPTER TWELVE

GERALD, WHERE IS MARCI?

The work on Gerald was done and he was coming home but where was home? His daughters were waiting and that was Peaches or Gail with Crème or Gloria. They both wanted their father to live by them. Gloria said that Gerald should live in his old home with her and her son who did the surgery. Gail was all upset and wanted Gerald close to her and Kenny for her father's protection. We all know where the problem ended up, in Jimmy's office. Jimmy was in his office waiting for it.

Kenny came into Jimmy's office and said, "Jimmy, help Gail, she wants Gerald next to us."

Jimmy replied, "Okay, no knocking ever and I will put a swinging door in for everyone to use. I have already talked to Gloria or Crème on the phone three times and now I am off the damn phone. What do you think I can do about this? It is the daughters and Gerald's issue."

Kenny replied, "Gerald is mixed up, he will do whatever you say. If I knocked, would it help?"

Jimmy said, "I will talk to Gerald's daughters. I need Gerald as close to me as possible for now. They can work out where he lives later. That is all I am saying on this subject, now go away."

Gerald was home and Jimmy had him stay with him at his home. Gerald could go and live next door by Michael who lived by Gary with Tammy, next to Gail with Kenny. Well readers, it is funny they don't fight about who sits on what chair by who. Now, these are smart people, doctors, lawyers, education people. Now we know why the world is a mess. We have left the running of the world to them and readers, we need to take it back!

Calvin knocked and came to Jimmy saying, "Boss, Jimmy I need to tell you something now."

Jimmy replied, "I had a hell of a day. Can it wait for morning? I am in bed with my Sylvia."

Calvin answered, "Is Gerald to be in his bed alone?"

Jimmy replied, "Yes, who else would be in bed with Gerald, my old dear friend?"

Calvin said, "I don't know who she is but they aren't sleeping. I don't think Kelly should see this and Edward is guarding the door as I tell you about it. We don't have to go in there to stop them, do we? Because if we do then I think that should be Edward's job, not mine."

Jimmy got out of bed and said, "You didn't see right."

Calvin said, "Yes, we do know what a woman without clothes on looks like. I called Edward."

Jimmy replied, "I live in a crazy house. Let me see."

Jimmy walked over to Gerald's bedroom and looked then looked again. There was a woman in Gerald's bed and they weren't sleeping in that bed. Jimmy sat down on the floor and said nothing.

Calvin asked, "Should we call Eddie and Kenny for a meeting on this to vote on something?"

Edward said, "Jimmy, should we call Michael the doctor? You don't look good on the floor."

Kevin asked, "What is wrong, Jimmy?"

Calvin and Edward pointed to Gerald's bedroom, Kevin looked in and looked again. Eddie and Kenny came running in. They looked at Jimmy on the floor. Kevin pointed to the Gerald's bedroom door. They looked in and looked again. Kelly came to look in but Calvin took her away to the kitchen for food. That was what they needed, something to eat as they thought this over and went to Jimmy's office.

Jimmy said, "Thanks Calvin, Edward, and Kelly, we can take it from here. Go back to sleep."

Kenny asked, "Where did the woman come from?"

Eddie said, "I know, Jimmy, you wanted Gerald to have a good first night home but this is great."

Jimmy replied, "I don't know who she is or how she got here. Did Gerald call a service?"

Kenny said, "I don't think we should tell my wife Gail, this is about her father, Gerald."

Kevin said, "If I was in that hospital as long as Gerald, that would the first thing I would do."

Eddie said, "What is the big deal, ask Gerald in the morning. We aren't going to stop them."

Kenny replied, "I am not asking my father-in-law about his sex life. We aren't stopping them."

Kevin said, "That is two votes on no to stopping them, so Jimmy, are you talking to Gerald then?"

They all left and went to their homes to bed. Edward and Calvin planned to catch the woman on her way out but they must have missed her because in the morning Gerald came out alone.

Jimmy asked, "Hungry, Gerald? We have a lot of food here. Did you sleep good?"

Gerald replied, "The best night's sleep ever. I had a sexy dream about a beautiful woman."

Jimmy asked, "Did you have a guest over last night?"

Gerald replied, "Jimmy, I don't know anyone but you guys. Who would I have over?"

Jimmy couldn't read Gerald's mind because of the surgery he had, it may hurt him, so what to do? As Gerald left with Kenny, Jimmy went in to check that bedroom. There was a woman in that bed with Gerald last night and they weren't sleeping. Gerald thought it was a dream so it was someone with skills. Jimmy found blond hair and other DNA to have checked out at the lab.

Kenny came in and knocked on the desk asking, "Who is she? A call girl? Where did he find her?"

Jimmy replied, "No, she is someone who helped me take care of the people at the hospital. She has cared for Gerald for years. I didn't know she was caring for Gerald that good."

Kenny asked, "This nurse has been having sex with my father-in-law against his wishes?"

Jimmy answered, "No, Gerald has enjoyed it and it wasn't against his wishes."

Eddie came in and asked, "What do we know about the woman?"

Kenny replied, "Believe it or not, Jimmy runs a full-service hospital, all a guy's needs are met."

Kevin came in and said, "Were Tim's needs all met too at that hospital?"

Jimmy answered, "I never thought to ask to Tim. I didn't know this was happening."

Jimmy had Gerald stay at the doctor's building which they got furniture for that day. Jimmy said Gerald needed some private time. Which I think means time to meet this nurse of his. Virgil and James Edson came home from a mission. James went straight to Sarah and his boys but Virgil was looking around. Something is up. Then Leo and Victor came home with Virgil, telling them something is up so they went to Edward who told them about Gerald's woman.

Virgil said, "Gerald has a girlfriend. I guess this old guy is fun and we like him already."

Kevin replied, "Okay, but let us not say anything for now. I don't know this Gerald at all."

They all agreed but were smiling too much around Gerald who smiled back at the Eds with Kelly and Calvin. Kevin and Eddie were smiling a lot too but Kenny was concerned. Gerald was now staying at his own home and Jimmy had Calvin with Kelly watching for this nurse. Did she come to Gerald's home at night? Gail wanted to stay with her father, Gerald, but Kenny wouldn't have it. Virgil was watching for her too because Lisa was home with her grandpa.

Virgil cried, "Calvin and Kelly, I see someone else in Gerald's bed. She is taking off her clothes."

Kelly said, "I want to see too."

Calvin put his hands over Kelly's eyes and said, "Go Virgil, tell Jimmy."

Virgil was afraid of Jimmy and went to James and said, "I need your help. The old guy, tell Jimmy."

James was waking up and said, "What, Virgil? Why are you in my bedroom and in our bed?"

Virgil said, "Calvin told me to tell Jimmy about the old guy having sex again. You tell Jimmy?"

James said, "No."

Sarah was awake and said, "Go with Virgil and I will tell my dad. Go now and see what it is."

James got dressed and went with Virgil to Gerald's home to see Calvin there with Kelly's eye covered. James looked in the window and looked again then Jimmy came.

Jimmy said, "I got this, go home."

Virgil asked, "Are you going in there?"

Jimmy replied, "I have to talk with her and Gerald but I can wait for a bit."

Virgil said, "I'll wait with you, Jimmy. We will talk with them two about this behavior."

James asked, "Should I stay too?"

Jimmy replied, "Yes, but Virgil help Calvin get Kelly home safely. Then come back for us."

They left and James asked, "Needed to get Virgil out of here for a few minutes?"

Jimmy replied, "Yes, the nurse has skills and she is appearing in Gerald's bed but he doesn't know she is real. Gerald appears to be good with it but I have to talk with them both."

James answered, "What should I do?"

Jimmy said, "Be my lookout and stop anyone from coming in so I can talk with them. I also mean not listening. If anyone asked you want you are doing, tell them you are my lookout."

In the house, Jimmy knocked on the bedroom door and said, "I know you are in there with Gerald and we need to talk now. I am coming in and if you disappear then I will come after you."

Gerald said, "Jimmy, why are you in my sweet dream?"

Jimmy replied, "Because you aren't dreaming. She is real and you know it. We need to talk."

Gerald asked, "Are you taking her away from me? I want to keep her."

Jimmy answered, "You can keep her. We need to talk about it, that is all. What is your name?"

Gerald replied, "Her name is Amy. And she has skills like you, Jimmy. She cared for me."

Jimmy asked, "Amy, can you stay here with Gerald all day? He could still use your help in care."

Amy replied, "Yes, I love Gerald. If he wants me to stay."

Gerald answered, "Yes, but what about my wife Shella?"

Jimmy said, "Good news there, she is dead and I would never do anything to help her."

Gerald said, "Thank God. But how will I tell my daughters? I love Amy. She has been with me."

Jimmy replied, "I will help you tell your daughters and Kenny with Eddie. We got this."

Mother's Day had passed as all Mother's Day do for the new mothers but Father's Day was coming up. Gerald would be home for Father's Day and his two daughters wanted a party for Gerald on Father's Day. Gail with Gloria were in Jimmy's office waiting.

Jimmy said, "Ladies, I thought I locked my office door."

Gail replied, "Kenny taught me how to get into a locked office. We wanted to sit and wait."

Jimmy said, "There are chairs to sit and wait outside this door of my office."

Gloria replied, "We like these chairs better to sit inside your office to wait."

Okay readers, I told you there would be a chair sitting problem in the group sometime.

Jimmy asked, "What can I do for you ladies today?"

Gail said, "Could you have a party for my dad this Father's Day? We can help pay for the cost."

Jimmy replied, "We don't need any money because we ran into a lot of gold some time ago. Yes, I could have Calvin with Kelly and Edward do that. But first, I need you two ladies to do something for me. Your dad has a girlfriend, be nice to Amy with understanding for them."

Gail asked, "Where did they meet?

Gloria asked, "Are they having sex?"

Jimmy replied, "They met at the hospital, she is his nurse. Yes, they are having sex."

Gail asked, "Are they living together now?"

Jimmy answered, "I am not sure but they are sleeping together every night and having sex."

Gail and Gloria got up and walked out of Jimmy's office not asking anything more. Jimmy called Kenny to tell him Gail was coming home with her sister. Kenny said nothing, hanging up the phone.

Kenny ran into Jimmy's office saying, "You did what? We are doing what? What should I do?"

Eddie came in and asked, "Sure a lot of questions there, what is up?"

Kevin came in with Tim to see what was happening. Kenny looked sick. Eddie was smiling too much.

Jimmy replied, "I told Gerald's two daughters about Gerald's girlfriend, Amy. We are having a Father's Day party at the church this year. Any more questions?"

Tim asked, "Gerald has a girlfriend named Amy?"

Eddie said, "When you were in Jimmy's hospital you didn't get sex with a female nurse?"

Tim replied, "No, I didn't. Jimmy, which box on that form didn't I check for that treatment?"

Kevin said, "With Jimmy's forms, always read the small print. No lies but not the whole truth."

Jimmy answered, "Shut up all of you and get out of my office. I am sitting right here as you talk about me. At least talk about me behind my back."

Eddie replied, "Jimmy, we aren't that kind of people. You are our oldest and dearest friend."

Jimmy said, "Bull shit, get out. Try to learn to talk about me alone. Kenny, are you okay?"

Kenny answered, "I am not sure. But I am pleased Gerald's stay for so long was enjoyable."

Calvin with Kelly and Edward planned the Father's Day party. They did have new fathers in the group and Gerald was home with two daughters still alive. The day started with church and then the food as a group. Sam, T-Jay, and Mickey wanted to do security for Amy was new. After church and prayer before eating they all talked. Gerald took Amy to meet his daughters Gail and Gloria. The Father's Day party had everyone having a good time except for Gerald's daughters. Lisa, Virgil's girlfriend appeared to know Amy. Jimmy needed his nap with Sylvia. The next day Kenny came to Jimmy's office and knocked on the desk after he walked in.

Jimmy said, "Will this day ever get the hell over? Nice knocking Kenny. What do you want?"

Kenny said, "I understand from Gerald that he is going to ask Amy to marry him. Her family?"

Eddie said, "I want wedding cake. I don't care about Amy's family as long as they share cake."

No more was said as Gerald got a ring then took Amy to his old home in the garden then got down on one knee. But Amy didn't understand this so she too got down on one knee.

Gerald said, "Will you marry me, Amy?"

Amy replied, "Yes, but why are we on one of our knees only?"

Virgil, Lisa, Calvin, and Kelly were listening and laughing so hard as Gerald tried to explain it. The next day, Gerald was telling everyone he was getting married to Amy, his girlfriend. Now, Eddie was happy, more cake to eat. Kevin liked a good party. Kenny was a little worried about her family. Jimmy called George to come and meet with him at the church again. George was there waiting.

Jimmy said, "George, Gerald is going to do the update on the medical information we need for Marci's surgery. Gerald is marring Amy. She has skills. Do you know Amy or did Marci?"

George replied, "Not much, I think they were sisters or cousins. They were very poor."

Jimmy said, "The sooner we have this wedding the faster Gerald will do his work."

George answered, "I think we are the only family she has. Marci and my children with Lisa."

Jimmy said, "I need all of you to come. We need them married on Labor Day weekend."

Gerald and Amy had their wedding on that Saturday but not at the church. It was in the gardens at Gerald's old home. No bride's maids or best men just them being married by the old priest without a hearing aid. Amy wore flowers in her hair with a white short cotton dress. Gerald wore a nice suit and they had Edward's help saying the marriage vows. There was food and dancing with a big white cake. The food was all vegetables and no meat, dairy or eggs which was a little different but still a lot of food to eat. They drank only water. But then that big white cake to eat was all Eddie cared about. Kenny was still looking for the meat. Kevin was trying to help Kenny. Betsy had talked about beef. No one said where's the beef or meat?

Kenny said, "Kevin and I can't find any meat at this wedding, not even fish."

Eddie replied with his mouth full of cake, "I've never seen Lisa eat meat at all. They are weird."

Amy threw the flowers and Lisa caught them. Virgil was all happy but Eddie looked sick. Is it too much cake or the thought of Virgil marrying this Lisa? Gerald and Amy left for a honeymoon.

Eddie said, "Maybe if we got Marci back, George would go away with his granddaughter Lisa."

Kevin said, "I don't know Virgil like you know your grandson, but I think he is in love with Lisa."

The work started on Marci and it was going to be more than one surgery. After the first one Marci was doing good but disappeared. Jimmy disappeared after her but where was Marci? George was all upset and waiting in the church, praying. Gerald came in but he didn't know what to do. All the people with skills were looking for Marci as Sarah left to help, Virgil came over.

Virgil said, "Lisa was sick again this morning, throwing up in the bathroom. She sleeps a lot so I told her to go see Michael the doctor. I have been feeding her and she is eating a lot of food. But Lisa likes to eat silly things like ice cream and pickles together in one dish."

James sat down and asked, "She is still taking that pill, right?"

Virgil replied, "Lisa forgets sometimes and now she is throwing up everything in the morning."

James asked, "Do you use any protection?"

Virgil answered, "No, Lisa is on the pill."

James said, "Let us go find Michael to see how Lisa is doing. Tammy is here with the boys."

Lisa was sitting in Michael's office crying with Marie trying to help her feel better. Sarah came and was mad at Lisa for not helping them look for Marci with the others. James and Vigil walked in and over to Lisa but she ran to the bathroom. James looked at Michael and he shook his head yes.

James said, "I think Lisa and Virgil are going to have a baby. Lisa forgot to take that pill."

Sarah replied, "Oh shit. Okay we can't take Lisa then. It would be too much for her."

They all went home thinking about this. Virgil crawled into bed with Lisa and held her. Calvin was told about Virgil and Lisa having a baby or was he reading minds again? We all know where Calvin went, to Jimmy' office with Kevin, Eddie, and Kenny in there. Calvin knocked on the door.

Jimmy replied, "Go away."

Calvin went away but Kenny went to get Calvin and said, "Come in and tell us all about it."

Eddie replied, "At least it can't be my grandsons anymore."

Jimmy looked up and said, "Want to bet on that one, Eddie?"

Just then Tammy ran in and said, "Dad, you are needed; they found Marci. Come right away."

Jimmy said, "Calvin, tell only Kelly but we will do this when I get back. No more talk."

They completed another surgery for Marci and she was better this time. Marci was very upset; she wanted her whip back from Calvin. So, Calvin tried to remember where the hell it was. Now the Eds all want to see Marci's whip. Virgil and Lisa were eating a lot of food but not talking about the baby they were having. Halloween came without an issue and Thanksgivings was great but no one was talking about the issue of Lisa's baby. They were all acting like nothing was wrong at all. Readers, I think Virgil really wants his baby.

Majestic Twelve met again but this time Jimmy brought Marci with them. Jimmy told the group Marci was to be his pick for the woman of group but they needed more women in Majestic Twelve than one. It was time to have as many women in the group as men. The group all voted for Marci for they felt a woman was needed to replace the member who died. Marci wasn't talking but a woman not talking is scarier for the men than these aliens they were watching for.

Eddie said, "This Marci always scares that hell out of me. She is like a witch on a broom."

Kenny said, "I think Marci is really out of it for now. Is she going to be okay?"

Jimmy said, "Calvin, find Marci's whip, I think that would help her. I am not sure but we will try."

One thing for sure we know readers, is that Virgil and the bad Eds aren't on the nice list again for Santa this Christmas. Maybe all the Eds are on the bad list again; they should have told George or their grandpa Eddie about Virgil with Lisa's baby and they didn't. Sometimes not doing something that you should have is as bad as doing something you shouldn't have done.

Victor is doing the Christmas trees again, C-Jay, Mickey, and Edward are decorating the homes with Virgil writing it all down how to decorate from the women. Again, Virgil threw the notes in the trash and they did whatever. The women were baking cookies. Everything was normal. Gifts were being brought and the new parents were having fun with this as everyone was. Marci wanted to see her granddaughter Lisa but it is clear she will notice Lisa is pregnant.

James went to talk with Virgil and said, "Do you want this baby?"

Virgil replied, "What difference does that make? I can't take care of a baby and wife."

James said, "I could help you. You did help Sarah and me. What do you want to do?"

Virgil said, "It doesn't matter. I am "bad Virgil" again. I am always on the bad list for Santa."

James said, "If you could have a say, what would you do? You could date someone else."

Virgil replied, "I don't want anyone else, just Lisa. I want this baby with Lisa. No one cares."

James said, "But I do and so does Sarah. We are all your family and we will help you but how?"

Virgil answered, "I want Lisa to marry me and have our baby. I am worried I will drop it or not feed the baby."

James said, "Virgil, that was a bird you forgot to feed and you were a little boy."

Virgil said, "I loved that bird. It was my pet. I forgot to feed it. My bird died because of me."

James said, "I think the bird maybe had other problems that killed it. But we have to shoot to kill people all the time and it is no big deal."

Virgil replied, "I don't like bad men but I like pets. I am like C-Jay and he is my friend. We like animals and not so much people. I get to go out to his grandparent's farm to feed the animals."

James said, "I was wondering why you two were good friends and now I know. C-Jay is very nice and he is good with children. He could help you too. We could get a ring for Lisa."

Virgil said, "I have a ring with a nice stone from great-great grandma Mrs. King. Could Gary make it nice like he did for you with Sarah's ring? Don't tell or they will take Lisa away."

Gary did the ring for them. Virgil and Lisa now planned to run away and get married. They had decided to keep their baby. Lisa didn't want to stay there for she was sure they would take her away from Virgil. Was Lisa reading minds or was she afraid? The Eds were all going to help them and the plan was set for Christmas as everyone would be busy with family, gifts, then church. The church started for them at midnight and all came that could. Then others went the next day; there was a meal after both but because the group was all mixed up no one knew who was going to what church time or meal. Christmas was very nice with the new babies' first Christmas all going well. Calvin with Kelly and Edward planned the parties as always but with no restrictions. They all came at different times to the two parties. Jimmy was noticing something but said nothing. What are the Eds up to, bad, bad Eds again. New Year's Eve and New Year was fun but no Virgil Edson. Gerald knocked on Jimmy's office door with the others and Jimmy waved then all in.

Eddie asked, "Does anyone know the mission Virgil, my grandson, was on this holiday?"

Kenny said, "He isn't out training any of my students with Edward. Edward is here."

Kevin said, "Could Virgil have got hurt or something on the job? We better find him."

Gerald said, "Maybe Virgil and Lisa went to meet Marci with George this holiday."

Tim said, "Jimmy, maybe you should check with them and see."

Jimmy replied, "No."

Eddie said, "I'll call my other grandsons in to see where Virgil is. I am sure they know."

Jimmy replied, "No, Virgil is fine. Let it go."

Kenny asked, "Jimmy, if you know where Virgil is, then tell us."

Gerald said, "I can have Amy talk with Marci and George about it."

Eddie said, "What did my grandsons do this time? Bad, bad Eds."

Kevin called, "Calvin, get into Jimmy' office. Calvin will tell us."

Calvin said, "I don't know anything about where Virgil is and no one is talking about it."

Eddie said, "I am going to my grandsons and get answered, Calvin and Kevin come with me."

Tim said, "You know where Virgil is, don't you, Jimmy?"

Kenny asked, "What in the world is Virgil doing anyway, in trouble again?"

Gerald said, "Lisa is pregnant and they ran away to get married."

Jimmy replied, "I have a good idea where Virgil and Lisa are. They are okay."

Jimmy was blocking Kevin from reading minds but Calvin was able to and he knew where they were. Virgil and Lisa were out at C-Jay's grandparents' farm, living in C-Jay's home he built for Cindy when they got married. On New Year's Eve Lisa and Virgil got married in the church C-Jay had built for Cindy when they got married. Edward, as a deacon could marry people for a couple marries each other in the church witnessed by a deacon. Lisa and Virgil were both over twenty-one years old so no problems there. The wedding was small and only the

Eds were there with C-Jay but Calvin was sure Kelly was there too. Why didn't she tell him? Eddie left all upset because the Eds told him nothing. Kevin stayed to try to find out, but he had no luck either. The Eds weren't talking.

Calvin asked, "Why didn't you tell me? I would have loved to see Virgil and Lisa get married."

Kelly replied, "Because, my love, you are a tattle tale. Edward knows that and he can't tell you everything like we can't tell him about our skills. We are still best friends. Jimmy trusts you."

Tim said, "Let it go. Jimmy will never tell and he does know where they are at. I think Jimmy is helping the Eds with this for Virgil and Lisa. Eddie and Barbie wouldn't be okay with Lisa. George or Marci will never be okay with Virgil so they have left."

Kevin asked, "What about the baby? Are you in on this too, to deliver that baby or Michael?"

Tim replied, "No, I think Jimmy will deliver the baby himself as he did Betsy's baby."

Sam was talking with Micky and T-Jay, he said, "I knew those Eds were trouble and no good."

Micky said, "Where the hell could they be? Jimmy hasn't told us to find them either."

T-Jay said, "Virgil is doing what he has to for the woman he loves with his baby. Let them go."

Readers, does T-Jay know where they are or he is more understanding of the situation? My guess is as good as yours at this point. The new year has started and all isn't good in their world. People are divided. The rules are becoming more important than the people they serve. Virgil and Lisa are happy at the farm. Virgil goes to work with his cousins and the agency doesn't give out information. Eddie is head of this agency but he doesn't over push his power.

Marci went to Jimmy's office, didn't knock and said, "Jimmy, I want my granddaughter back. Are you going to help me or not? I haven't gotten my whip back from Calvin."

Jimmy replied, "I see you flew in on your broom as all witches do without knocking first. It is good to have you back again. I missed these unpleasant talks. I am not going to help you. But I will get your whip back from Calvin if you help me with Linda at the hospital for Tim."

Marci got so mad she called Jimmy some very bad words and readers, I can't repeat them. But Kenny was writing them down and asking how to spell some of them. Kevin was trying to help Kenny with the spellings of all these bad words. Eddie was in shock. Was it the bad words or that Jimmy wouldn't help them find Lisa and Virgil?

Marci left mad as Jimmy was smiling then said, "I missed her, our talks are so unmeaningful."

Kenny said, "Jimmy, I missed some of those words Marci called you. Does anyone remember more than what I wrote down? Thanks, Kevin, for helping me with the spelling. You know a lot of bad words and how to spell them."

Jimmy replied, "Don't worry, Kenny, this will happen again and again. Many more times for you to get more bad words written down. Marci is back with us."

Eddie said, "I want the kids back too but her language isn't good. Can you get her to clean it up a bit? It made me feel dirty. What do you think, Kevin?"

Kevin replied, "Women have called me some of those words before. No big deal."

Calvin knocked on Jimmy's office door. Jimmy waved him in.

Calvin said, "I found Marci's whip. Do I give it to her?"

Jimmy replied, "No, not until she helps me with Linda. Hide that damn whip she wants so bad."

Time went on for the church and meals but it was different without Virgil. Everyone missed him so much but the Eds and Calvin with Kelly did work with Virgil on missions. C-Jay was Virgil's friend and was not missing him. But then C-Jay was out at his grandparents' farm all the time. Mickey was still best friends with Victor. The Majestic Twelve meetings were going good and Jimmy had most of the members. They didn't always agree themselves. But if Jimmy really wanted something, they voted his way. Marci wasn't afraid like the others were at the few first meetings, she fit right in. Marci was in Jimmy office a lot and they were fighting every time about something.

Kevin went to Eddie and said, "Virgil is going to be the father of Lisa's baby so why not welcome them back. They are married and they are staying that way. Virgil loves Lisa and she him."

Eddie replied, "I am afraid Marci will kill Virgil. Those people are weird. They don't eat meat."

Kevin answered, "I don't care what they eat as long as it isn't me. They all love animals."

Kevin went to James and Sarah's home to ask for help to get Marci to let Lisa stay with Virgil. They both agreed to help but Sarah would talk with George first and James went with her. But Jay was planning to marry Gerald the Third around her birthday. How did this make Calvin feel? Calvin wasn't saying anything but planning a wedding party for her and Gerald the Third. Ricky was helping and Jay would marry there and then again with her mother, Teresa Mary at Gerald the Third's home. Jimmy had asked Marci and George not to come. Jay was his granddaughter too. Betsy was cooking up a mess of food for the two weddings for Jay. One at their church with a meal and dancing then another at Gerald's the Third home with a meal and dancing. Jimmy and Sylvia would attend only the first one. Jay would wear one of Sylvia's old wedding dresses which they all could see Jimmy wasn't pleased about it but said nothing. Jay had no bride's maids, just Ricky her brother walking her down that church aisle to meet Gerald the Third. The old priest did a nice job. But there were two guests and it was Virgil with Lisa. Everyone was overjoyed and the party was on. Jay's wedding colors were pink and blue. Jay thanked Virgil and Lisa for coming back for her wedding.

Virgil said, "We couldn't miss our favorite cook's wedding, now could we? Never ever would we do that. We love you Jay and Gerald the Third or Fourth or Fifth, whatever."

Lisa said, "If this Gerald the Third isn't good to you, let us know and we will kill him."

There was dancing on the tables again. Lisa was very big with the baby and Jimmy was worried she may fall but she didn't. Lisa was right there with Virgil every step of the way. Two of a kind. The next day, Jay had another wedding with Ricky walking her to be married again to Gerald the Third. Betsy did the food but Calvin with Kelly didn't come to this. They ate beef and ham.

After that Marci was in Jimmy's office screaming at Jimmy about Lisa being there with Virgil. Jimmy sat there not saying a word until she was done with her screaming at him.

Jimmy said, "Keep this up and you will never see that great-grandchild of yours. Maybe a girl."

Marci said, "Those bad, bad Eds or Virgil. They are no good."

Jimmy replied, "That is up to you. I like Virgil and Lisa. They go good together."

George replied, "Virgil has been nice to me and I know he is trying to be a good man for Lisa."

Later that day, Virgil called James and said, "Lisa has pains and I think our baby is coming."

James replied, "Bring Lisa to Jimmy's office. We are all home and can help."

They were off the phone and went into action. The Eds were waiting every step of the way as Virgil brought Lisa in to see Jimmy with Michael and Tim there. It was a baby girl. George came down to talk with Virgil but he was in the delivery room and Virgil didn't faint. He was there for Lisa and she knew it. Their baby girl was born and Virgil was holding the baby as Lisa was resting. Maybe Virgil wasn't a baby himself maybe he had grown up a lot for his child.

Jimmy said, "Virgil, if you want you can take the baby out to see your cousins."

Virgil said, "I don't want to go away from Lisa. Can I stay here with her?"

Jimmy went out and told the people waiting, "Lisa is doing good and it is a healthy baby girl."

They waited until they could see Virgil with the baby and Lisa. Virgil was so proud of his family now.

James asked, "When can we take them home, Michael? I mean Lisa and the baby with Virgil."

Michael looked at Jimmy and replied, "Anytime now. They are good to go."

They started to leave as Marci with George walked in and Jimmy with Calvin and Kelly gave Marci a headache from hell. George said nothing at all. James had Virgil and Lisa with the baby go to the car. They would fight anyone who tried to stop them. Eddie came with Kenny and Kevin. Tim and Gerald were behind them. What was going on? Jimmy was standing there and he looked mad.

Tim said, "Let us all go back to Jimmy's office and wait for him there. He will tell us what is up."

Gerald said, "Into the cars, guys. Don't make Jimmy mad. Marci and George already did that."

Kevin took Eddie and Kenny to the car but Kevin had never seen Jimmy like that before. He was in the killing mood. Kevin was even afraid of Jimmy. Jimmy's mind was on hurting someone. They went back to Jimmy's office and waited for him. Tim and Gerald came in to sit down; no one was talking. Eddie looked at Kenny who looked at Gerald. What the hell happened?

Eddie asked, "What the hell is going on? Did Jimmy have a fight with Marci over something?"

Kenny replied, "I think Jimmy won that fight clearly. Is George going to be okay with Marci?"

Kevin said, "I never saw Jimmy like that before and I never want to see him like that again."

Edward walked in and answered, "Grandpa, it is a girl and mother with baby are doing great. Virgil was in the delivery room the whole time with Lisa. He didn't faint or anything. Maybe he isn't a baby himself and can take care of a wife with a child. We are all going to help them."

Eddie said, "I want them to come home. I miss Virgil and we can make this work."

Kenny added, "I think Marci and George are the problem, not you, Eddie. We know you love your grandson, Virgil with Lisa and the baby. Eddie is great grandfather to a baby girl, again."

Kevin asked, "What about Barbie? Will she be nice to Virgil and his new family?"

Eddie replied, "If Barbie isn't, then I will see them myself."

Kenny said, "Jimmy is their protector so I think they are good. But I know Cindy is helping him."

Kevin asked, "What do we do? Is Jimmy coming here to talk?"

Gerald said, "Let us wait here for him. Jimmy will come when he is ready."

Tim said, "Don't mess with Jimmy today. He is in no mood for anything."

Jimmy came in and said, "Marci and George will be nice to Virgil, Lisa, and baby girl or I will personally kill them. Marci and George wouldn't be coming around here for a long time."

Eddie said, "It should have been me protecting my grandson Virgil and his new family, thanks."

Kenny said, "Jimmy, what do you need us to do to help Virgil and his new family?"

Kevin said, "We need Jimmy and Marci to make up for Tim or Marci wouldn't help Jimmy with Linda. Tim needs his wife Linda, you guys understand that, right?"

Eddie said, "I am so proud of Jimmy. He is a true friend to protect those kids like that."

Kenny replied, "Jimmy, we are with you all the way on protecting those kids."

Gerald said, "Give Jimmy time, he will have Marci doing what he wants. I trust Jimmy."

CHAPTER THIRTEEN

BAD GROUP BACK TOGETHER

Virgil was home safe with his wife, Lisa and their baby girl. Virgil did know how to change diapers and Lisa was feeding the baby with C-Jay's grandparents there. Virgil and Lisa had the baptism at C-Jay's grandparents' church with Cindy and C-Jay as sponsors. They were naming the baby Violet Lara Cindy Edson. Eddie waited in Jimmy's office the next day.

Eddie said, "We are their family. We don't need this Marci but for a medical thing and if she wants the whip back from Calvin, she will do what Jimmy wants or never get the whip back."

Kevin asked, "How important is that whip to Marci? Can't she just get another one?"

Calvin came in with Kelly and said, "No, I think it is like a witch and her boom."

Kevin asked, "What if Marci comes after you, son?"

Kelly replied, "She is weak still and we can take her anytime anywhere. We got this."

Eddie said, "Jimmy, I want the group together. I want Virgil to come back with his family."

Jimmy replied, "Can't trust Marci but I am meeting with George today."

Jimmy met with George and George said, "Jimmy, can't we work something out?"

Jimmy replied, "Yes, we can but I need you to take Marci home with you to cool down."

George said, "Marci wants her whip back from Calvin and he won't give it to her."

Eddie said, "Why wouldn't Marci help Jimmy with Linda?"

George replied, "Because Marci is mad at Jimmy."

Kenny said, "Something has to give here and I don't think it will be Jimmy."

George said, "I'll get Marci to talk with Jimmy but you have to get Jimmy to talk to Marci."

Kenny said, "Could you talk to Marci about Linda and the whip she wants, Jimmy?"

Jimmy replied, "I can meet with her at the hospital with Kevin, whenever Marci wants."

Jimmy told Cindy if Marci tried anything with Virgil, Lisa, and the baby Violet, kill her. Jimmy met George and he talked to Marci. Marci started her bad language and Jimmy walked away. Kevin sat there and waited for Marci to stop talking.

Kevin said, "Okay Marci, you got all the bad words out. Some new ones which Kenny would love to know about. Can you spell the last seven words you called Jimmy? I can find the meanings."

Marci asked, "What the hell is wrong with you? Are you crazy?"

Kevin replied, "No, but I did date a lot of crazy women so I am good with this. Kenny wants to learn new words and he is starting with swear words."

Marci said, "Okay, I want your son to give me my whip back, now."

Kevin replied, "My son will do that as soon as you help Jimmy with Linda. This is just business."

Marci looked at George and said, "I am going with George to see our children but when I come back, Jimmy and I can work this out. Just business that is all it is."

Kevin replied, "Don't think about hurting my son or anyone if you ever want to see your whip."

Kevin went home and was pleased but Jimmy wanted a big Mother's Day party at the church so Calvin, Kelly, and Edward started to plan it. All were to come which included Virgil and Lisa with baby Violet. This Mother's Day did last more than one day but then they got a little carried away. Jimmy went home to sleep with his Sylvia and we all know who Jimmy put in charge of the group, Kevin. Now this has never worked out before so why did Jimmy keep doing it? Maybe he wanted them all to have a good time and be friends. Tim was praying for his Linda.

Calvin came in to Tim and said, "Don't worry so, Linda will be okay. Linda is the only mother Betsy and I have ever known. We will help you, and Jimmy loves Betsy's cooking, so we have that."

The group was coming to the Thursday church and meal now as Tim waited for Marci to come back to do Linda with Jimmy. Virgil and Lisa with little Violet were coming back to be with everyone but Virgil had to go on missions within the week. Eddie told Lisa they will protect her and Violet. Lisa went to Virgil and they checked it out. Virgil's home was next to his twin brother Victor so Lisa would have family there. They decided to move back home. Victor and Virgil planned never to be on a mission at the same time so one of them can watch their wives. Everyone was helping with the baby and now Salina, Victor's wife, wanted a baby. Salina had told Victor she was on the pill, so no big deal. Did she go off the pill without telling him? Can women be trusted to take the damn pill? Victor came home to find Salina wasn't nice again so he went to Michael for help.

Victor said, "I need those crabby pills for Salina. I know she is on the pill for birth control."

Michael looked at Salina's files and said, "No, Salina isn't. Victor, sit down and I need to tell you something you won't like. Women like babies and I don't know why but they want babies. You can't trust a woman to take that pill or to tell you the truth, they don't see it as being a liar."

Victor replied, "This is why I don't listen to you, Michael. What the hell are you telling me?"

Michael said, "Victor, your wife may be pregnant and was never on the pill."

Victor said, "No, she would never do that to me. We talk about everything. We are friends. She is sleeping all the time and isn't loving me up as always."

Edward came in and said, "Maybe Michael should check her out and see if she is sick."

Victor agreed and Salina came in very agreeable. They sat there waiting as Kenny and Eddie came by to see why Edward, Calvin, with Kelly were at Michael's office. Was someone shot?

Michael came out with Marie and said, "Eddie, can you stay a minute? I have to tell Victor he is going to be a father. Salina wanted a baby. She told him that she was on the pill but wasn't."

Eddie replied, "That isn't fair."

Michael said, "Who is telling Victor that he is going to be a father?"

Eddie said, "I think my chiropractor, his wife should and not us. This was her idea anyway."

The summer was here and all was good. Edward told all the other Eds but not Victor. Marci was coming back to help Jimmy with Linda and then Calvin would give back her whip.

Marci asked, "When do I get my whip back from Calvin?"

Jimmy replied, "When we get Linda all done that is when you get your whip back."

Marci said, "This isn't my home anymore?"

Jimmy said, "If you can accept Virgil with Lisa and their baby then yes, it is your home again."

Jimmy went home and told the group to watch Marci very closely. If she did anything, tell Cindy or him without question, shoot to kill. They had a church and meal on the first Thursday of the month with Virgil being home. Marci came to church and sat by Jimmy with Sylvia.

Eddie whispered to Kenny, "I didn't know witches could come to church. Doesn't the Holy Water make them melt?"

Kenny whispered back, "I think we have to pour it on the witch to make her melt. We can get Holy Water on our way out to eat."

Kevin whispered over to them and asked, "What are we doing to do about Marci? You think pouring Holy Water on her will melt her?"

Edward turned and whispered, "Grandpa Eddie, stop whispering in church. Kenny and Kevin stop it!"

And readers, we thought the Eds were bad but look at those older people whispering in church. That is a no, and they are the ones to keep the younger people in line, no adults in this group. Eddie, Kenny, and Kevin were at the Holy Water trying to take some Holy Water out in a jar.

Virgil went up to Marci and took her to a chair to sat down to eat. He even went over to get her food to eat. Then Lisa with the baby came over and they all sat down to eat with Marci. All the Eds were now sitting down around Marci as if she was now one of them.

Kenny said, "Kelly, you got your gun ready to shoot her?"

Kelly replied, "Yes grandpa, locked and loaded, ready with the silencer on."

Calvin said, "I think we are all getting along so this is good."

Eddie said, "Don't let her fool you, witches are evil."

Kevin said, "I got the Holy Water in this jar. Where is her broom?"

Jimmy said, "Stop it now. That was a figure of speech and nothing more."

No one understood what Jimmy just said and by the looks on their faces they were ready to fight. Then Virgil stood on a table, telling the group that this is my grandmother-in-law and they will treat her with respect. Jimmy agreed with Virgil. Marci was now all smiles and nothing melts the heart like a great-grandchild. Marci was now one of them and they were all trying hard to get along. The group was back together again. But then Bonnie noticed that Salina was fat and asked that question. Heaven help them but at least they were already in church.

Bonnie asked, "Are you having a baby, Salina and Victor? No one told me. How nice."

Victor said, "No, we are eating a lot of food. We like to eat."

Salina said, "Yes, we are having a baby, Victor and I. Sorry Victor, I guess I was to tell you. Calvin why didn't you tell Victor? You are the tattle tale."

Calvin said, "They told me that was your job and not to tell anyone."

Now you know what the group did, they looked at the ceiling then the floor to the right then the left and waited. No one was talking. Victor got up and walked outside. The Eds and Calvin with Kelly followed him. What to say to Victor? He was upset but was it about the baby or that Salina, who he trusted completely, didn't tell him or even talk to him about it first? They all stood there with Victor and no one was talking. Salina went out to see if he was mad.

Salina said, "Want to talk about it, Victor?"

Victor replied, "I think it is too late for talking."

Eddie came out and said, "We can work this out, you two. Now let us go home and rest. I don't want Salina upset over this, Victor. She is having your baby like it or not."

Victor said, "Can you take her home grandpa Eddie? I need a minute or two first."

Eddie took Salina home and told her to give Victor some time and he would be good with it. Victor didn't come home, he left on another mission. James and Leo went with him this time. They were gone for weeks. Then Calvin and Kelly were calling to help them for back up. There was another shootout and someone was shot. Eddie was with Salina as she was sure it was Victor.

They came through the door with Kelly holding Victor's hand as he was being carried in by Leo. Michael was there to help. Jimmy would put Victor in his hospital and go to God for help. Sarah was waiting for James to come home with Calvin. They waited and each day felt like a week or month. But it was only a few days until Calvin came home with James and they were both okay. Kelly ran to Calvin and Sarah was in James' arms, but what happened?

Sarah asked James, "What happened? Was it a bad mission?"

James replied, "I can't talk about it but we got it done. Victor made a little mistake. His mind was still at home and that got him shot. Calvin had to disappear and reappear with me. I wish you were the one, my first time, but Calvin did or I would have been killed. Thank God for skills."

Halloween was coming and they missed Fathers' Day and all the summer over this issue with Victor still in the Hospital. Virgil was the only one Jimmy would let go to see Victor. Kevin knocked on the door and Jimmy waved him in.

Kevin said, "We need to get these Eds another job. I don't like Calvin and Kelly out there."

Jimmy replied, "I can get Victor home by Christmas. We can't do anything about their jobs."

Kevin said, "Why do Kelly and Calvin have to go out?"

Jimmy answered, "Because they can disappear and reappear with one other person. I had them drug Leo and Edward so they wouldn't know but James knows everything."

Kevin asked, "What do you mean drug them?"

Jimmy replied, "A little shot to the arm and they would be out in the time it takes them to disappear and reappear someplace else out of danger. But Kenny and Eddie don't know this, just Kelly with Calvin. Then James also understand what they can do if needed to save lives."

Kevin said. "Can't we find them something else to do around here?"

Jimmy said, "Talk to Kenny about Eddie retiring and have him get Virgil and Victor in there. They are more like desk jobs but nothing else is available in that line of work."

Kevin went to talk with Kenny and he agreed this could work but then Calvin with Kelly would be on more missions. Eddie started the paperwork on this for their grandsons. Halloween started out sad as James took his sons on their first trick or treating. Michael was there with his son and Edward with his little girl. C-Jay and Mickey joined them with their babies. Ed and Ricky went along.

Ricky was so happy this was his first mission to protect kids. Pumpkins and candy for the people at that place they once called Marci but now were calling Our People's place. It was a good night because Victor woke up. Eddie went up right away with Sarah and he told Victor that Salina couldn't come there because she was too sick with the babies. Eddie did tell Victor it was twins. Victor went to sleep. Victor was talking to Virgil a lot but not to anyone else. Virgil stayed with his twin brother day and night. Then Jimmy was ready to do the surgery of taking one of Virgil's kidneys and giving it to Victor. Eddie didn't like it. He could lose two grandsons but Virgil was doing it and not asking anyone if he should, not even his wife, Lisa. Jimmy brought Victor in for surgery and he was sure it would go well for both Victor and Virgil. The two Geralds were there doing the surgery, it took hours but it did go well, for both Virgil and Victor were fine. Salina went into labor with the twins and it was very early but the two baby girls were born. They were very small and needed to stay in the hospital. Michael and Tim were on it as Jimmy was still busy with Virgil and Victor. This Thanksgiving, they had a lot to be thankful for and that was all the group was back together. A big meal with church was planned. Betsy and Jay cooked up many turkeys with everything and a thankful prayer was said. God had been very good to them this year. Virgil and Victor came down to eat and everyone was happy to see them. But Salina was afraid to talk with Victor. Was he mad at her? Did he still love her? What about the twin baby girls? They all walked into church as Victor came to sit by his wife, Salina. Victor took her hand.

Salina said, "I am so sorry."

Victor kissed her and replied, "I am sorry too, do you still love me?"

Salina said, "Yes, but what about the baby girls? Should we give them up?"

Victor said, "No, they are our children and we love them. Just give me time."

After church they all went to eat together. Then Victor and Salina went to the hospital to see their baby girls and what were they going to name them? The group would help them but they were busy partying with Virgil and Lisa dancing on the tables with their little girl Violet. Nothing had changed. Just bad, bad, Eds, Calvin said. Victor and Salina would take the babies home from the hospital for Christmas but this year I think there will be no coal in any Eds' stocking, even Virgil was on Santa's good list, helping his twin brother, Victor. Oh, okay maybe Salina should get black coal in her stocking but no one was saying anything about it. I still wouldn't bet money on those Eds ever all being good for Christmas or on Santa's good list. They were all back together again and that was good enough.

Now that all the Eds were okay and Jimmy was working with Marci on Linda. Victor and Salina brought their baby girls home before Christmas. Could they name them now? Victor was weak and didn't touch his daughters but was looking at them a lot. Salina was afraid to say anything to Victor about them. What to name the girls, who was going to ask Victor? Eddie and Kenny went into Jimmy's office to get him to talk about Victor. Kevin was in there waiting. Gerald ran ahead and knocked on Jimmy's office door, before anyone went in.

Jimmy said, "Come in and what do you want me to do for you this time?"

Eddie said, "Someone has to ask Victor what he is naming his daughters before Christmas. We think it should be you."

Jimmy said, "Hell no, I had to help with the surgery in keeping Victor alive so I am not doing it."

Kenny said, "We always vote on things so let us vote. Kevin can count the votes."

Gerald asked, "How many people vote?"

Kenny said, "Only Jimmy, Eddie, and me, so that is three. Kevin can count that high?"

Kevin said, "Very funny, Kenny. I can count."

Jimmy said, "I vote Eddie talks to his own grandson Victor on this."

Eddie said, "I vote Jimmy talks to my grandson Victor on this."

All eyes were on Kenny and he said, "This isn't going good for me. I vote Eddie does."

Tim came running and said, "Linda is talking now, Jimmy come with me."

Jimmy replied, "With pleasure. See, I have other things to do with Tim."

Eddie answered, "I can wait for you to help me."

Kenny said, "Eddie, I don't think Jimmy is coming back to help you with this."

Kevin said, "You lost that vote so you talk to Victor."

Eddie replied, "Go to hell, Kevin. There is always something with my grandsons."

They went to see what was up with the group and nothing was different. Virgil was getting the direction on how to decorate the homes and wrote down when to take the decorations down. They marked the calendar, then he took his notes and threw them in the trash can. C-Jay, Mickey, and Edward did all the work as they had done every year. Victor was to cut the Christmas trees and sing his song on cutting you up for Christmas. Now, how can Eddie stop this much fun for Victor and talk about something he knows Victor doesn't want to think about? Then there was the cookie tasting and how could Eddie stop them all from eating cookies? Eddie helped with the cookie eating.

Kenny came to talk with Kelly and Calvin, he said, "I know for Kelly's birthday last month you guys got new furniture to do your home next to me, to live after you got married. But why wait until Kelly is twenty-one, why not marry sooner? Kelly is twenty years old now."

Kelly looked at Calvin and said, "We could pick a date if you want to."

Calvin said, "Kelly, any day you want I will be there to marry you. You pick the date and time."

Victor came over to Virgil and said, "I need to name my baby girls, the twins. What do you think of the names Mary and Christy for the babies?"

Virgil said, "I like it but you know they are going to ask for middle names."

Victor said, "Does this sound silly, but Mary Christy and Christy Mary then for confirmation names, maybe the two sisters of Salina's for their names."

Eddie was overhearing this and said, "I love those names, let us do it now."

Victor said to Salina, "Do you think these names are silly?"

Salina said, "No, I love them, let us do it this Sunday in church before Christmas."

So, Virgil and Lisa were the sponsors for Mary Christy Suzanne Edson. Then Mickey and Betsy were sponsors for Christy Mary Samantha Edson. But I am sure next time Salina will be talking it over with her husband, Victor, before they have any more children.

Christmas and New Years are again two big parties that start one day and go into the next. The babies were all the more fun as they were moving around and playing with all the gifts for Christmas. Good things were happening as they all came together in joy to the world. James and Leo went to work but this time it was with Kelly and Calvin. Edward wanted to go too and he said Virgil or Victor should teach because with only one kidney they can't be out there. Agency rules and now what? Eddie could only teach two at the office and they did want a woman. Eddie was sitting in Jimmy's office as he walked in with Kenny.

Jimmy asked, "Eddie, you look like it is the end of the world."

Eddie said, "I can't use both of my grandsons. The rules say I must have a woman at the top."

Jimmy replied, "Edward wants to go back out and stop training so I think we need Victor to train Kenny. He has twin girls and is needed here. Take Virgil and Lisa as the top leaders."

Kenny said, "That will work."

Eddie replied, "I don't want Edward out there."

Jimmy answered, "He is going whether you like it or not, so don't try to stop him and let us be agreeable. Calvin with Kelly are out there and Edward wants it too."

Eddie said, "Virgil wouldn't want to be in an office at all."

Jimmy replied, "I will talk with him about it and James can help me."

Jimmy left and went to James and Sarah's home then knocked on the door. Sarah came to the door and talked to her dad through their minds. Then she went to get James.

Jimmy said to James, "You know what we are and we need Virgil to do Eddie's job with Lisa. They want a woman with the leadership too. I want Lisa because she has skills and will keep Virgil safe. I know he isn't an office guy but he can run that office to change the rules."

James asked, "What do you want me to do?"

Jimmy replied, "Talk to Virgil and get him to do the job. With one kidney it is the only way he can stay in the agency. Rules do change and let him know he will be the one changing them."

Kelly asked, "How are we going to get Lisa up to where she needs to be as an agent in time?"

Calvin said, "Kelly, you can personally train her with your grandpa Kenny. He is the best."

Virgil said, "I can be a good boy and then when I am in, I will change those damn rules."

Linda came home to Tim on March first at Calvin's home but Calvin was never there anymore. He was living with Jimmy and studying hard. Majestic Twelve was going great but another member was very sick. Jimmy was doing whatever he could to keep them going until Kelly was twenty-one years old. Ricky wanted to live with Kevin and his mother Teresa Mary was upset, so what should Kevin do? Kevin wanted his son with him but what about Bonnie, so he went to talk with Bonnie about it. Bonnie did love Ricky and was okay to have him living with them. So, Kevin told Ricky okay.

Calvin knocked on Jimmy's door and he waved Calvin in.

Calvin said, "Teresa Mary is on the phone for you. She called Leo's home first and he put her through to you. Are we changing all the phone numbers? Should I tell Sam?"

Jimmy replied, "No, I will talk with Teresa Mary. Don't change any phone numbers, she has Leo's and Kevin's numbers. Leo put her through to my phone, that is all he did."

Jimmy waited and said, "What can I do for you, Teresa Mary?"

Teresa Mary said, "I know you hate me but you would do anything for your kids. Is that me too?"

Jimmy replied, "As long as you aren't mean to my Sylvia. What can I do?"

Teresa Mary said, "I can leave Sylvia alone if you help me. I don't want my son Ricky to live with Kevin and his new wife Bonnie. I want my son home with me. But Kevin is a good lawyer and I can't fight him on this in court."

Jimmy said, "I think Ricky can live with his father if he wants to. I will talk with Kevin on it and about Ricky. I think I can get Ricky to stay home with you if I make a deal with him."

Teresa Mary asked, "What kind of deal could you make with Ricky? Am I so bad?"

Jimmy replied, "I can get Victor to let him help out at the training after school. I will tell Ricky we can only do that if he agrees to stay home and live with you. How is that?"

Teresa Mary answered, "I like it and think Ricky will do it. Why are you helping me?"

Jimmy was off the phone but said, "We got off to a bad start. I will take the blame for that."

Kenny and Eddie came running to see what the hell it was. Bonnie had told her dad, Eddie, about Ricky coming to live with Kevin and her. Kenny and Eddie came in to sit down. Jimmy had told Calvin to find Ricky for him to talk to in his office.

Kevin came in and Jimmy said, "Sit down, you won't like this but I have to do it."

Kevin said, "I am glad you guys are here. Jimmy is going to tell me something I wouldn't like."

Jimmy spoke, "Kevin, you aren't having Ricky live with you and Bonnie. Ricky stays home with his mother, Teresa Mary. She called me and we made a deal. I have no right to make this deal but I did. I will have Ricky work with Victor at the teaching for spies. Any problems, Kenny?"

Kenny replied, "No, Jimmy. I am good with it."

Eddie said, "I think that is best for Ricky to stay with his mother until he is eighteen."

Kevin answered, "Okay, if that is what you want, Jimmy. I can see my son anytime I want to here at school or at the training center but if Teresa Mary ever hurts him, I am taking her to court for my son. She will be a good mother to Ricky. I am checking up on her every day."

Jimmy said, "I agree if you find Teresa Mary doing anything not good for Ricky, you can't trust her."

Calvin brought Ricky to Jimmy's office and Jimmy said, "Ricky, I need your help in something. Victor, as you know, got hurt very bad and he is needing help with teaching at the spy school. Could you do that after your studies? But this is the hard part. The agency has silly rules and you can't live with Kevin or any of us for this work. You have to stay at home with your mother until you are eighteen to do this work. If there is a problem at home just tell me."

Ricky replied, "I want to work as a spy guy and I can help Victor after school. My mom is weird but she is nice to me. I can live at home with her until I train to be a secret agent man."

Kevin said, "I am not sure of that, Ricky. We need to talk about it."

Jimmy said, "That is years away, so you got time. You may not like it but Victor needs help."

Eddie was busy teaching Virgil and Lisa the business he did. Kenny was working with Victor on teaching at the spy school. Kevin was watching Ricky with his mother, Teresa Mary. Jay was living there at her home with her new husband, Gerald the Third. Jimmy called Kevin into his office.

Kevin said, "Boss, what is it? I am still not sure of this Teresa Mary."

Jimmy replied, "We can keep an eye on Teresa Mary. I need Ricky to do the Easter thing."

Ricky came into the office and Jimmy said, "Ricky, I know you are going a great job, I need help with Easter and candy for everyone. Can you do that like Calvin did for me?"

Ricky said, "Yes sir, I can do it like Calvin did. How do I get the bags of candy in their homes?"

Jimmy replied, "Betsy can do that with her cooking stuff. We need the Easter plastic eggs filled with candy to hide at the church for the Easter egg hunt. Little Ed can help. Betsy and Jay buy all the stuff needed. You put bags in their homes with Betsy. I will pay you as I did Calvin."

Ricky said, "Victor puts most of my pay in a bank account for me and I get a little of the money to spend. He tells me that is what secret agents do. They plan ahead always."

Jimmy replied, "Yes, I can do that for you, Ricky. That is a good idea. I did that too as an agent."

Kevin had tears as he said, "I am so thankful we have those bad Eds. They are good guys too."

Eddie came in said, "Kevin, did you forget to knock on Jimmy's office door, he made you cry?"

Kenny said, "I will go back out and knock, Jimmy, don't make me cry."

Tim said, "Jimmy, this knocking thing isn't that important. Get over it."

Gerald said, "Maybe it is something else. Jimmy isn't that mean to anyone."

Jimmy replied, "I am putting a special alarm in at my door so I know before anyone comes to my door and I can see who it is or lock my damn door. Gary will have it done for me by Easter."

Tim went over to Kevin and said, "See, no more knocking and Jimmy will never make us cry."

Jimmy said, "What do we want to eat for Easter after church for our meal? The girls need to know to cook it. You guys vote and tell me, anything. Good cooks are very important to us."

The guys agreed and they sat down to think about it. Kenny did want meat of some kind. Gerald wanted vegetables. Eddie wanted an Easter bunny cake. The notes went to Betsy and Jay. They were taking this to a whole new level in what to eat. Remember how they loved the Easter egg hunts, the big kids? The little kids will be more active this year too as they are growing up fast. Maybe that was why Kevin had tears in his eyes, Ricky growing up so fast.

Kevin said, "I called you all to meet for a reason, Ricky is working now with us. I have gotten him a special work permit because of his mother. Victor is doing a great job with Ricky."

Victor said," Ricky is good at it and a born teacher. He has the gift in helping people understand things. He puts things in simpler terms to understand what they are to do."

Virgil said, "Ricky likes to do things with humor. Making people laugh helps them learn easier."

Kevin was hearing things about Ricky he didn't know. These Eds knew Ricky better than him. Then Kevin noticed Victor was letting Ricky drive the car. Kevin went to pray and cry.

In the morning it was church and Easter egg hunting. All the kids were older so it was more fun for them and the big kids were still helping too much as Linda was talking with Calvin and Kelly.

Kelly said after prayer, "Attention please everyone, Calvin and I want to tell you when we are getting married. We want you all to come and enjoy that day with us. Calvin, tell them."

Everyone was laughing now as Victor called out, "Calvin, take your orders now and do it. You are getting married and we all know who is the boss then. We are all married with kids."

Calvin said, "I don't care who the boss is as long as Kelly marries me. We have set our wedding date for June first at four pm. Please mark that date and be home for our wedding. The only woman who Betsy and I have ever known as children is our mother, Linda. And I am so happy to have Linda back. Where is Linda? Right here, thank you, Jimmy. I love you, Kelly."

Kelly kissed Calvin and said, "I love you too, Calvin, and always will."

Calvin had his true love forever which is what he always wanted and someone to pray with. After all the Easter meal and fun, Kelly with Calvin went to plan their wedding on June first, at four pm. Kelly had the wedding dress and now who would all be in this wedding? I guess readers, it isn't going to be a small wedding. Kenny was more than ready to pay for this wedding and he couldn't have been happier. For Gail it was the wedding she and Kenny never got to have but now she was going to enjoy this to the fullest. Kelly was staying home to plan this not small wedding but Calvin didn't care. He wanted Kelly to have the wedding of her dreams. Kevin did cry for three days again but he got over it as he always does.

CHAPTER FOURTEEN

WHAT HAPPENED TO THEM?

Calvin wanted Linda to act as his mother in his wedding. This time it was Tim who was crying. Linda was so happy and everyone she didn't know were also happy she was back with them. All the Eds were so nice to Linda and made her feel like one of the family. Linda was to help in planning this not small wedding with Gail and Tammy, Kelly's mother.

Kelly wanted Michael's son little Tim to be the ring carrying boy and Edward's daughter Ellie to be flower girl. Kelly also wanted all the kids to be in the wedding as little flower girls and ring boys. James and Sarah's three boys were in the terrible twos or threes They were all over the place and a handful. Virgil's baby girl Violet could walk but Victor's twins Christy and Mary were starting to get around. Cindy and Betsy's kids were walking good but still very small. Little Ed would be the leader of the kids for he knew the job best as a ring carrying boy. Ricky would be Calvin's best man. Kelly's bride's maid was to be Betsy, Calvin's sister. Calvin went to talk with Jimmy on where they should go for a honeymoon. Jimmy's office door opened as Calvin walked close to the office. Okay, that must mean he can go in and talk.

Calvin said, "New door system to your office? I like it. We both know the Eds will never learn to knock first so why try. Where do you think Kelly and I should go on our honeymoon?"

Jimmy replied, "What are your ideas and maybe you should talk to your dad about this."

Calvin said, "We thought about a trip around the world, going to Our People's place and trying to see the winded horse, or going to Germany."

Jimmy asked, "Why Germany?"

Calvin replied, "It was Germany where Kelly and I went on our first mission with James Edson."

Jimmy thought a minute then said, "A trip around the world is what Margo and I did that may be bad luck. On Our People's place where the winged horses are is what you found with Jay. I say Germany, a place you both loved. Anyway, Kenny wants great-grandchildren."

Kevin came in and said, "Cindy is on the phone for you, Jimmy, but why on the phone?"

Cindy answered, "I am pregnant again. I have to limit my actions; it is twin boys."

Jimmy replied, "I am so happy for you and C-Jay. Yes, you need to rest a lot, we can help you."

They were off the phone. Jimmy gave orders for Calvin to stay home from missions and to help Cindy. Betsy was sad because she was sure Mickey didn't want any more children and after what had happened with Victor, she wasn't ever doing what Salina did.

James asked, "Calvin, how are the wedding plans going?"

Calvin answered, 'I want to go to Germany on our honeymoon and the other stuff I don't really care about, whatever Kelly wants. I will be there at the church to marry Kelly and that is what I want in this wedding, to have my true love forever which is only Kelly. I have to be home now."

Calvin and James Edson found Kelly a very nice necklace set for her to wear with her wedding dress. The stones were black and purple with white pearls. Kelly decided for her colors to be purple and black. A chocolate cake with chocolate frosting and purple candy roses on the cake with a water fall of grape fizzy juice. The food Betsy and Jay were cooking was beef.

The guys had a party of how to care for a baby and what do; they already know about babies. Virgil and Victor helped Ricky with the party. There was a lot of food and beef to eat with chocolate. The drink is a non-alcohol beer. Virgil was showing off his skills in diaper changing. Victor was showing how to feed babies. Edward was teaching how to be quiet as babies sleep. C-Jay was showing them how to do what you are told by your wife. Mickey was teaching them how to not talk in a marriage. James was showing them how to run after three little boys and Leo was telling them how to start with the right women. This had to be a silly party but the guys were very serious in their actions. Jimmy, Eddie, and Kenny couldn't stop laughing.

Kevin with Tim were crying and Gerald was sitting there with Gerald the Third taking notes. George came down to see what the hell they were all doing as Micky, T-Jay, and Sam did security for this party they didn't want to attend. Michael and Gary explained the delivery room and they all went to sleep. The women's party wasn't as much fun until they decided to sneak over and watch the men. Then they had to try not to laugh and get caught watching as Calvin took it all in from the group. The men's party went on all night but in the morning, they all went to sleep in one big room on the floor. Kelly and the women went in to cover the guys. They didn't want any of the guys sick at her wedding. Betsy got a good breakfast made for them or I guess it was more like lunch as the guys got up to eat. Then it was clean themselves up good and be at that church. They all did look good and everyone was ready for the wedding of the year for Kelly and Calvin.

The music started and all the group was trying to sing as the little children walked in with the help of their parents. Did they have a rehearsal dinner on this and I am sure they ate beef at this dinner. One of the little girls was eating the flowers and the other two were crawling all around the church. Michael was trying to get little Violet not to eat the flowers as Virgil with Lisa helped. Victor was busy running after his twin daughters with his wife. The little boys were walking in, too nice, and they got to Calvin then Roy peed on Calvin's shoes. Ron and Rob stomped on Calvin's other shoe.

The flower girl, Ellie, walked in, little Tim, the ring bearer with Aim and Mitch. Betsy walked after the two little kids so nicely as with the other little kids, it was like herding cats to get them to be good. Kenny walked his granddaughter up to Calvin with Gary, Tammy and Gail behind them. Linda, Tim, and Kevin were trying to get Calvin's shoes clean in time to meet his bride, Kelly in her great-great-grandma's wedding dress. It was a beautiful wedding; Edward started the wedding vows. They both say "I do" and Calvin kissed his bride, Kelly, with Kevin crying so hard.

Sam said, "I like Calvin and Kelly's wedding with Edward as the deacon."

T-Jay said, "I enjoyed watching James Edson run after those three little boys of his with Sarah."

Micky said, "Guys, you know we like them all now. But this is a lot more fun watching them."

The dancing started before the meal so the girls could get the food on the big table; Kenny had his beef with everything else. Pretty purple flowers were everywhere. As Calvin and Kelly continued to kiss. Ricky was now dancing with a pretty little girl about his age.

Kevin went to Jimmy and asked, "Who is that girl Ricky is dancing with? Do you know her?"

Jimmy replied, "I think it is Tim and Linda's only daughter's child. I invited her for Calvin. Linda is the only mother Calvin has ever known."

Kevin asked, "Jimmy, is my son, Ricky, kissing that girl? Is Virgil helping him to know how to kiss this girl? What the hell are they doing?"

Jimmy said, "I know you like Tim so being a future in-law with him should be good for you."

Kevin called, "Virgil, stop helping Ricky. He knows enough. No more teaching; bad, bad Eds."

Betsy came over to Kevin and said, "Ricky is learning and the Eds will be there helping him."

Eddie came and said, "Kenny, this is a nice wedding. What do you think, Jimmy?"

Jimmy replied, "I am enjoying seeing Kevin run around trying to stop things for a change."

Tim said, "Kenny, this is a nice wedding. Who is the guy running after the three little bad boys?"

Eddie said, "Oh, that is my grandson, James, running after his three sons with Sarah."

Tim said, "I've never seen little boys get into so many things so fast. They are real movers."

Eddie replied, "Yes, all the problems those grandsons of mine give me, this is sweet. Oh, there goes Victor running after his twin girls. Is Virgil's kid eating a bug? Oh, Lisa stopped her."

Kenny said, "I want that too. I hope I get some great grandchildren from Kelly and Calvin."

Eddie said, "There goes Leo after little Ed because he wants to kiss the girls too. So much fun."

Kevin said, "Come and sit down to eat, Jimmy, Eddie, and Kenny. Tim and Gerald, find your wives. God help me get through this wedding. Who has to say the prayer? Me, oh no, Jimmy help me, I don't know the before meal prayer."

Calvin said, "Dad, please lead us in the before meal prayer."

Gary stood up and said the before meal prayer with Kevin for he and Tammy knew the prayer.

Ricky said, "I will make my speech now. Brother Calvin with your lovely wife, Kelly. I only hope you have as much fun together always as I am having at your wedding."

Kevin called, "James, help me with Ricky."

James called back, "If you run after my three little boys, I will take care of your one son."

Kevin looked and Roy was playing in the grape fizzy waterfall with his mouth. Ron was drinking the water in the flowers on the tables. Rob was now looking up all the women's dresses. Sarah looked all tired out and James was running in all directions. Which one would you stop first?

Sally hit T-Jay and said, "Stop laughing at James Edson. It isn't funny, help him."

T-Jay replied, "I am so happy to have you back, dear. I am enjoying Calvin and Kelly's wedding."

Vicki said, "That James Edson is very handsome and just plain hot."

Sam replied, "I think you are right, dear, that drink little Roy spit in James's face must be hot."

Micky said, "I really like it when we are all together. Oh, there goes Victor after one of his girls."

T-Jay said, "No, that is Virgil's baby girl, Violet. I know because Virgil and my son C-Jay are good friends. His daughter likes to eat animal poop but they do stop her from eating it."

Jimmy came over and said, "I am glad the group is really coming together for Calvin and Kelly at their wedding. Having a good time, guys."

T-Jay replied, "I am having the best time sitting here, watching all the fun."

Jimmy asked, "Do you think I should help Sarah and James with their three boys?"

Sam replied, "No, I know how bad James wanted to be a father. His dream came true."

Micky said, "I have never seen a guy so involved with his children. I think he is loving it."

Jimmy said, "I guess you are right and Sarah is going over to help him. I get tired watching those little boys run around. I think it is time for my nap with Sylvia."

Leo came over and said, "I will help James and Sarah with their boys as soon as I find Ed. Does anyone know where my son little Eds is?"

Edward said, "Leo, come here, little Eds is kissing the girls again. Then help James and Sarah."

Virginia said, "Don't say anything about the bad, bad Eds; they have their hands full with their own kids now. Poor Victor and Salina, that Christy is biting them again and look at Mary crying."

The meal was over and it was time to put the kids to sleep or was it the parents that needed it? Kelly and Calvin cut the cake. Oh no, Rob had already started to eat their cake. Where is James everyone called out. His kid is being bad again. Calvin and Kelly were laughing as James came.

Kenny said to Eddie, "Are you having a good time today?"

Eddie replied, "The best time ever, sitting here and watching all the action. I am loving it."

After nap time and the kids to have a change of clothes, then back to start eating cake with dancing off all that sugar. Kelly and Calvin started their first dance as the Eds all sang a love song for them. Then the little kids tried to dance. James was trying to help his sons dance nicely with the little girls. Little Tim was dancing very nicely with Ellie, Edward's daughter. Aim and Mitch were dancing. Violet, Christy, and Mary were dancing with all of James' sons in a circle, so cute. After eating cake and watching the kids dance or run around in circles, they took them home to have Jimmy's people babysit so the adults could dance the night away. Leo wanted to take little Ed home but he wouldn't go home. Ricky was staying so he was too. They are needed to dance with women.

Leo sat down by James and said, "If you think it is bad now, wait until your boys get older."

James said, "Why did we want to become fathers again?"

Edward came over and answered, "It is a sickness that we got. It is gone now. Why does my little daughter have to dance all the time with little Tim? Michael wasn't even watching."

Leo said, "At least you got your kids to bed and home. My son is still here and he thinks he is a big boy now. God help me."

Victor came over and said, "Guys, why are you not dancing with your women? We have to dance with our women. It doesn't matter how tired you are, get off your ass and dance."

The Eds got up and found their wives to dance with them all night. They danced to the oldies but goodies and sang. All that chocolate should keep them going all night long. The dance went into the morning, now having breakfast before Kelly and Calvin left for their honeymoon. Kelly threw her flowers and Ricky caught those flowers with a girl. Oh my God, it is Tim and Linda's granddaughter. Kevin started to cry. Edward took Kelly and Calvin to the airport to Germany.

Calvin looked out and said, "Edward, I got this. Go home to your wife and daughter now."

The group slept a lot after the wedding. In two weeks, Calvin carried Kelly over the threshold into their home. Eddie called them all into his office, and it was a big office. They all came in looking confused.

Eddie said, "We need to change people doing jobs. Virgil and I got some of those rules changed. So, Virgil and Victor can go back out. Who wants to teach and help me?"

Kelly said, "I want to teach for my grandpa Kenny. Calvin has to help Cindy."

Edwards said, "Grandpa Eddie, I want to work with you and have my wife Suzanne there for mental health. We think mental health is a big issue for agents."

Edward was at Eddie's side every day helping him as Kelly was with Kenny and Ricky. Calvin helped Cindy and Kevin was always there for Jimmy. The summer was almost over as Ricky came to Jimmy's office and let himself in as Jimmy was working on something with Calvin.

Ricky said, "Kelly is sick, she is throwing up all the time and Kenny is happy about it. Why?"

Jimmy looked at Calvin and said, "Get Kelly to Michael now, Calvin."

Calvin went to see Kelly at work with Ricky and asked, "You have been sick all summer. Isn't time to see Michael?"

Kelly smiled and said, "I already did that and I am not sick. We are going to have a baby. But not just one baby. We are having twins."

Calvin hit the floor and was out cold. Kenny called Michael. Ricky was looking at what happened so he called Jimmy. Edward came running with Eddie. Michael came and helped Calvin with smelling salts. Bonnie ran to find Kevin who was on his way.

Kelly said, "Calvin and I are going to have twin babies."

Kenny said, "I knew you could do it, Calvin. I am so pleased. I want great grandchildren."

Calvin wasn't talking and Edward whispered, "Kiss Kelly and tell her you are so happy, then we will really talk about it."

Calvin did what Edward told him to as Jimmy said, "Ricky, help your dad for he will need three days of crying, but he will be okay."

Calvin whispered to Edward, "I am not ready to be a father and then twins."

Edwards said, "Ready or not, here they come."

Victor was first on advice, he said, "Have a lot of sex now for when those babies come, no more."

Virgil's advice was, "Eat all the same food she does. It tastes good, enjoy eating with her."

Edward said, "Be loving and understanding even when she is a pain in the ass. Be nice."

James said, "Pray more. Don't go in that delivery room with her, don't do it, man."

Leo said, "This is the good part. It is downhill from here."

Mickey told is brother-in-law, "Keep your mouth shut. Anything you say can and will be taken wrong. Just smile and be careful with that too."

C-Jay said, "Do whatever she tells you to do. No more or less. Take your orders from her."

Michael said, "Calvin, we have never lost a father in this. Kelly is very healthy, don't worry."

Calvin said, "What if she would die? I can't raise two kids myself and I can't live without Kelly."

Jimmy came in and said, "We will never let Kelly die. Kenny wouldn't hear of it."

Ricky said, "I can do the hard stuff. Kelly can just teach the written stuff. I got this for you."

Betsy said, "I will cook all the meals for you. Don't worry about losing your true love, Kelly."

Edward said, "Wow, so much has happened since we first met. I can't think of my life without you."

Calvin replied, "I don't even want to think of my life without all of you, but I need Kelly for she is my true love forever. We pray together at the church all the time as you and I do."

The two best friends, Calvin and Edward walked into the church to pray again.

Halloween was coming on their church day this year and all would be home for church with the meal then trick or treating for the kids. T-Jay was okay with more grandchildren as Cindy with C-Jay were having twins. T-Jay knew what the women were saying about James Edson. The women loved to watch him run after his little three boys and as he bent over to pick up one, they'd all look at his ass. Sarah got up then went to help James and give the women a not nice look. Now if there was sweet revenge then T-Jay was having it over James Edson for taking Sarah away from him, even if T-Jay did get Sally back that way. Every time James had to run after one of his three sons, T-Jay smiled. It was pure joy for him. As Calvin would say bad, bad Eds but this time T-Jay thought of it in a good way. James' sons were a joy for T-Jay to watch.

Sally hit T-Jay and said, "Stop laughing at James Edson running after his sons. Those boys are all over the place. They have so much energy and are wild."

T-Jay replied, "Boys will be boys, dear. They are kids, wait until they grow up then the fun really starts. I want to be here to see it all."

Sam and Micky were laughing so hard. Their wives weren't pleased either with this behavior of their husbands. But none of them wanted to miss a thing with the new group. Jimmy was happy, he had his group all coming together. Okay, maybe not for the best reasons but the guys, T-Jay, Sam, and Micky did want to be around Calvin and the Eds. They all loved going to church with the meals on the first and third Thursday each month.

Halloween had the kids all happy and they were all over the place. Victor was non-stop running after his twin daughters. Virgil's little daughter, Violet, got a booger from baby Christy's nose and ate it. This made Mary cry but it wasn't her nose so why was she crying? Ellie had stopped Violet just before eating it. Ellie, Edward's daughter, slapped Violet's hand so she was crying too. Christy had noticed her booger was gone and wanted it back so she hit Violet. Violet hit back and little Tim tried to stop the girls from fighting. Then James' three boys came to help little Tim, or did they want to fight with the girls? Roy had one girl down and Ron had Violet on the floor too with Rob grabbing Ellie. James was trying to stop them as the guy were laughing so hard at this. Little Tim was trying to hear what Christy was crying for, what did she want? Who took what from her?

Micky asked, "Should we tell them what is wrong?"

Sam replied, "No, Victor and Virgil are on their way. James is going down in the fight."

T-Jay said, "I love it, I like it, I want some more of it."

Micky asked, "Who is doing security these days for our church and meals?"

Sam replied, "My kids are, my son and daughter. I think my daughter does it so she can look at James Edson's ass as he bends over to get his sons. My son does it to stop my daughter."

T-Jay said, "Well, that is why we have to watch this all the time. Keep checking it all out. I don't think James Edson's ass is that nice, but I am not a woman."

Sam said, "We better stay on it and watch those Eds. My daughter is being silly as all the women are in this group."

Micky said, "Well, with all the running James does after his sons, weight isn't his problem."

T-Jay replied, "Yes, but Sarah is always worried about women looking at her husband. I like it."

Sam said, "A little anger issue from the past, T-Jay?"

T-Jay answered, "No, not angry at all, pure enjoyment with these meals and church."

Micky said, "Come guys, they aren't so bad, the Eds. Oh, look here comes Edward and Calvin to help with Leo, now it will stop. Did the kids kill James? He is on the floor not moving. Oh, he is up now, looking shaken but not stirred in his James Bond 007 style."

Sam said, "The meal is over already? I guess it is nap time and then trick or treating. Who wants to help me with security tonight?"

T-Jay answered, "I would love to. I can't wait to see James Edson run after those three little boys all over the homes with candy. Lots of candy they will be getting from everyone and eating as they go. More energy for those boys. Let me go in the church and thank God."

Micky said, "I don't think that is the right thing to thank God for, but who knows."

Halloween night went wonderful for T-Jay and he was laughing all night long as the kids went out. Jimmy's plan was to wait until Kelly was twenty-one to have her as their new member at Majestic Twelve because another member had died. Kelly was going to the meetings with Edward's wife and waiting in the café as the meetings were done. The other members saw her but then Jimmy had the vote already. He didn't need anyone else to vote to get Kelly in for more than three fourths of the members were Jimmy's friends. But Kelly still smiled at the other members. Calvin made no secret that Kelly was his pregnant wife but she would keep her last name Anderson.

Kelly had her twenty-first birthday with no party at all, she wanted to be home with Calvin then see her parents and grandparents. The group awaited their church and meal then gave Kelly a surprise party with cake. Betsy made a big cake but then they did have many cake lovers. There was dancing and fun but the kids again took over the party with James running all over after his boys. James and Sarah's sons were bad Eds which Calvin worried would his babies be?

Calvin asked, "Kelly, are we having boys or girls? Has Michael checked them out?"

Kelly replied, "One of each, my love, a boy and a girl."

Cindy was eating cake and cried, "It hurts."

Virgil said, "Stop eating cake. Remember you ate too many cookies then the baby came out."

Michael said, "Let me check you out, Cindy. The babies are not due for another month or so."

Cindy went to the hospital with Michael and C-Jay but he wasn't going in that delivery room. They all waited for Cindy to have her babies but they got cake to eat again. This time it appeared to go faster but then they all were busy eating cake for Kelly's birthday. Cindy and the babies were doing great as Tim came out to tell C-Jay he had twin boys. C-Jay sat there holding little Aim. Now C-Jay was throwing up. The group wasn't laughing, they felt sorry for C-Jay as they held their kids. Calvin looked at Kelly and she was smiling. C-Jay was now out cold on the floor. Virgil came over to take little Aim as Gail came to help C-Jay.

Kelly said, "The babies were born on my birthday, how nice."

Gail replied, "Not good. I need to put C-Jay in the hospital too."

Virgil said, "I can watch little Aim for them. She can play with Violet, my daughter."

Edward came over to Calvin and said, "Wow, that was something different. But then this group of ours is full of surprises. Two babies born on Kelly's birthday. C-Jay was spending too much time around James and it is catchy, this more than one baby at a time."

Calvin said, "I can understand Victor having twins because he is a twin but none of us are."

Cindy said, "We are naming the twins, Kim and Jim. Kim Karl Kenny Peterson and Jim Tim Eddie Peterson. What do you think of those names?"

They all looked at C-Jay and he was still sicker than Cindy who had two babies. This was hard on the fathers of the group. So now they called C-Jay and Cindy's kids, Aim, Kim and Jim. Cindy would have Kelly and Calvin as the god parents for Kim. Virgil and Lisa as god parents for Jim.

Jimmy now had seven grandsons and three granddaughters. Was it the seventh grandson of Jimmy's that would be the silver one and they didn't need to have seven children? Only time will tell. Kelly and Calvin's twins would be Jimmy's first great grandchildren.

Kelly was now twenty-one and at the next Majestic Twelve meeting Jimmy had her on the program as the newest member to be voted on. Calvin made a speech that Kelly was his pregnant wife with twins and Kenny's granddaughter. Then Calvin nominated his wife Kelly Anderson to be the next member. Kenny seconded it. They all opened their folders and voted all for Kelly. Now this hadn't happened before so why did the other members let it happen this time? Maybe because Jimmy already had the vote and they wanted the people who went with Jimmy to vote their way sometimes. But then it could be because everyone liked Calvin and Edward, nice young members as secret agents or is it that they all knew Calvin would be the leader after Jimmy. Don't get on the bad side of the future leader of Majestic Twelve. The leader of Majestic Twelve does have power over the group and members on when and where to have the meetings.

Thanksgiving came and there was one big meal with the kids all over the place again. Sarah was telling James that she will get the boys. He didn't have to pick them up all the time. Sarah told James she wanted to lose weight so she would run after the boys. Okay readers, we all know the real reason, those women looking at James Edson's ass. Poor James Edson, if he only knew what the women were now thinking about him. James would stay out of sight. It did go okay but the women were disappointed. James noticed now the guys were looking at Sarah's ass.

James said, "Sarah, my love, we need your father's people to run after the boys with us to pick them up. It is too much for you alone and I have to work, so I get very tired doing this."

The Eds aren't the only bad, bad ones that should get black coal in their stocking this year from Santa. These church going women all need to be on Santa not good list this year and not just Sarah's little Eds. Christmas comes with kids all over the place.

Nothing had changed, Victor still cut the Christmas trees, singing his cut you up song. Virgil still took notes on what the women want, in decorations with C-Jay, Mickey, and Edward doing all the work. The women still baked all those cookies for the guys to taste. The Christmas decorations would be down before Easter for that Easter bunny to come. Ricky's job was still doing Easter stuff. It was the end of February when this virus was first noticed in our world.

Kelly had the twins. It was so close to Jimmy's birthday and he was all pleased.

Calvin went into the delivery room and didn't faint. Calvin was right by Kelly's side as his son and daughter were born. The group waited with cake from Jimmy's birthday. Okay, Jimmy got no cake but he was still happy his first great-grandchildren. Kenny and Jimmy shared this, but Eddie was laughing. Kevin was crying again for three days. Calvin and Kelly named the baby boy Ken and the baby girl Kell Anderson-Carlson. Godparents would be Edward and Suzanne for the boy, Ken Calvin Kevin Anderson-Carlson. The girl godparents would be Betsy and Mickey for Kell Kelly Tammy Anderson-Carlson.

A big Baptism party was planned again and all were good with the kids running all over the place. Calvin looked a little sick but he had his Kelly to help him and his best friend Edward with all the Eds. Then there was his father Kevin and his step mother Bonnie, with the once called boys Jimmy, Eddie, and Kenny with their women. Calvin wasn't alone and then there was his sister, Betsy, who loved babies and Ricky, who was not little anymore. Calvin worried would his kids be a handful like James' three boys? Calvin and Kelly's twins did have skills. But then so did Cindy and Betsy's kids. What would that mean for the group? Would they ever tell the others in the group about these skills? So far James Edson was the only one who truly knew about the skills that didn't have skills, the other fathers were in the dark on this. How were they doing this and did C-Jay and Mickey really know but weren't saying anything? Would Jimmy tell them all one day as he did about Eddie and Kenny? Was Jimmy waiting for the right time or was that going to be Cindy's call as the leader of the people with skills? For Jimmy was now moving most of the control to her.

The boys, as Mrs. King once called them, were getting older now, Jimmy, Eddie, and Kenny. They were training others to do their work and they would be there to advise them every step of the way. Cindy was doing the business of Jimmy's people at that place and being their leader with her silver. Calvin was doing everything else Jimmy did and that meant meeting with the presidents of the United State of America. Jimmy was training Calvin to become the new leader of Majestic Twelve even before he died, that way Jimmy could help advise

Calvin every step of the way. Majestic Twelve was still scarier than all hell but it was a job someone needed to do. Jimmy had a new thing he called past president of the group which was what he wanted to be in Majestic Twelve and have Calvin the new president. How would that work? Well, Jimmy did have most of the members, so I guess he could do whatever he wanted and that is what he wants to do.

Kelly was training spies with Ricky as a teacher and doing all the other things Kenny did. Tammy and Gary watched the twin as Calvin and Kelly worked. It was a loving family with grandparents involved.

Edward was doing Eddie's job at the agency with his wife Suzanne as a mental health doctor for the women as in the leadership role. They were all together. The Eds were out there trying to keep the world safe for us. Mostly, the Eds were gone two weeks out of each month then home for two weeks. They did change partners but James and Leo were always with Virgil or Victor on a mission. Virgil and Victor were never both gone from home at the same time to help with kids.

Kevin was the one who watched over Jimmy, Kenny, and Eddie to guard them. Kevin loved his job and would always be there for them with Bonnie. The guys, T-Jay, Sam, and Micky were still doing their jobs and enjoying laughing at the Eds with their kids. But C-Jay and Mickey were now running around after their children too which only please the guys that much more. Their church and meals after were well attended by the group. Was it the church or the food they loved so much or watching the little kids running all over the place and their parents working hard to keep things under control? Calvin knew he and Kelly would join the group in watching and running after their twins but Calvin was good with it. He had the group, as all were friends now.

Tim, Linda, and Gerald were happy to be home and needed. Gerald was happy with his wife Amy. Marci was with George at his home with their children but came to see Jimmy more than Jimmy would like her too. Jimmy and Marci still fought about anything and everything but this was her home too. Tammy was with Gary caring for the twins, Kim and Kell, that had become a handful.

The question, was Sylvia also in that hospital after that car accident Jimmy and her were in as a teenager with his mother's help? Was Sylvia the mother of Jimmy's second son who died and had been taken to that hospital as the others were? Did Jimmy's mother help Sylvia as she helped Tammy so many years ago?

Could that be why they never could find her before? Jimmy's mother is gone now and that question isn't answered. Or was Sylvia a secret agent or spy too in the field of the spy world? There are secrets with this group and always will be.

So where are they all now? My guess is working hard and raising children. What will the new generation be like? What are they doing? Enjoying friends and family with so many little children to grow up. But I am sure of one thing, they are all watching out for Jimmy, Kenny, and Eddie with their women. These boys, as Mrs. King once called them, are so important to this group and always will be. They may not all love each other in the group but they all love Jimmy, Eddie and Kenny.

Are they aliens from another world or place? Well, we don't know for sure but Calvin does know now, because he was in the delivery room with Kelly when his babies were born. As we know, Calvin and Kelly's twins have skills, so he knows for sure. Will Calvin tell us or is it a need to know thing like being a secret spy?

What about the place called Our People's place? Is it a hospital Jimmy works at as a genius? You know Jimmy is very secretive. Could Calvin be an alien or is he with them in Majestic Twelve, watching for aliens on Earth? They are now all in the shadows. If you don't know that they are there, then we will never even see them. That is the way they want it but they are out there protecting us every day, thank God.

This is a fiction story, right? But let us hope it got you to think about things that are right in front of you each day. The people in your family and life. What is their story and their past? Maybe it is more than we ever dreamed, like Jimmy's life and his friends.

But how about you? What did you do during this time of stay home and social distancing? Did you learn about your family and history of your family or friends? The world is different but that is okay. We can be different and still be okay. We can change and still be happy. We can handle anything they throw at us, right readers? But if you don't have to go through it alone that is much better. Friends and family can help but sometimes they can be the problem. Where to go from that?

God is always here, we just have to go to God. Calvin does and it doesn't make the problem go away or even smaller but it does help us be stronger to work through whatever life throws at us anytime, anywhere. We got this. We can change if we want to. We have free will from God.

Calvin said, "Readers, please when you are in church or praying to God take a minute and think of others. Just say a little prayer for us. We need all the help we can get and that is something we can all do for each other. A prayer for the unknown person in need. God is always here and your best friend forever even if we aren't yet a saint or may never be one."

THE END